The Doubly Dead Angel-Thief

Marc Whelchel

Open Books

Published by Open Books

Cover photo "Delmar Loop" © by Paul Sableman
Learn more about the photographer at flickr.com/photos/pasa/

ISBN-10: 0615722814 /ISBN-13: 978-0615722818

To Mike Kempfer, riding his Kennedy Roofing van through the skies, hopping out at stoplights to pick cigarette butts and detritus from the clouds.

Contents

Author's Note

THE FESTERING EYESORE OF 703 DELMAR BLVD. IS ENTIRELY fictional, as is Kun-Woo's eatery. I have no reason to believe Vietnamese food in the Delmar Loop is a harbinger of dysentery.

Chapter I

JAKE KENNEDY HAD DIED FOR THE FIRST TIME THAT week, and the world was a colder, uglier place because of it.

I stood at the window of my studio apartment above the Korean noodle joint in the Delmar Loop, watching the rain fall.

"If life doesn't take the life out of you," I told the Purple Guy, "nothing will."

The Purple Guy stared back blankly, a plywood shell of a man who couldn't care less about my melodrama. For all his charms, the Purple Guy could be an asshole.

A playful knocking—*knock, knock, knock, knock, knock... pause... knock, knock*—came from the door, tearing me away from my one way-conversation. I dried a tear, as I'd been doing all day.

"Who is it?" I said, knowing who it was.

"Jehovah's fucking Witness," barked Aldous Lewie. "Open the door, V."

Lewie was still wearing his funeral clothes, and smiling, as always. And, as always, it had an unnerving effect, like he was about to kiss me, or tell me a secret I didn't want to hear, or poke his ever-present firearm in my side.

I wondered, not for the first time, if my dear old friend was a sociopath.

He rushed in from the rain and smiled wider, appraising my dingy abode. Downstairs, pots and pans rattled from the kitchen of Kun-Woo's Noodles.

"Kan Pong Gi!" someone hollered. "Kan Pong Yook!"

Next to Kun-Woo's, at Camilla's, some loud, angry band was starting sound check. By 9:00 p.m., my floor boards would quake, assaulted by ninety-five decibels of indie-punk clatter.

Such is my life. Kan Pong everything by day, F-bombs and power chords by night.

"It's brilliant!" hollered Lewie, the loudest man west of the Mississippi. "I love what you've done to the place. It's only half as depressing as it used to be. Last time, it made me want to stick my head in a boiling pot of ox blood soup. This time, I just want to poke my eyes out with steel chop sticks."

"Definitely the effect I was going for."

Lewie was with me a year ago when I signed my lease and the room was serving as headquarters for an all-inclusive insect alliance. It was the first dirt-cheap dwelling I came across after my wife and I finalized our divorce. On the bright side, it was a block from my friend Bobby's watering hole. Unfortunately, it also sat atop both the city's most repugnant eatery and deafening music venue. Imperfect as the situation was, I'd learned to accept it, even if it meant sometimes tucking myself into bed while bands with names like Pussy Bleeders and Coma Rage belted out Black Flag covers twelve feet below my pillow.

Fast-forward a year, and the vermin were evicted, mostly. In their place, the Purple Guy stood in the corner, his wooden limbs covered in a mélange of beads, neckties, and loud Hawaiian shirts. A sombrero sat atop his pear-shaped head. His creator's name, J. Kennedy, appeared in faded Sharpie on the back of his leg.

Craigslist freebies—couch, coffee table, dresser, bed—furnished the room. A small bookshelf topped with my old friend, the little green alien candle with the chipped skull, stood beside the Purple Guy. An Andy Warhol print, *Four Elvis*, hung crookedly on one wall and a Jake Kennedy print, *Buddha Pest*, on the other. Once upon a time, in a sleepy suburban basement, they hung straight. But that was before Steffi and I split, Jake ate a bullet, and the universe got weirder than all Al on me.

"Curses," growled Lewie as his cell phone rang. "Duty calls. Sorry, this may take a while."

After stints as a painter, window washer, bartender, barber, computer repairman, cook, mechanic, roadie, retail clerk, banker, security guard, delivery driver, bellhop, forklift driver, banquet captain, I.T. analyst, restaurant manager, blackjack dealer, car salesman, glass-blower, bus driver, and finally police officer, Lewie found his calling as a private eye. He spent most of his time taking pictures of unfaithful spouses frolicking and fornicating. The line between P.I. and pornographer was a fine one.

I stepped outside onto my tiny balcony to give him

some privacy. The downpour had slowed to an icy drizzle. The sky was an apocalyptic gray: the perfect day for a funeral.

On the main drag below, the Delmar Loop was coming alive, mocking the death vibes around me. Outside the vinyl shop, the Hare Krishnas in their colorful *dhoti* were beginning to chant their mantra. T-Bone, an elderly street musician and something of a local legend, was setting up his portable loop machine under the awning outside Kun-Woo's, preparing to turn himself into a one-man wall of sound. Two pimply-faced teens emerged from the head shop across the street, clutching brown paper bags and looking guilty. A young brunette disappeared into the body paint bar. As unhappy as it made me, life went on.

"V.C!" T-Bone was looking up at me, smiling and waving. "Looking dapper, my man!"

I, too, was still wearing my funeral attire. Part of me believed that once I took it off, the deal was sealed and Jake Kennedy was officially gone.

"Yeah, but for all the wrong reasons, amigo."

T-Bone nodded emphatically, though I suspected my cryptic remark missed its target.

"Praise the Lord," he said, and I guess that settled it. He turned away to continue setting up.

Inside my apartment, Lewie's laughter rang out. "When I die," he shouted into the phone, far too jovially, "just dig me a hole and give me a push. I don't even care if I'm face up!"

My stomach retched and I envisioned an earthworm slithering into Jake Kennedy's eye socket.

Visions of Jake had been dancing in my head since I learned of his death. First, he was playing tenor sax with a jazz band at Bird Lounge, then lead guitar with a punk trio at Sub-Mission. Then he was teaching my seven-year-old nephew the "Mechanic's Grip" card cheat. Then he was confessing to me in a whisper that his father, Big Jamie, was responsible for three-quarters of the whores and dope in the Midwest. Then he and I were driving in golden silence through corn fields and cow towns to the house where Bob Ford killed Jesse James, Jake's hero. The sun was high that day, the scent of freshly cut grass in the air, the flowers blooming. Jake's smile was contagious. The universe was humming a happy tune.

"How about that funeral, eh?" Lewie's voice pulled me back to reality. He was off the phone and standing in the doorway, smoking a Marlboro Red and ashing all over the place. "Talk about an eclectic cast of characters, eh?"

He wasn't lying. Big Jamie's crew was there, looking menacing in their ill-fitting suits. Jake's friends from Burning Man were there, too, honoring him (I think) by wearing their burner attire: polyester spacesuits, glowing disco gear, corsets, tutus, kilts. Intermixed with Big Jamie's scowlers, they looked especially comical. I was sandwiched between a man wearing a jacket made from porno magazine clippings and a girl sobbing quietly from under a uni-horned minotaur mask. Grieving with a straight face was a challenge.

Big Jamie alone represented the Kennedys. His wife, Jake's mother, died mysteriously when Jake was a baby.

His kin in Boston disowned him long ago. Maybe I was mistaken—like the time I thought marrying a girl I'd known for six weeks was a good idea—but once or twice, I thought I saw the big man fight back a smile.

I leaned in close to the man with the porno jacket. "How big a life insurance payment you think he's getting?" I whispered.

"Inappropriate," he murmured. Moments later, he nudged my side. "Hell, who am I to judge? Truth is, I got the dead guy wrong. You see that nerdy dude over there with the rainbow hair? I thought he was Jake. I'm just happy Rainbow Bright is still breathing. Who the hell's Jake?"

I started to speak, but he cut me off.

"Actually, don't tell me. I don't want to know. It would just ruin my good mood."

Jake's girlfriend, Arianna, wasn't so buoyant. She sat in the front row with Jamie, staring into space, looking lost in a chemical fog. Like the rest of us, she was probably still in shock that a man who didn't seem to have a negative bone in his body would swallow a bullet. Lewie getting busted with a crawl space full of dead bodies made sense. Merry prankster Jake Kennedy committing suicide was unimaginable.

At the cemetery, several of Jake's musician friends greeted the congregation with a rendition of "Death Is Not the End." The vibe got heavier. On a grassy knoll in the near distance, a silhouetted figure played saxophone while a priest sprinkled holy water on my friend's wooden overcoat.

As if on cue, the skies opened. The minotaur girl

said between sobs that the angels were crying for us. I didn't have the heart to tell her that if they were doing anything, it was pissing.

"Fuck it," I said to Lewie, back at my apartment. "Let's go drink."

So, I said goodbye to the Purple Guy and the little green alien candle with the chipped skull. I assured my *Four Elvis* painting that when I returned, there would be eight of them.

Then we left. Had we stayed, I probably wouldn't be alive to tell this tale.

———————

Maybe time heals all wounds, but music also helps. For months after Steffi and I fizzled out, I barely took my old iPod off the deck. Night and day, it was salve in my throbbing mental cut. Without good music, every day would be Provo, Utah for a lot of innocent people.

Bad music, on the other hand, is a grinding death. It's worse than a dinner date with an old friend who wants to sell you a timeshare, or a bowl of Kun-Woo's ox blood soup.

And bad music was evidently what Lewie had in mind to kick off our night.

"Lewie!" I screamed over the deuce-deuce-deuce of the electro turntable. "I will grant you rights to my firstborn child if we can leave this hellhole right now!"

Techno was an unwanted bedfellow in the Loop. Rocco's Lounge was thinking outside the indie rock box, and the results were ominous. Besides a smattering of young clubbers in shiny neon rave gear, Lewie and I were alone with a cacophony of synthesizers and software.

"No deal!" shouted Lewie, bobbing his head to the music and eyeballing a dangerously young blonde. "What am I going to do with your firstborn? Use it as a hockey puck? Sell it on eBay?"

"I'm out of here!" I shouted. "Meet me at Bobby's place when you've had enough of this crap!"

Before leaving, I approached the young lady.

"You see that big teddy bear over there with the goatee?" I shouted, pointing to Lewie, who smiled and tried to wave her over. "He's a cop. And a serial killer. And he has genital boils. And he likes you." I turned back and gave Lewie a double thumbs-up.

Outside, the sidewalks were alive, the bars and cafes filling up. A dozen teens were crowded around T-Bone, who was hard at work building his wall of sound, alternating between guitar, violin, and glockenspiel. He had the energy of a twenty-year-old. When he paused for a break, the teens erupted in applause, dropped money into his guitar case, shook his hand and queued up for selfies with him. For a subsection of society—the kind that gave a shit about old black men with loop machines on sidewalks—T-Bone was a rock star.

"Not a bad haul for five minutes of work," I observed when they walked away.

"Looks like I might not have to sell my second summer home after all," T-Bone joked. "Praise the Lord for Ladue kids who throw around their parents' money."

I met T-Bone the day I moved in. He was sitting on the stairs in the tenants' entryway, fiddling with his harmonica. He smiled warmly and introduced himself—"Name's Thomas Jones—boring, right?—but everyone calls me T-Bone." He was tall and thin with a deep, sonorous voice. I liked him instantly. Considering my track record of judging character, he'd probably plunge his harp through my uvula while I slept.

T-Bone scooped the money out of the guitar case but left a few singles behind.

"Advice if you ever become a street performer," he said. "Put your tips in your pocket as soon as your audience walks away. Leave a few bills out, though. If you put it all away, it makes people think, 'Why should I tip this guy? Nobody else is.' Leave all the money in the box, and they think, 'Shit, man, this guy makes more money than I do.' Plus, it gives thugs the idea to follow you to the Metro station and rob your ass."

"I'll keep that in mind. You're sounding good, by the way."

"That's kind of you to say. Truth is, though, with these old arthritic fingers, I don't know how much longer I can keep dragging my ass and all this equipment out here every day."

He held up his hands to show me his wrinkled, swollen digits.

"Might be easier to go back to playing harmonica, I'm thinking. Only problem is, there's only so many songs you can play on a mouth harp. And my lungs ain't what they used to be, so I get winded pretty quick. Can't imagine why."

"No?"

T-Bone winked and took half a cigarette from his pocket.

"My condolences, by the way," he said. "You're dressed up for the wrong reasons, you say. Funeral?"

"Friend of mine, yes."

I felt shaky all of a sudden. As tears welled up in my eyes, I pulled up a picture of Jake on my phone. He was posing with his latest artistic creation and my future roommate, the Purple Guy. Both creator and creation sported flowery shirts and sombreros. If there was a hint of depression in my friend's eyes, I couldn't find it.

"Looks like a nice guy," said T-Bone. "And almost as handsome as I am. The white fellow standing next to him looks all right, too." He put a sympathetic hand on my shoulder. "Hang in there, friend."

"I will," I said, slapping on a brave face. "Like Richard Manuel."

T-Bone groaned. "You are not OK, V.C."

Walking away, I realized Jake's funeral program was still in my pocket. On a whim, I turned around and placed it inside T-Bone's guitar case.

"There," I said. "While you play tonight, Jake's smiling mug will be looking up at you."

T-Bone smiled warmly.

"I think he'd enjoy that," I said. "He was a musician like you. And an artist. And, mostly, a thief."

Before I could elaborate, a fresh group approached to see the one-man orchestra in action, so I said goodbye and headed towards Bobby's bar, where some friends and acquaintances were gathering for Jake stories. Although Bobby's bar was about as jazzy as Utah, it was called Kind of Blue and featured the likeness of Miles Davis on the door. Bobby didn't know Miles

Davis from Jefferson Davis, but he let his ex-girlfriend name the joint, and she was going through a jazz kick. As Bobby grew to hate the girl, he grew to hate the name. I told him that it could be worse. He could be the proprietor of Young Man with a Horn.

Naturally, people mistook it from the outside for a jazz bar. Inside, it was clear its actual theme was squalor. Nails jutted from the walls. Insulation poked through the ceiling. Mismatched tables dotted the floor. Patches of multicolored mold broke up the barren walls. It was the least welcoming place in St. Louis, and I loved it. It felt like home.

As always, Bobby, a former Navy Seal with wide, crazy eyes and a scar that stretched from his right temple to his chin, was manning the bar and eye-fucking any stranger dumb enough to try to give him some business. I loved Bobby like a brother, but he was better suited for the blood-soaked streets of Fallujah than the tourist-friendly Delmar Loop.

He extended me a quick "Hey, brother" and tossed me a bottle of Guinness without asking what I was drinking. I didn't object. Business was rare at Kind of Blue, but alcohol outages were constant. You just drank whatever Bobby gave you.

I took a seat at the bar next to a handful of vaguely familiar faces and half-listened while they shared Jake stories. Mitch Hartley, St. Louis's resident Elvis impersonator, told us about the time Jake picked his pocket and snuck two grand into his wallet when Mitch was in a pinch. We all agreed that despite Jake's talents as an artist and musician, his most impressive life skills were as a thief.

Bobby's story was the one that stuck with me. It was also the one that would come back to haunt us.

"Jake and I and my friend Max were here last week," he said, "when this dude in an orange robe and hemp necklaces down to his pecker walked in. He had tall, curly, Marge Simpson sort of hair and looked like he time-warped here from a 1960s acid trip.

"Before I could run him off, he says he wants to buy us a drink, and then he buys us another, and another. He gets drunk and starts rambling about having powers that some maharishi in India *betrothed* him. He tells us he can read a person's past and future by rubbing their head and ingesting their aura. No shit, man, that's what he said. '*Ingesting* their aura.'

"He says he can prove it, so he sits down next to Max and starts rubbing his head and whispering in his ear. Then he slides over to Jake and does the same thing. He's got his nose and his mouth pressed against Jake's ear, and he's rubbing Jake's head with his palms and breathing heavy, like he's trying to huff Jake's brain out of his ear, man. So, I get close enough to hear what the dude's saying, and his eyes roll back in his head and he starts convulsing, like he's getting stunned or having a seizure. And he freezes for five or six seconds and then slowly opens his eyes, and he says, in this creepy voice that barely sounds human,

'I am the all seer… I am the all seer… I am the all seer… You will die… You will die young… You will die young and you will return a prophet… A warrior prophet… And you will lead… You will lead us against the iniquitous depraved… And you will die… tonight!'

"At this point, man, I'm rattled. I don't buy into that metaphysical spook shit, and I don't scare easy. But I'm freaked. And Jake's just sitting there, totally relaxed. All the while, the guy is talking in a trance, saying that he's the all-seer and Jake is a warrior prophet who will die tonight, blah blah blah. Then, all of the sudden, he stops talking and his eyes get wide and he, like, body-twitches a couple times and lets out this loud grunt, like a death rattle. Then he wavers back and forth like he's about to crash, looks around like he's not sure where he is, and bolts out the door.

"Max was freaked as fuck, man. He was like, 'Dude, what was that? The all-seer says you're going to die tonight, bro!' And Jake just smiles and pulls a wad of cash and a bunch of credit cards out of his pocket and says, 'He's definitely not the all-seer. If he was, he would have seen me rob his ass blind!'"

The bar erupted in laughter. "Seriously, he robbed the guy?" someone asked.

"Hell, yeah. Jake said he suspected the guy was a con the minute he walked in. He knew for sure when he saw him sneak a hand into Max's coat pocket. When he came over to Jake, Jake figured he'd make a move for his wallet, too, so he took it out of his pocket and slipped it under his thigh. Sure enough, not long after the guy pretends to go into a trance, Jake feels his hand go into his jacket.

"So, Jake fucks with him. He snags the dude's own wallet, empties it, then puts it back in the only pocket the guy hadn't checked. No shit, man, this happened. Finally, the guy checks that pocket and finds what he's looking for—Jake's wallet, right? Of course, he's really just stealing his own, completely empty wallet. Then he makes his dramatic fucking exit, thinking he scored."

"The way Jake picked pockets was a thing of beauty," said Mitch. "I never thought pickpockets like him really existed. I figured they were just imagined for TV and movies. But I don't know how many times I was hanging out with Jake and he'd steal my wallet or my keys just for the fun of it. Always gave them back, though."

Bobby poured the house a stiff round of his notorious bootleg moonshine. "A toast," he said. "To Jake. We'll miss you, brother."

Lewie, no longer grinning, showed up soon after. "Genital boils?" he said. "Really? And I'm a cop? And a serial killer?"

"In my defense," I said, "you used to be a cop. And you *might* be a serial killer. And you've never said you *didn't* have genital boils. Also, and I can't stress this enough, I didn't think she'd repeat what I told her."

"Are you kidding me? I can get information out of anybody. It's my greatest ability. People tell me everything."

"Probably because you stare at them with that creepy smile until they blurt out everything they know, in hopes that you don't bury them in your crawl space."

In truth, I trusted Lewie with my life. As I'd learn in a few days, I had good reason to.

I shouldn't have trusted him with my phone, though. It was on the bar top when it rang, and he snagged it before I could react.

"Psychopaths and Necrophiliacs. First, we croak 'em,

then we poke 'em." He handed me the phone. "I really hope that's somebody important."

"I always suspected you were into some depraved shit," said the caller. "This explains so much." It was Kalista Chestnut, my object of affection and sexual frustration. For the first time in days, a hint of a smile crossed my face.

"Sorry, my secretary has a macabre sense of humor, especially when he's menstruating."

"Lovely."

"What can I do you for, Ms. Chestnut? Just calling to profess your love?"

"Hardly, jackass. But if you promise not to behave like a circus animal, you can buy me dinner tomorrow."

"Tempting. Are you sure Sergio won't mind?"

"Sergio and I are split again. We're each doing our own thing, I've *told* you that. For instance, I'm trying to arrange dates with cute, lonely losers with amoeba brains, and he's probably plotting how to throw them in front of moving vehicles."

There was silence as I thought back to our first and only proper date, two years ago. Things were progressing nicely until Kalista's Venezuelan stalker-boyfriend snuck up behind us outside a restaurant on the Hill and pushed me in front of a moving car. It swerved at the last moment, narrowly avoiding splattering the streets of the Hill with a different sort of red sauce. Confused, I spun around as Sergio's fist flew towards my face. I ducked the blow and braced for a fight, but neither of us threw another punch. We just stood toe to toe, eyeing each other up for several seconds, before

Kalista grabbed his arm and led him away.

Six weeks later, I woke up in a budget motel in Anaheim, married to a girl I barely knew.

Steffi and I met at a gallery opening that Jake dragged me to the night after Sergio tried to off me. I was between jobs, going nowhere, sleeping late. Steffi was seven years younger than me, working as a pharmacy tech, pocketing pharmaceuticals, and partying all night. She dyed her hair purple, played guitar, rolled her own cigarettes. I was smitten.

We spent the night together, then the next night, then every night for the next several weeks. Life passed in a haze of Adderall by day and Vicodin and tequila by night. She invited me to California to visit her girlfriend, and outside a novelty shop on the Venice Beach Boardwalk, I proposed. We bought a souvenir ring and got married the next day at an instant wedding chapel in Long Beach. Steffi laughed conspiratorially over her vows. We consummated the marriage in our rental car. It was our six-week anniversary.

Shockingly, it didn't work out. Once we made the foolish mistake of sobering up and getting to know each other, our storybook romance crumbled. In hindsight, it's clear that we simply wanted different things. I wanted kids, backyard barbecues, and a quiet, normal life, even if I was too lazy and listless to make it happen. Steffi, on the other hand, wanted to snort lines of Dexedrine at 3:00 a.m. and sleep with my friends. That old story.

"Let's call it a date," I told Kalista. "Seven-ish at..." I looked out the window and spotted the hoity-toity

French fondue place across the street "… Fromageres sound good?"

"The restaurant sounds good. Your pronunciation of it, not as much. See you there. Don't get married tonight."

"You got a hot date, huh?" said Lewie as I hung up. "When's the wedding?"

"Six weeks from now, as usual. Save the date."

The rest of the evening passed in a haze. We drank moonshine with moonshine chasers and then stumbled down Delmar Blvd., past the bronze stars on the St. Louis Walk of Fame, to bars and more bars, where we had the type of deep, dumb conversations about life and love that only drunks can tolerate, and only while they are drinking. Lewie sang "Love is an Open Door" at a karaoke bar with a male hooker he once arrested for solicitation. I locked lips with a little person. We watched a Celtic punk band perform Hank Williams covers and then saw the encore of the Los Campesinos! concert at the Pageant, where "Romance is Boring" brought down the house. And then back to Bobby's, where Lewie switched to beer and I switched to moonshine right out of the bottle.

I barely remember the trek back to my apartment, or running into T-Bone, who was jabbering excitedly, saying, "Your friend, V.C., I saw him! I saw the dead man! He was even wearing that same hat as the picture! He went upstairs towards your apartment!" And I only vaguely recall fumbling with the keys to my door, realizing it wasn't locked anyway, and then tripping over whatever lay sprawled out on my kitchen floor.

I don't remember much about the end of that night,

but I do remember there was one question burning in my mind. It stayed with me even as a plainclothes cop barged through the door and threw me to the floor. And it stayed in my mind as he put me in handcuffs and dragged me outside. It was a question that I would ask myself for a very long time.

The question was this:

What was the blood-soaked, bullet-riddled body of Jake Kennedy doing on my floor?

Chapter 2

BEING ARRESTED FOR THE MURDER OF A MAN WHO'S supposed to already be dead is more than someone with a head full of moonshine and heartache should have to endure. It left me crushed, like I had just won a trip to Branson, and as far as I knew, Grand Marnier was the only remedy. So, I saddled up to the bar at Fromageres, where I was supposed to meet Kalista, and ordered a double shot. Silently, I toasted doubly dead friends, tossed it down, and asked for another. I've never bought into the alcoholic theory that the best cure for a hangover is more booze, but these were special circumstances.

My nerves were shot. Earlier that afternoon, I was released from the custody of the SLPD, having convinced the portly, curmudgeonly homicide detective Joe Beerman that I was not a killer and I didn't know what prompted Jake Kennedy to rise from his coffin just to die a second time. The detective asked me to repeat my story multiple times, and he grew edgier and more doubtful each time. In retrospect, it's easy to see why.

For most of my twelve-hour confinement, I was left alone in a featureless little room like you see in the movies, only I wasn't treated to any good cop, bad cop routines, fist-pounding interrogations, or sexy rogue detectives who seduced and coerced a confession out of me. On some level, it was wildly disappointing.

Beerman just stood outside the half-open door for what felt like an eternity, talking on his phone and casting incredulous glances my way. I wondered if his abnormally round, red face that looked like it would pop if you stuck it with a pin cushion would be the last face that I saw.

Finally, he burst through the door and told me to go home and meet the decontamination tech whom he was sending to clean up the mess.

"I don't know what angle you're playing here," said Beerman, "and I don't think I really care. Do yourself a favor, though, and never, ever cross my hairs again. *Shitbag*. Got it?"

"Chat soon," I agreed.

"And one other thing. This little mess stays between you and me. Don't talk about it with your mommy, your girlfriend, your boyfriend, or even that stupid little purple statue you play hide the pickle with. And if some nosy reporter approaches you, mum's the word. Tell him to go tickle his dick with a live chainsaw."

I couldn't put my finger on it, but I sensed a certain ill-natured quality to detective Beerman. I rushed off before he could extend any additional pleasantries.

Lewie had been hanging around the station, visiting former colleagues and no doubt making trained, armed professionals uncomfortable. He drove me home, where a uniformed gentleman who looked like Seth Rogen was waiting with a horde of biohazard containers, high-strength deodorizers and disinfectants, and an industrial cleaning machine that Lewie identified as "the human shrapnel digester." A closed sign hung in the window of Kun-Woo's. Otherwise, it was a normal Saturday morning in the Delmar Loop.

Lewie volunteered to let him in, which I appreciated. I wasn't sure I had the stomach for it. He emerged a half hour later carrying fresh clothes and a few odds and ends for me.

He slapped my back playfully. "You all right, killer? Never mind, of course you're not. Let's head over to my place. You can shower and change while Seth Rogen works his magic. And don't worry, I asked him to give the toilet bowl a good once-over and dust the furniture, too, while he's at it."

As we walked down Leland Avenue to his car, Lewie whistled happily, not a care in the world. "Actually, it doesn't look too terribly bad in there," he said. "I was expecting worse, to be honest. Most of the brain matter and whatnot is confined to the kitchen area. Hardwood looks fine. Did you realize your kitchen floor is slanted and sort of caves in right in the middle? Happy accident, because it caused the blood to pool in the center. Should be easy enough to gobble up."

"Lucky day," I said.

"Very! Not so lucky for poor Kun-Woo, though. Some of it soaked through the floorboard, dripped into his kitchen, and landed on some pots and pans, evidently. Next time you have the ox blood soup, it may have a hint of Jake in it."

I fought the urge to vomit. "Isn't it a little soon for your sick humor, Lewie?"

"Never! Humor is the best medicine there is, even if it is sick. If you can't go through life with a grin on your face, you may as well die twice."

"What the fuck even happened last night, man? My brain is jelly."

"Well, we drank a lot. Sang some karaoke, bowled, threw some darts, listened to some tunes, made some friends, kissed some midgets. All in all, a pretty good night, I'd say."

"I'm talking about Jake, man! Why the hell was Jake Kennedy lying dead on my kitchen floor, Lewie?"

"Oh, yeah. *That*. Well, it appears Jake faked his own death, probably to throw off whoever was trying to kill him, but was ultimately unsuccessful."

Lewie's matter-of-fact tone made me want to throttle him. "No worries," he added, "we'll figure out what happened."

"We? You mean, the police?"

"You're cute, you know that? The police!" Two teenage girls glided by on rollerblades as Lewie hollered at them, "The police! Can you believe this guy?" He chuckled heartily. "No, sir! The police have no impact on this case, I assure you, unless Big Jamie brings them in. Otherwise, detective Beerman will keep this under wraps. My guess is, Jamie will want to extract revenge on his own terms, and the SLPD will look the other way. And that, *Agent* Almond, is where we come in."

I didn't entirely follow, and despite the many questions and objections I suddenly had, I was in no shape to voice them. I felt worse than just hung over, like someone had slipped something in one of my countless drinks. We arrived at Lewie's car and I sank into the passenger seat, where I remained for the next few hours, too tired to move and too anxious to truly rest.

Now, after a long shower, I sat on a barstool, awaiting my hot date and nursing both another GrandMa and a slowly building panic attack. The Pixies' "Where Is My Mind," a nasty thing to hear at a time like this, played in the background. Fragmented thoughts flooded my head. I couldn't think straight. Breathing became a chore. I had the jittery sensation that my soul was trying to jump out of my body. For a moment, I truly believed I might up-chuck it onto the bar top. God was blowing fear into my brain, and my only defense was to sip my poison like a good little Christian and wait for the lions to feast on my entrails.

Perhaps some friendly conversation would help. I raised my glass to the only other bar patrons, a young couple who'd been giggling quietly and talking in baby voices, making an annoyance of themselves as only young lovers can.

"Top of the morning to you, young lovers," I said. "Kill any dead people lately?"

They smiled stiffly and turned away. The bartender pretended to wipe something down. I suddenly wished somebody's boyfriend would throw me into rush hour traffic.

My filter, I realized, was obliterated by sleep

deprivation, tension, and booze. So, I excused myself from the bar to seek refuge in the pisser and get my head straight. I looked in the bathroom mirror. My eyes were bloodshot and my mop of disheveled hair in need of a trim, but I still looked surprisingly presentable. My dancing bear necktie hung straight. I practiced a smile, and it wasn't completely crooked, either. I was still young enough, barely, to look better than I felt.

Relax, I told myself. Breathe. It could be worse. I could, for instance, be waiting for my promiscuous ex-wife, not the lovely Ms. Kalista Chestnut, to join me for dinner. Plus, the background tunes had shifted gears, trading Black Francis for Ma Rainey's "Booze and Blues."

Things were looking up. I began to breathe easy again. A toilet flushed.

"Every time a toilet flushes," I observed out loud, "a shitty little angel gets his wings."

Whether this was true or simply an old wives' tale, I wasn't sure. But before I had time to seriously ponder it, a wiry little man emerged from the stall and started washing his hands in the basin beside me.

"I went to bed last night and I was in my sleep/Woke up this mornin', the police was shakin' me..."

"Good song," I said. "Very fitting under the circumstances."

"How are you?" he murmured.

"Been saner, friend."

He gave me an ingratiating half-smile and hurried away. I took some more deep breaths and made a silent inventory of the questions cluttering my mind: If Jake was murdered last night, who the hell did we bury yesterday morning? Was his drug-dealing, knuckle-busting father involved? Did Jake show up just to surprise me, or was he hoping to slip in and out under the radar? Is it possible the body I tripped over was the same one we laid to rest? Did somebody uproot the body, load it with lead and leave it in my apartment? Did Beerman believe my alibi?

All sound questions, but I doubted even the most lucid mind could answer them, much less my own. I returned to the bar, where I was surprised to find a fresh GrandMa waiting for me. The bartender had poured himself one as well.

We clinked glasses. "To health, happiness, and dying once and being done with it," I murmured.

He didn't look convinced.

———————

The mood lighting was playing tricks on my unsteady eyes, changing Kalista's long, silky hair from honey brown to Swedish blonde and back again. The pendant around her neck shined like a diamond in the sky, or a police officer's flashlight in my eye. I was entranced.

I hadn't seen her in two years, and until a few weeks ago, when she called me out of the blue, we hadn't even spoken. My marriage, farcical as it was, didn't sit well with her. Kalista and I straddled that awkward line between just friends and something else for a long time before we finally went on a date. My marrying a stranger a mere six weeks later wasn't a romantic irony that she found particular amusing.

But when people go through hell together, they can't stay apart forever. And Kalista and I endured something far worse than even Bobby did in the darkest corners of the world: we worked side by side in the trenches of Java Bloc, St. Louis's favorite hipster haven coffeehouse, where spontaneous poetry slams pop up like roadside bombs and a never-ending parade of bearded, tight-jeaned bohemians queue up to order flat whites.

In spite of detective Beerman's orders, I spilled the story of my nightmare night into Kalista's lap as soon as we were seated. She didn't interrupt or ask questions, but just stared at me with those cutting, twinkling green eyes that had given me goose bumps years ago. Had my neurons not been firing booze-soaked, bone-tired blanks tonight, they would have given me goose bumps again.

"Are you insane?" she said when I was through. "Is this a joke?"

"Yes. And no. I wish it were."

A waitress appeared with a wine list. Kalista waved it off. "I'll have a brandy," she said. "Better make it a double."

Too much a gentleman to let a lady drink hard liquor alone, I said to make it two.

Kalista was having difficulty finding her words. "This is a lot to take in, V.C.," she said finally.

"Is it?"

"Why aren't you at home, licking your wounds? And playing with your noodle one last time?" If anything exceeded Kalista's beauty, it was her bluntness.

"What can I say? I'm excited to see you."

"Aren't you scared?"

"Scared? Why?"

"Think about it. Which is more likely—that someone followed your friend Jake into your house with the intention of killing *him*? Or someone broke into your house with the intention of killing *you*, and Jake just happened to be there? Fifty-fifty, I'd say."

I hadn't thought of that. "Until a few moments ago, I was very excited to see you, Kalista."

Our drinks arrived.

"Drink up, love," she said. "You don't want to die thirsty."

The woman at the booth across from us kept checking her phone and sighing loudly. Finally, her date arrived with a blooming flower bouquet. What an ass.

"Should I have brought flowers?" I said. "Want me to sneak a lily while they're not looking?"

"Flowers are lame. Unless there's an exciting story behind them. I prefer half-drunk men who bring me complicated tales of murder and intrigue."

"Is that sarcasm? And who are you calling *half* drunk?" I raised my glass. "Here's to murder and intrigue and..." A light bulb went off in my head. "The saxophone player!"

Kalista turned around. "What? Where? Who? Why?"

"At the burial site! I just realized something. There was a saxophonist standing on a grassy knoll overlooking the cemetery, playing a song while they put Jake, or whoever it was, underground. It was Jake! That son of a bitch played the saxophone at his own funeral, just like his hero Jesse James, who allegedly sang at his."

Kalista downed her drink in a single gulp. I got the

feeling she was rattled. "Hang on," she said. "Back to the coffin. It wasn't empty? You're sure there was a real person in it?"

"I think so. The top of it was closed, of course, and there was a picture of Jake sitting on it. The middle and lower parts were open, though, and you could see a body from the head down."

"Seriously? That's an option? That's a little comical and a lot creepy."

"I suppose when you want to make people think you aren't faking your death, and you're the son of Big Jamie Kennedy, anything is an option."

"Maybe it was a fake body, a dummy."

"Yeah, maybe."

Kalista shook her head slowly, her face flushed pink from the brandy. For the first time, a smile crept across her face. "I like your problems, V.C. They make my own seem so small and manageable."

"Let's talk about something else."

"Sure. Tell me about your wife."

"Ex-wife."

"Speak."

"Let's see. She's a pharmacy tech. Plays guitar, enjoys long walks on the beach, yoga, pina coladas, champagne..."

"Are you quoting the background music?"

"... and, most of all, my friends' genitals."

"Oh?"

"We met the day after your boyfriend..."

"Ex-boyfriend."

"... tried to murder me. We hit it off, drank too much, did too many mind-altering drugs. I was sort of joking when I asked her to marry me. She was sort of joking when she said yes. Neither called the other's bluff, and we ended up married for a minute. Pretty standard, boring, modern love story, really."

"Too bad it didn't work out. Here's to better luck next time."

Our eyes met. Under the table, her foot teased my leg. We were having a moment, I could feel it. But then her cell phone vibrated in her purse, killing it.

"I better check that. It's probably one of the seven guys I called last night before I got to you," she said, killing it further.

In search of her phone, she pulled a stack of envelopes and junk mail from her purse.

"There's nothing like letters from angry creditors and junk mail addressed to people who don't live there anymore to remind you that you're alive and wanted in the world, huh?"

"I don't have angry creditors. I just ignore my mail for a week before taking it out of the box. The mail lady was trying to jam this crap in there when I was leaving today, so I felt bad and took it. Ah, here's my phone. Nope, not a suitor, just my meddling parents. 'How's the date going?' they're asking. What should I tell them? That he won't stop staring at my cleavage?"

"I'm doing that? If I am, it's only because it's distracting. I mean, in a good way."

"You're a smooth-talking, hopeless romantic, V.C."

"I am."

"No wonder that little hooker married you after a month."

"I'm sensing some unresolved anger here, Kalista."

"You're very astute, V.C."

"I've missed you, Kalista."

"You better have, jackass."

"Hang on, isn't your father a drill sergeant? Don't mention the cleavage thing. I don't want an angry, meddling father pushing me in front of a car this time."

"Nah, they're just happy I'm having dinner with someone who's not a raging psychopath. Which reminds me, did I ever tell you that Sergio burned my initials into his forearm with a grill lighter?"

"Christ. And you call me a hopeless romantic."

"What can I say?" said Kalista, shrugging. "I have a type, I guess."

"You told your parents about me, huh?"

Kalista blushed, or maybe she just had a brandy allergy. "Don't get a big head. They surprised me with a visit. I had to get them out of there."

"Did they give you a curfew? Did you get an extra hour since it's not a school night?"

"Shut it, clown."

Fromageres was one of those date-friendly joints where you cook your own food and pay extra for it. Our waitress arrived with a plate of raw chicken, lobster, vegetables, and sauces. Kalista, an old pro at this apparently, went right to work, spearing meats and veggies with cooking forks and dropping them into the hot broth in our table-top kettle. I followed suit.

"How's work?" I said. "Right before you started giving me the silent treatment for no good reason..."

"Careful."

"... you started working at that interior design firm."

"I'm still there. It's enjoyable enough. It's a job."

"I've been looking for a good interior designer to bounce some ideas off. The more leisurely west wing of my estate needs some more pop, you know?"

"You want to make the 'west wing' of the studio space above Kun-Woo's *pop*?"

"Darn. I didn't realize you knew where I lived these days."

"What about you? Peddling espresso somewhere again?"

"I'm working freelance as a resume writer. Got certified and all that jazz. If you ever need someone to help you write a resume that gets ignored but looks better than all the other resumes getting ignored, I'm your man."

"At least you're sort of using your degree now."

"True. I smoked a lot of pipes and played a lot of video games to earn that English degree."

We lost track of time, catching up and reminiscing on old times. Before we knew it, we were finishing double brandy number four and Fromageres was closing.

"What's next on the agenda now that you've got me good and drunk?" asked Kalista.

"Remember that Sasquatch looking guy who used to come into Java Bloc and drool over you?" I said. "The one with those awful pickup lines?"

Kalista laughed. "I forgot about that animal. What about him?"

"What was that line? 'Want to come over and play carpenter? First, we'll get hammered, then I'll nail you.'"

Kalista rolled her eyes. "Yeah, that's pretty bad."

"Well," I said, "how about it?"

She didn't hesitate. "Not happening, big fella. You've got a better chance of getting Sergio in your bed tonight."

"Really? In that case, how can I get a hold of him?"

"Oh, I didn't mention? I have no idea. Sergio has gone missing."

Never mind that I was one nervous breakdown away from a one-way ticket to the Odd Fellows Insane Asylum. With the help of some good tunes and a bottle of Cabernet, it was beginning to look like the Purple Guy, *Four Elvis*, and the rest of my roomies may have some company tonight after all.

We were in my freshly disinfected murder scene of an apartment, dancing to the sounds of that same Hank Williams punk cover band now playing under our feet at Camilla's. I'm not a quality dancer. Dancing with me is not unlike wrestling a wounded six-foot duck. But despite my lead feet and lame, white moves, Kalista was still with me and enjoying herself very much. Wine was not the only thing we were sampling. We'd also had a taste or two of each other's tongue.

And then my world went akimbo. During a brief pause in the action, between "Lovesick Blues" and "Cold, Cold Heart" (or "Cold, Cold, Motherfucking, Cocksucking Heart," in its punk form), I made a brutal mistake: I took a leak.

Pissing, in most societal circles, is a harmless endeavor. At worst, a bowl gets missed, a stone gets passed, or a fetish gets satisfied. But different rules apply when there is a Purple Guy lurking in the shadows like a date-stealing predator.

When I returned from the pisser, the mood had clearly changed. Kalista stood in the corner, her mouth agape, a faraway look in her eye. She was gazing at the Purple Guy with desire in her eyes.

"And who," she said, "is this sexy young man?"

OK, so maybe it was unfair to blame the Purple Guy for what happened next, even if it is therapeutic to point the finger at your deadbeat roomie when life goes south. In truth, if anyone deserved blame for Kalista's sudden transformation from dashing, dancing, diva to hot mess, it was the Christian Brothers.

The eight shots of brandy suddenly made their presence felt in a bad way. Kalista dropped to her knees, her face contorted in a grimace that made me think my kitchen floor would soon be splattered with the second most objectionable bodily fluid of the weekend.

"Oh, God," she moaned. "I haven't felt this way since high school. When did I become such a lightweight? And why the hell did I drink brandy? I don't drink brandy."

"You don't?"

She laughed and climbed to her feet before falling, half-limp, deliberately theatrical, into my arms.

"Friday at work, I was rummaging through a desk and found an old *Sherlock Holmes* paperback. And I got bored and read a story or two and everybody kept drinking brandy. And then driving to that fondue place, I heard that 'Brandy' song on the radio. And I thought maybe the universe was trying to tell me something."

"In my experience, if the universe is telling you something, it means you ate some funky mushrooms. Or maybe..."

"Shush."

Kalista stood on her tiptoes and planted a wet kiss on my lips, then climbed into bed. "Nausea passed."

"That was quick."

"Sure was," she said, burrowing under the covers.

I wasn't sure if I was invited to join her. "What now?"

Kalista yawned. "Tuck in the kids. Close the garage door. Nappy nap time..."

I thought she was joking, but within a few minutes, she was snoring softly. I poured myself a final, highly unnecessary shot of whiskey, sat down on the couch, and took a moment to appraise the day's highs and lows. Having Kalista back in my life was beautiful and surreal. Beyond that, the cons prevailed. My apartment was now a murder scene, and it felt like a hospital. The "brain scrubber" had done an unnaturally thorough job disinfecting the place. Lewie had referred to me as Agent Almond, a surefire sign that he had a cockamamie plan up his sleeve. Worst of all, there was the sound of a man screaming bloody hell ringing in my ears. And it sounded an awful lot like T-Bone.

I snapped out of my stupor and flew down the stairs to the tenant lobby, where, sure enough, T-Bone was convulsing on the ground, breathing heavily, clutching his side.

"Crazy ass mothers!" he moaned. "What the hell was that about?!"

"911! Should I call 911? Are you shot?"

"No, just kicked and beaten in like a damn dog... Don't call 911, I'm cool... No, don't help me up yet, just give me a sec..."

"You got mugged?!"

"Not even. These three crazy mothers tried beating the black out of me. They kept shouting 'Where is he? Where the fuck is he? We know you're his friend!' You better tell us!'"

"Jesus! Who? Whose friend?"

"Hell if I know, man."

"Are you OK?!"

T-Bone lifted his shirt gingerly to reveal a dozen angry bruises taking shape on his stomach and chest. Luckily, the goons appeared to have missed his ribs. I helped him to his feet and guided him up the stairs and onto my couch, where he collapsed in a heap. Kalista barely stirred.

"We need to call the cops, right?" I was frantically scooping ice cubes into a pile of fast food napkins, devising the world's most ineffective cold pack to cover the worst of his contusions.

"Don't bother. Ain't a damn thing they can do... Aw, hell," said T-Bone, noticing Kalista, "I didn't know you had company. Let me just lie here and bleed for a minute, then I'll get out of your hair."

"Stay. They could come back, and you're hurt. Did you get a good look at them?"

"Oh, yeah," said T-Bone between measured breaths. "I saw them. Soon as I ducked inside the building, they followed me in. I even held the door for one of them.

35

Thought he might be a friend of yours."

"How'd you chase them off?"

"They kept asking where 'he' was, so I told them. I said, 'All right, you win, I'll tell you where he's at. He just took the MetroLink to the Wellston station. Go there, walk three blocks south to the big gray tenement complex, and knock on the third door on the right. You'll find him there.'"

"Whose place is that?"

"Hell if I know. But I figure a couple country honks and one skinny Latino stalking through Wellston looking for a fight on a Saturday night won't make it back to the Loop any time soon, if ever."

"Good thinking, T-Bone." I pressed the makeshift ice pack onto his nastiest wound, on the upper torso.

"Gaaaahhh," he moaned. "Jesus, it burns."

"Drink this, it will help." I brought a bottle of whiskey to his mouth. "I'll be right back."

I hurried to the drugstore for gauze, dressings, and a few other wound care products that Google recommended for grizzled street performers who just had the black stomped off them by mystery goons. When I returned, all was quiet on the Camilla's front. Both my houseguests were sleeping soundly. I cleaned and covered T-Bone's wounds and rolled Kalista onto her side. I doubted she had consumed enough alcohol to choke on her tongue, but I was swept up in my new role as caregiver. Then, not wanting to disturb either of my sleeping beauties and too exhausted to care about comfort, I kicked off my shoes and lay down on the floor, where I slept for the next ten glorious hours, my head in the living room and my feet in the kitchen, in nearly the exact spot where Jake Kennedy had bled out and died twenty-four hours earlier.

———————

I awoke to two things: the sound of my own screams, and the whooping of a whippoorwill. Or maybe it was a robin, a pigeon, a pterodactyl, or just some crazy house sparrow that didn't get the memo to fly his feathered ass south for the winter. Whippoorwills were good enough for Hank Williams, though, and they were good enough for me.

The screams were a byproduct of a nasty nightmare I had, starring a black swan that flew through my window and casually nestled up to me on the couch. He rubbed his beak gently against my forehead, face, and neck. I tried to scream for help, but my voice failed me. The swan lay still for a moment, took a deep breath, and yawned. He then raised his beak and proceeded to peck out my eyeballs.

My heart was racing and I was drenched in sweat when I awoke.

"I dream," I said, more out loud than I expected, "therefore I am."

I smelled cigarette smoke. Straining my head, I saw a familiar figure sitting on the couch, and it wasn't T-Bone. I blinked, shook my head, blinked again. He was still there.

"What the fuck," I murmured.

"You dream," the familiar figure corrected me, "therefore you *scream*."

Chapter 3

Excerpt from the pilfered journal of Patio Williams, CFO of RW Enter-
prises, younger brother of Big Jamie's business partner Radio Williams.

I AM IN GRAVE DANGER AND THIS TIME IT'S NOT MY PER-
secutory delusion acting up, as Dr. Chaudhary calls it.
Any moment I expect there will be a knock on the
door or maybe a violent crash right through it and Big
Jamie Kennedy's enforcers or maybe B.J. himself will
burst in, guns firing. I wouldn't blame him. My brother
killed his next of kin, I'm sure of it. It's only fair that
Mr. Kennedy should return the favor even if his son
was a reckless thief who probably had it coming.

At least I guess it's good timing that as I run out
of pages in this diary or mental health journal, as Dr.
Chaudhary calls it, my life will soon expire too. Dr.
Chaudhary told me to start this journal almost two
years ago to document my fears and come to terms with
them. He says that writing about your aversions reduces
the stress associated with them. My affective dysregula-
tion or inability to regulate my emotions, he says, will
improve when I put my thoughts to paper. Coupled

with cognitive behavioral therapy, as Dr. Chaudhary calls it, the journal should help me manage my phobias.

But sometimes I wonder if Dr. Chaudhary just looks up a bunch of psychiatry or psychology terms in a textbook or the internet before I come in so I think he knows stuff even though maybe he knows he's not fooling anyone.

Either way though the journal hasn't worked and off the top of my head and not counting my impending death at the hands of my brother's so-called business partner these are the things that I fear today: Crowds; being alone; silence; loud noises; strangers; sex; heights; public speaking; flying; storms; success; failure; bridges; being buried alive; the afterlife; God, or the lack of; and my older brother.

Jilly is now chewing gum and smacking her lips and I can hear the music from her headphones and it is making my misophonia, as Dr. Chaudhary calls it, flare up. I have to get out before the bugs crawling under my skin drive me to jump out the window.

———————

They changed the Goo Goo Clusters in the vending machine in the lobby from number 96 to number 38 which makes me think that I will soon be killed at the ripe young age of, yes, 38, which I am now.

Joe Van Nuys or Joey Vanilla as everybody called him used to get the Kit Kats which aren't nearly as good as the Goo Goo Clusters even though Kit Kats are everywhere in Chicago and Goo Goo Clusters aren't anywhere. The Kit Kats were number 24 and Joey

Vanilla was shot and killed by his girlfriend's boyfriend at age, you guessed it, 24.

Is it possible that the vending machine in the lobby is a cosmic death predictor? I believe anything is possible so I did not make the purchase.

Jilly just said "I thought you were going downstairs to get some of those Goo Goo Clusters you like so much" and I said "Oh, yeah, I got distracted and forgot." And then she said "I'm going down there soon, I can get them for you if you like" and I said "That would be great."

But now I'm struggling with my conscience and I'm about to tell Jilly to forget it. I don't want to be responsible for Jilly dying when she turns 38 even if she does chew her gum too loud.

––––––––––

My hand is shaking and it's difficult to write. I just got off the phone with Big Jamie and when I told him we needed to talk about Radio he said "The Radio is about to get turned off. And be careful or the Patio may get torn down too."

Then he laughed like he had said something very clever and told someone to "shake it baby" but I don't think it was me.

––––––––––

And now Jilly is tapping her employee badge against her desk in tune with the song in her ear and every time I think she is finished she starts again. If she keeps this up I will ask her to go get me some Goo Goo Clusters after all.

To make it worse I'm reminded that the lanyard around my neck itches something terrible and also looks like a noose and could very easily be used to choke me to death. But Radio is a control freak and he insists that all the office and admin staff including him and me wear them. As if wearing an official looking badge makes us legit. Even though A) we have plenty of businesses now that already are legit and could thrive in this city even without Radio's dirty dope money getting filtered through them and B) everyone in Chicago already knows Radio is a criminal and he wouldn't have it any other way and that's why he posts pictures of himself with El Chapo and Big Jamie Kennedy and Whitey Bulger and other criminals and dresses like a silly 1970s pimp. If anybody deserved to get robbed it's Radio and if Jake weren't already dead I'd be rooting for him to get away with it.

What kind of idiot hides 3 million in a 200 dollar Walmart drop safe anyway?

I'm tempted to throw the silly badge away but Radio has a terrible and dangerous and illogical temper and I fear what he would do if he returned to Chicago to find me not wearing it. He is already upset with me I'm afraid since I told him it was dangerous and stupid and just plain wrong to strike that deal with the Delgado brothers to buy those Mexican girls.

For the tenth time today I tried to call Radio and it went straight to voicemail. My brother is a cruel, selfish, impulsive man and it wouldn't surprise me at all if he is laying low in some exotic place hiding from Big Jamie and living high off the money that should have gone to the Delgado brothers for those Mexican girls I told him not to get involved with in the first place.

Or maybe he didn't get the money back, in which case I shudder to think what will happen if Radio is a no-show and the Delgado brothers and their Tijuana sex slaves pop up in San Diego only to be greeted by no Radio and no money.

Part of me really hopes this journal falls into the wrong hands and our whole stinking operation comes tumbling down.

Chapter 4

I FELT LIKE I'D BEEN TRAMPLED BY A BUDWEISER CLYDESDALE.

Maybe I was hung over. Or maybe I woke up on the wrong side of the floor.

There was no sign of T-Bone or Kalista, but Lewie now sat on the couch, smoking a cigarette and ashing into an oil burner that he must have found on the street. It didn't seem wise, but then again, I'm no arsonist.

"If you prefer," I said, "we can probably find a can of gasoline you can use as an ashtray instead. Might be safer."

I sat up slowly and rubbed my pounding forehead.

"Rough night?" said Lewie loudly. "Not enough blood in your alcohol stream this morning? And why are you on the floor, dude?"

"Long story. What time is it?"

"Ten o'clock or so."

Lewie stood up, stretched, and did a little hop. He was a little too lively, and much too loud, for such an ungodly hour.

"Ten o'clock," he repeated, "and while you've been

Captain Produce, vegetating the day away, I've been Mr. Productivity, knocking it out of the park."

As my friend towered above me, shadowboxing and grinning like a lunatic, I fought the urge to wrestle the firearm from his jacket and send him to Jesus and Jake.

"That's clever," I said. "I hope you didn't lose too much sleep coming up with it. Did you even knock, or just stroll right in?"

"Neither! I noticed the door to the balcony was ajar, so I scaled the building and came in that way."

"Of course you did. And I suppose there's a reason you didn't knock like a normal human being."

"Of course there is. I didn't want to wake you."

"Of course you didn't. And I suppose there's a reason you've decided to invade my life in the first place?"

"I thought you'd never ask." Lewie rushed to the kitchen and returned a moment later with a thick manila folder, which he set in front of me dramatically. "Voila!"

"What's that? Your latest resume?"

"No, sir! It's the case notes I've been compiling on the murder of Jake Kennedy, along with the full rap sheets of every known and suspected associate and acquaintance of Big Jamie Kennedy, courtesy of a certain friend in federal places who shall remain anonymous. Somewhere in here is the key to unlocking the mystery of the untimely demise of our hero-for-hire in dashing attire, Mr. Jacob Patrick Kennedy..."

"Hero-for-hire in dash...? Jesus, Lewie, what did you do, stay at home thinking up these little one-liners?"

"Of course not. They came to me while I was sitting

on your couch waiting for you to stop screaming and wake up."

Annoyed, I pushed the papers away. I was more concerned with quieting the bass solo pounding in my skull than perusing the criminal records of a bunch of thugs whose crosshairs nobody with the slightest interest in self-preservation would voluntarily enter.

"Who fucking cares, Lewie," I grumbled.

"Well, well, Mr. Grumpypants, aren't we a negative Nelly! Need a cigarette or something?"

"I'd rather have a very large building to jump off."

"Pick your own poison," he said with a shrug, lighting another cigarette off the tip of the first one. "But the answer to your question is, *we* fucking care. Because, my good lad, if we're going to solve this mystery, it would help to have ..."

"Stop there. What do you mean, 'if *we're* going to solve this mystery?'"

Lewie held out his hand and helped me to my feet. "Inspector Aldous Lewie, at your service."

"It's going to be more like *Specter* Aldous Lewie if you don't start making some sense."

"*Specter*? I don't follow."

"It means I'm about to turn you into a ghost."

"Now that's clever, V!" Lewie let out an excruciatingly long, loud laugh. "Very, very clever. You're a clever fellow. And for the record, I never trusted the masses of learned people who insist you could fuck up a one-car parade."

"Lewie, why don't you just let the police do their jobs? Isn't there something better you can do with your time? Like run a weed whacker over your back hair?"

"I don't have a weed whacker. And, besides, as I do remember telling you, the St. Louis Police Department is not investigating the death of Jake Kennedy."

It was too early to argue. I limped to the kitchen, splashed some cold water on my face, and took inventory of my surroundings. The bed was made with a woman's graceful touch, the covers tucked neatly under the pillows, the corners pulled tight. The wine glasses were cleaned and put away and T-Bone's bloody bandages discarded. The Purple Guy in his loud Hawaiian shirts stood in his usual corner, staring and judging.

The intense aroma of industrial grade disinfectant filled my nostrils. I hadn't noticed it last night, but the "brain scrubber" had cleaned up more than just blood and guts. The mold on the bottom of my refrigerator door, which I had been meaning to alphabetize, was wiped clean. All four gun-slinging Elvises on the wall glistened in dust-free glory. The frame of Jake's *Buddha Pest* painting, featuring the enlightened sage's beaming face attached to the scaly body of a long-nosed weevil, had been cleaned, too. Even the little green alien candle with the chipped skull had been given a Windex once-over. It made his waxy eyes shine even brighter.

"The world is a pearl," I said, "and life is a diamond, when little green alien candle eyes are smiling."

"Excuse me?"

"Forget it. Any chance you ran into a sandy-haired white girl and an older black dude with bruises all over his body on your way in?"

"You are into some kinky stuff, my friend. But sorry,

it was just you here. There's a nice love letter on the counter, though."

Written in pink lipstick, it said,

You're a resume writer, and you don't have a pen? Thanks for a fun night. I'll call later. Don't get married today.

Kisses,
Kalista

"Sounds like the date went well, eh?" said Lewie playfully, jabbing me in the ribs. The gun in his jacket continued to beckon me.

"Glorious. It was your typical case of boy likes girl, girl likes boy, girl gets drunk and falls in love with Purple Guy instead, then girl passes out in bed."

"Really? That old story? You look like hell, by the way. You want some coffee? You have coffee here, right? I'm going to make some coffee."

As Lewie rooted through the kitchen, I opened the balcony door, inviting the blistery winds to slap my face and spark me to life. It was one of those bright, brisk days that looks like Hawaii and feels like Alaska. They say if you don't like the weather in St. Louis, wait fifteen minutes and it will change. In the winter, for instance, temperatures go from cold to miserably cold to unbearably cold to hey-look-I'm-pissing-icicles-cold in less than an hour. I thought of my parents in Florida, who were probably rolling out of bed and making plans to snorkel, take a stroll on the boardwalk, or have a pink drink on the white sands.

They had no idea what they were missing.

The Delmar Loop was still half asleep, though I could hear the faint sounds of some soft jazz band at Berry's, the new gastropub down the block where the good people of our fair city were probably cutting into omelets, sipping mimosas in their church clothes, and sharing pictures of their children. I felt profoundly out of place, a creature of the night cheating the cosmos by sneaking a peak into a world that I didn't deserve and where I didn't belong. Below me on the street, a pair of rabbits bounced to and fro with an enthusiasm that felt alien to me. For some reason, they reminded me of Jake. Everything lately reminded me of Jake. My knees almost buckled. Perhaps the reality of the situation was finally setting in. It took some effort to fight back a tear.

Lewie appeared with two cups of coffee and put his arm around on my shoulder. Infuriating as he was, he really did *get it* when it mattered most.

"I feel it, too, man," he said. "Sucks. Life is not all beer and skittles, eh?"

"Where the hell do rabbits go for the winter?" I mumbled. "Do they hibernate, or hop their little white asses South, or just suffer through it like the rest of us?"

"Don't know. They certainly don't just whither up and die, that's for sure."

"Well," I sighed, "that's good news."

"Cheer up," said Lewie. "Get dressed and ready to go. I'll go hit up the market and come back with breakfast. I've got a lot of things to fill you in on, Agent Almond."

"What's this 'agent' talk?" I started to say, but Lewie was on the move and no longer listening.

"Back in a flash... partner!" he hollered as he walked out the door.

I popped a couple ibuprofens and took a long, hot shower. When I got out, my headache was gone, surprisingly. For the first time in days, I felt clear and focused, ready to brave the day. I found Lewie in the kitchen, flipping eggs and meats in three skillets. The oven was on and fresh coffee was brewing. The iPod speakers had been fired up, too, filling the room with the fitting and uncomfortable sounds of Modest Mouse's "Satin in a Coffin."

"There you are, V! How would you like your eggs, partner?"

"Devilled."

"I don't know how to devil an egg. If you like, though, I can ask Anton Lavey to give them a Satanic blessing."

"In that case, raw is fine."

"Feeling better, I assume?" Lewie said with a wink.

"Did you just wink? Why did you wink?"

"I love those powers of observation! You see, this is why I think you'll be a terrific detective one day, Agent Almond."

My lips, I realized, were numb. "What did you do, Lewie?"

"Suspicious much? OK, fine. There's no sense hiding it, I suppose. I put a little something in your coffee."

"You *what?!*"

"Oh, don't worry. It was just a sprinkle or two of some sort of prescription speed I came across. Maybe twelve sprinkles. Fifteen, tops. Best hangover cure you'll find. I think it might even be legal in some countries."

I probably should have bludgeoned Lewie with a skillet at that point, but the waves of euphoria racing through my veins made me want to hug him. Instead of doing either, I stood there shadowboxing the Purple Guy and grinning like a lunatic.

"Have a seat, my good man," said Lewie cheerfully, plating up breakfast, an impressive spread of eggs, croissants, ham, sautéed apples, hash browns topped with ricotta cheese, and coffee with cream, sans amphetamines. Lewie's mystery meds had curbed my appetite, but I ate heartily for the first time in days anyway.

I'd forgotten what a talented chef Lewie was. Of course, his myriad eccentricities made his many talents easy to forget. Except for maybe Jake—whose interests were mostly "just" creative—I'd never met anyone with more fields of expertise than Lewie. He could rewire a house, apply physics laws to real life situations, rebuild a transmission, hold his own against chess masters, and build complicated tech gear from scratch. Problem was, he was too flighty to maintain an interest in anything for longer than a year or two, tops. Lewie collected skill sets the way Steffi collected sex partners.

If the real world were a police dramedy where the eccentric cop irks the brass but saves the day, Lewie would have been an SLPD legend. At the very least, with his God-given intelligence and innate ability to read people, he could have made detective. But when you live on Aldous Time, which dictates you show up thirty minutes to three weeks late for everything, career advancement in any field tends to be elusive. His perpetual tardiness wasn't his fault exactly, though.

The concept of Time was simply beyond him. If he was ninety miles away he would tell you he'd be at your door step in fifteen minutes. And he really believed it.

"So," he said, silencing Isaac Brock so we could talk, "you want to come work with me?"

"Work with you? What am I, bat shit crazy? I have a job, Lewie."

"Writing resumes? Lame. And like you told me, you're bored with it anyway. It's a side gig at best."

"So, you want me to be your assistant?"

"Assistant? You? Heck, no! I want you to be my partner. Look here," he said, reaching into his pocket, "I even made you your very own business cards."

Wearily, I took a look. They read:

Super Special Agent VC Almond
Mastermind Sleuth
Jack of Some Trades
Bah Mitzvahs ★ *Graduations* ★ *Crime Solveing* ★
Spelling
Private Investigator Ordinaire
"At. Your. Disservice."

"What do you think? Pretty sweet, huh?"

"I think it's a joke, but I'm not sure I get it."

"What's not to get? It's funny and, besides, if you want to be a mastermind sleuth..."

"Which I don't."

"... you need a business card to give yourself an air of legitimacy."

"Legitimacy? Lewie, nobody would take someone with this business card seriously."

"Come on, V! Nobody reads business cards anyway."

"If I were smart, I would have learned long ago that arguing logic with you is an act of pure fucking idiocy."

"Don't be so hard on yourself. You'll get there someday. You want to know the trick to solving mysteries, V.C.?"

"Not even a little."

"You open your eyes. And you ask questions. You put yourself out in the world. That's it. That's all there is to it. You know why? Because deep down inside, everybody wants to tell everybody everything. As you like to point out, I handle my fair share of infidelity cases. And you know how I close them?"

"You peek through windows with a video camera and then post the footage on PriscillasPornPalace.com?"

"Only occasionally. Usually, I just ask the person. Let me give you an example..."

"Save it, detective. And for the record, it's not human nature that makes people answer to you, man. It's the fact that you sit there grinning at them, like you're doing right now, and it's scary as hell. And then you stop grinning every now and then... right, just like that... and it's even scarier. Thanks for the advice, detective, and thanks for the job offer, but I'm not interested."

"Inspector, please."

"Whatever. Inspector. Still not interested. It's not my thing."

"Great. Consider yourself hired! We can hash out the details later, partner. For now, let's just focus on finding out who killed Jake."

My headache was coming back. "Lewie, why are you so damn sure the police aren't trying to find Jake's killer? Everybody knows Big Jamie has connections in the SLPD. Why are you so damned convinced they're ignoring this?"

Lewie pushed his plate away and started to light a cigarette. "I forgot to ask. Mind if I smoke in here?"

"As a matter of fact, yes."

"Good," he said, lighting up. "Let me answer your question with a question. How much did you pay to have the essence of Jake power-scrubbed off your floor?"

"What? The police covered the cost, I think. Why?"

"Because that's not how it works. The building owner should front the bill. And if he can't afford it or doesn't care that there's a puddle of melted man flesh on his floor..."

"That's as inaccurate as it is revolting, man."

"... it stays there. In this case, the building owner— Mr. Kun-Woo, right...?"

"Yeah, he owns the place."

"Mr. Kun-Woo should have been the one to hire a biohazard team to sanitize the place. There would be paperwork, insurance claims, inspections, interviews, all sorts of red tape. Do you know what Kun-Woo thinks happened Friday night?"

"You talked to him?"

"Again, Mister Productivity here. Kun-Woo thinks a pack of rodents got cut up in a damaged ventilation shaft and bled out into his kitchen."

"What? That's asinine."

"That's what a cop who matched the description

of Joe Beerman told him, anyway. Another question: How many media outlets have you talked to? I presume channels two, four, five, and ESPN have been knocking on your door for an interview, right?"

"Well... no, but..."

"And I'm sure there's no way in hell Beerman told you to keep this whole thing under wraps, right?"

"He may have mentioned it. But so what? The cops want to keep everyone out of the way. My guess is, they're trying to make sense of this mess as we speak."

"You want to know who called the police Friday night, V.C.?"

"Chuck Berry? Uncle Tupelo?"

"Nobody."

"Nobody? Someone obviously heard gun shots and called the police."

"With as loud as Camilla's gets on the weekends, it's doubtful anyone would have heard a gunshot, or thought much of it. Did I ever tell that I used to *shtup* a cute little dispatcher by the name of Jeannie? She's a doll. A bit of a biter, but, hey, nobody's perfect, right?"

"You're a master of awkward segues. Where are you going with this, Lewie?"

"Jeannie was working dispatch Friday night. Nobody called it in. She thought I was joking when I asked about the murder in the Loop. And the police who saw you at the station thought you were just a belligerent drunk who got into a bar fight with an off-duty cop."

"I don't follow."

"Because your eyes aren't open, grasshopper. Consider

this: I spoke with the state medical examiner yesterday as well..."

"Let me guess. You used to *shtup* her, too?"

"Gross, dude. The M.E. is a 'he,' and he's about ninety. Naturally, yes, I'm *shtupping* him. Anyway, during pillow talk, I probed him, pun intended, for his thoughts on the Delmar murder. He didn't know what I was talking about, either. Nobody from the M.E.'s office stepped foot in this apartment, and Jake's body is not in the M.E.'s possession like it should be. The body is missing, V.C."

Lewie paused for effect, staring me down.

"Go back a second," I said. "If nobody called the police the other night, how did I get arrested?"

"You tell me. Who arrested you, V.C.?"

Through a dense fog of drunken memory, I replayed my voyage home: stumbling past a pale, shaken T-Bone; struggling up the stairs, dizzy and disoriented, trying to make his cryptic words about seeing my dead friend register; staggering inside, tripping over something, spiraling towards the ground and catching the trademark sombrero of Jake Kennedy out of the corner of my eye; attempting to get to my feet, to get a better look at the bloody carnage; falling back to the ground as a knee dug into the small of my back and an elbow bore into my neck, courtesy of a plainclothes cop who was screaming bloody murder...

"Detective Beerman."

Lewie sat there, grinning and satisfied while I sat there, frowning and confused.

"Nobody called it in, yet Beerman was there. What does that tell you, Agent Almond?"

"Fine. I'll play along. It tells me one of two things. First, though—is Beerman connected to Big Jamie?"

"Like Siamese cats."

"Twins."

"Whichever. They're poker buddies, and Beerman spends half his life in the VIP lounge of BJ's Cabaret. At the risk of sounding cliché, it's a safe bet that the good detective is in Big Jamie's back pocket."

"So," I said slowly, thinking things through, "moments after Jake gets whacked, detective Beerman, Big Jamie's good friend, mysteriously shows up and makes all the evidence, including the body, disappear. Ergo... either Beerman went dark side and he's a traitor and a killer, or at the very least, he's somehow involved. You're sure nobody called the police about this Friday night?"

"Not a soul. Last night while you were off playing footsie, I was canvassing the neighborhood, talking to bar owners, waitresses, and anyone else who was around Friday night. Nobody knows a thing about any shooting. Besides, a homicide detective—who was off-duty, by the way—would never be first responder. And this place would still be crawling with cops, CSI techs, forensics specialists, lawyers, media, and gawkers."

"Shockingly, Lewie," I said, starting to clear the dishes, "you may have a point. Based on the evidence, my untrained eye would agree that the SLPD is not actively investigating this crime. I just don't agree that it's our job to sort it out, man."

Even as the words escaped my lips, though, they didn't sound quite right. Jake was a special hombre. He helped me soldier through those first few dark months after my divorce. And he chose my apartment as the place to show up dead for the second time in five days. I owed it to him to do *something* to catch his killer.

"Although," I continued before an agitated Lewie could respond, "I suppose you, Kalista, and I are the only people besides Beerman and the killer—or just possibly Beerman—who know how Jake really died. If we don't investigate this, nobody will, right?"

"I knew you'd come around!" roared Lewie. "Let's get down to brass tacks, then, shall we? The first order of business, of course, is to arm you." He opened his jacket and pulled out a silver pistol. "Colt Defender .45, one of my special little friends through thick and thicker. You've got a license to carry, I presume?"

"What? No, you lunatic! What do I need a firearm for?"

"Are you joking?" Lewie laughed so loud the jazz band at Barry's may have missed a beat. "Dude! The son of a well-known, well-connected crime boss showed up dead on your kitchen floor! Do you know what happens to innocent schmoes who get mixed up in organized crime? They get full-time jobs as Mississippi River fish food."

It was a tough point to argue. Despite my general ambivalence towards firearms, I tried the gun on for size, held it in my hand, pointed it at the Purple Guy.

"Kalista thinks my life might be in danger as well," I said.

"Oh, yeah. About *her.* We should probably talk about your new girlfriend, too."

"What about her?"

"Something's not right. I'm not sure what, but

the timing is too coincidental. The very same night some beautiful woman from your past catapults back into your life, your born again/dead again friend gets whacked. Does that seem odd to you?"

"I hadn't thought about it, but, no, not really. Kalista never even met Jake. T-Bone getting the black stomped off him, on the other hand..."

"T-Bone? The street performer? What happened? And does this have anything to do with you sleeping on the floor?"

I filled Lewie in on last night's misadventures while he sucked down another cigarette and stroked his goatee.

"Interesting," he said. "One night Jake gets killed in this building, the next night T-Bone gets a beat down. This is cause for concern, partner. Things happen in threes, you know."

"Actually, things happen in twos. Two things happen, and then everybody says, 'Watch out, things happen in threes.' But then the third thing doesn't actually happen. It's a scientific proof. Google it."

"Maybe later!" Lewie hopped to his feet. He had a jarring tendency to go from zero to sixty in a flash, like an alarm clock was sounding in his brain, alerting him that he's thirty minutes to three weeks late for something. "We both to need to get going. I'm going to be late if I don't hit the road. And the M.E. is not exactly a patient man."

"I don't follow."

"I have a confession. I'm not really *shtuping* the M.E. I only spoke to him on the phone. And he told me he has some interesting info to share about Jake's body—Jake's first body, that is, the one that wasn't really Jake. He said he couldn't talk about it over the phone. Sounded dicey."

Lewie ran his hands over his pockets, spot checking for essentials. "Wallet... keys... pepper spray... phone... taser... gum... Glock... audio recorder... Good to go. So, yeah, here's the plan: We have two dead bodies. Our ultimate goal is to find out who killed Jake Kennedy, the second body. And in order to find out who killed the second body—assuming that these deaths are related, and why wouldn't they be? —we first need to find out who the first body belongs to. And there are only two people, I believe, who know the true identity. One of them is the M.E., whom I'm supposed to meet..." Lewie checked his watch. "Oh, shit. Ninety minutes ago. The other person, who you can meet with today, is Big Jamie."

I nearly spit up last night's brandy. "Come again? You want me to voluntarily stick my nose in Big Jamie's business? He's liable to kill me, Lewie. The man is crazy, yes?"

"That's what makes it perfect. You're crazy too! Nobody's too crazy for you. Being too crazy for you is like being... I don't know, too Jewish for Jesus."

Lewie had gathered his things and was standing by the door, ready to leave.

"And what exactly am I supposed to ask him? Who he really buried—after probably murdering, of course— on Friday when he was pretending it was Jake?"

"If it comes up, sure! That would be terrific. At the very least, you should inform him that his son is *really* dead after all. There's a good chance he's in the dark about that."

Lewie must have noticed the dubious look on my face.

"Come on, you'll do great, Agent Almond! Remember, Big Jamie is our ally. If Beerman turned his back on him and helped Big Jamie's enemy—whoever that is—murder Jake, most likely as retribution for whoever got buried Friday, then Big Jamie will be eternally grateful for the info."

I wasn't buying it. "Why can't you go with me? A little moral and perhaps physical support might be appreciated, you know."

"No can do, partner. I need to scour these files for clues and also conduct a few interviews myself —the M.E., the Seth Rogen guy, a couple others who might know who Big Jamie was at war with and may have motive to kill Jake… Oh, that reminds me! You've got neighbors in this palace, right? Pay them a visit. It's a long shot, I know, but see if they saw or heard anything helpful Friday. Talk to your buddy T-Bone, too. Find out what he saw Friday. Capiche?"

"What I *capiche*, Lewie, is that getting involved in this crazy fucking mess is liable to kill us both."

"Of course it is! And the whole world is a crazy fucking mess that's liable to kill us all. Question is, what are you going to do about it? Go on *Oprah* and cry about it? Or get off your ass and get to work?"

"I don't think *Oprah* is on anymore, Lewie."

"Well, then, it's settled. Off to work we go!"

And then he was off, bounding down the steps and whistling a happy tune, pausing only long enough to holler, "Meet me at Kind of Blue around nine-ish! We'll compare notes and beat back the DTs!"

Moments later, a car engine sputtered to life, tires skidded across the pavement, and silence fell on my corner of the world. For the first time, my apartment felt like a murder scene. Standing on the very spot where my friend was slain, my knuckle hairs stood on end and the juices in my stomach churned uneasily. Last night, while the floorboards were jumping and I was locking lips with Kalista, 703 B Delmar Blvd. felt like home sweet home. In the cutting silence of a lazy Sunday morning, it just felt oppressive and... well, haunted.

It was probably just my imagination. Or maybe the weekend's many libations were making a power move in my gut. But maybe it was something else...

"Is that you, Jake?" I said aloud, feeling a tad foolish. From the corner of my eye, I thought I saw the Purple Guy roll his eyes and shake his head. "If that's you, Jake, just give me a sign..."

The air was thick, my mouth dry, the silence deafening. I waited, and waited, and waited. And then...

My phone vibrated on the kitchen counter. Even with the mystery powder keeping my nerves at a hyper-focused even keel, I jumped backwards in surprise.

"Now that," I answered the phone, "is a mighty impressive sign. How's the Great Beyond, amigo?"

A pause, followed by the gruff, nicotine-stained voice of our prime suspect: "Almond. This is detective Joe Beerman."

Rut-roh. I froze for a second, then raced to the patio

to close the blinds, in case Beerman was perched on a rooftop, spying on me through the lens of an assault weapon, Jason Bourne style. I did my best to sound at ease.

"Joe Joe! So good to hear your smiling voice again, sir."

"Cut the crap, Almond. Haven't bought any plane tickets today, have you?"

"Plane tickets? No."

"Good. Because I'm going to get to the bottom of this cesspool, and when I do, I get the feeling I'm going to find your ass swimming around in it. And when I do, I don't want to find out that you're hiding in some whorehouse in Mexico."

"Don't worry. I've never even liked Europe."

"Yeah, well, if you don't cooperate then you're not going to like me, either."

I was tempted to inform him that I wasn't his biggest fan already, but thought better of it. Best not to stroll too deep in this cesspool, I thought.

"And don't go running off to South America, either. I'm going to want to talk to your ass again before this is over."

"But I've always wanted to see Dakar."

"And one more thing, tough guy. Don't say a god-damn thing to the media. Let me deal with those nosy news fucks. Fortunately for you, this is St. Louis, and there's already a fresh murder. Some gangbanger's girl-friend in Jennings got her head chopped off last night. Lucky little twist of fate for you, huh?"

I grimaced. Why such a macabre tragedy made me lucky, or how it classified as a twist of fate, was beyond me. "Fate is just a four-letter word," I offered.

"They chopped it right off her pretty little neck and mounted it to a stop sign on the Rock Road. Not your typical gangbanger hit, huh?"

"I suppose," I murmured.

"Yeah, well, it's not my case, so I don't really care."

"I suppose," I said again.

"Yeah, well, you better suppose."

There was nothing left to say. Maybe the detective was a lonely man who just needed someone to talk to. Sunday mornings in solitude, I've learned, are difficult times to be a human. Nevertheless, he hung up the phone without a goodbye.

Without further ado, and before I had a chance to talk myself out of it, I gathered my things, slapped on my game face, and went out the door to brave the day. It didn't occur to me to bring the Colt.

Four hours later, when I returned, I was covered in blood, tears, stripper glitter, and Dalmatian dribble, but at least I was still alive.

Chapter 5

I WASN'T THE ONLY ONE CRAZY ENOUGH TO LIVE ABOVE Kun-Woo's and Camilla's. There were four of us—Hazim and me in the small front rooms facing the main boulevard, and Angry Dave and the girl with the dragon tattoo in the roomier ones overlooking the back lot. They had the leg space, we had the view. The balance of power was intact.

Like any good American, I did my best to pretend my neighbors didn't exist and dutifully lowered my head and walked quickly in the other direction when we were in danger of crossing paths. But, as Lewie stated, to get answers in this world, you have to put yourself out there.

I started with Hazim, the most approachable of the three. Our interactions rarely went beyond token greetings, but he struck me as a nice enough fellow. Occasionally, while I was sitting on my balcony watching the world turn and making vague plans to rejoin it, he would jog by on the street below and wave amicably. He usually wore dangerously short shorts and sported a haircut that was one missed trim from a full-blown mullet. Although we barely knew each other, the cardboard-thin wall between our rooms made it impossible not to pick up on the other's habits and hobbies. Hazim's included listening to classical music, watching English Premier League matches, and having steamy late-night flings with a medley of misses.

I knocked on his door and then immediately regretted it, remembering he was a night owl who was probably dead to the world on a Sunday morning. To my surprise, he opened the door with a wide-awake smile and greeted me like an old friend.

Inside his apartment, classical music played softly on an antique turntable. A fuzzy area rug dotted with yin-yang symbols covered the floor. Adding to the Zen-like environment, or else gently mocking it, was a framed print of the Dalai Lama on the wall. The epitaph under His Holiness's smiling face read:

Sit like tortoise. Sleep like dog. Watch like hawk. Screw like rabbit.

"Have a seat, friend, and tell me, what is good? What can I do for you today?" Hazim spoke with a thick Bosnian accent in precise, measured tones.

"It's a long shot," I began, "but did you see anything unusual around the building on Friday night? I mean, beyond the usual Delmar Loop weekend weirdness?"

"Friday night? Let's see. Oh, yes, Friday night, I was on the streets, partying with some of the many fine ladies in our wonderful city. Attempting to lay the mack down, as you Americans say. Why do you ask, V.C.?"

Lewie's Mississippi River fish food comment fresh in my brain, I told Hazim that my apartment had been broken into but spared him the gory details. He sounded genuinely disappointed to tell me that he had nothing pertinent to share.

"Have you checked with Josie, though?" he suggested. "I believe she was at home with her girlfriend Aliyah on Friday. Aliyah has been battling a sinus infection. Maybe they saw someone lurking around."

"Right. Good idea. Check with Josie. Will do." I thanked him and headed for the door. "Quick question: Who's Josie? The girl with the dragon tattoo?"

"The fine young lady from apartment C, of course! And yes, I suppose she does bear a resemblance to the girl from that movie. She's a very sweet girl. Josie and Aliyah are lesbians," he added with a good-natured laugh, "but they have promised that if they ever switch sides, they will come to me first. I am not holding my breath."

Hazim shook my hand vigorously. "Come by any time, my friend. I will keep an eye out for intruders in the future. Oh, and you may want to ask Dave from apartment D if he saw anything. He usually drives to Kansas City to see his daughters on the weekends, so he probably wasn't here Friday, and he's not always the friendliest person, but it's worth a shot."

As I shuffled down the hallway to apartments C and D, I felt like a prick for having never befriended my neighbors like Hazim did. Fortunately, Angry Dave was there to reaffirm my faith in the merits of a solitary, non-neighborly existence.

I knocked on his door twice, didn't receive a response, and was ready to move along when I heard his boorish voice call out, "Who the hell is it?"

"V.C.! From down the hall."

"*Who?*"

"Land shark."

Angry Dave opened the door just enough to reveal a sliver of his scowling, mustachioed face. "What do you want?"

I fed him the same line about my place being vandalized.

"Can't help you," he said curtly. "Don't know shit. Bye-bye."

Pleasantries taken care of, he shut the door in my face and locked the deadbolt.

"Don't let him get you down," came a squeaky little voice behind me. "He's like that to everyone."

The girl with the dragon tattoo—Josie, apparently—stood outside her door holding a purring, cream-colored cat. Jake gave her the dragon tattoo moniker the day he helped me move in because she resembled, from a distance anyway, the title character from the David Fincher movie. Up close, her features were much softer, but she was still the poster girl for visceral overload: tattoos, piercings, and spikes covered nearly every inch of her bony frame.

"Hi," I said. "I'm V.C., from down the hall. I was hoping you could help."

"V.C.? What does that stand for?"

"Nothing. I was conceived in Virginia City, but my parents weren't depraved enough to name me that, so they went with V.C."

"Interesting. I was a Super Bowl baby."

"Oh, yeah?"

"Yeah. My dad played lineman for the Cowboys in '94. They were down thirteen to six at halftime. He was superstitious and thought it was because he and my mom didn't have their ritual pre-game quickie. So, he threw her a fuck during halftime while the Judd's sang a duet. The Cowboys scored twenty-four unanswered and nine months later, I popped out."

"Oh, yeah?"

"I'm sorry. Is that too much info?" She held out her hand. "Name's Josie. You can call me the girl with the dragon tattoo."

"Oh, yeah?"

"Stop that. And I'm joking, of course. Hazim just called and said you were on your way. And that you call me the girl with the dragon tattoo. Don't worry, though. I've been called worse. I'll even take it as a compliment. Come in."

I stepped inside her apartment, which smelled of cat litter, perfume, and marijuana. Clothes, dirty dishes, and empty food wrappers were strewn about. A copy of the book *Rebuilding the Walls of Time: Hypnosis, the Powerful Mind, and Past Life Regression* sat on the counter.

"Good thing I cleaned up today," Josie deadpanned. "I wasn't expecting visitors."

"I'll just take a minute of your time. I'm not sure how much you heard, or what Hazim told you, but my apartment was broken into Friday. The police are no help, of course, so I was wondering if any of my neighbors saw anything unusual."

Josie was grinning ear-to-ear. "Anything *unusual?* Yeah, I did see something *unusual.* This one guy who lives in my building got his wasted ass handcuffed and dragged down the stairway. He looked like shit. I wonder if he even remembers it."

"Wait. You were here? You saw that?"

"Hell, yeah. My girlfriend and I were walking up the stairs when that fat ass cop dragged you down them. You looked like shit."

"So I've heard."

"And the cop said to us"—she lowered her voice in a shoddy attempt to mimic Beerman—"'this is what happens, ladies, when you don't pay your bar bill and put your hands on a police officer.'"

"That's plain slander. I've never walked out on a bar tab in my life."

"Did you at least punch a cop?"

"No."

"Damn. That would have been sexy. I was even get-ting ready to show you my dragon tattoo. Instead, you get demon bunny."

She lifted the side of her shirt to reveal a red-eyed, saber-toothed zombie bunny tattooed on her midriff.

"That is one demonic bunny. Back to Friday, though—did you notice anything, you know, suspi-cious before I got arrested?"

"Not a thing."

"Figures. Thanks anyway. I'll leave you to your kit-ties and your demons." I made for the door. "See you around, I'm sure."

"Slow down, Virginia!" Stealth-like, she slipped in front

of me, blocking my path. "Aren't you going to ask me if I saw anything suspicious *after* the cop dragged you off?"

"Did you?"

"I did. But first, tell me what really happened. You're hiding something."

"The less you know, the better. Trust me."

"You are *soooo* cliché. Demon bunny is rolling his eyes so hard right now. Come on, you can tell me."

"Fine. Here's the truth. A friend of mine died last week, or so we thought. We even had a funeral for him on Friday. Closed casket, sort of. That night, I went out and got wasted..."

"You looked like shit."

"... and when I got home, I found my friend's dead, freshly murdered body on my floor. The cop—detective, actually—that you met showed up out of nowhere and hauled me to jail for some reason. To complicate things, he's an associate of my dead friend's father, an organized crime boss..."

"Fine. Don't tell me."

"Honest to Anton Lavey, this is one hundred per-cent true."

"Whatever. The truth is probably boring anyway. Here's what we saw: Half an hour after you and the cop left, some dude built like a brick shithouse showed up and went into your room with a giant trunk. He was in there for about twenty minutes and then came out with the trunk. Aliyah and I stood in the main doorway by Kun-Woo's and watched him struggling to lug it down the steps. Looked heavy as shit. He dragged it right by us and said, 'Police business. Piss off.' Acted like a cop, but didn't look like any police I've ever seen. You know the guy?"

With a queasy feeling in my gut, I visualized some ogre casually rolling a bloody corpse box down Delmar Blvd., Jake juice trickling onto the Walk of Fame as socialites toasted health, happiness, and the dearly departed all around him. For all I know, he wheeled the trunk right past me.

"Maybe," I lied, for some reason. "What exactly did he look like?"

"Like an asshole. Like he lives under a bridge and eats steroids and children for breakfast. Tall, pale, shaved head. Flying snake tattoo on the back of his skull. Judging by the blank look on your face, I'm going to go out on a limb and say he's not a friend of yours."

She was right. I had no idea who he was. Jake's killer? Another crooked cop? Some low level organized crime trash collector?

Little did I know, in less than one hour, my questions would be answered and the mystery man would be a mystery no longer. As I gazed into the barrel of his gun, he would tell me everything I wanted to know. And then he would pull the trigger.

———————

Outside, the forces of nature battled for dominion. The skies boomed and belched and frosty raindrops drizzled down, but a ray or two of rebellious sunlight fought through the clouds, glistening the wet pavement. As the rain fell harder, the sunlight grew brighter. Life was a CCR tune.

For my own part, I was walking on pure sunshine.

Just twenty minutes after becoming a private investigator—a largely unwilling, untrained, pseudo version of
one, anyway—I had unraveled a lead, or scored a clue,
or whatever the adage was. All we had to do now was
pick Skull Tat out of Lewie's files, with Josie's help if
necessary, and we had the body snatcher, and possibly
the murderer, positively identified. All was well.

Well, maybe not *all*. There was the obvious question
of what to do with this new info once we obtained it.
Contact the police? Surely not everyone in the SLPD
was as corrupt as Beerman. Reach out to Lewie's friend
in federal places? Present the facts to Big Jamie and sit
back and watch while he painted the streets red? Send
an anonymous letter to those nosy news fucks Beerman
warned me to avoid? Post the story on Facebook and
see if I could get one hundred people to like it?

And then there was T-Bone, who was conspicuously
absent from his musical stoop, which I hoped wasn't
unusual on a sleepy Sunday morning. I'd never paid
much attention to his schedule before, but then again,
I never had reason to fear that he was lying in a ditch
bleeding to death. Last night, when I returned from
the pharmacy, he seemed OK. *Ish*, anyway. But in the
sobering clarity of the morning, it felt criminally neg-
ligent to let him go without professional medical care.

The universe must have sensed my unease
and figured it owed me one, because at that very
moment, my phone vibrated with good news. Not
only did I have an email from Lexxxi Hardy confessing that she "wants to try new $ex game with
stud boys girls at wild invitation orgy. Free Cial$!$is"

but there was also a text from Kalista:

> *Hope I'm not waking you. sorry about last night, I'm*
> *a $*#%*… I feel awful. Poor me… Had breakfast*
> *with T bone. Best date in years! He said to tell you*
> *he's ok, just sore. Call you later.*

Although life and love and a slew of other four-letter words have jaded me beyond repair, I had to smile
just thinking about dancing with Kalista last night and
tasting her soft cherry lips, which paired particular well
with Cabernet. It was a moment I wanted to put in a
bottle of Grand Marnier and drink forever. Naturally,
my impulse was to respond to her text with a marriage
proposal. Somehow, I resisted.

Instead, I texted Lewie:

> *Big news. New suspect. Is there a guy with a flying*
> *snake tattoo on his skull in your files? He was at*
> *my apt Friday and stole a dead Kennedy.*

His response wasn't what I expected, and it made
the gravity of the situation quite clear:

> *Whoa. Dude. Don't. Go. Anywhere. Especially Big*
> *Jamie's. Abort. Mission. We're. Fucked. Abort!!*

Unfortunately, in standard Lewie fashion, the text
didn't come through until three hours later. By then,
I had already passed, quite literally, through the jaws
of Death.

Chapter 6

I HAD SOME TROUBLE FINDING MY CAR IN THE PARKING lot behind Ditzy's Root Beer. It hadn't seen much street action since I moved to the Loop and stopped venturing beyond the stretch of Delmar Blvd. from Kingsland to Skinker.

At the tail end of my marriage, that old clunker was my sanctuary. Most evenings, after Steffi and I got our requisite squabble out of the way, I hopped inside it, drove around aimlessly, and blew off steam. While I was away, Steffi whored around aimlessly and blew off the neighbor. It was a win-win situation.

Luckily, the engine turned over on the first try. I felt like I'd been reunited with an old friend as I merged onto the Interbelt, heading north towards the county with Titus Andronicus wailing in my eardrums.

Coincidentally, an old copy of the *St. Louis Punk-Disgrace* lay on the passenger seat. Despite its name, it wasn't a low-budget spoof of the *St. Louis Post-Dispatch*, but instead a *Crime Times* – style rag that published colorful commentaries and news bits about Mound City's seedy underbelly.

Its writers/editors, brothers Reginald and James Hudson, were ardent admirers of amusing alliterations apparently, because headlines included such gems as "Soused Suburban Sad Sack Skids into Stop Sign" and "Hood Rat from Hell Goes Very Medieval on Vending Machine" (subtitle: *Psychotic shorty wins overnight stay in city's finest lockup*). Disingenuous slogan—*Rehabilitating by Humiliating!*—notwithstanding, it was entertainment gold, at least in small doses.

It was also the first publication to identify Big Jamie Kennedy as the ring leader of a global criminal empire. Before that, he was anonymous outside of St. Louis. Even within the city, most people only knew him as the impishly-grinning pimp surrounded by double D's on the BJ's Cabaret billboard alongside Interstate 40 near Sauget.

In its wake, word slowly spread that the East side was run by the mafia, or at least some pseudo version of it. Perhaps it was a coincidence, but a few weeks later, the History Channel aired a documentary about the modern American mob. Several minutes were devoted to Big Jamie. Soon after, news reports surfaced that the Justice Department was actively investigating him. As far as I know, nothing ever became of it. But Big Jamie would never fly under the radar again.

This is the article, poetic warts and all:

On a steamy, starry, South Side Saturday night, a frazzled fiend buries a bullet in the bevy of a bystander's brain. It doesn't matter that the vic, 64-year-old

Donald Hadigan, is cleaner than a whistle wading in trisodium phosphate. The desperate dope fiend needs his fix, and the dead presidents in Hadigan's pocket are his ticket to get faded tonight.

Ten miles east, on O'Fallon Ave, buckets of blood paint the serene, sequoia-lined street a raging red. Surrounding the pails of plasma are 5-0 and lookout boys, nauseated neighbors and bored blunt heads. But the gangsta who pulled the trigger is out of sight, and surprise surprise, it's quieter than a church mouse during Sunday service as the SLPD murder squad scours the 'hood for a willing witness. They knock on doors and take down names, but everyone knows they are spinning their wheels. Thomas Baby T Bragg, 19, is just another dead dope dealer who wore the wrong colors and stood on the wrong side of the street on the wrong day of the week. His murder will go unsolved, and by the time the credits roll on the morning news, his replacement will be slinging fresh rock and St. Louis will have forgotten Mrs. Bragg's baby boy ever existed.

Dangerous drugs and verminous violence are sad staples of life in the Lou, and there's beaucoup blame to go around, from the pinky-pointing politicians to the lowliest lookout boy. We all know that. But what you may not know is that the lion's lot of the dope and coke in our city (and maybe the entire Midwest) comes courtesy of one measly man.

He's a man the DEA and FBI (some of them, anyway) have been monitoring and surveilling for years. According to one fed who acquiesced to assisting on account of absolute anonymity, he's a man whose powder-powered payroll includes local police and federal agents from every law enforcement agency that you, your neighbor, and your Aunt Ava's hairdresser can collectively conceive.

His name is Jamie Kennedy aka Big Jamie to those in the know. According to my loquacious, bodacious contact, Kennedy's payroll includes cocaine cultivators in Bolivia, poppy-planting Afghanis, and an elaborate network of nefarious U.S. government officials who ensure safe passage of his putrid, poisonous product all the way from the U.S-Mexican border to the crumbling corners of St. Louis, Chicago, Kansas City, Cleveland, and as far north as Detroit.

Our source estimates that 80 percent of the blow and dope crippling our communities comes from Mr. Kennedy and his corrupt criminal counterparts. Law enforcement officials who aren't on the tawdry, tasteless take have linked him to prostitution and illegal bookmaking from coast to coast as well.

Local businesses Big Jamie owns include strip clubs BJ's Cabaret and Sexy Trixie's, an escort service called Diamond Girls, Shi-Lo Sharky's, a collection agency, Fly Buy, a chain of skimpily-stocked grocery stores where four brawny behemoths mysteriously man the counter, Cicada Club, and a slew of inner city parking garages.

Next time you and your ballers are fixin' to blow your bank on gyrating, G-stringed strippers, remember where your greenbacks are going. Mr. Kennedy cares less about this community than a paraplegic cares about perfecting the polka.

Check back next week for more on Big Jamie Kennedy, because you can bet your bottom banknote that this newspaper (unlike other petrified publications that refuse to touch Big Jamie with a 12-foot stripper pole) isn't done dragging St. Louis's vilest villain into the limelight.

If you really would have bet your bottom banknote, you'd be broke. To this day, Big Jamie's name hasn't appeared in the pages of the *Punk-Disgrace* again. Maybe he strong-armed the Hudson boys into silence. Maybe he paid them off. Maybe they were blackballed on other stories by suddenly uncooperative police. Or maybe, as the conspiracy theorist inside me believes, Big Jamie, craving notoriety after years of anonymity, masterminded the article himself.

Stranger things have happened.

I felt like Luca Brasi rehearsing his lines at Connie Corleone's wedding.

"My deepest condolences, Mr. Kennedy," I practiced out loud, "but your son is officially food for worm's thoughts. I found him murdered in my apartment on Friday night, several hours after his funeral. Detective Joe Beerman, whom I understand is a friend of yours, can tell you more. He showed up at my place for some reason just after I did. I believe Jake's body is in the possession of a man with a flying snake tattoo on the back of his skull. Out of respect for you, I have not discussed the matter with the police, The

Police, or any of Sting's other associated acts."

In truth, despite my attempts to humor myself, I wasn't feeling very light-hearted anymore. If Big Jamie didn't believe my story or, worse, thought I was implicit in Jake's murder, I knew I'd be sipping GrandMa in the Great Beyond within the hour.

I first met Big Jamie when I was nineteen years old. Jake hadn't seen him for nearly two years. We went to his south side watering hole, Big Jamie's Cicada Club, to drink White Russians and act like we belonged. The first time I saw Big Jamie, he was dragging a man in a chef's hat by the ear. He forced him to the front entrance, hurled him to the pavement outside, and ordered the bouncer to "go play piñata with his fucking skull." Moments later, Big Jamie was shaking hands and cracking jokes with us like nothing was wrong and a brain matter mosaic wasn't getting painted in the parking lot.

I'd never been inside his sprawling estate, but it was impossible to miss. A massive brick building with round-arched windows and pointed turrets, it was the solitary structure atop a steep manmade hill situated a stone's throw from the Clark Bridge in West Alton. Its backyard swimming pool was the Mississippi River. A high-voltage fence weaved around its perimeter through a widespread bamboo thicket. From street level, a winding, paved trail lined with hardy mums and delicate dahlias led to a security gate about a hundred yards from the front entrance. Even Jake had to pass through it when he visited, which was hardly ever.

The layout wasn't accidental or for the sake of

aesthetics. The sharp hill, meandering driveway, and security checkpoint safeguarded Big Jamie from sneak attacks by warrant-wielding feds. From a dozen different vantage points, a person inside could spot a vehicle zigzagging up the hill. If Big Jamie ever got raided, he'd have ample time to make some calls, hide some contraband, or dump some severed fingers into the bowels of the Muddy Mississippi.

As I inched up the driveway, thunder filled the sky, lightning flashed, and buckets of rain started to fall. In the daily battle of sun versus rain, hope versus melancholia, a winner had been crowned. It didn't help calm the butterflies in my stomach, which were starting to feel more like hornets. I had a sickening feeling that I was making a serious misstep and should turn around and go home. Instead, against every iota of instinct, I soldiered on.

Unexpectedly, the security booth was unmanned and the mechanical gate wide open. I paused beside it for a long minute, debating whether I should stay or I should go and, then, if *Combat Rock* was an exercise in selling out or evolving. Finally, I chose the latter. I also chose to push the intercom buzzer once, twice, three times.

Radio silence.

I pushed it again and yelled, "Hello! Anybody home? Are you there? Are you still serving breakfast?!"

Silence.

"This is V.C., Jake's friend," I announced. "I'll just go ahead and pull up! Also, and I really can't stress this enough, I come in peace, man!"

I approached the house slowly with my flashers and high beams on, trying to make it clear that this wasn't a sneak attack. Eventually, I came to a halt next to a water fountain in the shape of an elephant. Whimsical choice for a drug lord, I thought.

I watched the house for several minutes without seeing even a flicker of movement. Maybe nobody was home. It was Sunday, after all. Big Jamie was probably taking a leisurely drive, singing falsetto in the church choir, or forcing some schmuck's finger into a torturous vice grip. The usual Lord's Day activities, you know.

I should have said that I gave it the old college drop-out try and gone home, but instead, I jumped out of my car and ran to the front door. I was drenched by the time I reached the covered patio—a portmanteau, was it? No, that wasn't right. Pimlico? Pomodoro? Somewhere, my owl-eyed Intro to Architecture professor from freshman year was having a cornice.

I rang the doorbell and waited. No answer. I knocked loudly several times. Still, nothing. Content now to move along my merry way, I turned back towards the car and was getting ready to run through the rain when something caught my eye. There were four somethings, actually. And each was barking louder, running faster, and foaming at the mouth more angrily than the one before.

Doberman Pinschers. Good old-fashioned junk-yard dogs.

I had no idea where they had come from, but they were boring down on me at full stride from a couple hundred feet away. My car was at least half that distance.

Advantage, dogs.

I dropped my head and broke into a dead sprint, but I couldn't get traction on the wet pavement. I only made it a few yards before I slipped, fell, and landed face first in a bed of landscaping rock.

Woozily, I looked up to see my canine killers nearly upon me. Before I blacked out, three thoughts crossed my mind:

The first was that years ago, I heard the comedian Norm MacDonald perform an amusing routine about Doberman Pinschers. I should track it down if the dogs don't eat my ears. Lewie was right, laughter really is the best medicine.

The second was that Big Jamie's patio is called a *portico*.

The third thought was actually more of an observation: the Dobermans weren't alone. A man was leading them. He carried a shovel in one hand, a revolver in the other, and he was built like a brick shithouse. His skin was pale as a ghost.

For a split second, he turned his head, and I could have sworn that I saw, through a thick haze of raindrops and blood, a hissing serpent with angel wings tattooed on the back of his skull.

———————

I sat on a bench in a dark train station, staring into the abyss. Several people loitered about with blank, disassociated looks on their faces, like undead horror movie extras. The train was scheduled to arrive at any moment, but I knew it would never show. I ran like hell.

Invisible enemies followed in close pursuit. Somehow,

I made it to the Loop, but I couldn't find my apartment building. An old hippie slurping vodka from a brown paper sack walked up to me and said, "Usually, when I meet people, I claim to be the rain. They usually punch me out!"

A giant police officer stepped between us, club raised. He wore a nametag that read KLC.

"Prepare for punishment and incarceration," he said in a robotic monotone.

"This is an outrage!" the hippie cried.

"This is America!" I added.

"America the beautiful," said the cop, his mighty club falling upon us.

And then I was dancing with Kalista and life felt right again. All the horror shows and crooked cops in the world couldn't get me down.

"But you're missing something!" hollered Kalista.

I realized we were on a crowded dance floor. "I'm missing what?!"

"Something obvious!"

"About what? About Jake?"

"Of course!" She leaned in and kissed my lips, my cheeks, my forehead. Her tongue felt soft and warm and far too wet, like a... dog. "It's because your eyes aren't open!"

"What?!"

"You're missing something obvious because your eyes aren't open! Open your eyes, grasshopper! Open your eyes! Open your eyes!"

"OPEN YOUR EYES!!!"

I opened my eyes.

I was lying on a comfy couch with a bandage wrapped around my head, and I had company. A Doberman was nibbling my shoe playfully, his chompers a few centimeters from severing my little toe. Another was making out with every inch of my face, licking me frantically like I was an ice cream cone melting in the sun. I could feel the saliva high up my nostrils and deep in my throat.

"Well, well, well," came the surprisingly effeminate voice of the man with the flying snake tattoo. "Look who decided to join us."

My wallet, keys, phone, a few of those ludicrous business cards that I brought along for no good reason, a large black revolver, and, most disconcertingly, my pants, were spread out on a cocktail table between us.

"My pants ... why don't I have my pants?" I managed to say.

"Um ... duh! I had to check you for weapons, didn't I?"

"Weapons?"

"Oh, don't worry. Believe it or not, I'm a big ole sister if you know what I mean."

I didn't.

"Fine, you big baby. You can have your pants back."

He tossed them to me and called off the disappointed dogs as I struggled to get up.

"I miss the nightmare train station," I murmured.

"What's that? Oh, don't mind Death. He never can get enough of the boys. I wonder where he gets that from."

"So, you're ..."

"Gay? Is that a problem?"

"No. I was going to say … Never mind. How long was I out?"

"About an hour. You got yourself a nice little divot in your forehead. I put a few stitches in there for you. They self-dissolve, I think. You're welcome. You really didn't need to run off like that, you know."

"Oh?"

"Truth is, they might look scary, but these little munchkins of mine are big ole' softies at heart."

"Good to know."

"Your boyfriend over there is Death. This is War here, and that's Famine. Conquest is the runt of the litter. He's the one with the shoe fetish."

My head, just north of my left eyebrow, was throbbing. I wondered what my captor's qualifications were to stitch a bloody melon. It sure as hell didn't feel right. Maybe the wound was infected with Death dribble. On the bright side, the fact that he bothered to fix me up probably meant he wasn't planning to park a bullet in me.

A dozen questions raced through my mind.

"Did you kill Big Jamie?"

He looked genuinely befuddled. "Did *I* kill Big Jamie? Are you afraid I beat you to it? Of course I didn't kill James. Do I seem crazy to you?"

Yes, I thought. More than a little. Instead, I said, "What were you doing with that shovel then?"

"My my! Aren't you a nosy Rosie!"

"Where are we?"

"James's basement."

There was an elegant marble bar, fully stocked, along one wall. Pub tables, plush armchairs, sofas, and stages with stripper poles were spread throughout. A DJ booth was set up in the corner.

"Big Jamie's basement is a strip club?"

"You really are a mastermind sleuth, aren't you?" He forced War gently from his lap and stood up. "We really do have fun down here. Even us sisters. It's a shame you won't be around to ever experience it."

He picked up the gun and gazed at it lovingly for a few seconds. Then he pressed it against my forehead.

"What the... wait!" I pleaded. "Who are you?"

He rolled his eyes. "Seriously? You're going to act like you don't know who I am? What a lame stall tactic. I'm Sal, of course!"

He paused, perhaps expecting a reaction.

"Salvatore Aquino? *El número dos*? Big Jamie Kennedy's main man! Big Gay Sal?"

I stared back blankly, which was evidently the wrong response. He pulled the trigger. Then again, and again, and again, and again. And then he burst out in laughter.

"Oh! My! Buddha! You should see the look on your face, double-0-seven! Whoo! You didn't think I'd really kill you right here, did you? This thing isn't even loaded. Look!"

He opened the cylinder to reveal five empty chambers and a shiny silver bullet resting idly in the sixth.

"Whooooaaaa," he said.

"Whooooaaaa," I said.

"Dude ... I almost killed you in the house. *In* the fucking house. Do you have any idea the trouble I'd be in?" He sounded devastated. "Not cool, Sal! Not cool ..."

I got the feeling Big Gay Sal was off his meds. "Hey, there. Everybody makes mistakes, man," I said.

With shaky hands, he emptied the chamber and tossed the lonely bullet over his shoulder. "Now," he said, collecting himself, "where were we? Oh, right. You were about to squeal."

"Squeal?"

"Squeal!" he shouted. "Who are you?"

Big Gay Sal jumped to his feet and towered above me, getting the dogs all worked up. "Who sent you? Chicago? San Diego? Tijuana? Spill it, spy!"

"Lewie," I said, "Lewie sent me."

In a flash, he was waving a hypodermic needle in front of my eyes. "There are ways for me to get you to talk, Spynet Sam! Sodium thiopental! Ever hear of it? It's a little something we in the biz like to call truth serum!"

He was inches from my face, his crazy-wide eyes locked on mine... and then he broke out in cackles of laughter once again. "I'm just joking, of course. Truth serum! What is this, a cheesy dime novel? There's no such thing as truth serum! It's insulin, man! Helps me bench-press an elephant."

"I tell you what, I think I'm just going to mosey along…"

I gathered my things quickly and backed away slowly, though I didn't know which way to go. Sal was poking and prodding his six-pack abs, looking for a good injection site.

"Sounds like the rain has stopped," I continued, "and

obviously Big Jamie's not here. I've got a few other things to, you know, get off the checklist today. So, it was nice to meet you. And the dogs, of course. Thanks for the stitches and for, you know, joking around with me with the gun and all. I'll see myself out..."

Sal rolled his eyes. "The exit's over here, Hardy Boy! And you know I can't let you leave. Not before you tell James everything you know about Chicago, Tijuana, or whoever's signing your check!"

"Chicago? Tijuana? Wind and donkey shows, man. That's what I know. Who do you think I am? My name's V.C. I was a friend of Jake's, that's all. I came to see Big Jamie to... um, you know... offer my condolences."

"Bullshit. Only a pro could get past the electric fence and through the security gate without getting noticed. You work for the feds? NSA? Don't lie. That business card of yours looks pretty CIA to me, Man from U.N.C.L.E.!"

"Man from ...? CIA? What the ...?! I'm just a guy, man. And the gate was open! I pushed the buzzer half a dozen times! I yelled into it. I even made a joke about breakfast."

"Breakf...?" I didn't think Big Gay Sal's face could get whiter, but it did. "Fuuuuuck..." he said slowly. I could see the hamster wheel in his brain starting to turn. "Did I... the gate... are you sure? It's open? I forgot to close it? Fuck! I did, didn't I? The buzzer won't work when it's open.... Oh, *fuck fuck fuck fuck*..."

Suddenly, my captor was on the move, scurrying to the doorway and cursing under his breath as the dogs followed in close pursuit.

"Wait right there!" he called. "And stay away from the third floor!"

There was silence for several minutes. I considered hiding, but to what end? Fleeing was pointless as well. The only way to freedom was through the gate and down the long driveway. I couldn't possibly escape unnoticed.

I considered sneaking up to the third floor—which, according to the papers, was where Big Jamie found his son dead from a self-inflicted gunshot wound—but it wasn't worth the risk. Sal could be back any minute, and I had no clue where I was going. So instead, I did what I do best—I poured myself a snifter of Grand Marnier and waited.

Eventually, Big Gay Sal returned. He took out his phone and pointed it at me.

"Smile," he said, and disappeared again.

Moments later, he returned, looking sheepish.

"Fine. You're not a spy. I was wrong. And I'm sorry." He teared up a little, confirming I had tumbled down the rabbit hole. "Now let's get you cleaned up, V.C. Big Jamie wants to see you pronto."

———————

Princess Estella was her name, and her life was roses and ponies until the bloodsucking Count Shagula turned her into a vampire. Naturally, she despised him for a solid five minutes, but his charm was too great to resist. She fell madly in love with him, and when he asked for her hand in marriage, she wept for joy.

Their wedding ceremony was also a coronation.

First, they exchanged vows, and then Shagula was pronounced king. A grand, orgiastic celebration ensued. Together, Shagula and Estella screwed and bit the masses, turning the entire kingdom into horny vampires. Everybody frolicked and fornicated and nibbled each other's necks while a vampire who resembled Michael Jackson circa 1985 sang pop tunes and moonwalked across the floor. Nobody was in any position to complain.

Estella was the protagonist, the one we were supposed to *really* care about. She definitely saw the most action. And she had a moral dilemma. Although she was now a happily married vampire queen, a piece of her heart, she confessed to her scantily clad handmaiden, still belonged to her true love, Prince Longrod.

Right on queue, the handsome prince materialized in her bedchamber.

"My love!" he exclaimed. "How my heart leapeth with joy to layeth my eyes upon your fairest of faces and most bountiful of bosoms! Word has reached my ears that the abominable Count Shagula is near! We must escape, my love, before it is too late!"

First, though, they enjoyed a threesome with the handmaiden.

"I feel almost human again," whispered Estella into Longrod's ear.

"*Almost* human?"

A look of shock and horror appeared on his face as he realized Estella was a vampire.

"Curse you, Shagula!" he cried out.

The camera panned out to show Shagula standing

in the corner, laughing manically. Evidently, he'd been in the room, playing looky-loo, all along.

A battle broke out between Longrod and Estella. Inexplicably, they wore chain mail now. Longrod wielded a giant stake.

"You may have a long rod, Longrod, but you will never defeat my queen!" taunted Shagula.

Longrod must have agreed with the Count's assessment, because he promptly turned the stake around and plunged it through his own heart. The chainmail was gone now. What the hell.

"I would rather perish," said Longrod with his dying breath, "than live another day with the knowledge that my true love is the bride of Shagula!"

Weeping, Estella removed the stake from Longrod's heart and plunged it through her own.

"And I would rather perish," she said with her dying breath, "than live another day with the knowledge that I shall never hold Longrod in my hands... I mean, my arms... again!"

It was Shagula's turn. He picked up the stake, pressed it against his own chest... and then tossed it away with a mirthful laugh.

Was this his plan all along? The ending was open to interpretation, I suppose. As the credits rolled, Shagula peered into the camera, mua-ha-ha-ing like Dracula. He was lean and wiry and didn't look like he had started an insulin regimen to bench press an elephant yet, but the pug nose and deep-set eyes were unmistakably those of Big Gay Sal.

"Well," said Sal excitedly, ejecting the tape from a

Stone Age VHS player, "what did you think?"

I hesitated. My experiences with the pseudo-comedic 1980s short softcore porn film genre were surprisingly limited. And my honest answer—"I will forever have difficulty looking you in the eye"—somehow seemed uncouth.

"You hated it!" said Sal, dejected. "Don't try to deny it, I can tell, you hated it."

"Not at all. It was good. The acting was really good. Especially that strapping young lad who played Shagula." We clinked champagne glasses. "Tour de force performance, man."

Big Gay Sal's frown turned upside down. "Not bad for a big ole sister, huh?"

We were riding in the company limo to Trixie's. Big Jamie "was hosting open tryouts for new talent," said Sal. Our driver, a stone-faced Latino covered in tats, picked us up right after Sal told me Big Jamie wanted to see me. He didn't look pleased, and I got the feeling this wasn't a regularly scheduled workday.

After Sal realized I wasn't James Bond, a Hardy Boy, or any other fictional spook, he decided that my real identity must be his new best friend. Over flutes of Dom Perignon, he told me his life story. Not your average, everyday bodybuilding gangster-prankster with a couple dozen screws loose, he had stints as a B-movie actor, Hollywood bodyguard, and semi–pro wrestler (where he first assumed the Big Gay Sal moniker) before joining Big Jamie's crew more than a decade ago. He didn't stop chatting for a single minute.

"Do you want to see my wrestling debut?" he said

excitedly, reaching for another tape. He reminded me of a child showing off his toys at a sleepover.

"I was hoping you'd ask."

"It was in a high school gym with about eighty people in the crowd. The promotion was called the Wrestling Wrestling Wrestling Foundation. I know, creative, right? It formed in '87 or '88 and was out of business by '89. Check it out, I was the heel, the bad guy, but those good ole country boys loved me. I guess they recognized it takes balls to wear a pink tutu in motherfucking Dixie. Or maybe they secretly wore the same thing under their huntin' vests."

Next up was a children's commercial starring an eye-patched Sal and his pirate crew singing a sea shanty about plundering the corners of the world for cereal, or action figures, or something. I wasn't sure, and didn't care. Nor was I sure what such a thing was doing in a crime lord's limousine.

What the hell had Lewie gotten me into? What the hell really happened at my apartment Friday night? As the limo pulled into the parking lot of Trixie's Gentlemen's Club, I had a powerful premonition that my questions were about to be answered.

I have never been more wrong.

———

A large neon clock emblazoned with the silhouette of an exotic dancer in the crab walk position hung in the entranceway. Her long, slender legs functioned as the clock's hands, so that at 6:30, for instance, she wasn't a lick of fun. At 3:45 and 9:15, on the other hand, she was open for all kinds of business.

I entered Trixie's at the freakishly acrobatic time of four o'clock. By the far more plausible 4:30, I was heading out the door, feeling like it was my brain that had been twisted in a dozen impossible directions.

The club wasn't open yet, but fifteen or twenty glittering young ladies lounged around, smoking cigarettes and waiting for their chance to gyrate jubilantly in their G-strings, as the Hudson brothers would say. Big Jamie sat at a table in the far corner, his eyes fixed on the girl on stage, who was swinging her hips to Joe Cocker's "You Can Leave Your Hat On." She wasn't a lyrics person, evidently, because she had taken her hat off, along with everything else.

With his flowery shirt, safari hat, and sleaze ball grin, Big Jamie looked like a silver-haired Jabba the Hut on a tropical vacation. Or the leader of a dystopian society where women were either given jobs as sex slaves or devoured whole. Unwanted male inquisitors like me were probably thrown into a desert pit and digested slowly over the course of several millennia.

"When do I get to shake my ass up there?" shouted Sal as we neared Big Jamie. "When do the boys get to have some fun, James?"

Big Jamie rolled his eyes, but he didn't stop smiling or chair-dancing. "You haven't missed a Tuesday night boy bash in thirteen years, Sally. I think you know when your little *sistahs* take the stage."

Sal pulled out the chair closest to his boss and gestured for me to sit. Big Jamie acknowledged me with a playful slap on the cheek. So far, so good.

"How we looking so far?" asked Sal.

"Beautiful as *evah*, Sally." Big Jamie moved to the Midwest three decades ago but still spoke the occasional phrase in a thick, R–less Boston accent. "All's quiet on the Chicago front."

Mr. Cocker quit his howling. Big Jamie waived the girl over.

"What do you think of *Kimbah* here, Sally? You think we can find a spot for her on a Monday *aftah-noon*? Or maybe the Sunday shift *aftah* church?"

Kimber stuck out her bottom lip, playing along.

"I don't know, James. Sunday mornings are pretty competitive," said Sal. "The other girls might mutiny."

"You aren't even *open* Sundays," said Kimber. "Today is Sunday."

"I think I'm in love!" declared Big Jamie. "Brains and beauty! What do you think, kiddo?"

Three sets of eyes looked at me, and I made a valid point that they probably hadn't considered.

"Umm," I said.

"Don't mind him," Sal intervened. "He's had a rough day. You don't even want to know how he got those stitches on his forehead."

Big Jamie scribbled something on a piece of paper and tossed it on stage like a dollar bill. "Bring that to Tony, that leathery *slickstah* by the door. He's the night *managah*, he'll get you set up, tell you about our stock options, 401k, profit sharing plan, and probably ask you some inappropriate personal questions that make you feel like a play toy. See you Friday night."

With a firm slap on her ass, Big Jamie sent Kimber

away. I found it hard to believe this mutant was remotely related to Jake.

"Do me a *favah*, Sally," he said. "I'm sure kiddo has a cell phone in his pocket. Lock it in the vault for a few minutes, will you?"

I must have looked as uneasy as I felt. "It's OK," said Sal, reassuringly. "Standard operating procedure. You're out of the fire pit now. Cross my heart."

For some reason, I trusted Sal. Never mind that two hours ago he was a trigger squeeze away from accidentally offing me. As he walked away to put my phone in the vault, I found myself hoping he'd hurry back.

"Don't take it personal, kiddo," said Big Jamie. I wondered if he knew my name. "You'll get it back when we're done. You never know who the *bastids* might have a roving bug on. You're probably safe, but I didn't get to where I am today by taking chances, you understand?"

I didn't.

"So do us all a *favah*, kiddo. Keep a hundred feet from your phone if you feel the need to *talk business*. If you know what I mean."

What?

"Of course, I don't have to tell you that, though, do I? You're probably the *smahtest* son of a bitch in this room!"

"Oh, yeah?"

"Oh, yeah. Beerman told me everything! To be honest, I loved your idea, at first anyway. You read the situation and called an audible. Nothing wrong with that, kiddo. If the plan goes haywire the first time, try again, right?"

Big Jamie took a cigar from his shirt pocket and started to light it.

"I appreciate brains like that. Balls, too. You *evah* need a job, you come to me. Truth is, though"—he leaned in close and lowered his voice—"it was nothing but a fluke. Some no-name nobody saw a dead man walking and tried to make a name for himself. It wasn't premeditated, and he wasn't in contact with anybody on our *radah*. The *bastids* are clueless as *evah*. The plan worked."

"The plan?"

"We think it worked, anyway. Fairly certain. Ninety percent certain. Ninety-five after a couple drinks. For a while, just to be sure though, some of us will be laying low with the Okies. If you catch my drift."

Big Jamie ruffled my hair playfully and continued spouting utter gibberish:

"It was Jake's own damn fault, really. He should have vanished for a few days, months even after a stunt like that. You kids would have *undestood*, right? But the kid just had to pop his head out on one of the busiest nights of the week in one of the busiest *pahts* of St. Louis, where every shithead mope knows his face. And look what happened."

For a moment, there was silence as Big Jamie puffed his cigar and I pondered the possibility that one or both of us were having a stroke.

"Ah, well," he continued, "no *hahm*, no foul, right? It's not the first or last time some foolish prick with a stupid fucking idea gets his brains blown out, right?"

I'd never heard anything so callous. Big Jamie just leaned back and sighed contentedly.

"How'd you like to stick around for a while, kiddo? You can help me *saht* through these beauties. Help me decide if they have the right *assets* to be part of the Trixie's harem. How's that sound?"

"It sounds... back up a second... So, we already *know* who killed Jake?"

He laughed and slapped my back. "'Jake killed himself, of course." He rubbed his eyes, drying mock tears. "My poor son... boo hoo hoo..."

"But... then... wait... at my apartment, I mean... who did it?"

"Who gives a fuck! Some no-name, like I said. *Fahget* about it, the plan worked!"

"What plan?"

Big Jamie shot me a peculiar look. I'd seen it before—on my own father's face, when he caught me with my teenaged hand in the liquor cabinet.

"My, my. Aren't you a nosy Rosie, as my big gay friend over there likes to say."

"He does like to say that."

"Listen, kiddo." For the first time, Big Jamie looked me in the eye. "You don't need to know everything about the original plan. Just reap the rewards and be happy. Drink the wine, let the world be the world, praise the God of all things, or however the fuck it goes. Understand?"

"Not... entirely."

"Fine. You win. And what the hell, I'm in a celebratory mood, so here's the essence: I'm an asshole, but I ain't a *slave owner*. I'm a *humanist*, you see. You want to hear the honest to God truth, kiddo?"

"That's why I'm here."

"I've done some questionable shit in my life. Google me, if you haven't already. But one thing I've never done is make a single person do a single fucking thing they didn't want to do on their own. You want to ruin your political career getting caught with a *hookah*? Stick a speedball in your arm and turn blue? Dance naked for meatheads who won't give you a second glance ten years from now? Go right ahead. Your call. I'll collect that check gladly. That's *free will*, kiddo. And who the fuck am I to stand in the way of that?"

Big Jamie stared me down, awaiting a response.

"I'm sorry. I thought that was a rhetorical question."

"Suppose one of my girls gets a crazy idea to do something new with her life, maybe go back to school, have some kids, sling rock in the projects, *whatevah*. You know what I do? I shake her hand, smack her ass one last time for good luck, and send her on her way with my blessing. I sure as shit don't force her to slob some scumbag's knob just to make my fat ass wallet a little *fattah*!"

His voice was getting louder. I'd touched a nerve somehow. What fresh weirdness was this?

"And do you know what happens, V.C.,"—hey, he knew my name!—"when some lowlife shithead disagrees and thinks he can strong *ahm* me, *Jamie Fucking Kennedy*, into going along with some hair-brained idea without expecting me to make a goddamn peep?!"

Most of the room, I realized, was watching us. I nodded empathically, attempting to send the message that Big Jamie was yelling with me, not at me.

99

"I'll tell you what happens. First, he gets robbed. And if he's got a problem with that, he gets a *bullet in his brain*! End... of... story!"

Beads of sweat were forming on Big Jamie's brow. His shirt was soaked.

"Plus," he continued, lowering his voice, "it's bad business. Do you think my police friends, my political allies, my respected business contacts—*pillahs* of the community I'm talking about here—would let that type of thing stand, V.C.? Do you think they would shrug their shoulders and look the other way? Is that what you think, V.C.? *Is it?*"

"In my life, I have never thought that once."

"Good. I'm glad we're on the same page."

I detected a tone of finality. Sure enough, he slapped my cheek playfully again and whistled at someone across the room.

"Tony Tone Tone!" he called out. "Quit pining for hand jobs and bring *ovah* the next contestant!"

Maybe it was just the Death sputum caked into my facial pores, but I had a craving for a long shower.

"I'm a busy man, kiddo," said Big Jamie. "Lots on the agenda. Hands to shake and wheels to grease. But I wouldn't miss an open call for new talent for all the coca fields in Bogota." He chuckled and tussled my hair again. "What a life, kiddo. What a life... Feel free to stay or go. Like I said, if beautiful women are your thing—and hey, I ain't judging you if they ain't—I suggest you keep your ass right there."

"Thanks, but I have a... thing... There's this place, actually, that I, um..."

"Say no more, kiddo. You got a thing at a place." Big Jamie ruffled my hair again. "Say no more," he repeated. "Say no more."

A young lady wearing a feathered boa and little else appeared beside us, carrying a gold-plated tray with an iPhone on it.

"Sorry to interrupt, Mr. Kennedy," she said excitedly, "but your special phone, the one that you said should never ever ring, just rang! The caller says it's urgent."

Big Jamie grinned and took the call while I took the opportunity to get the hell out of Dodge. Walking quickly towards the exit and the relative sanity of Big Gay Sal, I couldn't help but overhear his conversation. He was talking in code, it seemed. Is that what he'd been doing with me, too?

"The radio is about to get turned off," he said. "And be careful or the patio may get torn down, too."

I went home and iced my forehead, iced my Grand Marnier, and was preparing to ponder the day's myriad absurdities when Lewie sent me that *Abort!!* text message. He followed it with another:

> *Change of plans. Meeting with Seth Rogen tonight. No go on Bobby's bar. Breakfast tomorrow? 8:00 a.m., Cousin Willy's Diner. Bring yer thinkin' capp. Lots to discuss. Partner.*"

It was just as well. I did want to hear Lewie's perspective on the day's events, but my bed was beckoning.

I kicked off my shoes, crawled under the covers, and was getting ready to dream sweet dreams of my favorite dead Kennedy when my cell started to buzz. It was Kalista.

"Patty's Porno Palace," I answered. "Hold, please, Patty's coming."

"You're real hilarious. But we need to talk, V.C."
She sounded serious.

"I couldn't agree more. Open communications are the foundation of any loving, giving, long-term relationship, Kalista."

"The Oasis Hotel downtown, tomorrow, six o'clock. Can you make it?"

"Sure. We'll call it a date. And we'll call you a Chestnut and me an Almond."

"Real funny. But I got something in my mail that wasn't so funny."

"Let me guess. It was a fifteen percent off Kohl's coupon, even though you were totally due for a thirty."

"Not quite. It was a letter, and it was from Sergio." Her voice wavered. "It was written in blood. And it read, 'I'm going to kill V.C., and then I'm going to kill you.'"

Chapter 7

THE STRESS WAS CLEARLY GETTING TO ME. I SHOWED UP AT Cousin Willy's at 8:00 a.m. sharp, somehow forgetting that Lewie's standard time of arrival is three hours to three days late.

I sat alone at the counter for a couple hours, pounding coffee, contemplating my inevitable demise, and making small talk with the waitress, a sweet old lady whose nametag read Mighty Millie. Next to me, a trio of old grumps groused about everything that's wrong with the world: neighborhood association fees, speed traps, gun laws, kids these days, the price of coffee, and, especially, immigrants. They tried to reel me into the conversation at one point, but my response— *"Nada de ingles, s'il vous plait. Du dummkopf!"*—successfully startled them into silence.

Finally, around 10:30, the 314 area code jumped out of its collective skin as the loudest man west of the Mississippi burst through the door and bellowed, "Smells delicious in here! I'm so hungry I could eat a newborn!"

A young mother at a booth near the door instinctively pulled her toddler close.

"Only joking!" said Lewie, noticing her reaction. "At the most, I'd eat a limb. I'm no cannibal."

His face lit up with surprise when he saw me sitting at the counter. To Lewie, it was a remarkable phenomenon that a human being would actually be present at the place where he said he would be, at the time he said he would be there.

"Partner! Been here long? Sorry if I'm running a few minutes late," he said, settling into the seat across from me. "Coffee please, my good miss!" he called to Mighty Millie. "Black as night and thick as snot, preferably."

"A few minutes? Where the hell have you been, man? You said you were on your way two hours ago. And you live two minutes from here!"

"Oh, yeah? Did I say that? Classic sleep talk! Sorry, man, but I had to make a pit stop."

"A pit stop? Where?"

"If I remember correctly, I had to get my ex-girlfriend Kelly to a Moby concert at Riverport because she was singing a cappella during the second set. Bizarre, huh? But neither of us were wearing clothes, and we were driving a Flintstones car, so I had to use my feet. And our teeth kept falling out. Any idea what that means? And then you showed up, actually. Somehow, we ended up at the Himeji Castle..."

"Do you realize the textbook definition of asshole is a person who shows up two hours late because he's at home dreaming of some girl he went on *one* date with *three* years ago and still refers to as his ex-girlfriend, like some made-for-TV-movie stalker?"

"First of all, V.C., Kelly and I went on two dates.

Second, stalking is no joking matter. It's a fact, fourteen out of one thousand women are stalked in their lifetimes and often suffer a litany of long-term..."

"Seriously, Lewie?"

"... negative effects, including an inability to embrace intimate situations and an unshakeable sense of isolation. Third, I'm almost positive that the *textbook* definition of asshole revolves largely around the expulsion of feces and other undesirables from the digestive tract. Fourth, forget about it. I'll make it up to you, partner. Guaranteed. Fifth... what the fuck happened to your head, dude?"

Sal had actually done a surprisingly good job suturing me up. He even sent me home with a bottle of prescription wound cleanser—it was for dogs, but still. Despite all this, the gash was, in medical jargon, unsightly as all possible fuck.

"You mean, it's noticeable?"

"For Frankenstein's monster, not so much. For you? Yeah, a little bit. What the hell happened? Those same hooligans who roughed up T-Bone get to you?"

"Some landscaping stones in Big Jamie's front yard got to me. River rocks, I think they're called."

"What?! You went to Big Jamie's? Didn't you get my text?"

"Yes, Lewie, I got your text. In typical imbecilic fashion, though, you sent it five hours late."

"Well, I didn't expect you to go rushing over there like a lunatic!"

"You sent me over there like a lunatic! I was happy to lay on the floor all day. You're the one who got me all hopped up on prescription speed and insisted I ..."

"Points taken," said Lewie, nodding his head in agreement. "Points taken. You make valid points, partner. Ah, well. *C'est la vie*. Live and learn, yes?"

Mighty Millie hobbled over with fresh coffee. Lewie jumped at the opportunity to behave like a nuthouse refugee.

"How's your syrup selection here?" he said. "Do you stock sorghum? Boysenberry? Cajun praline?"

"Well... we have sugar-free. And regular, of course."

"Amoretti crème brulee?"

"No, I believe it's maple."

"Curses!"

Lewie strained his neck to look out the window. "Is that gourmet food shop still across the street?"

"Lewie, I swear to God, if you leave this restaurant to go buy some bullshit syrup..." I began to say, but it was too late. He was gone.

"He's mentally ill," I explained to Mighty Millie. "Freak condition. Literally believes he's a five-year-old. His doctor suggested I drag him out back and shoot him, but every time I start to, he gives me those sad puppy dog eyes and I just can't pull the trigger."

Twenty minutes later, Lewie returned triumphantly, a dozen bottles of obscure imported condiments in tow.

"What the hell, Lewie?!"

"Let the feasting begin!"

"Oh good, you found your syrup!"

Mighty Millie must not have picked up on my sarcasm, because she now spoke to Lewie in a tone normally reserved for small children and politicians.

"Are you boys ready to order?" she said. "Would you like some pancakes? They are very, very yummy."

"Actually," said Lewie, "I changed my mind. The Western omelet sounds good. I'll go with that."

"Poison it," I said. "Do the world a favor and lace it with arsenic, cyanide, mamba venom, whatever's back there."

"Now, don't you pay attention to your friend, young man!" Mighty Millie told Lewie. "He's only joking. We don't have poison here, especially for a special young man like you!"

"She's a fun one," said Lewie as Mighty Millie limped away. "Probably a former kindergarten teacher or something."

"Something like that, Lewie."

"Now back to business," he said, his voice now barely a whisper. "The reason I told you to abort mission is that Flying Snake Tat is a *major player* in Big Jamie's camp. Like, huge. He's sort of a consigliere-underboss combo. His name is..."

"Shagula."

"... Sal Aquino, but he goes by Big Gay Sal. Don't let the nickname fool you. The dude's an absolute pit bull..."

"I think he's more of a tummy rub-loving Dober-man, actually."

"... and people fear him as much as they do Big Jamie. If he was involved in Jake's death, that means either Big Jamie ordered him to kill Jake—chilling, right?—or there's a power coup going on. High treason. 'Let them eat cake.' If so, Big Jamie is probably next on the chopping block. Either way, we shouldn't rush in blindly. If Big Gay Sal did kill Jake..."

"He didn't. Some no-name killed Jake."

"What?"

"Don't worry about it. The plan worked. Drink the wine, praise the God of all things, let the world be the world. Or however the fuck it goes."

"What the fuck are you yammering about, man?"

Over coffee and omelets, I brought Lewie up to speed. He was silent for a long time after I finished.

"Something just doesn't add up," he said finally.

"Yeah? What's that?"

"Kimber," he said. "It's a terrible name for a stripper. Rhymes with timber. Are you sure it wasn't Kimber*ly*? Or Kimmie? Or Elektra? And something else: If Shagula married Estella, and Estella was the princess, how did Shagula leap-frog his vampiric ass all the way to the throne? It's inconsistent with the laws of monarchial succession."

"I'm glad you're taking this so seriously, Lewie. I hope you bring the same cerebral vigor to the table when you're investigating my murder."

"Come on! You're not really worried about that Sergio character, are you? He's just trying to get under your skin so you're less likely to try and get under Kalista's. Nudge nudge wink wink."

When we got up to leave, Lewie insisted he leave his ridiculous syrup collection for the next condiment connoisseur. Mighty Millie gave him a big hug and told him what a wonderful boy he was.

Outside, familiar storm clouds were forming. Thunder rumbled in the near distance. Lewie whistled while he walked, perfectly oblivious to the shit storm about to descend.

"Did you drive or take the Metro?"

"Metro," I said.

"Let's walk to my place. I'll give you a lift back to Delmar. We need to discuss how to fend off Sergio. If you're not carrying that Colt yet, it's time to start."

Lewie lived in an historic little brick bungalow on a tree-lined cul-de-sac in Maplewood, a short jaunt from the boutiques and eateries on the main drag. We took a shortcut across a weed-strewn parking lot and a muddy field covered in wet leaves and gumballs. A church bell tower rang twelve times. Otherwise, the streets were eerily quiet. In retrospect, I had the feeling we were being watched.

"Also," Lewie continued, "we need to formulate a plan to sneak into Big Jamie's house so we can explore the third floor. I have the feeling that whatever Sal Aquino didn't want you to see up there is one of the keys to making this mystery a slice of history. Plus, I need to tell you about the medical examiner. He didn't even examine dead Jake number one's cadaver. He was strong-armed by—you're not going to believe this—the FBI and the *mayor's office* into signing his name on an autopsy report that he didn't even read. He was sworn to secrecy and told it was a matter of national security. And then I tried to visit..."

"Hang on. If Big Jamie's legitimate FBI connections swore him to silence, why'd he open up to you?"

"I'm a persuasive fellow. And I'm not FBI. I'm C-I-motherfucking-A."

I waited for the punch line, but it didn't come.

"Come on, you didn't think I've worked at every

place in the phonebook just because I can't keep a job, do you? I go where the Agency sends me. And then I move along to the next assignment. St. Louis is a hotbed for Agency interests."

"You're fucking with me... right?"

"Of course I am! But if *you* half-believed me, imagine how easy it was for me to deceive the one-hundred-thirty-two-year-old chief medical examiner. Anyway, after that, I swung by Jake's girlfriend Arianna's place. You know that little bead shop she runs under her apartment?"

"Yeah. What about it?"

"It's closed. For good, apparently. And when I knocked on her door, a neighbor popped her head out and said Ari hadn't been home in four days. She also said that I wasn't the first person to come looking for her."

"Jesus. Ari's missing now?" I thought of how she looked at the funeral—stoned, lost, chemically catatonic—and got the sickening feeling that she wasn't off catching a country jubilee in Branson. "Do you think she's..."

"Dead?" said Lewie. "Meh. It's possible. Doubtful. Probable. Impossible. Definite. Who knows? Good news is, though, we're collecting plenty of puzzle pieces, partner."

"Puzzle pieces?"

"Sure! Think about it. What's the first thing you do to solve a puzzle?"

"I don't know. Find the corner pieces."

"Even before that, though—you open the box and shake the pieces out, right? That's what we're doing for now, V—shaking out the pieces and getting them in a nice, neat little pile, so that when the time comes, we can look at them from different angles, decipher which are the corners, the centerpieces, the extra piece or two that every good puzzler has left over in the end, etc."

"That's a surprisingly thoughtful perspective, Lewie."

"You think so? I just made it up. It sounded a little smug coming out of my mouth. I wasn't a fan."

"Nah, it's good. Solid. You should keep it."

"I talked to Joel as well yesterday, you know the brain scrubber who looks like..."

"Seth Rogen, sure."

"You know what he thinks happened at your apartment? Or what detective Beerman told him, anyway? That some Satanist fuckers broke in and performed a sacrificial ritual with the blood of a ram. Beerman swore him to secrecy, too. And get this—he paid him five thousand dollars in cash, no paperwork, no questions asked."

We hung a left on St. Cyril Court and were a stone's throw from Lewie's front door when all hell broke loose. It happened quickly, as it's apt to do. First there was the sound of an engine firing. And then tires squealing. And then Lewie and I spun around to see a dark sedan with a shiny grill cover and tinted windows barreling towards us.

"I wonder who that guy robbed," I said.

"Cool! Is that one of those new Continentals?" said Lewie.

"Kids these days."

"You know, it reminds me a little of the Jaguar XL."

"Is it just me, or he is coming straight at us?"

"No way. Not in that car. He's messing with us... no, he's not! *Move!*"

Lewie lowered his head and delivered a flying spear to my midsection that sent us both tumbling to the ground behind the temporary safety of a stately red maple. A stabbing pain shot through my side. I felt like I was breathing battery acid. Compared to the crazy son of a bitch who just saved my life, though, I was gold.

Lewie was on his knees, struggling to get to his feet and having difficulty. He was now the one who looked like Frankenstein's monster. Blood—too much of it—spurted from a gaping hole in his forehead. A thick puddle of it had formed around the unforgiving tree root that he head-butted on the way down.

The Continental had skidded to a halt a few inches from the tree trunk. It wasn't sure how to proceed. It reversed several feet, straightened out, started to pull away. Stopped. Moved a few more feet. Stopped again. Jerked a few feet forward. Stopped again.

The driver's door opened. Then the passenger door. Then a backseat door. Maybe I was just concussed, but our three assailants seemed to be walking in slow motion. From my angle, I couldn't see faces, just sneakers. One step... two steps... three steps... A heated argument in Spanish, in an unfamiliar accent... Venezuelan, was it? Sergio and his friends?

I snapped out of it. Lewie was on his feet, swaying back and forth like a wounded cowboy in a TV Western. He grasped for the gun on his belt, ready to go out in a blaze of glory, six shooter firing, but his coordination was shot and he couldn't grasp the barrel.

I sucked in what little air I had, lunged for the gun, and fielded it cleanly. Slow motion became fast forward. In a flash, our attackers were on the move, scurrying backward. Police sirens rang out.

Lewie was moaning, cursing, stumbling in circles like a cartoon chicken with his head cut off. Rage boiled up inside me. Some no-name bastard had already erased Jake from my world. And now Lewie? I fired three shots into the Continental's sleek new grill. To this day, I wonder what I would have done with the final three bullets had the Continental not sped away.

"Lewie! Are you all right, man?"

As always, he was smiling. But it was a different sort of smile.

"I told you I'd make it up to you, partner," he said with a laugh. "Guaranteed."

And then he collapsed in a heap.

Chapter 8

Newspaper clipping found in the pilfered journal of Patio Williams, CFO of RW Enterprises, younger brother of Big Jamie Kennedy's business partner Radio Williams.

Hundreds Rescued, Dozens Arrested in Human Trafficking Sting

More than 250 sex trafficking victims have been rescued and 60 members of the infamous Delgado cartel of Tijuana arrested after a dramatic series of events last night in San Diego.

The victims were being smuggled from Tenancingo, a central Mexico town known as the "sex trafficking capital of the world," to an undisclosed U.S. location when authorities intervened.

Two of the FBI's Most Wanted, cartel leaders Manuel and Marco Antonio Delgado, were among those placed under arrest. The brothers are expected to face felony charges of labor and sex trafficking, obstruction of justice, and homicide. They are suspected in the execution-style killings of 27 men—members of rival cartel Coyote Roja—in Chula Vista, California in 2012.

Authorities say they received an anonymous tip that the Delgados and their top lieutenants were traveling through a secret underground tunnel from Tijuana to an industrial park near the border to "finalize a major sex slaves-for-cash deal with a well-known organized crime boss."

The alleged crime boss did not show. A joint team of undercover FBI, DEA, and U.S. Customs & Border Protection officials, however, did.

Assistant FBI director Hillary Best told reporters that she thought the tip was a hoax at first.

"It sounded bogus, too good to be true," she said.

Agents were surprised, then, when they found the entrance to the secret tunnel exactly where the tipster said it would be: underneath a large metal recycling dumpster in a nondescript Otay Mesa warehouse.

"Like other Tijuana-to-San Diego super tunnels we've uncovered," said Best, "this one is highly advanced (and) includes railway tracks, elevators, and even an office filled with thousands of potentially incriminating documents. It's an impressive structure. And it's ours now."

"I look forward," Best added, "to working with international law enforcement and prosecutors to ensure these criminals jail sentences, wherever they may be served, are very long and very arduous."'

The identities and nationalities of the victims have not been released. Best said that they ranged in age from young teens to the middle-aged.

Best was tight-lipped about how the capture-

and-rescue mission played out but did indicate that it *"went smoothly."*

"Not a single shot was fired," said Best. "The Delgado crew was clearly surprised. I don't think they realized what was happening until they were locked up in the back of FBI vans in route to a federal detention center."

"Clearly," she added, "they trusted that their buyers had ensured the sale would go without a hitch."

It's unclear who this alleged buyer is or what role he or she may have played in triggering this mass arrest.

Manuel and Marco Antonio Delgado are also wanted in Jalisco, Mexico, where their cartel shot down three Mexican military helicopters with rocket-propelled grenades earlier this year, killing 7 more.

(continued on page 12B)

I don't care if it continues on 12B, I just want to chew alprazolam and climb under the covers and wake up with new nerves and a bowl full of serotonin and a better brain that doesn't care about Jilly's gum smacking and her loud music that makes my brain sweat and twitch and makes me want to send her to the vending machine of death for Goo Goo Clusters.

"What are you reading?" Jilly shouts over the music she calls "Ree" because she said, "Pat, do you like Ree?" and even though I don't know what Ree is I lied and said "yes, I like ree," just like I lied when she said, "patio's such a funny name. would you prefer to be called pat?" and I said, "yes, I would like that."

Apparently "ree" is dance music that jilly thinks is fun and appropriate for an executive office.

But I guess I do need to do more mindless fun so my "somatic anxiety" as Dr. Chaudhary calls it doesn't lead to my "rumination," or is it the other way around? Or maybe I'm getting the words mixed up but does it really matter anyway if BIG Jamie Kennedy AND now the Delgado crew or whatever is left of them burst through the door and mow us down?

And riddle me this, Dr. Chaudhary, what does it mean when it turns out the paranoid guy with the "persecutory delusion" really is being persecuted? And he really should be paranoid? Maybe it means I was right all along.

And what does doctor Chaudhary know of fun anyway, since every time I go to his office he's listening to the radio and the talking heads are worked up and saying things like, "well, what is God, how do you define God?" and then another guy says, "God is the undefinable" and then another guy says, "God is the undefinable everything!" and then another guy says, "God is the undefinable, arbitrary everything!" and then they all laugh. How is *that* fun and how is that supposed to make anybody feel good about anything??? What an asshole, right?

———————

I just got back from the small bathroom in the hallway because how can I use my office one when jilly is sitting right next to it painting her nails and smacking her gum and not even trying to look busy? Of course, I'm the boss and she's the assistant, and I never have stuff for her to assist on so maybe it's my fault which is why I don't say anything. Well, also because I fear confrontation and I fear women and I fear everything and I fear admitting it even in writing, much less out loud.

So while I'm on the toilet which already makes me uncomfortable some lady from the cleaning crew knocks on the door and yells "housekeeping!" and I say, "I'll be out soon!' and then she stands outside the door tapping her feet and sighing heavy until I'm done and when I walk out the door she's just standing there looking mad and mean and sure I'm paranoid and there are things that I imagine but this much is true: that woman hates me.

Still no answer from Radio, Big Jamie won't take my calls anymore even when I call the secret line, and Eli's phone finally answered but it wasn't Eli. The guy who did answer just said, "'sup, nigga?" and when I paused he hung up and for all I know eli and his boys don't even know the kennedy kid is dead and they're hunting a ghost!

And to make it worse, Radio the "anonymous tipster" put the knife in the delgados back and stiffed them on the deal for those Mexican girls and tipped off the feds too! Or maybe the Kennedy kid did it before Radio killed him and my careless psycho brother just decided not to tell the delgados "No Deal!" I guess if you're already making enemies with Jamie you may as well start a war with the delgados too?

Things are too complicated and I just want to tell Big Jamie my side of the story, if I can do that and he realizes I'm not my brother, I'm just a guy who's along for the road and barely even wants to be, maybe I'll be OK. Maybe we'll all be OK and maybe I can go back to worrying about just my head and not my head getting blown off.

———————

Radio just texted after all this time and said, "I did what I had to."

Isn't that all any of us ever do, big brother?

Chapter 9

"It's been a long day, Jack. It's probably been a long day for you too, man. And I'd love to help you. I really would. But you got to tell me what you want. Just shout it out. Or pantomime, man. Throw me a bone here, Jack..."

Gummy Jack just jabbered, toothless and incoherent, before slapping his knee and bursting into laughter. He composed himself just long enough to slap *my* knee and crack up again, all the while swaying back and forth like a drunken hobo.

"He wants money, mon," said a dreadlocked young man with a Haile Selassie T-shirt on the other side of the platform. "Give him a buck and he'll be happy."

"Not true," I said. "I've given him money before. He tears it into tiny pieces and tosses it in the air like confetti. Right, Jack?"

Gummy Jack grunted something that sounded like, "Who, me?" and then burst into a new fit of laughter.

"I bought him a Trainwreck sandwich a while back," said a middle-aged woman sitting on the end of the bench, reading a Fabio paperback as she waited for the eastbound train. "He pretended to eat a bite and then flung the whole thing across the street like a Frisbee. A *Frisbee*! There was tomatoes and mayonnaise all over the sidewalk. All *over*! Um-hmm! Right, Jack?"

This fresh accusation was too much for Gummy Jack to handle. He fell to his knees, laughing so hard that I thought his ninety-plus year-old innards would explode out of his body and decorate the platform.

Gummy Jack was something of a neighborhood pet. He stood five feet tall, reeked of Old Spice and cigarette butts, and wore a ratty, double-breasted Zoot suit and a faded porkpie hat—a living, breathing Tom Waits tune. Every couple years, city officials hung new No Panhandling! signs all over the Loop and brought in the U City cops to squeegee the beggars into the gutter, but Gummy Jack remained, the last leaf on a skeletal tree from a bygone era.

I'd been sitting on the bench at the Metrolink station, waiting for the train to take me downtown for my date with Kalista, when he appeared out of nowhere and practically sat on my lap, even though seating space was ample. For the past ten minutes, I'd been trying to figure out what he wanted. Maybe, like much of the world, he'd simply gone crazy.

"Dude wants a ride, Sherlocks," said a teenager in a red hoodie with his eyes glued to his phone. "He wants to get on that train. Dude don't want no damn sandwich. Especially with that nasty ass mayonnaise."

Gummy Jack nodded and jabbered excitedly. The woman with the Fabio book was aghast.

"Mind your manners, young man!" she scolded him. "No respect! No respect at all anymore. None at all!"

"Kids these days," I told her.

"You want a job, kid?" I asked the teen. "You'd make a great private eye. You're a natural. I know a guy who's hiring. He might be a sociopath, and after today, there's a sizable chunk of his head missing, and he'll probably send you to your demise for no good reason before your first paycheck. But a job's a job, right? What do you say?"

He didn't look up from his phone, just rolled his eyes and shook his head in disgust. "I say I got a job. *Kid*," he sneered. "A real good one, too. Fast food. I only have to take this train and then two buses to get there. They even pay me a whole nickel over minimum wage. And if I keep on until I'm fifty, I might be promoted to part-time weekend assistant manager."

I turned my attention to my toothless little friend. "Let's go get you a ticket, Gummy Jack. I've had enough sarcasm for one day already."

"No respect at all anymore!" repeated the woman with the paperback. "And it's a crying shame. A *crying* shame..."

The Metrolink finally arrived. It was nearly empty, as I'd hoped. I took a seat in the back corner, craving a few minutes of solitude, but Gummy Jack, oblivious to the tenets of personal space, squeezed in beside me. For the next twenty minutes, he giggled and stammered in my ear. I couldn't understand a single word he said. When the train lurched to a stop at Union Station—not my exit—I made a beeline for the door, opting to leg it out the final eight city blocks. To my relief, Jack did not follow.

Outside, the skies were still drizzling and the wind was gaining momentum, but I didn't mind. A solitary stroll was just what I needed to decompress and wrap my head around the morning's monkey business.

As soon as the Continental had sped away, leaving Lewie lying there in a bloody heap, I started screaming for help. Evidently our run-in had already crossed the authorities' radar, though, because sirens were blaring. They sounded close. In a panic, I tore off my shirt and wrapped it around the abnormally large gash on my friend's abnormally large melon. But I didn't know if my makeshift tourniquet was too tight or too loose, and I had a very real fear that Lewie's think machine, medulla oblongata and all, would slip through the bloody chasm in his forehead and plop down into my lap.

Lewie was half-conscious when the police and medics showed up, and I was half-delirious, shivering in the cold and screaming at my friend to stay the fuck alive, because I'm not going to dig a hole and push you in it, not today anyway, you no-good, sick, twisted bastard, you tardy, crazy, sociopathic son of a bitch...

The paramedics moved at hyper speed, bandaging and suturing Lewie, sticking needles in his arms and penlights in his eyes and then hoisting him onto a gurney and loading him into the back of an ambulance, which sped away without me despite my objections.

Two police and one medic stayed behind—the former to grill me, the latter to tend to the watermelon-sized strawberry on my side, which I'd collected when my rather well-rounded cohort drove me into the unforgiving earth. All things considered, though, I was lucky. My ribs were bruised but not broken, and after a generous intake of oxygen, the wind that had been knocked out of me was restored.

A baby-faced officer who didn't look a day over twenty-one brought me an SLPD sweatshirt and a blanket while his partner, a slightly older, wiry, jumpy little guy with a razor thin mustache, continued to question me.

"Who fired the gun?" he demanded.

"I told you the whole story already," I said. "I fired the gun."

"Who fired the gun?"

"I fired the gun."

"Who fired the gun?"

"I fired the gun."

"Who fired the gun?"

I looked to the babyface for help. "Why is he having such difficulty understanding that I fired the gun?"

The babyface shuffled his feet but said nothing.

"Who fired the gun, V.C.?"

"What the fuck is wrong with this guy?"

"Who fired the gun, V.C.?"

"Who do *you* think fired the gun?"

"Who fired the gun, V.C.?"

"I fired the gun."

"Who fired the gun, V.C.?"

"How would it benefit me to lie about firing the gun, man?"

"Who fired the gun, V.C.?"

"Fine," I said, "you win." I pointed at the babyface, who hadn't said a word. "He did it. He fired the gun. I told him not to. I said, 'Don't fire the gun. Your partner will be pissed. He's going to ask me a dozen times who fired the gun, and when I tell him I fired the gun, he's not going to believe me. He's too smart.' But he fired it anyway. Three times. Bang-bang-bang. Happy now?"

He wasn't. For the second time in four days, I was pushed into the back of a police car and escorted in handcuffs to an interrogation room at SLPD headquarters to think about what I had done.

An hour later, the door behind me opened.

"Please don't ask me who fired the gun again," I said. "Does it even matter? Would you just tell me if my friend is dead or not, please?"

"He'll be fine, we think," came a familiar, highly out of place voice. "He won't win any beauty contests, but that ship sailed as soon as he escaped his mamma's womb, don't you think, sweetheart?"

I spun around to find an unexpected duo standing there: Big Gay Sal, who looked genuinely happy to see me again, and detective Joe Beerman, who looked poised to win a vein-popping-angrily-out-of-his-head competition.

"Speak!" barked the detective. "What happened? Who was the driver? Who were they?"

"No, really, detective Beerman, the pleasure's all mine. Wonderful to see you."

"Speak fast, shitbag. Who were they? What did they look like?"

"I don't know. I didn't get a good look at them. There were three of them. Spanish-speaking. They were wearing hats, I think."

"How helpful! Did you hear that, Sal? All we got to do is find the three Spics in this city who wear hats!"

"Calm yourself," said Sal. He took a seat in the chair across from me and leaned in close. "Detective Beerman called us as soon as he heard what happened," he said in a low voice. "What we're trying to figure out is whether the assailants were somehow tied to our... mutual friend, shall we say?"

"I don't know anything, Sal."

"It's OK. Just start from the beginning. Tell us what happened."

"There's not much to tell. We were just walking down Lewie's street when some lunatics in a shiny black Continental tried to run us down. Lewie knocked me out of the way at the last second. Saved both of our lives. He hit his head on the ground, on a tree root sticking..."

"That's terrific," interrupted Beerman. "Your boyfriend's a real American hero. Truly touching. Do you have enemies, *pal*?"

"Well, there's this homicide detective who seems to have it in for me. Fortunately, I'm pretty sure the vein in his forehead is going to pop before he has the chance to..."

"Do you have enemies?" shouted Beerman, pounding his fists on the table. These were the theatrics I missed my first time around.

"Yes," I said. "I do. A madman from my past is hellbent on making my present tense..."

"I don't have time for poetry, hipster! Let me ask you again..."

"That's not... I'm not..."

"What are you hiding from us, Almond? What aren't

you telling us? What's your secret, kid?"

"My secret?"

"Tell us something we don't know, Almond!"

"OK... uh... well... I have a hypnic jerk some nights. It makes me twitch when I'm about to fall asleep. It's usually accompanied by a falling sensation. Some theorists believe it's not just nerves misfiring, but a remnant from our ancient primate days. Basically, our brain thinks that we're falling out of a tree while we're asleep..."

"Are you *trying* to get a black eye?"

"Come on, detective. Don't tell me you're one of those world-in-seven-days types."

"I have the same thing," said Sal. "I assumed it was related to the supplements I take, or stress maybe, but I like your theory better."

"We are the missing link."

"The so-called madman," growled Beerman. "Who is he? What's his name?"

"His name," I said, "is..."

"Hold," said Sal. "Why don't you write it down, V.C.? Find a pen, please detective."

"This room is secure," said Beerman. "Nobody but us is listening in."

"Find a pen, detective!" repeated Sal, louder.

I was surprised to see Beerman hurry off diligently.

"He's right," said Sal. "The room's secure. That window right there isn't a two-way. But sometimes I have to remind the good detective who's *really* signing his paycheck, right?"

The man with the flying snake tattoo on the back of his skull squeezed my shoulder and gave me a playful noogie. It occurred to me that there was no way in hell he spilled Jake Kennedy's blood. But then what was he doing dragging Jake's carcass down Delmar Blvd. last Friday night?

"Your friend will be all right," he continued. "No worries. We got a man stationed outside his door already. Anyone who steps foot on that hospital floor with big ideas goes straight to the morgue with a case of *lead poisoning*. Get it? Ha!"

"Sal," I said slowly, tentatively, "I have a question. More of a statement, actually."

He leaned in close again so that we were nearly nose to nose. "Tell me," he said.

"I know... I know that... you were at my apartment on Friday ... I know you took the body, Sal."

I wasn't sure what to expect. Anger? Denial? Mock confusion? The police chief to burst in and drag me to the city dungeon? A valid explanation?

Sal's actual response blew me away. "Well, duh!" he said, completely unruffled. "We couldn't just leave his body there, could we? What's wrong, did I traipse mud across the floor or something?"

Before I could respond, detective Beerman barged in and slammed a pen and notepad on the table.

"Start writing, Almond."

"I can't remember his last name."

"You're about as helpful as a pecker at a dyke convention, you know that?"

I looked at Sal. He looked at me.

"I don't get it," I said.

"I don't, either. What does it mean?" said Sal.

"A guy with a pecker could help move chairs or something," I said. "That would be helpful."

"Is it a joke?" said Sal.

"Just write the name!" hollered Beerman.

"Anything for you, detective."

On the notepad, I wrote...

> *Sergio*

... and then added:

> *...from Venezuela. San Cristóbal, I think.*

Beerman's face promptly turned crimson.

Sal just chuckled. "You got style, kid," he said. "And balls. I can see why Jake told me he was such a fan."

Silence filled the room for several seconds as amusement, confusion, and anger sized each other up. Finally, anger spoke. His eyes were wide and felt like daggers piercing my soul.

"Is that," said Beerman, "your idea of a threat?"

He didn't wait for a response. He just hurled a chair across the room. I jumped to my feet.

"Go!" he railed. "Get out of my police station, you shitbag hipster son of a bitch! Go! Get out! Get the fuck out! Fuck off! Fuck off! Fuck off!"

I was beginning to think we were stranded on opposite sides of a seismic communication gap. But the detective was clearly in no mood to build bridges, so I didn't say a word. I just walked out the door and fucked off as quickly as I could.

———————

After eight blocks of rain, wind, and drivers who honk

and scream at pedestrians who have the nerve to utilize the city's crosswalks, the Oasis Hotel was a sight for sore eyes, even if it had a reputation as a traveler's last resort.

Decades ago, the Oasis was St. Louis' "celebrity inn." Its lounge, "Coda," was the place where people went to see the stars and where the stars went to be seen. Sixty years of neglect later, it was the place where tenants of the skyscraper across the street went after work for happy hour chicken wings and two-dollar shots of Fireball on Mondays and Wednesdays.

My eyes scanned the dimly lit room and spotted Kalista sitting at a booth near the piano, underneath a fresco of jazz legends who once played the room. Multiple painters must have created it simultaneously without discussing size and scope, because Ella Fitzgerald's oversized bun was twice as large as Benny Goodman's entire upper body and Count Basie was the size of a housefly buzzing around Dizzy Gillespie's bulging bullfrog cheeks. For some odd reason, Yanni was included.

Kalista wasn't alone. A young man with an ivory tuxedo and a full mane of coifed black curls sat across from her. He was gazing at her with a seductive half-smile. I instinctively despised him.

"I'm not interrupting, am I?"

"V.C.!" Kalista hopped to her feet and gave me a peck on the cheek—not the lips, I noted. "Meet Duke Kettle. Duke plays piano here on weekdays."

"Duke," I said with a nearly imperceptible nod.

Duke barely raised his eyebrows in return. We'd come a long way since our caveman days.

"I didn't think they had live music here anymore," I said.

"Trying to spruce the place up," said Duke.

"This place has changed over the years," I said. "From Duke Ellington to Duke... Kettle, was it?"

"Nice stitches," retorted Duke. "Snitch on someone?"

"Oh, right, I get it. Because snitches get stitches. Funny. Clever. *Duke*."

"Duke's going to sing me a song," said Kalista. "Isn't that sweet?"

"Not just one song." He took her hand and brought it gently to his lips. "If you were *just* a beautiful woman, I would sing you a song. For a goddess like yourself, only the entire set will do."

Kalista batted her eyes. I looked around for a Louisville Slugger. Before I could find one, Duke excused himself to go play his little songs. I hoped that he played like shit and the crowd of about twenty booed him back to the snake pit from which he slithered.

"Friend of yours? Is he the reason you chose this place?" I said.

"No," replied Kalista, "I just met the guy. And my office is right across the street." She regarded me with an amused grin. "How cute. You're jealous. I've never seen you jealous. I didn't know you had it in you."

"I'm not jealous," I said quickly. "I'm aggravated."

"I believe they call that a half-truth, sweetie."

"I could be your husband for all that asshole knows."

"He knows I'm not married. It was the first thing he asked me. Besides, you fired the first shot."

My new nemesis's voice filled the room. He

welcomed everyone to Coda, talked about how priv-
ileged he was to play such an historic space, blah blah
blah. Then he dedicated the evening's songs to a "very
special woman in my life, the talented and beautiful
Ms. Kalista." He asked her to stand. She blushed and
waved to polite applause. He jumped right in to Buddy
Holly's "Oh Boy!" To my disgust, he was spot on.

I must have looked as vitriolic as I felt.

"Don't get pissy with me," said Kalista. "What am I
supposed to do? Tell him to fuck off?"

I shrugged.

"Here's an idea, V.C. If it bothers you so much that
he's flirting with me, why don't *you* tell him?"

"Forget it," I said. "Let's take a look at that letter
from Sergio."

"What happened to your forehead? Are you all right?"

"Long story. It's been a long couple of days."

"Sergio didn't do that, did he?"

"A landscaping stone did that. The assist goes to
Death, Famine, War, and Conquest. The Dobermans,
not the Horsemen. All Sergio tried to do was run me
over with a Lincoln Continental. I think it was him,
anyway. He did successfully manage to put a friend of
mine in the hospital."

"Oh my God! Is he OK?"

I shrugged. "He was never really *OK*, per se."

A cocktail waitress arrived with a glass of wine for
Kalista. "From the gentleman at the piano," she said. "I
think he likes you..." she added in a singsong voice as
she started to walk away.

"Excuse me," I said. "Wait. Please."

She turned around and looked right through me. "Yes?" she said curtly. "What?"

"Grand Marnier, straight. Please. Pretty please. With a cherry on top."

She disappeared without a word.

"Ouch. Is that your ex-girlfriend or something?" said Kalista.

"I'm not sure I like this place, Kalista," I said.

"That cut looks nasty, V.C. Have you seen a doctor?"

"No. I got some random crazy ass gangster to stitch it up for me."

Kalista glared at me for a second and then turned her attention to the piano man. He'd moved from "Oh Boy!" to "Oh, Donna," changing the refrain to "Oh, Kalista." "Oh, Brother" was more like it.

The waitress returned with the skimpiest shot I've ever seen. "There," she said, slamming it on the table with enough force to send a few precious drops spilling over the side. "With a cherry on top."

Sure enough, there was a maraschino cherry floating in it.

"Enjoy," she said with a patronizing smile and walked away.

"Are you *sure* you don't know her?" said Kalista.

"I suspect that your not-so-secret admirer has something to do with her attitude. I saw him talking to her right before he went on. Who knows what he told her about me. But fuck it. Let's take a look at that letter."

Kalista fished it right out of her purse. Evidently, she'd finally emptied that giant stack of mail. "What do you think?"

"I think you can fill Busch Stadium with pedestrian pianists like this one."

"Seriously, V.C. Stop it. What do you think of the letter?"

Other than a missing apostrophe and a misplaced comma—*Im gonna kill V.C. and, then I'm going to kill you*—it was rather unremarkable. I shrugged and flipped it back to her.

"We've got nothing to worry about. That's obviously not real blood. It looks like some cheap red dye, or maybe a saturated watercolor paint."

"Clearly, we're safe in that case."

"What I've been wondering is, how did Sergio even know we were going out? And is one date really worth killing a guy over? I mean, even for a raging psychopath, that's pretty extreme."

Kalista shrunk in her seat. "I'm sorry, but I sort of... told him... we were... OK, this is really embarrassing, and if you take it the wrong way, I get it. But Sergio showed up at my apartment Friday night, right after we got off the phone. He was coked out of his skull and acting crazy, rambling about how he wanted me back, that he *deserved* me and I *belonged* to him and if I couldn't get it through my pretty little skull that I was his, he'd beat some sense into me, so I..."

"He hit you?!" I said, feeling my blood start to boil.

"No. Never. Well, almost never. Sergio's the type who puts his fist through a window, slashes a tire, kicks a dog, or picks a bar fight with some other Neanderthal like himself when he's pissed. He'd threaten me all the time, sure, but he rarely got physical with me. Anyway, he told me..."

"A special surprise from your future boyfriend!"

Our waitress was back, this time with a generous shot of Fireball for Kalista and a bill for one Grand Marnier for me. Apparently, I was cut off.

"Did I do something to piss you off?" I asked her.

"What do you think of Duke?" she asked Kalista, ignoring me. "He's a doll, huh? I know if I was single, I'd..."

"He's terrific," I interrupted. "Not a douchebag at all. But if you don't mind, we're in the middle of a conversation."

"*He's* the d...?" she started to say, but then held her tongue and turned away with a contemptuous glare on her face. "I'm sure your little conversation's a matter of life and death," she said as she stomped off.

Kalista did not look entertained, either. "Would you please stop being a dickhead?"

"What did you tell Sergio, Kalista?"

She pushed my drink into my hand. "Drink up first. And enjoy it. It's all you get, apparently."

"Cheers," I said, without a hint of it. We clinked glasses. Kalista downed her Fireball in one swallow. She looked me dead in the eye, and despite my sour state of mind, I melted a little.

"I told him I was pregnant with your baby, V.C."

I nearly spit up my cherry.

"Don't read much into it," she said quickly. "I saw an out, and I went for it. That's all. Sergio said to give him one good reason we shouldn't be together. Other than the fact that I have a restraining order against him for stalking me, of course. He said it wasn't too late for us, we could work things out, he was going to change, all this other crap. 'It's not like you're pregnant with some other guy's kid,' he said. I saw an out, and I just went for it.

"Obviously, he didn't take it well," she continued, her voice trembling slightly. "He stormed outside and beat the shit out of his steering wheel for five minutes straight. I could see his car from my window. I locked my door in case he came back up. Next time I looked out the window, his car was there, but he wasn't. I was ready to call the police, thinking he was stalking through the hallways or something. I looked again a few minutes later and the car was gone. I get goose bumps thinking about it now."

Sure enough, her arms were covered in goose bumps. I gestured for her to take a drink.

"I'm sorry, V.C. I had no idea what I was getting either of us into. And I know you have enough bullshit in your life without me adding to it. I've tried to call Sergio a hundred times, I've left him voice messages, texts, emails, everything, but he won't respond. I've tried to tell him that I made it up, that I'm not really pregnant and I haven't even seen you in a couple years, but I guess he doesn't believe me. He always hated you, V.C. You remember how he was when he came to Java Bloc when we were working. He would sit there for hours, pretending to work on his laptop and just stare holes in you. He was always convinced I was cheating on him with you. At first, during my first few months with him, back when he still seemed like a sweet guy, he would just joke about it. And then as time went on, and the crazier I realized he was, you became his obsession. He would literally ask about you first thing in the morning and last thing at night. 'Did you see V.C. today? You dreamed about V.C., didn't you?' He thinks you're the devil. Literally, the devil."

"Horns, pitchfork, the whole nine yards?"

"And I don't think he's just bullshitting us with this death threat. His boss called me Saturday afternoon, looking for him. Same thing Sunday. Sergio has been skipping work. His boss thinks I've already reported him missing. Truth is, he's making arrangements to disappear. I just know it. My guess is, he's going to try to get back home to Venezuela after he kills us. He won't just rush out and kill us and then be content to get caught and rot away in a jail cell for the rest of his life. Sergio has a plan, V.C."

Kalista paused to dab her eyes with a bar napkin. "And I'm scared," she continued, "I'm fucking scared. And, mostly, I'm sorry... Please say something. Anything. What are you thinking?"

"Honestly?"

"Yes, V.C. Honestly."

"Honestly... I'm thinking that you're kind of cute when you cry. I think I might have a tear fetish. What would it take to convince you to come back to my place and chop a few onions?"

Kalista rolled her eyes in mock disgust. "There's that weird ass sense of humor I know and tolerate. Under the circumstances, should I feel obligated to laugh?"

"You should. And speaking of laugh—what's with this comically brutal rendition your boyfriend is doing up there?"

The song was Elvis Presley's "Can't Help Falling in Love," and in truth, Duke was crushing it. But we hear what we choose to hear. And I chose to hear a talentless hack desecrating the King.

"Seriously, V.C. Let's talk about this. What do we do? We should call the cops. Right?"

"No need," I said. "The song will be over soon enough. And we'll never be able to prove how much pain it inflicted."

"I'm talking about Sergio, jackass."

I gazed longingly at the fully stocked bar. Thinking without drinking was unchartered territory for me.

"A week ago, Kalista, I wouldn't have thought twice about filing a police report. Now, I'm not so sure. I get the feeling there are still a lot of puzzle pieces to, you know, shake out of the box. And last time I mentioned Sergio to the SLPD, I was emphatically asked to fuck off."

"What are you talking about?"

"It's a very long story, Kalista."

"Then tell me, jackass. Tell me everything. The Dobermans, the Continental, your friend in the hospital, everything. We're in this together, V.C."

Maybe we were. But that didn't stop her eyes from drifting over my shoulder and resting on the piano player serenading her while I recounted the events of the past few days. I was just starting to tell her about my interview with Beerman and Sal at the police station when the piano man slid into the booth beside her and started speaking softly in her ear. I'd been so focused on my story that I hadn't even realized the music had stopped.

"Next set, I have something extra special planned for you! For a beautiful lady like you..." he began to say, but then something happened that he didn't anticipate.

I lost it.

I've never really thought myself an overly impulsive person, but my track record might suggest otherwise. Impulse is what made me drop down on one knee on the Venice Beach Boardwalk and ask a girl I barely knew to marry me. It's what made me walk into a Vietnamese takeout place for stir fry one lonely afternoon and walk out with a multi-year apartment lease. And it's what made me decide that Duke Kettle had just ordered himself a nonreturnable knuckle sandwich on the house, as my father would say.

Like my encounters with Jake's corpse V2.0, Sal and the Dobermans, and the death car, my brief squabble with Duke flew by in an adrenaline-fueled blur. Fortunately—or unfortunately, depending on perspective—we live in an age where every little scuffle between an overly flirtatious piano player and a guy trying to tell a girl about a mind-boggling conversation he had with a B-movie star turned gangster and a curmudgeonly homicide detective is captured on a cell phone and promptly splattered all over the internet for the world to see. Last time I checked, "Piano Player Wets Himself in Near Fight" had reached 1.3 million views.

When the video begins, Duke is holding Kalista's hand and whispering sweet nothings in her ear. Her face is frozen in an uncharacteristic frown, and she looks annoyed, which is something I didn't realize at the time. Maybe, had I noticed, my reaction would have been different.

At thirty-two seconds, I stand up, fists clenched. I grab Duke by his lapels and force him to his feet.

"She's fucking taken, you fucking scumbag!" I shout.

At forty-one seconds, I cock my fist. My back is facing the camera, so the unflattering scowl on my face is mercifully hidden.

Kalista lunges forward and yells, "Don't you dare, V.C.!"

My fist starts to fly. It stops short, harmlessly, like a baseball hitter's check swing. At the same time, Duke emits a high-pitched squeal, like a cartoon mouse shrieking "Eeeeek!" as the cat's claws start to pounce.

Moments later, a dark circle appears around the crotch of his ivory white tuxedo pants. Crouched over and whimpering, he runs out the door.

Kalista slaps my face—a crisp, resounding slap, like you see in the movies.

"What the hell is wrong with you?!" she yells as the clip ends.

But Kalista wasn't the only one seeing red. I had held back my fist, but I was still livid. I fought the urge to hurl a glass through the window. Or pummel the shit-eating grin off the face of the bearded grunger who recorded the whole thing and was now watching it giddily on his phone. Instead, I fished the last ten-dollar bill out of my pocket and tossed it on the table. Then I stormed off, barely noticing the bartender slap my back and tell me excitedly that it was about time someone gave that home wrecking son of a bitch pansy what he deserved.

Outside, the skies pissed down angrily. Lost in my thoughts, I barely noticed.

My brain felt like a transistor radio stuck between frequencies, broadcasting muddled snippets of three unhappy stations.

There was anger. Kalista's lie was the catalyst that fired up the engine of the death car that hospitalized Lewie and would inevitably roll over my spine. Was it unreasonable under such circumstances for me to expect her full and undivided attention, even while some pants-pissing Romeo was giving her bedroom eyes?

There was embarrassment. Awkward as the situation was, it didn't take long for me to realize that I could have handled it better. In what delusional dream world was Kalista taken by anyone, much less me, who had now seen her exactly *twice* in the past two years? And what kind of possessive psycho shouts out that sort of thing, anyway? Sergio. And me, apparently.

I was embarrassed for Duke as well. I just wanted to rearrange his face—it would have been the first real punch I'd thrown since high school—not ruin his life. If the guy who recorded the altercation posted it online, it could go viral and follow Pee Kettle to every gig he ever scored. The Duke of Micturition. Duke Kettle, piano wizz. It goes on.

Mostly, there was regret. *Stale* regret.

Deep inside, I knew that a vicious slap and a bitter exit were exactly what I deserved, karmically speaking. I had my chance with Kalista years ago, and I blew it. The night Sergio heaved me into oncoming traffic, I should have stood up to him. I should have told him that Kalista and I were both done with his threats and his bullshit. If he had a problem with it, fine. We could club each other like cavemen right there on Shaw Blvd. I should have saved Kalista that night. But I didn't. I just stood there and watched as she calmed Sergio down and led him away. Saving me. I didn't even follow up to see if she was OK. For all I knew, he broke her arm that night.

I just did what I always do—I drank, and I drank, and I forgot about it. I married a stranger. I let Kalista get away, and when the universe cut me a break and brought her back in my life, I blew it. Again. V.C. Almond, real American zero.

Everything was wrong. Nothing was funny. I rode the Metrolink with my head down to avoid human contact. Sergio could have casually walked up and planted a knife in my belly and I wouldn't have seen him coming.

I stopped at Bobby's bar for a drink. I wanted company. I wanted to be alone. I didn't know what I wanted. The Closed... Grand Reopening next Monday! sign hanging on the door made the choice for me. Alone it was.

Back at my apartment, I turned my iPod on shuffle. Fittingly, the Grateful Dead's "Dire Wolf" filled the air first. Ironically, Elvis Costello's version of "(What's So Funny 'Bout) Peace Love and Understanding" came next. Cruelly, Band of Horses' "No One's Gonna Love You" was third.

Everything was wrong. The whole damn world was wrong, wrong, wrong. I didn't have the energy to pour myself a whiskey or even wax poetic with the Purple Guy. I just lay on the couch and thought about the rain. I thought about Jake. I thought about Kalista. I thought about Lewie. I thought about answering the door, which was rattling on its hinges all of a sudden. Someone was pounding it ferociously. *Too ferociously*. Something—everything—was wrong, wrong, wrong.

Only it wasn't. Kalista stood in the doorway, but she wasn't standing for long. She dropped her bag and jumped in my arms, and then her tongue was buried in my mouth, my hands were buried in her flesh, hearts were racing, clothes were flying, and just like that the world was right again.

Chapter 10

I DECIDED TO HOLE UP INSIDE THE COZY CONFINES OF 703 B Delmar Blvd. the next day and take a little vacation. The way I saw it, good things happened when I stayed. Bad things happened when I strayed. Outside my sliver of paradise, there was confusion, depression, desperation, and death. Inside, there was everything I needed to live a healthy, wholesome existence—a few GB of quality tunes, half a bottle of Grand Marnier, and the company of the purpliest guy in town.

"The last time it rained like this," I said, watching the skies piss down yet again, "it lasted forty days and forty nights and ended with Noah taking an exotic cruise with two animals of every kind. You should have seen the look on the unicorns' faces when the saber-toothed tigers stepped on board."

The Purple Guy was silent, not even a little amused. Failed, clichéd attempts at biblical humor didn't appeal to his wooden, atheistic sensibilities.

My cell phone rang. It was one of the editors with the resume writing agency that fed me just enough work to keep me above the poverty line. She had a job offer for me—a dozen resume rewrites at forty bucks a pop, fifty if I was up-to-date on my certifications, which I was. With my anorexic bank account in desperate need of an entrée, I jumped at it.

So, I spent the next several hours editing attachments and poring over goals, work histories, and achievements, turning a pile of clunky, wordy, three-page resumes that would never get noticed into concise, convincing, one-page self-marketing tools that would never get noticed. I felt like a valued contributor to society again. Focusing my attention on something other than the dead and dying for the first time in a week was just the cathartic release my chaotic psyche needed.

In the afternoon, I took a break to call the hospital and check on Lewie. "I'm not sure which room he's in," I said, "but his first name is Aldous..."

"Um-hmmm," replied the receptionist. "I know the room. We *all* know the room. Praise the Lord, that man is asleep. And unless you're calling to say I get hazard pay for every second Mr. Aldous Lewie is awake, I ain't about to disturb him."

I was happy to hear that Lewie was already feeling back to normal.

Later, I texted Kalista: *Still breathing?*

If you are, I am, she replied. *The plan is to kill you first. So stay alive.*

In the evening, Hazim tapped on the wall separating our palaces. "Hey, V.C.!" he called. There was a smile in his voice. "You over there?"

"Howdy, neighbor."

"I just wanted to tell you"—it sounded like he was fighting back laughter—"there was an intruder in your apartment last night. She was intruding all night long, my friend. I was going to call the police, but it sounded like you had things under control."

"Oh... um... thanks, Hazim."

"Hey, V.C.?"

"Hey, Hazim."

"You are a dog, V.C."

"Oh... um... thanks, Hazim."

Mondays and Tuesdays were dark at Camilla's—no screaming knucklehead bands, not even a DJ. Kun Woo's was closed by 9:00 p.m. as well. Feeling more tranquil than I had in months, I dialed up some meditational music and hit the sack early with the Colt .45 tugged snuggly under my pillow and the enchanting sounds of Tibetan singing bowls and Chinese flutes filling my ears, tickling my serenity sensors and sending me gently into a long and dreamless sleep.

And that was Tuesday.

———————

I got up early the next morning, checked my body for bullet holes, and put the finishing touches on those last couple resumes. Cabin fever was just starting to kick in when Kalista called and invited me to lunch. So, I rode the Metrolink to the Sphire Building, the sleek skyscraper downtown where she worked, and waited for her in the lobby, the unofficial shiny foliage capital of America. Men and women in power suits and skirts floated by, strides purposeful, countenances somber. I felt out of place, and in my ratty jeans and faded Jesus Lizard tee, I must have looked it, too.

I was surprised to see Kalista step off the elevator wearing capris pants and a Bleed Blue sweatshirt. I was even more surprised when she hurried towards me and planted a seven-Mississippi kiss on my lips (yes, I counted). I'd been wondering where we stood after our tryst the other night. Evidently it was well outside the friend zone.

"Come up to my office with me," she said, taking my hand. "My boss said I could have the afternoon off. But only if I bring you up there so everyone can stare and judge you and make you feel uncomfortable."

"Naturally."

We rode the elevator to her office on the four-teenth floor, where I expected a wasteland of cubicles and ennui. Instead, there were open spaces, round tables, leather couches, and floor-to-ceiling windows flooding the room with natural light. An espresso bar stood in the corner. The company's name, Internal Reflexions, was etched in elegant calligraphy on a wall above a photo montage of completed projects. Splashes of color dotted the walls. The room clearly belonged to people well-versed in the art of modern comfort and design.

Kalista introduced me to her manager, a pig-tailed woman in her thirties with vintage rhinestone glasses and a fuzzy turtleneck that read BOSS in glittering pink letters.

"*Enchanté,*" she said.

"*La bibliotheque,*" I replied.

A man in a sequined shirt shook my hand and said, "I'd tell you my name, but you'll just forget it. I'm Kalista's work husband, but don't get mad, because I'm the biggest queer in St. Louis."

A guy with spiky hair and the whitest teeth I've ever seen pointed out that I was the first straight guy to walk through the door in ten years.

"No offense, Davey," he added.

The young man whom I presumed to be Davey didn't look up from his laptop, but just raised his middle finger.

"We've been waiting for Davey to come out of the cabinet for years," said the work husband. "We say cabinet, not closet, because he's such a tiny little guy."

"Clever," said Davey, still not looking up. "Believe it or not, a-holes, not all interior designers are gay."

"Now, Davey, that's just offensive."

"V.C., what do you do?" said a man in the corner who looked and sounded like the comedian Andy Dick.

"You mean other than Kalista?" said the work husband.

"Inappropriate!" someone called.

"Awwwwwkward," sang someone else.

"He shoots people who ask questions," said Kalista, ushering me to the exit. "We're leaving. Bye, bitches."

As we walked out the door, someone said, "He looks dopey as all hell, but she's done worse."

"He didn't look Vietnamese to me," said another. "Isn't he supposed to be Vietnamese or something?"

"Oh my God, Christian! Do you ever fucking listen? That's the *old* boyfriend, the one with the *restraining order*, and he's *Venezuelan*."

"Well, excuse the fuck out of me! But some of us are

busy working here, not gabbing all day about Chesty Chestnut's sex life."

"You didn't hear that," said Kalista. "And don't get a big head thinking I talk about you. Until this morning, they'd never even heard your name. Got it, jackass?"

"You're the boss, boss."

We walked to Kalista's car, which was parked two blocks away in a particularly shady lot behind the Huck Finn Inn. Ominous signs at the entrance warned drivers to park at their own risk, they were not responsible for stolen items or vehicles. Another sign read not to walk alone at night. A third sign read Beware Panhandlers! Under it, someone had scribbled *And Police!*

"Do you always park here?"

"Are you scared? No, I normally park in the garage over there. There's a hockey game tonight, so it costs twenty bucks."

"If Sergio wants to whack us both at the same time, this is his perfect chance," I said.

Kalista just tossed me the keys. "You want to drive?"

"Sure."

"Drive fast. I'm getting hungry. You won't like me when I'm hungry."

"I'll give you something to nibble on," I murmured.

"What?"

"I said, 'Where to?'"

"South Grand. There's a tapas place I've been wanting to try."

The skies were clear and bright for the first time since Jake, or the person lying in Jake's grave, died. We drove the convertible with the top down, soaking up the Indian summer sunshine while Kalista sang along to Top Forty. After a great deal of internal debate, I decided not to hold it against her.

At the restaurant, we ordered a hodgepodge of small plates—Korean rib sliders, toasted ravioli, lobster bites, and fried oysters. We turned down the wine list—"Too early," we agreed—and opted for honeyed ginseng tea instead. It suddenly occurred to me that I didn't drink booze yesterday. Such a phenomenon hadn't occurred since... longer than I could remember, actually.

"Let me ask you a question," said Kalista as she sucked Rémoulade sauce off a lobster bite and then swallowed it whole. "Have you..."

"Ever wanted to be a crustacean? Yes. Yes, I have."

"... thought about if things are going to be weird between us now?"

"Whatever do you mean?"

"Now that we slept together, jackass."

"Wait... we *what?*... Hold on... was that *you* the other night? Wow, this is very embarrassing, I don't know what to..."

"Seriously. Are things going to get weird? Are you going to get weird on me, V.C.?"

"That depends what you consider weird, Kalista."

"Try me."

"OK... If I cut off tiny pieces of my appendages and hide them in your apartment so that you think of me when you find them, would that be weird?"

"Why would someone have that thought? And then say it out loud? Yes, that would be weird."

"Then yes. Things will definitely be weird between us now."

Kalista stared, unblinking and unamused.

"Things have always been weird between us, Kalista. Right? And why not? The whole damn world is weird. Look at Portland. Look at Weird Al. Look at the City Museum. Roll with it. It works."

"Wow. That's deep. Jackass."

"My wisdom is eclipsed only by my idiocy."

After lunch, we went to St. Judoc's Medical Center to visit Lewie. When we asked for his room number at the front desk in the ICU, the receptionist threw her hands in the air like a preacher and declared, "Praise Jesus, that man is gone! He's been moved to a regular room on the east wing!"

"Where's that?" asked Kalista.

"Far enough, child. Far enough!"

Even with those foolproof directions, we made a wrong turn and ended up in the nursery. Kalista looked through the glass at someone's little bundle of joy, who was screaming bloody murder, and said, "Do you think ours will be that adorable, love?"

"Funny," I said, though it wasn't.

Eventually, we found Lewie's room at the end of a hallway on the other side of the complex. Nobody was standing guard outside his door, which I took to be a good sign.

My spirits fell, though, when I saw the angry purple bruises on the left side of his face and the golf ball-sized bump on his forehead, concealed under a protective gauze pad. Foamy spittle dribbled out of the corner of his mouth and came to a stop on his backup chin. He was snoring softly, like a precious baby ogre catching some Z's after a long day of clubbing villagers over the head.

"I feel guilty," I said. I must have been using my serious voice, because Kalista put a comforting hand on my shoulder. "If anyone should be deft at dodging vehicles, it's me."

"I feel guilty, too. It was my ex-boyfriend who did this."

"We don't know that for sure. It could have been anyone."

A dry erase board hung on the wall next to the bed. I recall the words contusion, concussion, hematoma, Ativan, and Percocet. Under a column titled Today's Goal is to Keep Me... the nurses had written *Away from other patients, Not as disruptive as yesterday* and *Asleep as much as safely possible.*

As we looked down on him, his eyes started to flutter. A low grown escaped his lips. "V.C.," he moaned, barely audible.

"Hey there, big fella. Hey, Lewie."

"V.C.... come closer..."

"Sure, buddy," I said, leaning in. "What's up, Lewie?"

With a weakened hand, he grabbed my wrist and pulled me even closer. "Listen to me," he said, his voice creaky and weak. "A boy... a boy..."

"A boy?"

"A boy has..."

"What about a boy, Lewie? Stay with me, buddy!"

He was having great difficulty fighting off

unconsciousness. What was he trying to communicate?
It must be important, I thought.

"Stay with me, Lewie!"

"A boy," he said, "has never..."

"Lewie! Stay with me!"

His body went rigid under the sheets as he mus-
tered all his might to speak. Finally, he managed to
share his revelation:

"A boy has never wept," he declared, "nor dashed a
thousand kim."

Kalista and I looked at each other, bewildered.

Suddenly, like a wound-up jack-in-the-box, Lewie
bolted upright, eyes wide open. "Dutch Schultz!" he
boomed. "The dying words of Dutch Schultz? Eh? Eh?"

"What the... Dutch... what?"

"Schultz! The Dutchman! Hello! The bootlegger,
killed by his fellow mobsters? Murder, Inc.? The hit
squad? Legs Diamond, Lucky Luciano? Rambling
deathbed confession, very stream-of-consciousness, very
bizarre, oddly beautiful at times? A boy has never fucking wept, nor dashed a thousand fucking kim? Eh? Eh?"

"Rings a bell, I think, sort of," I said.

"Holy stromboli!" shouted Lewie, seeing Kalista for
the first time. "You are definitely not ugly. Not even
a little bit!"

Kalista batted her eyes playfully. "Aren't you a
charmer," she said. "I like your giant bump."

"Lewie," I said, "meet..."

"Don't tell me! Is this Kalista?" said Lewie. "I don't
know what you're talking about, V.C. There's nothing
wrong with her nose at all. *I* think she's beautiful."

"Lewie," I said, "was there a guard at your door ear-lier? One of Big Jamie's guys?"

"Was! And yeah, that was a disaster. Miguel Zuman is the joker's name. I recognized him right away as one of Jake's dad's guys. When I woke up and saw him, I thought he was here to kill me. Not sure why. Tempo-rary drug psychosis, I suppose. Turns out, he was sent to protect me! Big Jamie thinks the guys in the car have something to do with Jake's murder. Can you believe it!"

"What did you do to Miguel Zuman, Lewie?"

"Ack," said Lewie, dismissing the question with a wave of the hand. "He'll be fine. Besides, if a guy can't stop a freaking hospital patient *with tubes* from choking him out, should he really be a guard anyway?"

Unfortunately, that's all Lewie wrote. His eyelids grew heavy, and this time he wasn't faking it. Before he could even extol the virtues of the last words of Dutch Schultz, he was back in the land of nod.

In the evening, Kalista drove me home. She pulled to the side of the road to let me out, keeping the car running. For the first time all day, awkwardness crept in. I wasn't sure whether to give her a kiss, a hug, a fist bump, or a marriage proposal. I decided on the first. But when I closed in on the delivery, she quickly turned away.

"What exactly are you doing?" she said.

Fortunately, the ability to communicate with beau-tiful women in tense situations has always been my greatest gift.

"Oh," I said. "Um... well, didn't... um..."

"This isn't goodbye. Go. Pack an overnight bag.

Quickly. If you *want* to come home with me, that is. But I'm not waiting forever."

"Yes, boss," I said. "You're the boss, boss."

I took the stairs three at a time.

And that was Wednesday.

"V.C.!"

I must have zoned out, because Kalista was shaking me and shouting in my ear.

"Oh... um... hi," I said. "How are you? What brings you here?"

"Are you all right? I just screamed your name, like, seven times."

"With your clothes on? That's unusual."

"Touché. Seriously, though. You haven't laughed at one of Cat's witty asides in twenty minutes."

Kalista had called into work "sick—very, very sick," a self-diagnosis that I tried not to take too personally. We spent the morning lying in her heavenly king-sized bed and watching a marathon showing of some offbeat Brit sci-fi comedy called "Red Dwarf."

"Sorry, my brain's not right. I haven't had a drink in two days."

"Oh, honey. Only an alcoholic would say that. And only a hopeless alcoholic would say that before he's out of bed in the morning."

"I was thinking about something Lewie said."

"Is it, 'A boy has never wept, nor bashed...'"

"*Dashed.*"

"...'a million...'"

"*Thousand.*"

"… 'kings?'"

"*Kim.* And no. He said that solving a mystery is just like solving a puzzle. You gather up all the pieces, spread them out on the floor or wherever, and piece them together."

"Wow. He's almost as deep as you are."

"I think we need to establish some ground rules about the use—overuse, really—of sarcasm in this relationship."

"That's a terrific idea, V.C. You're, like, MENSA material, honey."

"Lewie said we were still collecting puzzle pieces. But what if he's wrong? What if we have all the pieces already? And now we just need to snap them into place?"

I stood up and started to pace. "Do you have a pen and paper handy?"

Kalista patted down her nightgown, pretending to search its nonexistent pockets for the requested items. "Shoot," she said. "I must have left them in the pockets of my Monday lingerie."

"Something's not right," I said. "There's something my brain isn't digesting the way it should. Something obvious… something… just… obvious. Where are the pens around here?"

Begrudgingly, Kalista got out of bed and led me to her office, which was twice the size of my apartment and looked, with its jade plants, mirrors, candles, framed pictures of oceanic atolls, and vibrant colors, like a showroom in a Feng Shui fanzine.

"Everything you need is on the desk– pens, paper, a picture of Fredbird swallowing my grandmother's head at old Busch Stadium. I'm going to hop in the shower. Oh, yeah, and don't forget…"

She disappeared and returned a moment later holding the Colt .45 gingerly by the barrel. I'd packed it in my overnight bag and placed it on Kalista's nightstand while we slept.

"If Sergio shows up, shoot him, but please don't make a mess. I'm quite fond of the carpet in here."

While Kalista showered, I fired up a pot of coffee and found a sharpie and a pad of stick-it notes. On the top one, I wrote, *Fake funeral held Friday for Jake.* On the next, *Half-open casket; body visible, not head.* On the next, *Black stomped off T-Bone by three thugs.* And so on, arranging them on the floor in chronological order, until every puzzle piece I could think of was laid out in front of me.

"Occupational therapy?" said Kalista, who had finished her shower and was standing in the doorway, brushing her hair, naked from the waist up. "Can I help?"

"Yes. You can come back when you're hideous and hairy and mutant-like and not at all distracting."

Ignoring me, she bent over to get a closer look. "There's more," she said. "Give me the pen. Maybe it's nothing, but let's note it anyway."

When we were finished, we had an orderly little collection of valuable clues to ponder. Or a pile of bloody pains in the ass to ignore and avoid:

Fake funeral held Friday for Jake—"suicide"

Half-open casket; body visible, not head

M.E. not allowed to examine body

Jake plays sax at own funeral, a la Jesse James

Kalista tells Sergio she's pregnant with V.C.'s baby

Sergio goes MIA

Jake killed in V.C.'s apartment Friday night

Police not called, but Det. Beerman shows up, brings V.C. to jail

Big Gay Sal removes body

Det. Beerman hires brain scrubber to clean apt (eliminate all evidence)

Black stomped off T-Bone by three thugs

Sal accuses V.C. of being a spy

Sal thinks V.C. is from Chicago, San Diego, or Tijuana

Sal doesn't want V.C. to see third floor

Sal carries shovel while V.C. knocks on door

Big Jamie thinks V.C.'s phone is bugged (?)

B.J. says "some no-name" killed Jake and "plan worked"

B.J. infuriated b/c someone tried to force him into…. Something?

B.J…. "I ain't a goddamn slave owner." Big fan of "free will." WTF??

Sergio leaves death threat in Kalista's mailbox

Arianna goes MIA

Big black car w/ three thugs (same as T-Bone?) try to run over Lewie and V.C.

Sal and Beerman at police station together (car attack related to Jake/Jamie?)

Beerman furious when V.C. mentions Sergio

We stared at the mystifying potpourri of post-its at our feet for several minutes, saying nothing. Sadly, there was no "Aha!" moment forthcoming in my brain.

"Well," I said, "what do you think?"

Kalista knitted her brow in concentration and shook her head slowly. "I think," she said after a long pause, "that we are missing some pieces." She took my hand and pulled me close. "And I think," she added, "that we both deserve a day in bed."

"Your house," I said, "your rules."

And that was Thursday.

———

I awoke to find Kalista standing in front of the mirror, fixing her hair into a no-nonsense bun. She was wearing a gray and black skirt suit and dress shoes.

"Are Fridays Girl Power day or something?"

Kalista groaned. "Some rich bitch client is visiting the office this morning. On a *Friday*. Seriously, who does that to people?"

"Skip it. You're very, very sick, remember?"

"Sorry, honey. The real world beckons."

Regrettably, it was beckoning me as well. I had a text from the resume agency:

*Four rewrites needed by end of day. Call before nine
if you want them.*

In light of recent events, working on resumes felt like a silly way to expend my energies. But my shithole apartment didn't pay for itself, so I accepted the offer. Kalista and I ate a quick breakfast at the diner across the street, then she drove me to the Galleria Metrolink station.

"Will I ever see you again?" I said.

"Don't joke," said Kalista. "And don't die. I'm serious."

"Yes, boss."

I gave her a quick kiss, which turned into a long kiss. Finally, she pushed me away.

"Get out of the car. You're going to get me fired. Go. And keep breathing, jackass."

I was still in the parking lot when a crackling voice on the intercom announced, presumably, that the train was near, so stand back or jump in front of it, depending on your self-preservation preferences. I managed to hop aboard moments before the automatic doors rattled shut. A security guard at the exit frowned at me and shook his head. I was suddenly very conscious of the unlicensed firearm in my duffle bag. Fortunately, the guard didn't pay me any more attention, and neither did anyone else. They were probably wrapped up in death dramas and murder mysteries of their own.

A few minutes later, I stepped off the platform onto Delmar Blvd. feeling like an expatriate returning home after a long, happy voyage. It was another unseasonably warm, sunny day, and even though we were two weeks from Halloween, spring was in the air. There was a spring in my step as well. A little bit o' lovin' goes a long way indeed.

I heard Bobby before I saw him.

"If the motherfuckers don't think this place is classy

enough now, fuck them!" he bawled. "They wouldn't know class if it bit them in the ass!"

The door to Kind of Blue was propped open. Bobby stood in the entranceway, drinking a bottle of beer while a muscle head with a faux hawk pushed a polyurethane mop across the hardwood floor. I'm no master do-it-yourself-er, but I was fairly certain the recommended strategy for refinishing a floor called for removing the tables and chairs, not just hastily mopping around them.

The Kind of Blue signage above the door was gone, replaced by a flimsy plastic marquee that read Seal. The nails that used to jut from the walls had been removed and the loose insulation hanging from the ceiling pushed back into place. Framed snapshots of war heroes now adorned the walls. Oddly, a lone Miles Davis picture remained. Sandwiched between Normandy invaders and Seal Team Six, the Prince of Darkness looked uncharacteristically toothless.

"V.C.!" The former Navy Seal shook my hand and pulled me in for a bear hug. "Come in, check out the new digs. How the hell have you been, man? I've barely seen you since Jake went under. Get in here, you chicken-fucking motherfucker!"

Bobby had two modes: aggressively friendly and frighteningly anti-social. He switched between them on a dime. Maybe he had a screw loose. As I'd soon learn, though, he was a good guy to have in your corner when skulls started cracking.

"Seal, huh?" I commented. "The man does have soul. 'Kissed by a Rose.'"

"'Kissed by a Rose!' You're amazing, you know that! Grand reopening Monday night, brother! I expect you to be here. Bring a friend. Hell, you can even bring Lewie! We're kicking things off with an open mic night. Bands, comedians, some poet fucker or something. It's going to be the stuff of motherfucking legend, bro. I even hired some cute little bartender so the big bad Seal with the scars doesn't scare away all those pantywaist chicken shits anymore!"

Bobby laughed loudly and trudged across the wet, waxy floor to retrieve three bottles of Budweiser from the bar. "Chicken sandwiches on the house!" he announced with another boisterous laugh. Faux hawk chuckled dutifully. I didn't get it.

"Why the name change?" I asked, accepting a beer that I didn't particularly want, considering it wasn't quite 8:30 a.m. "Was the old one just giving you the blues?"

Bobby's face turned red. "Some neighborhood association fuckface cockslobberers have been crawling up my ass, threatening to shut me down if I don't quote unquote, class the place up a little. Fuck them! It's my fucking property, and I'll run it the way I want. You agree? You agree? You agree?"

"I agree."

"So yeah, I'm classing the place up a little."

I didn't follow the logic train, but opted not to question it.

"Well, it does look good in here," I said. "You know, with the new pictures on the wall. And the floor is clean and shiny in a few places, too."

"Damn right it looks good in here."

"Hopefully changing the name wasn't too big of a hassle. I imagine there was a lot of paperwork involved, huh?"

"Paperwork? Fuck if I know! What paperwork?"

"Oh. Ummm... I don't know exactly, but don't you need a new business license, liquor license, that sort of thing?"

"Fuck that! I fucking dare those Isis-loving mother-fuckers to come at me with some bullshit paperwork charge! I dare them! I fucking dare them!"

"Amen to that, Bobby. Amen to that, man," said Faux Hawk.

Bobby raised his bottle. "Here's to new beginnings, my brothers. Here's to Seal." Faux Hawk and I sipped our beers while Bobby chugged every drop. "Ah... Breakfast of champions!" he said. "Ready for another?"

"Actually, I need to work today," I said. "Thanks for the offer, but..."

"What have you been up to anyway, brother? How's life? Let's talk. What's new?"

"What's new? Well, how much time you got?"

"All night! Hockey game tonight. Let's go, you and me. I'll stop by your apartment at six. I know an usher at Scottrade, he'll get us in. His name's Donald, I'm an old friend of his brother's. Donald's a great guy. He'll get us in, no problem. He *better* get us in, if that pig fucker knows what's good for him! See you at six."

He showed up an hour early. I was sitting on the floor poring over those post-it notes when he barged in. Startled, I reached for the Colt .45 beside me. Bobby's eyes lit up.

"Jesus Christ, brother! What's going on here? What kind of mess are you wrapped up in?"

Bobby was a loose cannon, but it never hurts to have a hand-to-hand combat master on your side when there's a lunatic trying to kill you and the double-death of a crime lord's son hanging over your head. So, I fed him the entire story, sparing no detail. His wide, crazy eyes grew wider and crazier as the story progressed. He didn't say anything for a long minute after I finished, but just sat there grinding his teeth, doing a slow burn.

Finally, he spoke: "First thing we need to do is find that Sergio motherfucker and slit his throat! Self-defense!"

"Yeah, but... what if he was just blowing off steam or whatever when he wrote the death threat, Bobby? I mean, it's been a few days, and he hasn't surfaced, so maybe he's just..."

"First thing we need to do is find that Sergio motherfucker and slit his throat!" Bobby repeated, louder. "Self-defense!"

Fortunately, Bobby proceeded to drink a river of Budweiser and lose sight of committing first degree murder.

Aggravated assault, however, was still on the table.

He was lying on my sofa after the game, face down, piss drunk, and worn out from yelling "Shoot!" at inopportune times, when the band below us at Camilla's took the stage. They literally blasted Bobby off the couch.

"What the fuck is that!" he bellowed, pounding his fists furiously on the floor. "Hey, you tuneless cocksucker motherfuckers! Shut the fuck up! We're trying to sleep up here!"

Bobby focused his attention on me, and I made a futile effort to keep myself from laughing.

"What the fuck are they doing down there, V.C.? *Why is it so fucking loud?!*"

"It's not exactly acoustic night at Camilla's, Bobby."

My friend climbed to his feet and struggled into his shoes. "Well, it's about to become acoustic night at Camilla's!"

"Where you going, Bobby?"

"Where am I going? Where am I fucking going?! I'm going to bash someone's head into a snare drum until he shuts the fuck up!"

"Try the cymbal if that doesn't work, Bobby. I think it will be make them especially cognizant of your displeasure, man."

I don't know who Bobby threatened or whose head he smashed into which percussion accessory, but within minutes, the decibel level at Camilla's was cut in half. Bobby then burst through my door with a triumphant "Whoo! Much better! Fuck yeah!" and promptly fell asleep on my couch with a satisfied smile on his face.

"I'm glad you're on my side, Bobby," I said.

And that was Friday.

Lewie called the next morning to say he had been released from the hospital and had taken a taxi home.

"Let's go to Jewelbug's Palace to celebrate!" he said.

"Jewelbug's Palace? That kids arcade at the mall?"

"Kids arcade? Kids arcade! Jewelbug's Palace is for adults, too, V.C."

"Yeah. OK. I mean, I guess they won't kick you out just for being an adult, if that's what you mean."

"Rubbish! Did you know that adults who set aside twenty minutes each day to play demonstrate better critical thinking skills, enhanced creativity, and an improved ability to cope with relationship challenges?"

"Wow, Lewie. That's, like, truly eye-opening, man. Inspirational."

"Then it's settled! See you there. And besides, it will be a good training opportunity for you, Agent Almond. Playing video games and closing cases are basically the same thing. You'll see. And if you want to come work with me..."

"I don't."

"... then it's high time you spent some time under the learning tree, grasshopper. And bring that Kalista girl along, will you? My memory is a little fuzzy, but I distinctively remember we shared a special moment at the hospital."

"Careful, Lewie."

I called Kalista.

"Seriously?" she said. "You want to go that kids arcade at the mall?"

"It's for adults too, Kalista. Did you know that adults who play for just twenty minutes a day have better, you know, thinking skills, and... um... you know, thinking... abilities?"

"Then you better play for sixty, sweetie."

Jewelbug's Palace was, as I expected, crawling with hyper kids, irritated parents, and my favorite brain-damaged pseudo private investigator. He was sitting at some *Star Wars* video game, surrounded by twelve-year old boys and firing two guns without looking at the screen.

"Oh, no. What's that?" said Lewie to an awestruck youth by his side. "Are three storm troopers about to get me? Wait... what's that? There's a bounty hunter on my tail, you say? Oh, no! What are we going to do about that?"

"Lewie," I said, "I see you found some friends."

"Oh, hey, V.C.! I'll be through with these Mos Espa jokers in just a minute."

"Did you *see* that? Are you *watching* this?" one of Lewie's new pals asked me. "He just beat Darth Mal without even *looking* at him! And now he's halfway through level four and he's still on his first lightsaber! And he's still not looking!"

"You're lying," I said.

"Honest to God, I saw him!"

I stood among Lewie's impromptu fan club for the next half hour, watching him battle acid lizards, mutated sandmaggots, and "the most badass greater krayt dragon in the galaxy," according to one observer. The place smelled like soda syrup and feet. I was ready to slip away when Lewie finally defeated the game. His fan club erupted in applause.

Lewie slapped me on the back. "There's no better way to celebrate freedom than by impaling a couple dozen woolly veermoks, am I right?"

"How's your head, Lewie? Shouldn't you be resting up or something?"

Lewie blew off the suggestion with a flick of the hand. "Head's fine," he said. "Nothing major. A few cranial cracks here and there. Just a few chips off the old block, really." He was zigzagging across the room with a purpose, and I was having trouble catching up. "Oh, yeah," he added as an afterthought. "I had a pinch of hematoma as well. Ever hear of it? Google it. It's a bitch! No fun on that front, my friend!"

We came to a stop at some treasure-finding game called *Heroine's Treasure*.

"Listen and learn, Agent Almond. Some cases, you see, are like this game. You find a clue, you follow a clue. It leads to the next clue, and the next clue, and so on. Sure, every now and then you may bump into a wall or a flesh-eating ogre, but that's OK. It's part logic, part trial and error, see? Just watch."

I watched, and watched, and watched. I was so relieved to see Lewie alive and well that I only half-wished Sergio would sneak up behind me and plant a knife in my gut to get me out of there.

Next up was a game called *Mutant Melee*. As a sword-wielding Japanese samurai with the head of a tiger, Lewie conquered a wizard-dragon with a flaming beard. The key to victory, evidently, was to pound the controls spastically, like a caffeinated monkey with a drum set.

"Other cases," said Lewie, "are like *Mutant Melee*. You simply steam roll through them. Let me give you an example, partner. Say you're hired to trail a guy who's defrauding his company, claiming some bullshit injury. There are no clues to be found here. All you need to do is take your scimitar and lop off his head... or kick out the crutches from underneath him and watch him dance, partner."

"I'm not sure I want to lop anyone's head off, Lewie. Or kick their crutches, man."

"Sure you do! Come, let's move along."

Next stop was a James Bond-themed game. Lewie's character, armed with an automatic rifle, traipsed through a maze of control rooms in search of some dastardly commie scum.

"Some cases are like Bond," he said. "You stalk your target, keeping your distance, until the moment is right to"—Secret Agent Aldous Lewie popped up from behind a skid of wine casks and put a single bullet through his enemy's eye—"plant some lead in his head. Or, more likely, take a picture of him shagging his secretary. Questions?"

"One. Why, Lewie, did you save my life, only to immediately make it not worth saving?"

"That's the spirit! Come along, there's one more I want to show you. You'll appreciate this, Agent Almond."

The final game was called *Bomb, Bomb, Bomb and Away!* A parachute at the top of the screen dropped different colored explosives every few seconds. The objective was to maneuver the parachute to make three bombs of the same color connect, causing them to incinerate. The more bombs you cleared, the faster they rained down. When there was nowhere left to stack them, you lost.

"The death of Jake Kennedy," said Lewie, "is a classic *Bomb, Bomb, Bomb and Away!* situation, V.C. You have all these clues, puzzle pieces, bombs, whatever you want to call them. And they appear to be falling down on us in completely indiscriminate fashion."

Lewie dropped the bombs seemingly randomly, stacking blue on green and yellow on red and purple on black.

"And it builds and it builds. And it starts to look more desperate and dire with each dropping bomb."

Three-quarters of the screen was now occupied.

"And sometimes, you think you might have something, but it turns out to be nothing. A red herring, if you will." He dropped a red bomb atop two orange. "Close, but no cigarillo, right?"

Lewie was nearly out of space. Three or four more misplaced bombs and it would be game over—with a grand score of absolutely zero.

"Here's the thing, though, partner. Things aren't as muddled and fucked as you think they are. In fact, they're lined up pretty nicely. They always are. All you need is that one... magic... missing... piece..."

Lewie had enough screen space for one more bomb. He dropped it into place. Three reds touched each other and erupted. It set off a chain reaction. Cartoon explosives fell like dominos as groups of three connected. Another slack-jawed peanut gallery gathered around Lewie, watching *Bomb, Bomb, Bomb and Away!* light up like a slot machine and spit out a jackpot of midway tickets.

"You see, partner?" said Lewie, walking away and leaving the spoils for the masses. "Bleak and hopeless as things may look, you're always just one clue away from breaking the case wide open!"

And that was Saturday.

———

Kalista and I went to lunch the next day at Strawberry

Mountain, the burger joint across the street from my apartment. On the way out, we ran into Josie. Her mouth dropped open when she saw us.

"Virginia!" she scolded me. "How dare you cheat on me!"

The girl with the dragon tattoo then stalked away in mock anger before turning around to blow one or both of us a kiss.

"Don't ask," I said. "I think she might be a little crazy."

"She is a little scary. She could totally kick your ass, I bet."

We stayed inside the rest of the day, snuggled up on my sofa in front of a space heater, watching football, sipping hot cocoa, and occasionally asking the ghost of Jake if he had anything to say. The skies were gray and abnormally still. It felt like the calm before the storm.

It was.

And that was Sunday.

On Monday, the world got weird again.

Chapter II

THE RAIN WAS BACK. I STARED BLANKLY AT THE FLOOR in my apartment, like a junkie fixated on his shoe. I'd spent the morning poring over those post-it notes, and again, my brain shot blanks. Maybe two decades of liquid libations had created a permanent static, a sort of white noise, in the space between my ears. Or maybe Lewie and Kalista were right and too many pieces of the puzzle were still MIA.

Either way, as detective Beerman would say, I felt as useless as a pecker at a dyke convention.

A sudden clap of thunder shook 703 Delmar Blvd., snapping me out of my stupor. The kitchen crew at Kun-Woo's hooted.

"Cosmic boom!" shouted one of them.

"*Sonic* boom!" a coworker corrected him.

Outside, a middle-aged couple waddled across the street to Strawberry Mountain, skipping hand in hand as raindrops kept falling on their heads.

"There's something about getting caught in the rain," I mused aloud, "that turns us all into kids again."

And there was something about the next sound I heard that promptly turned my frown upside down.

It wasn't particularly melodic or coherent—just a few random plucks of some stringed instrument that I couldn't put my finger on. But for all I cared, it could have been fingernails on a chalkboard, or even some early 2000s emo band. Because it was coming from the tenant lobby, which meant only one thing:

"T-Bone!"

I dashed down the steps. My old friend was in his usual warmup spot by the door, fiddling with some two-stringed instrument I didn't recognize. Its head was fashioned in the shape of a curly-horned goat.

"T-Bone! You're back!"

I rushed to the old busker and threw my arms around him. He flinched a little.

"Shit, man, I'm sorry! Are you all right? Are you sore?"

"Just a little bit, maybe."

Hearing T-Bone's soothing, sonorous voice had a narcotic effect, like salve in a cut.

"Not all the black that got stomped off of me has grown back," he said. "Don't tell my wife, though. She'll try to put me back in bed and check my pulse every five minutes again."

"She sounds like an angel."

"That she is. A doting, loving, smothering angel. And you, my friend, are a sight for sore eyes. The Delmar Loop is a sight for sore eyes. Laid up in bed bruised and bleeding, even with an angel watching over you, is no way to live."

"I've been worried about you, man. How you holding up?"

"About the same as you, by the looks of that cut on your head. What happened? Don't tell me those same three hounds sic'd you, too."

"No, but... sort of. Maybe. Probably not. Shit, I don't know. Epic story, T-Bone. You want to come up for a cup of coffee? It doesn't look like this rain is going to let up anytime soon. Where's your equipment?"

"I'm playing inside today. The record store asked me to play this *tovshuur* for a couple hours. A *Tishoumaren* band from West Africa is performing later. I'm opening for them. You ever hear of Tinariwen?"

"Yeah, of course!"

"Well, it's not them."

"Oh."

"But they're supposed to be similar." T-Bone gazed lovingly at the instrument in his hands. "You ever hear someone play a *tovshuur*?"

"Can't say that I have. I like the goat, though."

"It's an ibex. A beautiful, talented young lady by the name of Arslan Zaya"—the name rolled off T-Bone's tongue like butter—"taught me to play it in Ulaan-baatar, the capital of Mongolia, damn near fifty years ago. I was a teenage Peace Corps volunteer. She was the first woman to tug at my heartstrings."

"Oh, yeah?"

"Oh, yeah. Arslan Zaya." T-Bone had a faraway look in his eye. "Miss Arslan Zaya," he repeated. "What a woman, what a time. You know, Arslan Zaya played another instrument masterfully, too."

"Yeah? Which one?"

"You ever hear of a skin flute?"

T-Bone was stone-faced for several seconds before he couldn't hold it any longer and cracked up laughing. I was so happy to see him that I joined in, even though I was less than thrilled with the image he just planted in my head.

"I never realized you were such a romantic, T-Bone."

"Don't tell my wife that, either." T-Bone gestured towards the stairs. "I've got some time to kill. I showed up early, hoping you'd be around to parlay."

"Good. I need to ask you some questions about what happened the other night, if you don't mind."

"Of course. Damnedest night I've had in twenty-five years of playing music on the corner of Delmar and Leland."

While I made a fresh pot of sludge, T-Bone fidgeted with his *tovshuur* and warmed up his voice with some barely audible throat singing.

"I've seen some crazy things in my time, V.C.," he said when he was through. "But a dead man dropping a Benjamin in my guitar case? That may take the cake. What in the name of Howlin' Wolf happened last weekend?"

"I'd like to tell you, T-Bone," I began. "But..."

"It's complicated?"

"A little bit, yeah. And for your own good, the less you know, the better."

T-Bone smirked. "That sounds like a line from a murder mystery."

"And not a very good one, admittedly."

"Your friend's alive after all, huh? Or does he have a twin?"

"Neither. No twin. At least not that I'm aware of. And he's dead. Again. I didn't realize it at the time you saw him, but he faked his death. But now he's dead for real. He was killed Friday, just a few hours after his funeral. Here in my apartment, actually. You were probably the last person, other than his killer, to see him alive."

"Christ on a bike, V.C.!" said T-Bone, stunned. "Why haven't the police…"

"The police aren't investigating the murder. Except for one detective who swept away the evidence and the body, they don't even know about it. My friend's dad is Big Jamie Kennedy, you know, the…"

"Christmas on a cracker, man! What happened to the less I know, the better?"

"Sorry," I said. "I'm new at this." I poured T-Bone a cup of coffee and returned to my seat on the floor, pen and post-it notes poised. "When you saw Jake the other night, did you talk to him at all? Did he say anything?"

"Not a word. Mind if I smoke in here?"

I did mind, but T-Bone was clearly rattled and could use a nerve tonic. "Anything to conceal the smell of that fish sauce downstairs," I said.

His fingers shook slightly as he fetched a loose smoke from his shirt pocket. "Your friend caught me by surprise," he said. "Before you went off to drink your worries away, you put that picture of him in my guitar case, remember?"

"The funeral program, sure."

"So, all night, every time I looked down, his face was staring up at me. He looked like such a nice, cool cat, you know? I really felt like his spirit was there, man, digging the music, *feeling* it, you know?"

"Sure."

"I was staring into his eyes in that picture when I saw a hundred-dollar bill float into my guitar case..."

"If you don't mind my asking, is that unusual?"

"Well, you never know who's going to drop a twenty, a fifty, or even a hundo on you. It doesn't happen every night, especially not in St. Louis, but yeah, it happens."

"And it was Jake, huh?"

"Damnedest thing, V. I went from staring at his face in a picture to staring at his face in reality. Damn near gave me a heart attack. I finished the song and called it a night."

"Did anybody see Jake give you the money?"

T-Bone shrugged. "Probably, but I can't be sure. Like I said, it threw me off big time."

"The guys who stomped you Saturday—you said you could I.D. them, right?"

"Two of them—the big ole' corn-fed white boys— for sure. The third guy was darker skinned, Hispanic maybe. He was wearing a ball cap and I didn't get a good look at him, but yeah, maybe I could pick him out of a lineup, too."

"Had you ever seen these guys before? They from around here?"

"That's what I've wanted to tell you, V.C. I'm pretty sure they saw me play Saturday. I had that picture in my guitar case again. And I think they saw it. At the time, I didn't realize what they were looking at. I tend to zone out, or focus in, really, when I'm playing. But at one point there were two or three guys peering into my guitar case, and they were talking back and forth, super excited, in Spanish. One of them shouted '*Luego!*' which is Spanish for 'Later!' and another said '*Demasiada gente!*'" which means 'too many people…'"

"Too many people?"

"Right. I didn't realize it then or give it much thought, but they must have meant, 'We'll stomp the black off of this cat later. There are too many people here now.'"

My heart raced excitedly. I felt like we were on the verge of a breakthrough.

"You said that when they were kicking you, they kept saying, 'Where is he?' and 'We know he's your friend.' Do you think…"

"… they were talking about Jake, because they saw his picture in my guitar case and assumed we were friends? Makes sense, doesn't it?"

"Maybe," I said slowly, "maybe not. Let me show you something."

I did a Google search for Sergio Mendoza on my laptop and clicked Images. His profile picture from some social media site appeared halfway down the screen, underneath pictures of Sergio Garcia, Tickle Me Elmo, and Amanda Seyfried for some reason. I showed it to T-Bone.

"Was this the Hispanic guy?"

T-Bone stared at it for a full minute, silent. "Maybe. Maybe not. Sorry, V.C., but I really don't know. Any chance you have pics of the two white dudes?"

I thought of the FBI files in Lewie's poss-ession. "Possibly."

"So, is this guy an enemy of Big Jamie Kennedy or something?" said T-Bone, still eyeballing Sergio.

"Actually, no. Not that I know of, anyway. This is the ex-boyfriend of the girl I'm seeing. He's expressed a strong desire to turn the girl and I both into Mississippi River fish food."

T-Bone's eyes lit up. "Man alive, V.C.! Is this what they mean by white people problems?"

———————

My cell phone rang. It was a local number I didn't recognize.

"Cheerio," I answered.

"Honey nut?" said a voice in a tunnel.

"Who is this?"

The voice on the other end didn't hesitate. "Defective detective Aldous Lewie, witty and gritty with a license to chill."

"Wow. That's just... lame, Lewie. Even with brain damage, that's bad. Why does your voice sound so weird? Where you are calling from?"

"Our office. I got us a phone finally! A landline. They still have landlines, V.C.!"

"Our? Us?"

"And I've got some interesting news for you."

"Please don't. It's too early for interesting news. How about some mundane news instead?"

"Too early? It's noon. And get this: detective Joe Beerman is now just Joe Beerman. He turned in his badge this morning."

"Whoa. Wow. Why?"

"Well... I don't know. An old SLPD colleague told me about it, but he didn't have the details, and I didn't press it. He's a pain in the ass, a real blue flamer if you know what I mean."

"No idea."

"It was an amicable split, evidently. Hugs, handshakes, parting gifts. They even pulled over a black man and pinned a bundle of heroin on him for old time's sake."

"Interesting," I said, recalling Sal's statement about who was *really* signing the detective's paycheck. "I wonder what his *other* boss thinks about that."

"Also, no hits on a black Continental with dealer plates yet. Chances are, they, whoever *they* are, have stowed it by now."

"Chances are."

"So, what are you working on?"

"Actually, I'm looking at..."

"You're right. Not important. How soon can you be at the office? We have work to do, Agent Almond. On the Kennedy case."

"What do you mean, Lewie?"

"Come here and I'll show you."

"Can't you just tell me? It's pouring outside. And your office..."

"*Our* office."

"... is at least six blocks from the Metrolink station."

"What's wrong with your car?"

"My car's been on its last leg for a year, Lewie. It's been overdue for service since before I married Stef. It coughs, spits, squeals, clunks, sputters, grinds..."

"Nonsense. It's fine. Cars are like cast-iron plants, V.C.

They thrive on neglect. And what's the worst that can happen? Trust me. It will be fine."

It wasn't.

Nonetheless, without the benefit of clairvoyance, I hopped inside that old Crown Vic and sputtered down the highway to Tower Grove South with Titus Andronicus blaring in my ears again, reminding me that "the enemy is everywhere." The rains poured down in a fury. I appreciated the empathy.

Lewie P.I. & Associates (of which there were none) was situated on the top floor of a two-story brick building surrounded by historic Victorian homes near South Grand. Fittingly, a divorce attorney occupied the ground level. It was a marriage of convenience for clients, who could collect evidence against their cheating spouses and then file for the Big D in one fell swoop.

Unfortunately, parking was nonexistent. I drove around the block several times before finally settling for a spot in a tow-away zone outside a Chinese Baptist church half a mile away. On the bright side, or so I thought, the rain let up moments after I parked.

I pressed the intercom at the front door and moments later, the divorce attorney—a tanned, blonde-haired young man who reminded me more of a beach bum than a lawyer—buzzed me in.

"Hey there!" he said, jumping to his feet to offer me a fist pump. "How are you?"

"Divorced already," I said. "Sorry."

He waved a playful finger at me. "Just don't do it again, young man."

A middle-aged black woman dressed in her Sunday

best stood outside Lewie's door, giving the defective detective a hug.

"Now don't you worry one bit, Mrs. Minafort," said Lewie in a surprisingly tender voice. "We'll find out the truth about your daughter. And when we do, we can confront her with it, and then the healing can begin. OK? Now go get some rest, Mrs. Minafort. You've earned it."

Mrs. Minafort placed both hands over her heart.

"You're one of the good guys, Mr. Lewie. I just know it. Praise Jesus, you are one of the good guys!"

"Who's that?" I said when she was gone. "The future Mrs. Aldous Lewie?"

"Her? Nah, that's just Mrs. Minafort."

"Well, that explains it."

"She thinks her daughter's on drugs. Under the wicked spell of the devil's lettuce."

"What are you going to do? Follow her? Try to catch her buying it from her dealer?"

"Meh." Lewie shrugged, dismissively. "That sounds like a lot of effort. I figured I'd just offer the kid some weed, and if she takes a toke, I'll…" He made a clicking sound like he was taking a picture. "But never mind that. Follow me!"

Lewie led me across his office to the cozy little split-level annex in the corner. He'd been attempting, unsuccessfully, to sublet it for months. He gestured for me to enter and stepped aside with a dramatic bow.

"Ta-da!" he sang.

I stepped inside to find a solid oak desk with a glass name plate on top that read Special Agent V.C. Almond.

Dolly Llama, a Jake Kennedy painting featuring the visage and cleavage of Dolly Parton attached to the torso of a wooly beast of burden, hung on the wall. A flowering peace lily sat in the corner next to an old reclining chair.

"Eh? Eh? What do you think, partner? Eh?"

In truth, it looked like a terrific place to punch the clock. There were only two problems.

"You're mental, Lewie. And I don't know a damn thing about being a private dick, man!"

"Rubbish! Being a private investigator is all about who you know, and I know everybody. I'll introduce you."

I took a seat in the swivel chair behind the desk and put my feet up. It was quite comfy, I had to admit.

"Why are you so obsessed with getting me to work here, Lewie?"

"The rent's almost due. And I've already told you, you're a natural! Tell me, what color hat was Mrs. Minafort wearing?"

I thought about it for several seconds, racking my brain. "She wasn't," I said. "She had braids, no hat."

"Exactly! Do you know how many people I've interviewed for this position? Seven. And do you know how many knew the color of Mrs. Minafort's hat?"

"One hundred."

"Guess again."

"Pi."

"Zero. And you know why?"

"Because they aren't naturals like me?" I played along.

Lewie shot me a puzzled look. "Because Mrs. Minafort wasn't *here* when they interviewed. Get it together, man. I just met her today."

"Why am I here, Lewie? What's going on with Jake?" I said, anxious to change the subject.

"Excellent question, partner! Those FBI files are fairly worthless. The FBI either didn't know what was going on with Big Jamie and his acquaintances, they were on his payroll, or they simply didn't give a fuck. Or maybe my contact deliberately withheld the juicy stuff."

"Can't imagine why he would do that."

"I've been interviewing Jake's friends, too, to see if they knew what was going down. I've been feeding them a line about his girlfriend hiring me to find out why he ate a bullet."

"And?"

"And nothing! Nobody knows a thing. The more I've thought about it, the more I'm convinced that none of us really even *knew* Jake. He had a girlfriend in St. Louis, an apartment in Asheville, played in a cover band in Austin, spent a lot of weekends in L.A. He was a rolling stone, bouncing around from town to town, never grounded for long enough for anyone to get a read on him."

Lewie lit a cigarette and offered me the pack.

"Don't tempt me," I said. "You know I quit."

"When's the last time you saw Jake?"

"At his funeral. He was on a grassy knoll in the near distance, playing saxophone while we put someone else's corpse underground."

"True. How about before then?"

"I had lunch with him and Arianna about two weeks ago before he died. He was his merry prankster self, man."

Lewie nodded thoughtfully. "That's the general consensus. But we still have some peeps to talk to."

"We?"

Lewie pulled a list from his pocket. It contained several names that I vaguely recognized, including the Elvis impersonator Mitch Hartley and Connor Ventura, an old acquaintance who held the distinction of being the first of many to sleep with my ex-wife while we were still married.

"Seriously? Connor? That prick?"

"Don't give me that look. Connor's a good guy. He's been trying to make amends with you forever. It's time you boys kissed and made up. And besides, if we're not going to talk to anybody your ex-wife slept with, then that pretty much rules out the 314 and 636 area codes."

"Don't forget the 618."

"That's the spirit!" Lewie handed me a manila envelope. "Names, occupations, contact info, it's all there. You know most of the people anyway, I think. Find out the last time they saw Jake and if he mentioned, uh..."

"Any plans to fake his own death?"

"Precisely, grasshopper!"

Lewie put his jacket on and fished out his car keys. "Any questions?"

"Where are you going?"

"To smoke a blunt, hopefully with my new friend Ms. Chelsea Minafort."

"This is why you're one of the good guys, Lewie."

He returned to his whistling ways as we walked down the stairs and out the door. "Which way are you parked?"

"That-a-way."

"I'm this-a-way. Let's meet at Bobby's place tonight for his little grand reopening thing. We'll compare notes. And I can tell you about our next move."

"Which is?"

Lewie slapped me on the back and flashed me a grin that made it clear he had malarkey on his mind.

"We break into Big Jamie's house, of course."

———

The familiar sound of sirens filled my ears. The less familiar smell of flaming Crown Vic filled my nostrils.

"I can't believe it! It blew up, just like the movies!" exclaimed a soccer mom walking towards me.

"It was just the tires," grumbled her companion. "They got too hot and exploded, blew air onto the open flame, gave the fire a big ass boost. Happens all the time when a car's on fire."

"All the time? How often do *you* see a car on fire?"

I turned the corner into the parking lot of the Chinese Baptist church and promptly froze in my tracks. "Chinese Jesus on a bike," I murmured.

A crowd of gawkers was gathered around my four-wheeled friend, recording its fiery demise on their cell phone cameras. A mighty plume of purplish smoke wafted high into the air. It smelled like a gym sock-rotten egg potpourri with a hint of flaming Jersey punk rocker.

Chapter 12

Bobby rolled out the red carpet for Seal's grand opening. It stretched forty feet down the sidewalk, giving patrons the very false impression that they were the subjects of great deference. To be fair, a few were greeted by the wild-eyed, tuxedoed proprietor at the door with a bear hug or an enthusiastic handshake. Most, though, merely received a contemptuous scowl.

Others were threatened with bodily harm if they transgressed in any way:

"Get drunk and act like a clown in there and I swear to God, a hearse drives you home tonight."

"Tip the bartender, or I tip you—off the side of a cliff, cocksucker."

Such warnings were followed by Bobby's raucous laughter, leaving guests to speculate whether their host was just prone to dark humor or legitimately deranged.

As the unwelcome masses filed in, Kalista and I sat at a table in the corner, waiting for Lewie. Not long after the fire department put an end to my car's Joan of Arc routine, he sent me a text:

Partner. Get to Bobby's early and save that table in
the back corner. I arranged interviews with more of
J's friends. See you at 6.

It was now going on seven o'clock, and as expected, there was no sign of Lewie—which was fine with me. I preferred my present company, even if our conversation was a little heavy for a guy with barely a slug of bourbon in his belly.

"Running people over in an expensive car doesn't necessarily sound like Sergio," said Kalista. "But stalking you across town and setting your car on fire? That's totally that pyro's M.O."

"The cops said I should write it off as an act of God. Chinese Jesus smote my car for parking in his special spot."

"Did they find any evidence? It was broad daylight. There had to be witnesses, right?"

"I don't think so. Honestly, the police aren't too concerned. The destruction of a rusty old LTD isn't Major Case Squad material. I got the feeling they thought I torched it myself. The insurance inspector seemed to think so, too. I'm just happy I didn't end up in jail for some silly reason."

"You're *happy*? I'm worried, and you should be, too." Kalista's eyes swept the room nervously. "I hate being worried. Screw worry." She tossed back a double shot of peppermint schnapps in a single gulp. "And screw Sergio," she added.

I refrained from pointing out that such thinking is what got us into a jam in the first place.

"That's right," I said instead. "Screw worry. No chance Sergio shows up here tonight, anyway. Bobby's on the lookout for him. I also alerted Lewie, T-Bone, and my neighbor Hazim. The minute Sergio pokes his head out, they'll contact me, and then I'll..."

"You'll what? Shoot him? And spend the next twenty years in jail? Not cool. We need to get the cops involved and file an official complaint, V.C. Stalking, destruction of property, attempted murder—we have enough to put him in prison for years. And you're going to get arrested for carrying an unlicensed firearm one of these days. Or get drunk and shoot your dick off."

"But..."

"No buts. You're going to get drunk and shoot your dick off."

"But..."

"You'll be a eunuch."

"But..."

"A *eunuch*, V.C."

"*Listen* to me. I've thought about this. While I was standing there watching my old rust bucket burn, something occurred to me. It's time to fight fire with fire. It's time to get Big Gay Sal involved."

"Big Gay Sal?!" said Kalista, incredulous. "The same Big Gay Sal who put a loaded gun to your head and pulled the trigger *five times*? And might be Jake's killer, for all we know? That Big Gay Sal?"

"That big gay guy, correct."

"Why?!"

"Honestly... I don't know. But I get a trustworthy vibe from him. I think he'd be happy to help."

"A trustworthy vibe? Happy to help? The vibe *I* get is that you're going to come out of this mess dead or dickless, V.C."

"There are worse things in life than being dead or dickless, Kalista."

Kalista wasn't amused. "I'm not amused. I need a drink. A real drink. A vodka martini. And a cigarette."

Kind of Blue/Seal was hopping for the first time ever, the bar three-deep. Bobby was making the rounds, glad-handing some and staring down most. Zeb Zeale, a local radio personality who was apparently playing emcee, stood on the makeshift stage, tapping his microphone and saying, "Testes, one two, testes, one two."

I was about to elbow my way to the bar for another round when Bobby stumbled over to us. He was buzzing with excited, inebriated energy.

"You cornball, cracker-jack, honky-ass mucka-lucka!" he shouted. "I am so glad you made it, brother!"

"Sounds like it."

He put me in a playful headlock, gave me a noogie, kissed Kalista's hand a dozen times, gave me another noogie.

"How about a couple shots of that legendary moonshine?" I said. "This young lady needs a real drink."

"I didn't tell you?" said Bobby. "This is a moonshine-free establishment, brother. I kicked my supplier to the curb. I found out the dude was giving me straight up backins laced with traces of salvia divinorum." He paused for effect. "Can you believe it?"

"I can't," I said. "Not at all. Unacceptable. Quick question: What's backins? And salvia divini-something?"

"Salvia divinorum," said Kalista. "It's a psychoactive plant that can make you trip balls. Full-blown hallucinations. Also known as the Sage of the Diviners. It's a shady as hell way to make low-grade 'shine seem more potent. Backins is slang for the watered-down whiskey that comes through the thump barrel at the tail end of a run. Your friend's supplier was selling him cheap whiskey mixed with a poor man's 'shrooms, basically."

I stared at Kalista, stunned.

"What?" she said. "I know things. I've been places. Deal with it."

"Dude!" said Bobby. "Are you thinking what I'm thinking?"

"Are you thinking that I hallucinated Jake's dead body lying on my kitchen floor?"

"Nah, I was thinking that this girl is way too good for you, brother. Seriously, what's the catch? She got syphilis or something? Or a gaping..."

"Hi," came a tinny voice from behind the ever-tactful Bobby. "I'm supposed to be meeting Lewie here. You're V.C., right? Do you remember me?"

A gaunt, long-haired thirty-something with a Dinosaur Jr. T-shirt and shark tooth necklace stood there, looking especially mousey next to the imposing former Navy Seal. It took me a second to recognize him.

"Tony Drethers? Hey, what's up, man? It's been a while! Have a seat."

I met Tony in the early 2000s, when he was in a grunge band with Jake called Grandma's Back Shavers. They released one underwhelming album, *The Last American Grungers*, before quietly dissolving. Tony was a chronic mumbler who played the drums like an absolute beast and had a sister named Maple, who went on a few dates with my brother Marlin in college. Tony owned a sex shop near the airport, where a gimp was probably tied up in the storage room. He gave me the willies.

"How you been, man? Good to see you," I fibbed. "How's Maple?"

"She lost her mind, man."

"I'm sorry to hear that."

"It's true. The crazy girl tried to electrocute her roommate in the bathtub. She was up to twenty benzos a day, man. Shit went straight to her head, I guess. They got her locked up in Bethalto in that home for the criminally insane."

"Christ," I murmured. "Is there no good news in the world today?"

"Of course there is!" shouted Lewie, appearing out of nowhere with an arm full of booze bottles. "Drinks have arrived! Bobbinator! V.C.! Tony! Girl who's too hot for V.C.! Salutations, all!"

"Your friends are nice," Kalista told me.

Lewie unloaded his stash of Crown, Ketel One, Fireball, and rocks glasses on the table. "Your girl behind the bar sold me these bottles at the not-at-all-over-priced cost of one-hundred bucks a pop, Bobby. Oddly, she then gave me this receipt for thirty-three chicken sandwiches and four bags of chips."

"Hell, yeah! That's my girl! You see," explained Bobby, "there's some bullshit statute in Missouri called the Liquor Control Law or some shit that says half your sales have to be food. So, we're just playing by the rules."

For some reason, I got the feeling that Seal's overture would also be its swan song.

Zeb Zeale's voice filled the room, welcoming everyone to "U City's hottest new bar, Seal." He then introduced the opening act, Richard something or another, who was either a comedian, a poet, both, or neither.

"I was on my third cup of coffee," he said in monotone, "when the kitty cat of my dreams ogrified into the rage-filled lioness of dreamless reality."

Huh?

"The day my brother was released from the mental ward, he got lost in the elevator on the way out. He rode up and down, up and down, up and down. Finally, the janitor swept him out with a broom. It may have been a Swiffer."

Oh?

"If you'd like to see me after the show, I will be in your kitchen, microwaving your cat."

Wait—what?

Up next was an all-male a cappella group, who dressed in Catholic schoolgirl blouses and sang Marilyn Manson's "The Beautiful People."

The world's most amazing banana juggler then stepped onto the stage with one banana, ate it, and stalked off in mock indignation.

A man wearing a Save the Pangolin hat lectured us on the dangers of microwave ovens—they decrease the bioavailability of nutrients or something—before the crowd drowned him out in a symphony of jeers.

The unofficial Poet Laureate of Bel-Nor then recited her magnum opus, "The Iambic Pentameter

St. Louis Blues." Unexpectedly, it wasn't about hockey. Expectedly, it drew crickets.

An 80s cover band decked out in headbands and Swatch watches showed up later with a small army of fans only to realize that A) this wasn't a paying gig, and B) there was no sound system at Seal anyway. They left in a huff, grousing about the jerk they spoke to on the phone who had given them bogus information.

They didn't miss much. By 10:00 p.m., Bobby was out of entertainers. He was also out of beer. The wine and liquor soon ran dry, too. Evidently Bobby hadn't thought to bolster his inventory to accommodate a couple hundred people instead of the usual six or seven. The crowd dispersed. Zeb disappeared. The bartender took her tips and did the same. It was an inauspicious start for U City's "hottest new bar," but fortunately for all, Bobby was too hammered to notice anything wrong.

Lewie and I weren't writing a success story, either. Tony didn't have a clue what Jake was doing in the days leading up to his death, and neither did the dozen others we spoke to. We did learn through several people, however, that Arianna was undoubtedly still alive and breathing and had moved back home to Georgia after the funeral. We also learned that cinnamon whiskey isn't just a spirit; it's a weapon.

Bobby closed early, boozeless and convinced that the night was a rousing success. He didn't bother to clean up, leaving dirty glasses, trash, and empty bottles strewn all over the place. We spilled out onto the street just as our friend Da'Quan showed up.

Da'Quan Marks was a graffiti artist with a devout

cult following and also St. Louis' most beloved itiner-
ant. Lewie, Jake, Bobby, the St. Louis County Police
Department, and I had all taken turns giving him a
couch or bed to call home from time to time. He
repaid us with good vibes, good company, and, in some
cases, good weed.

"I missed it?" he said. "Damn, what happened?"

"Bobby ran out of drinks."

"Figures. Come on, then. Let's go down to the Glass-
blower. My boy's tending bar tonight. He'll take care
of us."

"Ugh," I groaned. "That's a club, right?"

"On Mondays," said Da'Quan, "it's just a big open
space with hardly anybody in it. You won't even have
to dance, old man."

"Maybe we can find you a nice recliner in the
corner," said Lewie.

"Is there a black and white TV where I can watch
Matlock in my orthopedic Velcro shoes?" I said, playing along.

We piled into Lewie's car and drove east on Delmar,
a drunken clown mobile unaware of the weirdness the
gods of fate or chance had in store for us next.

Glassblower was nearly empty, as promised.
Da'Quan's friend was getting ready to close, though,
and didn't look happy to see us. After some negotiations
in which various green commodities exchanged hands,
he agreed to pour us a round. Lewie, Kalista, and Bobby
threw darts while I caught up with Da'Quan.

"I went on a blind date tonight," he told me. "The
girl was beautiful. I was stunned, man."

"Oh, yeah? How'd that go?"

"I'm here with you now, aren't I?" Da'Quan's eyes were razor-thin slits as he puffed an electronic cigarette—filled with hash oil, no doubt. "Problem is, my mind's diseased, dog. It's an unnamed, undiagnosed disease. Only men get it, and only when a beautiful woman's around. And there's only one side effect. You know what it is?"

"What is it?"

"A deterioration of the wits, man. I'm telling you, V. I got a chronic case of that shit. There we are, man, having a nice meal at Aioli on the Hill, and there's a world of topics of conversation I could go to. But you know what I talk about?"

"What's that?"

"My ex-girlfriend's titties."

I nearly spit out my Grand Marnier. "Why would you do that? What's wrong with you?"

"I'm diseased, I told you. It was like I could actually see myself crashing the train, but there was nothing I could do. My brain was saying, 'Shut the fuck up, D. Talk about you, your art, the weather, or be real smart and talk about *her*. Whatever you do, don't talk about your ex – girlfriend's titties.' But I opened my mouth anyway and..." Da'Quan mimicked an explosion with his hands.

"How did that subject even come up?" I asked.

"The waitress, man. The waitress came over and took our order, and I mentioned that she looks like my ex. And Brandi, that's the blind date, asked me what she was like. But T'Nesha, that's my ex, you remember her, right, she just ain't that interesting, man. The only interesting thing about her, really, is her..."

"Tits?"

"I hate that word. *Tits,*" said Kalista, sliding into the booth beside me and helping herself to Da'Quan's e-cig. "But what about them?"

"They didn't match!" said Da'Quan. "One of them was big and round, like an overgrown tomato, and other just jutted out like a... a... fleshy torpedo."

"The Fleshy Torpedoes," said Kalista. "Sounds like a girl power band."

"You know the worst thing about it, though?" said Da'Quan. "The part that proves how hopeless my condition is? The waitress didn't even look like T'Ne-sha. T'Nesha's black as the pit from pole to pole, like my grandmamma says. This waitress was, like, Filipino or something."

I'm not sure how long we stayed, puffing hash oil and joking around with Da'Quan. The next thing I knew, we were standing under an overhang outside, shivering in the cold and the rain and debating the best way to make it to the East side for a nightcap.

"Damn," said Da'Quan, "I got to leak again." He tugged on the front door. "Damn. Fool locked it already. How's that for gratitude? How's that for hospitality?"

"I've got to piss, too," said Lewie. "Let's just go on the side of the building."

"In the rain?"

"Think of it as a free shower."

"A'ight."

"Have fun crossing streams, lady boys," slurred Bobby.

Lewie and Da'Quan disappeared around the corner. Tires squealed a block or two away, but we didn't give it a second thought.

"I'm cold," said Kalista. "It's freezing out here."

"Go twerk on an Eskimo's icicle," suggested Bobby.

"Maybe I will twerk on an Eskimo's icicle."

We never found out if she really would have, though, because a familiar voice—Da'Quan's—cried out in the urban wilderness.

"Ouch!" he screamed. *"That fucking hurt!"*

Bobby and I looked at each other for a split second and then darted around the corner. Da'Quan lay motionless against the side of the building. Lewie was pinned against the wall, restrained by three hulking men in ski masks.

"We know he's your friend, dickhead!" shouted one of them. "Tell us where he is! Now!"

"I'm right here, you ISIS fucks!" roared Bobby, jumping into the mix.

He leapt into the air, kicked the first assailant square in the chest and then practically booted off his head with the same foot. In a flash, he broke the second goon's nose with a quick jab—it sounded like a peanut cracking—and then launched him face first into the wall. I couldn't tell if the moan of agony he emitted was of the Venezuelan variety.

The final assailant stood there frozen, gawking at the carnage around him. Bobby advanced on him, ready to channel his inner ninja warrior again, but Lewie had a different, far more bilious trick up his sleeve.

He jumped to his feet, lifted the man's mask, and

rabbit-punched *himself* in the stomach. On cue, a stream of regurgitated Fireball and beer shot out of his mouth, drenching his attacker in liquid agony. An uppercut to the chin later, the crisis was officially averted.

And then there were sirens. Bobby and I lifted Da'Quan's limp body off the ground and, like any group of moderately innocent Americans with a black guy in tow, ran like hell instead of waiting for the police. We flung Da'Quan into the back of Lewie's car, squealed onto the main drag, and disappeared into the night.

———

"Do you see what happens, V.C.?" said Bobby. "Do you see what happens..."

"Who am I, Larry Sellers?" I said.

"... when you get mixed up with scandalous girls with un-American boyfriends? Your friends and countrymen pay the fucking price."

Luckily, Kalista was in the bathroom with the sink running, out of earshot.

"Over the line, Bobby," I said. "Come on, this isn't her fault."

We were standing above Da'Quan's body on my couch, watching him breathe. His neck and arms were badly scraped, and his left eye was crimson red, courtesy of some goon's fist, but it looked like he'd be OK.

"Besides," I added, "we don't know if that was Sergio. It's just as likely they were looking for Jake. I mean, if they didn't know he was dead..."

"They looked pretty damn South American to me, brother," snarled Bobby.

"Come on, how could you tell that? It was dark, and they were wearing ski masks. Lewie, did you get a good look at the guy you ralphed on?"

Lewie sat on the edge of my bed, utterly unconcerned, laughing loudly as he read an article on *Cracked.com.*

"Lewie!" I shouted.

"What? Oh, him? Eh," he shrugged, "normal looking guy. White, nothing special. Oh, my God! This article is hilarious!"

Bobby looked me square in the eye.

"You're a wanted man, brother. Sleep with one eye open. And alternate eyes, because you don't know what side they're coming from."

"Bobby," I said, "I appreciate the concern, but I'm not convinced..."

"I need to go," he interrupted. "It's past this frog-man's bedtime."

"Ditto," said Lewie.

It had been a long night. After we fled the scene of the crimes, we drove around aimlessly, putting plenty of distance between the cops and ourselves, before doubling back towards U City. We carried Da'Quan up the steps to my apartment and had a final beer to calm our shattered nerves. It was now nearly dawn, and grogginess was kicking in.

We shook hands and I thanked Bobby for being such a bloodthirsty bastard. He and Lewie split, and moments later, Da'Quan started to stir. He sat up for a moment, looked around confusedly and started to say something but then thought better of it and went back to sleep with a goofy grin on his face. I patted his head.

"May a thousand beautiful *chicas* with perfectly matching *tatas* bless your dreams, sweet prince," I said.

"Much better word," said Kalista, climbing into bed. "*Tatas*. I'm not going to work, as you've probably guessed. You're a bad influence. Wake me when life makes sense again, will you?"

I put a blanket on Da'Quan, placed the Colt .45 under my pillow, and was ready to join Kalista when something caught my eye. Something was terribly wrong in my little corner of the world, I realized. Something I should have noticed earlier. Something that would send chills down the spine of any loving caretaker of a six-foot wooden purple statue.

"Kalista!" I screamed. "We have a huge fucking problem!"

It was the Purple Guy.

He was wearing a dead man's hat.

Chapter 13

MY MOTHER AND I HAVE BEEN SENTENCED TO DEATH for killing a donkey. It seems a harsh penalty, especially since the alleged victim is strolling happily alongside us in the desert, very much alive.

"You've got it wrong!" I scream. "The jackass is alive!"

A towering constable kicks the animal repeatedly with a cleated boot, crushing its spine. Tears flow freely down my face. I clench my fists in rage. Bile rises up in my chest.

"Don't be melodramatic," says my mother.

The constable is amused. My knees buckle as I look him in the eye and realize he's... my father? The fuck, man?

"Relax, son," he says. "I can assure you the creature felt nothing but pain. Feel free to fight shit flies and maggots for what's left of its body."

It's not too late. He is trapped under a car, wiggling in agony, gasping for breath, but alive, barely. And he has morphed into... a man? Wearing a... sombrero? *Jake? Jake? Jake?* No response. His breathing has stopped.

My father's booming voice echoes off the walls of

eternity, filling time and space and my soggy, rattled brain: "It... it... it... it... it... was... was... was... was... was... never... never... never... never... never... Jake... Jake... Jake... Jake... Jake..."

The desert is a mirage. I'm actually on first base, an adolescent playing baseball. I have a slight leadoff. The pitcher casually throws the ball to first, just checking the runner. My foot is glue, my legs rubber. He picks me off, the crowd goes silent. Bobby greets me at the dugout.

"Great American pastime," I say with a shrug.

"You are not a great American," he says. "Sit down and wait for the train."

I realize that the dugout is a train station. Kalista sits on the bench, wearing a poker face and a ball cap embroidered with her initials, KLC. Her dollish bare feet are resting in shards of broken glass. A fire rages behind her. She doesn't appear to mind. Does she even know?

"When is the train coming?" I ask.

"The train is not coming, jackass."

But the train and the fire are the least of my worries. Sergio is on top of me, and this is not a game anymore, not a nightmare, not a daydream, not a premonition, not a fear. This is reality, and his hands are around my neck, I can smell the stink of his fury and feel the sweat and blood from his grimacing face drip upon me, immersing my body in spectral puss and goo. Why is there so much blood? My legs flail but my upper body is comatose, and then, for a moment, in a flash, I'm at peace, I realize my heart is lighter than a feather, my sins forgiven, my addictions obliterated, and I smile, because the Forever can have me, I see dewy vines and crystal waters, severed limbs and a folding boat flailing in rogue waves of tears, and it's all just a figment, the world in all its sweetness and gore can fuck itself sideways, I was only ever a transient here, and baby I'm coming home...

And then there's a light, my fingers take form, Kan Pan something fills my nostrils, and Sergio recedes, a blip of nefarious black swallowed up in a sea of luminescence. I am freezing, I am scared, I am shaking, I am paper in the wind, I am firing my revolver at the ceiling, I am hyperventilating, and I am alive, good Christ, I am alive, and a new day is knocking...

———————

I looked the Purple Guy square in the spot on his pear-shaped head where his eyes should have been.

"Merrily, merrily, merrily, merrily," I told him, "life is but a dream."

He didn't say anything, just stood there sulking in a dead man's hat. No doubt, he was anxious for Kalista to get out of the shower so I would direct my attempts at conversation elsewhere.

"I don't know about you, Purps, but unlike some mystics, I've never held too much stock in the importance of dreams. Maybe it's just because my dreams are notoriously sour, and they offer me little hope in life. And what, my friend, is life without hope? It is merely a slutbag ho."

He rolled his invisible eyes in disgust. It was far too early, and his brim was far too alien, for pellets of morning wisdom to be thrown his way.

"Dreams, you see, are merely your brain's way of reminding itself that it can never be free of the crosses it bears, even in the land of nod. Nothing new can be gleaned from them. They are far less mysterious than reality. I've never had a dream that doesn't make complete and pointless sense, in fact. Take, for instance, the desert dream, which reflects my paranoia about getting mixed up with Jake's father's crowd. My father in the dream is actually Jake's father, whose cruelty—referring to Jake as a foolish prick, for instance—is spine-crushing, if you will. My inability to rescue Jake from under the car is symbolic of my inability to solve his murder. The desert is symbolic of a desert. KLC is Kalista's initials, nothing more. And my mother is there because Sigmund Freud must have invited her."

I paused to let my words sink in. Kalista, hung over, groaned as she got out of the shower. The Purple Guy said shit.

"The baseball dream," I continued, "is a recurring one I've had for as long as I can remember. As a child, it represented my fear of failing on the highly competitive Little League team I played for. As a teenager, it symbolized my inability to get past first base with Violet Cole. Today, first base is the present. Second is progress, the future. Because I'm so anxious to move along to second base—some hazy, unknown place I've never been but certainly must be sunnier than first—I'm stumbling through the now, lost, unable to find my footing. And how do you like that bag of beans, old sport?"

Judging by his non-responsiveness, he didn't like it much at all.

"Of course, like any decent psychoanalyst, I completely just pulled all that nonsense out of my ass. The only thing I can't figure out," I added, "is why Sergio was strangling me. Some dreams just don't make a lick of sense, I suppose. It must have been something I ate."

"What is something you ate?" said Kalista. She was standing outside the bathroom in a fuzzy pink robe. "Are you talking to yourself again?"

"Crazy people talk to themselves, Kalista. I'm talking to the Purple Guy."

"How you feeling?"

"Awake. Alive. You?"

"A little better. What were you talking to the Purple Guy about? How he ended up with Jake's hat on his head?"

"Dreams, actually. Let me ask you something, Kalista. Would you say that your current situation is sort of like standing in shards of broken glass, but you don't mind, because yours truly makes it bearable? Or would you say that I am the broken glass, but it's not *that* bad, considering you only recently escaped from a raging dumpster fire of a relationship with Sergio? Or would you say that my subconscious thoughts on the situation are entirely off target?"

Kalista knitted her brow in concentration. "I would say," she said, "that you're a fucking idiot when you open your mouth."

"Harsh."

"On the bright side, you only look like one when you're being quiet."

Heavy footsteps climbed the stairs, followed by a loud knock on the door, putting an end to Kalista's sorry attempts to butter me up. The doorknob rattled as the person on the other end tried to force his way in.

Kalista darted into the bathroom for clothes. I darted to the nightstand for the revolver.

"Fuck me, it's locked!" exclaimed our visitor. "This is the place, my God that's heavy, holy shit, man. Open the door, man! I can feel it, it's completely pulling me in! Can you feel that, Aldous?"

"Oh, yeah!" roared Lewie. "Definitely! Sort of! Not at all, actually. V.C.! Put your dick in your diaper and open the door! It's time to commune with the dead, baby!"

I opened the door just wide enough to stick the barrel of the Colt .45 through it. "Bang," I said.

"That's my boy!" said Lewie. "Shoot first, ask questions later."

The man accompanying Lewie pushed past me into the kitchen, unfazed, murmuring that he could feel it, *like, really fucking feel it, dig?* He wore a bright dashiki emblazoned with golden dragons and tortoise shell glasses held together in various parts with discolored Scotch tape. The thick dreadlocks atop his head were shaped into an elaborate beehive. It climbed higher than I thought the laws of physics would allow.

"Who's your friend, Lewie?"

"Uh... Excuse me? Sandy Galanos? Hello?" Lewie sounded exasperated, like he was a household name. "Soothsaying Sandy? The man, the myth, the legend? The friend I've told you about a dozen times, the one with the Ph.D. in the paranormal?"

"Sure, rings a bell," I lied, while the man, myth, and legend spun in circles in my kitchen, his arms outstretched like a child balancing on the safety rope in a swimming pool.

"Sandy, I want you to meet V.C.," said Lewie. "He lives here. He's the one who found the body."

Soothsaying Sandy didn't say a word, just continued to spin. I felt like Phish would break into "Fluffhead" at any moment. Sandy didn't snap out of his trance until Kalista stepped out from the bathroom.

"Her!" he shouted. "It's *her*, Aldous! She has the attachment. Can you feel it? Can you see it?"

Sandy sprung towards Kalista, placed his hands on her temples and started rubbing them frantically.

"V.C.," said Kalista, only mildly rattled, "please shoot this man in the kneecap."

"Gladly."

"No need for that," said Lewie, stepping between them. "We're all on the same side here, aren't we?"

"Are we?" I said. "Who the fuck is this guy, Lewie? What's going on?"

"I'll tell you what's going on! Last night, Tony Drethers said something that gave me an idea..."

"Was it, 'I better get home and tickle the gimp'?"

"He said, 'Man, I wish I could talk to Jake one more time. I wish I knew what was going through his head, man.'"

"And?"

"And it made me think, let's talk to Jake! As in, g-g-g-g-g-g-ghost Jake, Scooby!"

"Hell, no," said Kalista. "Homey don't play that, Lewie."

"Sure he does!"

"Where's his Ouija Board? Or his proton pack?" I asked.

"Ouija?! Proton?! Soothsaying Sandy Galanos does not use gimmicks, V.C.! Right, Sandy? Seriously, V., you know Sandy Galanos—from TV, remember? Destination America? The *Soothsayer* series? Visits some of the most haunted locations in America, communes with the dead, gives them control of his body? Plus, he's an SLPD legend! Do you have any idea how many murders this guy is responsible for solving?"

"I'm going to take a wild guess and say zero."

"Zero!? What the... ?! This man is legit, partner!"

"I'm sure he's a real Shawn Spencer, Lewie."

"You know that's right," said Kalista, channeling her inner Burton Guster to my immense approval.

Sandy stumbled backwards like he'd been punched in the gut. "Gone!" he bellowed. "Just like that, gone! He fled! Gone! Did you feel it, Lewie? He went right through me! Did you feel it?"

"Eh, little bit," said Lewie. "Sandy here is teaching me to be psychic," he explained. "He's..."

Sandy chortled derisively. "Don't be a spiritual *plebian*, Aldous. I am not teaching you to be psychic. I am giving your third eye a gentle nudge open so it can see beyond the"—he gestured to Kalista and myself with a sour look on his face—"grossly, worldly *ordinary*."

"Ignore him," said Lewie. "It's part of his charm."

Sandy suddenly took an interest in me, like he was seeing me for the first time. He leaned within a few inches of my face and peered at me with wide, piercing eyes. The scent of head shop incense and Febreze filled my nostrils. A palpable, repellant buzz emanated from the man's pores. I got the chills.

"What's he doing, Lewie?" I said. "Make him stop. Or, you know, shoot him in the kneecap."

"You're blue," said Sandy. "So, so blue!" He pinched my cheek and shook it playfully, like I was a small child. "Why so blue, chummy wummy bear? So sensitive, so caring, so..."—his eyes lit up—"scared! Boo!"

"I ain't 'fraid of no ghost," I said.

He turned to Kalista. "He's nervous about the baby he put in your belly, isn't he?"

I nearly dropped my coffee.

"*Baby!?!*" said Kalista.

"Oops, my mistake!" sang Sandy. "I guess you didn't know. You're only a couple weeks along. Let me be the first to say congratulations."

"A baby!" roared Lewie. "That's terrific!" He slapped my back. "Congratulations, pops!"

"Don't congratulate him," said Kalista. "This man is a lunatic. I'm not pregnant."

"Oh, please," said Sandy. "Your aura is white as snow, sister. You see that, Aldous? You see the white around her? You see it?"

"Sorry, Kalista," said Lewie. "Looks pretty white to me."

"You don't see shit, Lewie," I said.

Without warning, Sandy lurched backwards again, this time crashing into my bookshelf and sending the little green alien candle with the chipped skull careening to the floor. Lewie, Kalista, and I watched in confused silence as Sandy tottered around the room, crouched over, clutching his stomach. When he finally looked up, his face was painted with a wicked smile.

"He's back!" he said giddily. "Can you feel him,

Aldous? Can you feel him?" He turned to me. "How about it, Baby Blue? Can you feel it?"

"Ummm..."

"Come on, man! Feel it!" Sandy grabbed my hand and pulled me into the kitchen. "Put your hand out! It's a force field! Élan vitale! A spirit portal in your own little rat hole, plebe! Yes? *Yes?*" He squeezed my arm as hard as he could. "Feel it, man, *fucking feel it, Baby Blue!*"

"What the fuck is wrong with this guy, Lewie?" I said.

"No time for that!" said Sandy. "You've felt it before, yes? Cold spots? Otherworldly eyes feasting on your every move? Inexplicable sadness, anger, frustration?"

"I don't know," I said. "I think my sadness, anger, and frustration is pretty explicable."

"No time for that!" Sandy repeated. "Bring out the voice recorder, Lewie!"

"What's happening?" said Kalista. "Are you on acid, dude?"

"No time for that! Roll tape, minion! Roll!"

"Shouldn't we wait for Bobby?" said Lewie. "He said he wanted to see this."

"No time for that! Roll, minion, roll!"

"Oh, uh, right..." said Lewie, fishing a miniature audio recorder from his pocket. "Should we film this too, Sandy? Grab your phone and record this, will you, V?"

"I think this guy needs to leave, V.C.," said Kalista. "Seriously, this is how Sharon Tate got killed."

"Nonsense," said Lewie. "Google him. G-A-L-A-N-O-S. He's the real deal."

"So, we're supposed to believe he just got mowed

down by Ghost Jake?" I said. "Is that what happened?"

"I don't feel shit," said Kalista.

"The baby's messing with your ghost radar," said Lewie.

"Not funny, Lewie," I said.

"And not true," Kalista added.

"Silence!" demanded Sandy. "And you," he said, turning towards the Purple Guy, "must have patience, ghoul! Your time will come!"

"See?" said Kalista. "He's crazy. He's talking to the Purple Guy. Crazy people do that. I've seen it."

"That's a little hurtful," I murmured.

"Ignore her," said Lewie. "It's the baby stress talking."

"Are you rolling, Aldous?" said Sandy. "Are you recording, Baby Blue?"

"Check it out," said Kalista, looking at her phone. "He really does have a TV show. Sundays at eleven, *Soothsayer* on Destination America. Gifted medium, diviner, spirit healer, and clairvoyant Sandy Galanos visits America's most haunted locations to rendezvous with the dead, it says...'"

"Why's it called *Soothsayer*?" I said. "Isn't a soothsayer supposed to see the future? Not see dead people, right? Sounds convoluted."

"The reviews aren't great. The tomato meter on Rotten Tomatoes is fifty-five percent. That means it's officially rotten."

"Silence!" hollered Sandy. "Our guest does not have the energy to stay forever." He turned to my cell phone camera and announced, "What you will witness next, ladies and gentlemen..."

"Lady," said Kalista. "One."

"… will turn skeptics into believers and prove beyond a shadow of doubt that the dead walk among us!"

"Sounds rehearsed," I suggested. "Maybe tone it down a pinch."

"No time for that! Right now, at this very moment, the spirit of a murdered young man is standing beside me. I will proceed to ask him questions, and on my bidding, he will respond. I can see him, hear him, sense him in every way…"

"Not buying it," said Kalista.

"… while you will hear his responses on the EVP recorder that my colleague is holding."

I turned the camera to Lewie.

"Hi, Mom," he said.

"This is absurd," said Kalista.

"Jake's here?" I said. "I don't feel it. Do you feel it, Lewie?"

"Meh. Little bit, maybe."

"Silence, plebes!" demanded Sandy. "Our guest…"

"I'm not going to lie, Sandy," said Lewie, "I'm not really digging the plebes thing."

"He is ready to speak! He is angry, so angry… I sense… anger…"

"Wow," said Kalista. "Clearly, the dead are walking among us."

"Why again did he attack my bookshelf? Is he saying Jake did it? I'm lost," I said.

"Shhh," whispered Sandy. "Please… shhh… now is the time…"

He squeezed his eyelids shut, rocked back and forth slowly.

"What," he inquired, "is your name?"

Kalista started to say something.

"Hush, Mama," I said. "Humor him, will you?"

"What," Sandy repeated, "is your name?"

Nobody said a word. The air felt thick and still. Kalista flashed me her middle finger. I noticed that Sandy was covered in goose bumps.

"Who," he whispered, "killed you?"

Nothing happened. Nothing happened. Nothing happened.

And then something happened. Something unexpected. Something that would prove beyond a shadow of doubt that the *crazy* walk among us.

Bobby stomped up the stairs and appeared in the doorway. He froze when he saw Sandy, and then his eyes grew large. Shock, confusion, realization, and finally rage crossed his face. He bull-rushed into the room and speared the soothsayer, WWE-style, into the ground.

The building shook, the Purple Guy toppled over and broke his left arm clean off, the kitchen crew at Kun-Woo's hollered. Lewie, Kalista, and I stared in shock as Bobby, ever the gentleman, carefully removed Sandy's tattered glasses, tossed them to the side, and cocked his fist. As the terrified soothsayer struggled to escape, Bobby dug his free elbow into his Adam's apple.

"Ummm..." I said. "Hey, uh, Bobby...You mind filling us in on what's going on here?"

"It's him!" screamed Bobby, his neck veins bulging. "This is the guy! It makes sense now,V! It's got to be him!"

"It's got to be who, Bobby?"

When he spoke again, his voice was trembling with rage.

"The son of a bitch who killed Jake Kennedy, that's who!"

Chapter 14

Excerpt from the pilfered journal of Patio Williams, CFO of RW Enterprises, younger brother of Big Jamie's business partner Radio Williams.

I JUST GOT BACK FROM PSYCHIC TERRI'S PLACE, THE ONE on West Montrose with those old pots in the window. It's in the same building as Harley's Burgers, which I've always thought was funny, like you can go there and get a cheeseburger and a hex bag as your side. I walked inside and nobody was there, just Psychic Terri who was dressed in beads like a gypsy and she was talking to herself. Without looking at me she said, "what do you want?!" and I get cute and say "you're the psychic, you tell me," and she said "don't get cute!"

Maybe she thinks I'm looking at the pots in the window because she tells me they are spirit pots and they are homes for disembodied entities and they belong to her and she belongs to them. I say, "you mean ghosts are in there?" and she laughs at me and she rolls her eyes and pulls me by my shirt into the back room. I'm shaking even now when I write this. She puts me in a chair and lights this incense and turns on spooky

Egyptian music with clappers and flutes and whistling. She climbs in my lap like Radio's girls at the strip club only Psychic Terri smells like cigarettes and that head shop on Strickland with the Grateful Dead posters in the windows and her face and body are caked with deep wrinkles that cast shadows all over her flabby flesh. Psychic Terri kisses my ear + licks my cheek, she puts my palm to her face and she shoves it away and says palm readers are a joke and why am I trembling? She says I have nothing to fear, I need to look for the signs, my meds will never save me, I need to listen to the world, I need to shout it out!

Something rattles in the front of the shop and Psychic Terri tells me it's Joanie's pot. And she says, "what now, Joanie? The truth will set him free?" and then she tells me Joanie is a bible beater but she's right, the truth will set me free. And then she reached into my pocket and took 43 dollars out of my wallet and told me to run off and make way for someone who can get an erection for her.

———————

Jilly left and I turned the music down low and ran the vacuum cleaner even though there are no crumbs. I dropped the handle part of the vacuum and when I picked it up the cord got yanked out of the wall. I stopped vacuuming, thinking maybe that's a sign? Is that what Psychic Terri meant? Was the cord going to electrocute me? And then I called Big Jamie again and again and again, because the truth will set me free. He doesn't answer, it just rang and rang. How is that even possible these days? Just thinking about spilling my guts bring me closer to peace that I've even dreamed I'd feel. When I try to leave a voice message my voice fails me though. I feel like a news lady I once saw who freezes on camera and finally after an excruciating long period of silence she just squeaks a long and awful eeeeeee.

———

Radio doesn't answer or text anymore either. Maybe he's sipping RumChata, or maybe he's dead. Maybe whatever is left of the Delgados gang tracked him down. Business goes on, above the table and under it. But of course what do I know, I'm just the nervous, neurotic little brother. The lieutenants, Froggy, Jack Mackay, Weezey, those guys, probably know more. Maybe we're at war for all I know.

I keep calling ELI and his crew too and eventually someone answered, sounded like a black guy and I asked for Eli and he yelled to "stop wasting my minutes, nigga." Maybe telling Eli and his crew not to come back until they found Jake Kennedy was a bad idea. Maybe they don't even know he's dead and they're too dumb to figure it out. Maybe they're dead too, maybe Big Jamie killed them. Maybe they crashed Radio's Continental and they are afraid he will cut off their fingers like he did to Slim Philly when his counts kept coming up short.

Chapter 15

WHAT?!" CRIED KALISTA.

"Jake?!" cried Lewie.

"Who?!" cried Sandy.

"Mind blower!" cried I.

Bobby let his fists do the talking, thrice striking Sandy in rapid succession on the forehead. The flood-gates opened. Blood spilled onto the floor and spurted across the room in erratic bursts, like waterlogged silly string. A hearty splotch landed on Kalista's shirt. I remember thinking that I'd seen more juice in the past two weeks than I had in all my first thirty-five years. And I didn't particularly like it.

Sandy Galanos yelped in pain and struggled in vain to break free. Kalista shrieked. I dropped my phone and, with Lewie's help, tried to separate Bobby from his punching bag.

He wasn't having it.

"Back off, fuckers!" he shouted. "This thieving son of a bitch had motive to kill Jake!"

"I don't know what you're talking about!" pleaded

Sandy. "Please! I swear I don't..."

The accused's words came to an abrupt halt as Bobby drove a forearm into his windpipe. It was safe to say the soothsayer didn't see this coming.

Kalista was screaming bloody murder, kicking Bobby's side and begging him to heel. I was pulling his arm desperately, trying to create some separation, but making little progress. I felt like a child trying to free a toy poodle from a Rottweiler's jaws.

"Well, this is progressing unsuccessfully," mused Lewie.

Casually, with a carefree smile on his face and exactly zero pep in his step, he pulled a stun gun from his jacket.

"Bobbinator," he said, "I really hate to do this. You're a good friend, and you're a crazy bastard to boot. This will not make you happy."

"Do something, Lewie!" shouted Kalista. "He's turning purple!"

"You have to let go, Bobby. You can't kill B-list celebrities."

"Bobby, fucking stop it!" I shouted. "You're going to go to jail, man."

"Actually," said Lewie, "what's going to happen, is, on the count of three, I'm going to stun the snot out of him."

Bobby released his grip just long enough for Sandy to catch a life-preserving breath.

"Fuck off, Lewie!" he said between clenched teeth as he reapplied his chokehold. "He knows what he did!"

"One," said Lewie, steadying his aim. "Two..."

"*Stop, friends. Please.*"

An unfamiliar voice rang out, effectively hitting the

pause button on the gnarly scene. Bobby relaxed his death claws. Lewie lowered his gun. I forced a smile for the figure in the doorway.

"Howdy, neighbor," I said. "What brings you here? Cup of milk? Pad of butter? Film a snuff flick?"

Hazim entered with his hands outstretched in a show of supplication. "Please, friend," he said, approaching Bobby. "Let him go."

I once heard a story on NPR about a mugger who held up a beloved Indian yogi at gunpoint in New York. The mugger, who was being interviewed, said that the yogi smiled at him, looked him calmly in the eye, and asked what he could to do help him. Shame and embarrassment washed over the thief. He melted, broke down weeping. In that moment, his life was changed; he found his calling. He joined the Peace Corps, studied the Tao, skinny-dipped with rotting corpses in the Ganges, voted Green Party. His heart was awakened.

Something similar—albeit less permanently life-altering—happened to Bobby. In the presence of Hazim's kindness, he was instantly ashamed of himself. He shrunk visibly and, blushing, removed his forearm from Sandy's throat.

"You don't understand," he said, weakly. "He killed Jake... I think."

"It's OK, friend," said Hazim. "It's OK. If he killed this Jake, he will go to jail. You will get your justice, friend."

"Who are you?" said Bobby. "What's that accent, *friend*?"

"I am V.C.'s neighbor. Thin walls," said Hazim with a smile. "And I am Bosnian. My family and I lived in

Tuzla until '95, right before the massacre. We came here near the end of the war."

Bobby's face lit up. "Tuzla? I've been to Tuzla! You're talking to an IFOR vet here, '95 through '96. Best time of my life!"

"Perhaps we've met before, then, friend," replied Hazim evenly, seemingly unoffended that his genocide-stricken homeland was once this lunatic's personal Disneyland. "Now, please. Let him go."

"Fine, I'll let him go. For you, bro, I'll do it." Bobby climbed to his feet. "But get ready to call the cops. Because this son of a bitch is about to confess to the murder of Jake Kennedy!"

"Never heard of him," groaned Sandy, and then, looking at me: "Please, Baby Blue. Keep him away! He's an... an... an... anathema! Ghoul! Fiend! Flee, serpent! Flee! Egad! Egad!"

"You'll be fine," I said. "Rub some dirt in it."

"Anybody else confused?" asked Lewie. "Sandy, do you even know Jake Kennedy?"

Dazed and bloody, Sandy just moaned. Hazim ran next door for towels and salve. Bobby stood in the corner, looking guilty.

I did a quick inventory of the damage: one highly agitated, one-armed Purple Guy lying horizontal on the floor beside a dead man's hat. One little green alien candle with an extra chip in his skull who just happened to be in the wrong place when a renegade specter inexplicably ghost-tackled Sandy Galanos. One blood-splattered spirit whisperer. And one badly shaken girlfriend with tears on her face and fury in her eyes.

The blood, or maybe the sickening thud of knuckle-on-skull, had clearly touched a nerve.

"What the hell, Bobby!" she shouted. "There's blood everywhere. Look at this mess! You're psychotic, *brother*. You can't just attack people. What's wrong with you? What the fuck is wrong with you? And use your words, not your hands!"

Bobby pointed at Sandy, writhing on the ground. "This guy," he said, "is a thief. He tried robbing Jake just three days before he died! And Jake got the best of him!" Bobby towered over Sandy menacingly. "And then he got his revenge!" he bawled. "Didn't you? *Didn't you?! Admit it!*"

Sandy's mouth dropped open.

"You! You're the bar owner!" he spat. "That's where I recognized that lunk-headed, vacuous, dim-witted, mutton-headed..."

"Mutton-headed?" I murmured.

"... pea-brained, cretinous..."

"That's very descriptive."

"... inbred-looking, feeble-minded face!"

"This is going well."

"What did you do, walk out on a bar tab or something, Sandy?" said Lewie.

"Fuck no!!" cried Bobby. "The week Jake died, he came into the bar, claiming to be psychic, and..."

"Hold on," I said. "Is this the guy from the story you told everyone at the bar after Jake's funeral? The pickpocket with the powers from the maharishi?"

"Maharishi Anjana!" sang Sandy.

"Gibberish," said Kalista.

"I don't remember hearing any story like that," said Lewie.

"You were still at that techno bar, hitting on that fourteen-year old," I said.

"Gross. She was twenty-one, dude."

"Fifteen."

"Nineteen."

"Sixteen."

"Seventeen."

"Deal!"

"Shut it, pervs" snapped Kalista. "What happened, Bobby?"

"He came in the bar and started rubbing my other friend's head like a weirdo, 'ingesting his aura' to give him a psychic reading or some crap. Really, he was just distracting him so he could root through his pockets and steal his wallet."

"Is this true, Sandy?" said Lewie.

"It's not what you plebes think!" said Sandy.

"Not this again," I said.

"Bullshit," said Bobby. "It's exactly what we think. He tried doing the same thing to Jake. Only Jake was the Carl fucking Higbie of picking pockets. He saw this dude's scheme from a mile away..."

"Did you just say Carl Higbie?" I said.

"Who the fuck is Carl Higbie?" said Lewie.

"Jake saw your scheme from a mile away," Bobby repeated, "and he picked your pocket, emptied your wallet, and put it in his own pocket so you'd steal your own wallet, and then..."

"My head is spinning," said Lewie.

"Yeah, about that. My wallet, I mean. Do you have my black card still?" said Sandy. "The AMEX?"

"That's a pretty exclusive card, Sandy," said Lewie.

"Wait," said Kalista. "You have a black card, and you're picking drunks' pockets?"

"It's not like that!" said Sandy, and then, turning to Bobby: "Am I understanding correctly that the very same guy whom I predicted would perish…"

"And return a warrior prophet," I chimed in.

"… has indeed perished?"

"Bingo."

Despite his obvious discomfort, Sandy broke into a smile.

"So, I was right?! I called it? I called it!"

"You didn't call shit," I said. "In the story Bobby told, you said Jake would die before midnight *that very night*. He died several days later, man."

"So, I was a couple days off," said Sandy with a shrug. "It's not an exact science."

"And you also said he would return a warrior prophet."

"Warrior prophet?" said Kalista.

"Who's Carl Higbie?" said Lewie.

"He might return a warrior prophet," said Sandy. "You don't know, Baby Blue."

Hazim returned with a cold compress and placed it gently against Sandy's forehead. Sandy winced.

"We will wash out the cut really good," said Hazim, "and then dry it and put some Neosporin on it. Sounds good? And look on the bright side. Now we have an equal number of people in the room with head wounds and no head wounds."

"We should play Pictionary," I said.

"Carl Higbie is an American author and former Navy Seal," read Lewie from his phone. "He served two tours..."

"Fascinating," I said. "Bobby, what makes you think Sandy here killed Jake?"

"Isn't it obvious?" said Bobby, incredulous. "Jake robbed his ass. A few days later, he saw Jake on the street, followed him here, and got his revenge. In typical psycho-criminal fashion, he's even returned to the scene of the crime!"

There was a moment of silence as the room pondered the theory.

"Makes sense," said Lewie. "Maybe, anyway. Sandy, where were you the night of Friday, October third?"

"Do I need stitches?" said Sandy. "It feels like I need stitches."

"You're fine," I replied. "Rub some dirt in it. Where were you?"

"Where were you, Sandy?" Lewie repeated. "Tell us."

"I've been in Poveglia, fools!" said Sandy, agitated.

"Kentucky?" said Bobby.

"That's Paducah," I said.

"Northern Italy," said Sandy. "The Venetian Lagoon! We embarked on the first of the month and only just returned this weekend."

"Can anybody back up that story?" said Kalista. "Did anybody *embark* with you?"

"You mean other than the camera crew, my publicist, agent, producer, tech crew, and the spirit of mad Dr. Paolo? Nope. Sorry, plebe!"

"I kind of miss the time Bobby was pummeling you, Sandy," I admitted.

"I still can't believe this guy is famous," said Kalista.

"Ish," I said. "Famous-*ish*."

"I still can't believe you're a fake," said Lewie, shaking his head sadly at Sandy. "Pretending to be a seer so you can roll a couple lushes! I'm disappointed, young man."

"He's a fake?" said Kalista. "No way! Next you're going to tell me that Ghost Jake didn't really tackle him."

"I'm not a *fake*, Aldous," snapped Sandy. "Don't mistake harmless chicanery for fraud."

"Chicanery?"

"Grow up, Aldous. I'm not a murderer. Nor am I a swindler. I had no interest in your friend's grubby, worldly, arcane..."

"You're a fan of the adjective, aren't you, Sandy?" I said.

"... bloody money. I was simply entertaining myself with one of the oldest tricks in the clairvoyant playbook."

"Which is?"

"Sneak a peak in someone's wallet when they aren't looking and use whatever info you discover to make a bold psychic prediction. Works every time."

"It didn't work this time," said Bobby.

"The lady psychic did that in *Pee Wee's Big Adventure*," said Lewie.

"How is that helpful?" said Kalista.

"Madam Ruby," I said. "It worked for her."

"I was going to leave the bar, peak inside his wallet, and come right back, just for fun, pretending I didn't have any recollection of what happened but had all these revelations to share," said Sandy. "But then..."

"That doesn't sound fraudulent at all," I said.

"... I realized I'd been had. And I sensed a niggardly, iniquitous..."

"Not this again."

"... *reprobate* spirit attached to the bar owner over here. I wasn't about to go back inside and try to explain myself to such a... a... a... *mongrel*."

"He does have a point there, Bobby," said Lewie. "I've always said you can be rather—what was the word?—iniquitous? Hell, I almost had to fry you with my trusty Vipertek a minute ago."

"Please," said Bobby, sneering. "You could barely tickle my dick with that tiny taser."

"You're pants-on-fire mistaken, sir," countered Lewie. "Four milliamps and nine million volts are enough to sedate a velociraptor."

"The velociraptor was tiny, Lewie," said Bobby.

"Fine. A brontosaurus."

"Slow and stupid."

"A T-Rex on testosterone?"

"Now we're talking, brother."

"Sweet Jesus!" said Lewie, noticing the blood on Sandy's shirt. "You really did bleed a lot, Sandy!"

"You're just now noticing all the blood, Lewie?" I said.

"How does a forehead even bleed so much? It's just skin and skull."

"Sharp knuckles," said Bobby.

"Fuck," grunted Sandy as Hazim dabbed his cuts. "Does it look bad? What will I tell my fans?"

"Tell them you got attacked by a succubus, or an incubus, or the devil."

"Don't be preposterous, Aldous."

"Fans?" said Bobby. "You have fans? What fans? Who is this guy?"

"He's got a paranormal television show," said Lewie. "The *Soothsayer* series with Sandy Galanos. He's Sandy!"

"Never heard of him," said Bobby. "How come I've never heard of him? What channel?"

"Destination America. Right, Sandy?"

"I don't think I get that channel," said Bobby. "I don't get the premiums."

"Destination America isn't a premium. Is it?"

"Depends on the package you sign up for," said Hazim. "With CableBoom, it's included in the basic."

"I should look into that," said Lewie. "Do they make you sign a contract, though? I've been burned by contracts."

"I don't like your friends anymore, V.C.," said Kalista.

"Join the club, Kalista."

With Hazim's assistance, Sandy rose to his feet. "I feel like I got hit by a brick," he moaned, wavering unsteadily.

"Perhaps you should lie down," suggested Hazim. "You are welcome to rest next door at my place."

"So... damn... dizzy," he groaned.

"You owe him an apology, Bobby," said Kalista sternly.

"Aw, hell," said Bobby sheepishly, "I'm sorry, man. My mistake. My bad. I don't know what came over me, I just thought... I mean, it made sense that..."

"It's the room!" declared Sandy, giving Bobby an out he probably didn't deserve. "Something dark and foul lives here, attaching itself to all who cross its path!"

"That's just the Kan Pong Yook," I said.

"You laugh, Baby Blue, but you have an angry spirit on your hands, and I'm not talking about the meathead with the sharp knuckles."

To Bobby, he said, "Your apology is accepted, barkeep. Your mortal mind is simply overpowered. However, I have one stipulation: I really do need that black card back."

"Let's go," said Bobby. "Your wallet's still at the bar, I think. Come along, I'll pour you something on the house."

"Liquid restitution!" said Lewie. "Sign me up. This day isn't going to drink itself away, now is it? Care to join us, V.C.'s friendly neighbor?"

"Sure. It's noon somewhere," said Hazim.

"VC? Kalista? You coming? Oh, wait. You better not. Baby and all."

"Baby?" said Bobby. "What baby?"

"She's pregnant," said Sandy. "Refuses to accept it."

"Congratulations!" exclaimed Hazim.

As Kalista and Sandy bickered about whether or not her womb was occupied, Lewie stepped over the fallen Purple Guy and leaned in close to me.

"Call me later," he whispered. "We still need to talk about how to"—he cleared his throat—"eak-bray into ig-bay amie-ja's ouse-hay to investigate the ird-thay loor-fay."

"We aren't breaking into Big Jamie's house to investigate the third floor, Lewie," I said.

"Great! Call me later and we'll hash out the details! Also, we'll arrange a better time for Sandy to come back and communicate with Jake's spirit."

"That's not happening, Lewie," said Kalista, redirecting her attention to us.

"Women, huh?" said Lewie, rolling his eyes. "You put a baby in their belly and they think they can start speaking for you. Am I right, partner?"

Before Kalista had a chance to attack, I ushered my unwanted visitors and Hazim to the door. "Thanks for stopping by, gentlemen," I said. "This was lots of fun. I'm sure glad we got to do this. Feel free to stop by unannounced and uproot my life any time you like."

The last thing I saw before I closed the door was Lewie's face, grinning, as always, for no reason at all. When I saw him again a few hours later, I would give him reason to grin for real: I would give him the name of the man who killed Jake Kennedy.

Chapter 16

T-BONE WAS LOOPING A SAXOPHONE INTO HIS WALL OF sound and fresh leaves were crunching under our feet when panic attacked.

I remember thinking that it was strange how the most innocuous little thing can topple the mind. The straw that broke the Marlboro's back, as the saying goes. For William Foster, it was being denied the breakfast menu at Whammy Burger because he was approximately three minutes late. For me, it was seeing the empty space in the parking lot where my car should be.

I was already keenly aware that I'd fallen down the rabbit hole and might be sipping Grand Marnier in the Great Beyond at any moment, but seeing that empty space somehow made it real. I began to hyperventilate. A sharp pain shot through my chest. Fight-or-flight took hold. I felt like I was at the precipice of a bad trip—like, one to Branson, even.

In a world that frequently felt like it was collapsing around me, the Crown Vic was a constant. Jake and I traveled the High Road to Taos in that old rust bucket, from the mountains of the Nambe Pueblo to the ruins of Rancho de Taos. Steffi and I had just split. Jake had just finished a three-month sentence for attempting to relieve Screen City of two pallets of LCD televisions, which he didn't want, need, or even plan to sell. He just wanted to see if he could get away with the caper. He couldn't.

When I picked him up from jail, he was grinning ear-to-ear. The guards shook his hand, embraced him, pulled him in for group pictures. Three months in lockup was a grand old time for Jake. He was a rare breed.

"I'll drive," he said, and then he drove—westward, for fifteen hours, stopping only for cigarettes and gasoline and then chicken fried steak in Amarillo. Mountains and forests appeared on the desert horizon. We met a half-blind, hermetic watercolorist in Truchas who fed us split pea soup and peyote. Jake swallowed three buttons and vomited profusely. The hermit and the snow-capped South Truchas Peaks watched in silence. Jake couldn't have been happier.

"Do me a favor," he said between fits of vomit and laughter. "Don't tell Arianna we're here. She thinks I'm in jail until Thursday."

I laughed, both then and now. Kalista shot me a peculiar glance.

"You look pale," she said as we climbed into her car, fleeing the ugly vibes of 703 B Delmar Blvd. "You all right?"

My heart was racing, my stomach in knots. I felt like I did in the old days, when hangovers still affected me.

My own words surprised me.

"I think I'm having an anxiety attack," I confessed. "Or something. I don't know what. Something is wrong with me."

Kalista stared at me. Her eyes grew soft.

"Relax, sweetie," she said. "Of *course* you're having an anxiety attack. Your friend was killed in your own apartment and your crazy, other friend thinks it's your job to figure out who did it. The police detective who covered it up hates you for some reason. Some girl from your past popped up out of nowhere and now her psycho ex and his friends might be trying to cut your balls off. There's a gun attached to your hip, and you're afraid you're going to have to use it. You may or may not be mixed up in some organized crime scheme involving murder, drugs, police corruption, who knows what else. You just saw your *other* crazy friend nearly choke the life out of some other crazy person who believes that your dead friend is haunting you. Last night, Da'Quan was attacked. Before that, it was you and Lewie. Before that, T-Bone. Your nerves are damaged from too much drinking and not enough sleep. Your car is a pile of ashes. And to top it off, I'm pregnant with your child—not really, of course. My point is though, if there's not something seriously wrong with you right now, V.C., there's something seriously wrong with you.

"You're just stressed," she continued. "That's all that's happening. Your brain is a tangled web of emotions. You've got shock, grief, anger, confusion, apathy of course because this is you we're talking about, and maybe even a little bit of"—slowly, in a display that was equal parts seductive and corny, she ran her pointer finger from the cleft of my chin to my navel—"*excitement.*"

I could breathe again. "You do know how to say the right thing from time to time, Kalista."

"Feeling better already, aren't you?"

"Maybe a little."

"Hearing your problems out loud is cathartic. When you air your grievances, you give them back to the universe. Did you know that?"

"Goddamn hippie."

"Sit back, close your eyes," she said. "I'll tell you when we're at my house. Dream a little dream of me or something. Jackass."

I laid back, breathed deep, and smiled. I thought about how lucky I was to have Kalista back in my life. Maybe, I thought, if we survived this mess, I'd make it work with her. Like, *really* work. I'd get a real job, put a ring on her finger, buy her a house in the sprawls with a neighborhood clubhouse and a swimming pool and a neatly manicured lawn with peonies and whimsical little garden gnomes. We'd make a baby or two. She'd get fat. I'd take up Sudoku. Once a month, we'd have friends over for fondue. I'd grumble about my neighbor's leaves falling in my yard. Kalista would join the PTC. We'd grow older and rougher around the edges and happier every day.

It was a nice dream. But it wouldn't endure. Like a block of C4 explosives detonating in a field of puppies, a different thought popped up. It came out of nowhere, and it didn't make a lick of sense, but somehow, I knew, or thought I knew, that it must be true: The reappearance of Kalista Chestnut was no coincidence. Somehow, it was tied to the demise of Jake Kennedy.

Kalista pitied me for being a head case. I pitied Kalista for being a girl who dates head cases. We had pity sex on the couch in her living room. When in Rome, you know.

After lunch, she disappeared into her office and closed the door, saying she needed to work for a few hours.

"You don't mind, do you?" she said. "You can watch TV, point the gun at the door, pretend there's a purple statue here to talk to, whatever you want. *Mi casa es su casa*. I just need something mindless to think about for a while."

I knew the feeling, so I called the resume agency to beg for a bone. They were dry. Evidently the world had found a job, or stopped trying. Sitting on the couch, watching two talking heads on ESPN argue about LeBron James, I felt like useless cargo.

Kalista must have joined a conference call, because obnoxious chatter soon came from her office, followed by her pigtailed boss's squeaky voice fighting to rise above it. I took the opportunity to ponder whether the lovely Ms. Chestnut was a lying, murderous succubus or future ex-wife material.

On one hand, she never struck me as having a particularly sinister soul. One slow night at Java Bloc, we watched a low-budget zombie film on the television on the back wall that the hipsters always groused about, as if its mere presence was an existential threat to their very being. Kalista fought back tears when an innocent, albeit zombified, infant was drowned in a bathtub filled with holy water. Succubi don't cry for zombified babies in bathtubs.

On the other hand, random, fleeting thoughts are powerful things. If a baseless premonition that some- one is guilty of something heinous and completely out of character pops into your head, chances are, it has merit.

I decided to confront my suspicions head on. When the voices in the office died down, I tapped on the door and tiptoed in. Kalista was now holding the phone to her ear, looking bored.

"Hi, sweetie," I whispered. "Got a sec?"

She waved me in.

"Quick question," I said.

"Sure," she said, pushing the mute button. "What's up?"

"Hey, uh... I was just thinking... do you think... um... never mind, actually, I just..."

"What, V.C.?"

"It's kind of just a... you know, uh, formality... but, you know, actually, you're busy, I'll just..."

"Spit it out already, will you?"

"Fine. I'll spit it."

"OK..."

"I will," I said.

"Ready, set, go."

"Something's on my mind," I began.

"You're not proposing, are you?"

"Oh... uh, no, it's not that at all, I just..."

"Joking, jackass. What's wrong with you?"

"You mean, other than the fact that I'm starting to annoy myself?"

"Let it out, champ."

"Kalista," I said, mustering a voice, "I'm bothered by the timing of Jake's death and the reappearance of you in my life. I mean, the very same night you contact me after two years of the silent treatment, Jake dies? Doesn't that seem a little too coincidental?"

Kalista didn't miss a beat. "Oh, it's no coincidence, sweetie," she said matter-of-factly. "I'm part of a conspiracy to kill you and all your friends. Sergio and I are both in on it. We're in it for your money, mostly. Sergio and I killed this Jake guy, and later down the road, when I'm done having fun with you, we'll kill you. Did it really take you this long to figure it out?"

"Does Chesty think she's on mute?" someone squawked into Kalista's phone. "Kalista, we can hear you, girl."

"Oops. Sorry," said Kalista to her coworkers, and then, to me, with a juicy smile, "Anything else, love?"

"I'm good," I said. "Just wanted to make sure."

A few minutes later, she came out of the office with a faint smirk on her face. She squinted at me for several seconds, clearly attempting to read me.

"You weren't seriously accusing me of *murder* in there, were you?" she said.

"Of course not. Just messing with you. Having some fun. You know me. Fuckin' ha ha," I said.

Still, I couldn't shake the feeling that Kalista's

words, or at least some part of them, rang true.

———————

Lewie called.

"I just got off the phone with Tony Drethers," he said. "Three men came into his shop today..."

"Let me guess. A priest, a rabbi, and L. Ron Hubbard."

"Maybe. They were wearing ski masks. And they were limping. Almost like they had a run-in with a certain iron-fisted barkeep we know."

"Jesus."

"Bobby, actually."

"What did they do? Is Tony alright?"

"He's fine. But get this. They were asking for Jake."

"Oh, yeah? What did Tony tell them?"

"That he was dead, of course."

"And how did that go over?"

"He said they were surprised. And that they believed him."

"They did?"

"They did."

"Did they say anything else?"

"Yes. They said, 'Fuck this city. We're going home.'"

———————

Instinctively and quickly, before I could think myself out of it, I called Sal.

"Hello," he groaned sleepily.

"I'm not waking you, am I?"

"Nah," he yawned. "Who is this?"

"It's V.C."

A pause.

"Oh."

A longer pause.

"What's up?" he said finally. "How'd you get this number?"

"You gave it to me."

"I did? Huh. Well, what's up?"

"I need to talk to your boss."

"Oh, yeah? About what?"

"Honestly... I don't know. Just... things."

"*Things?*"

"Can you get him for me? Is he around? Or how can I get a hold of him?"

"Tell you what, kid. He's hosting his annual Halloween gala at the house tomorrow. Bring a friend. Maybe he'll have time for you. Who knows, maybe our *mutual friend* will sneak in for a visit, too."

"Yeah, who's that? Detective Beerman?"

"Detective Beerman!" chortled Big Gay Sal as if I said something clever. "Yeah. Right."

"See you there. I'll be the guy in the Power Ranger costume."

"Later, kid," said Sal, yawning again.

"Wait! Quick question before you hang up." I was trying to sound casual. "What does the name Sergio Mendoza mean to you?"

"Fucking fuck me, fucker!" cried Sal, springing to life. "Not on the phone, man! The fuck! The *fuck!*"

"Oh... right. The phone. My bad."

"Never heard of him!"

"OK, man, it's cool, it's cool..."

"The *fuck!* Never *fucking* heard of him! No idea! No clue! No fucking clue! None! Zilch! Wrong number! *Nyet!* Fuck! Never heard of him!"

For some reason, I had the distinct feeling that Big Gay Sal was lying. In the interest of self-preservation, I opted not to push it.

"Sounds great," I said as Sal huffed and puffed. "Thanks, Sal. Sir. Buddy. See you tomorrow. Bye-bye now."

My fingers tingled, my legs twitched, my eyebrows fluttered. I was on the verge of either a breakthrough or a breakdown. I felt it in my bones.

Kalista stormed out of her office and stomped past me in a fury, her eyes burning craters in my soul. It didn't take a college dropout to realize she just did a slow burn on our last conversation and worked herself into a boil. She stalked out the door and slammed it behind her, then returned a moment later with a mountain of unread mail, which she slammed on the kitchen table.

"Work problems, dear?" I said feebly.

"Fuck you, V.C.," she spat. "Dickhead."

"Dickhead? Is that a term of endearment, like jackass?"

"Go… to… hell, V.C.," said Kalista between clenched teeth. "You make me miss the psycho."

At least one mystery was solved, sort of: The three goons who stomped T-Bone, tried to run over Lewie and me, and attacked Da'Quan, were hunting Jake, not me. They made that much clear when they used their big boy words to ask Tony where he was. They had nothing to do with Sergio. Chances are, they were the people Jake was trying to elude when he faked his death. And yet they weren't the ones who actually killed him.

I took my collection of dog-eared, crumpled post-it notes out of my overnight bag and spread them across the floor again. Then, I added a few new pieces to the puzzle:

Detective Beerman retires unexpectedly

V.C.'s car goes up in flames

3 goons attack DaQuan, get mauled by Bobby

Sandy G. claims assault by Ghost Jake

Sandy G. confesses to being robbed by living Jake after trying to trick him

3 goons confront Tony, ask for Jake

Sal goes apeshit on phone when he hears name of Sergio

I don't know how long I sat there, mind and heart racing, eyes bulging, waiting for a bolt of enlightenment to strike. At one point, Kalista came out to make iced tea and happily ignored me when I asked how she was holding up. She retreated into her office and got back on the phone. Soon, she was laughing loudly and chatting it up with her coworkers, determined to not let a dickhead like me darken her day.

"Women," I said to the imaginary Purple Guy. "Can't

live with them, can't accuse them of conspiracy to commit murder."

I stared, and stared, and stared some more, waiting for the click that refused to come.

"I feel like I'm missing something obvious," I muttered.

"Then write down the obvious," said Kalista. "Like V.C. is a dickhead."

Lost in thought, I didn't realize she had returned and was flipping through her epic mail stack.

"Good thinking," I said. "It's like that Poe story, maybe. 'The Purloined Letter', is it? Maybe the truth is so obvious that it's hiding in plain sight. V.C. is an asshole," I said out loud as I wrote it on a post-it note, trying without avail to get a smile from Kalista. "Kalista is beautiful when she's angry at V.C. Kalista ignores her mail. V.C. is sorry he's a dickhead. Wait, where are you going?"

"Back to work," grumbled Kalista. "And to update my online dating profile."

———————

Darkness fell. My brain continued to itch. I hopped in the shower.

I've always done my best thinking in the shower. It was where I figured out that if I helped other people get jobs for a living, I'd never have to get a real one of my own.

It was where I realized that the faint, orgiastic moaning I heard wasn't just one of those things that go bump in the night but the sound of Steffi cheating on me with the neighbor in my bedroom.

And it was where I realized who killed Jake Kennedy.

"I know who killed Jake?" I asked the wash cloth.

"I know who killed Jake," I told the shampoo bottle.

"I know who killed Jake!" I cried out to the universe.

Adrenalized and hysterical, buck naked and covered in suds, I jumped out of the shower and sprinted to Kalista's office.

"I know who killed Jake!" I bellowed, throwing open the door. "Kalista, I know who killed Jake!"

Kalista was videoconferencing with fifteen or twenty people. I recognized the pig-tailed boss, the self-identified work boyfriend, the one they called Davey, and a couple others. An elegant, older woman whom I later learned was the same rich bitch client Kalista complained about last week, was front and center.

They all stared at me, mouths agape. I stared back at them. There was only one thing to say.

"I know who killed Jake!" I exclaimed.

Chapter 17

"HOT DAMN, DUSTY, IT *IS* ANOTHER ONE! BOOMER WUDN'T lyin', they got more bars on this here street as we got in all of Willows County!"

"Yeah, but ain't hardly nobody even *pat-er-nizin'* this one. Looks dirtier 'n deader 'n Rhonda's on Tuesday."

"A *slow* Tuesday."

"An' still I bet they ain't got Natty. I bet all they got's them fancy beers like back at that hotel we're at, the uh, uh..."

"Hotel Ritzo."

"Yeah. The Hotel *Ritzo.*"

The good ole boys in the doorway shared a laugh. The Hotel Ritzo.

The one called Dusty spotted us at a table in the corner. "Good evening to you fine gentlemen," he said in a countrified, mock debonair voice. "Can you fine gentlemen tell us if this establishment serves any real American beer? Or just them Japanese-y concoctions, them uh, uh..."

"Imports," said his friend.

"Yeah. Them *imports*?"

With their big shiny belt buckles and flannel shirts tucked into their tight jeans, they looked like *Dukes of Hazzard* extras.

Bobby took great offense to their existence. "Do we *look* like we're open to the public?" he bellowed drunkenly, slamming his fist on the table, sending a pint glass careening over the edge. "Do we fucking look like we're open?"

Kalista, T-Bone, and I had just arrived to find Lewie and Bobby sitting at a table covered in empty beer bottles and shot glasses. The brand-new neon sign on the front door alternately flashed Seal and Open.

"By all accounts," murmured T-Bone under his breath.

"Damn, Dusty, how's that for big city hospitality? Can you even 'magine old Sam Hutty at Poochie's running off good payin' customers like that? Can you 'magine?"

"Our money ain't good in here, fella?" said Dusty, turning crimson from the neck up. "Is that what you sayin' to us, boy?"

"Private party!" shouted Bobby, rushing towards his unwanted patrons. "Move along, you toothless country ass crackers!"

It didn't take a soothsayer to see what was about to transpire: fists would fly, glass would break, blood would flow, cops would show. All because... hell, I didn't know why. All because Bobby was incompatible with the human race.

"You best lower your voice and show some respect, son!" said Dusty. "Me and Sorrel here, we ain't scared of no scar-faced, city boy momma boy."

Bobby and his failed attempt at customers were nose to nose, snarling at each other, ready to throw down, when inspiration struck. I jumped up and applauded loudly.

"Masterfully done, Bobby! I didn't think I'd ever say this, but you're starting to get the hang of it. You're learning to put the bark in Seal after all. That's exactly what we're looking for!"

I slapped Bobby on the back and shook our confused visitors' hands. "What did you think, guys? Not bad, huh?"

Like the rest of the room, Dusty and Sorrel looked utterly bewildered.

"What you talking about, boy?" said Dusty. "You ain't makin' no sense. What kind of place is this place?"

"Oh, you mean you didn't realize?" I said, feigning shock. "We insult the customers here at Seal. That's why people come—or at least, that's why we hope people will come, when our trial run is over and we officially open. We insult you, you insult us, it's a grand old, faux hateful time. All in good humor, of course."

"You mean like that Last Resort place?" said Dusty, looking dubious.

"Sure. That's right. Exactly like it. Only we're even bigger dicks than them."

"Hmmm," said Dusty.

"Innarestin', I guess," said Sorrel.

"I don't know," said Dusty, shaking his head. "Dudn't seem right. Is it even *true*?" he said to my friends at the table.

Kalista just stared. T-Bone nodded uncertainly.

"Go fuck yourself," said Lewie cheerfully.

A smile crept across Dusty's face. "I'll be goddamned, son!" he exclaimed. "I thought we was straight up bein' runned off, didn't you, Sorrel? Woo! A restaurant where they treat you like the corner of the pigsty!"

"And I bet there'll be a line out this door just to get inside," mused Sorrel.

"Only in the big city, right, Sorrel?" said Dusty. "Though I tell you what, Sorrel, when they open these doors for real, we ought bring our women in here..."

"... and don't give 'em no warning about what this place is doing. I can only 'magine the fun these folks'd have crackin' wise about that lady beard keeps coming back on my Tilly!"

"Hell, Sorrel, her teeth is what they really'd have a field day playing on."

"Or what about your Tess's turkey neck? They ought put that bird on the goddamn menu!"

"An' serve up some of that cliff palate o' hers as a... a... what you call it... a side dish!"

Dusty and Sorrel spilled back onto the street happily, continuing to extol their wives' physical virtues. T-Bone and Lewie burst into laughter. Even Kalista, who was clearly still annoyed by a trifecta of unpleasant realities—me, myself, and I—couldn't fight off a grin.

Bobby, however, was not entertained. "What the fuck, V," he slurred. "A couple *ash*holes *shh*trut in here and *inshh*ult me and my busine*shh*, and you *shh*end them off with a handshake? What the fuck is that? What are you doing?"

"Keeping you out of jail," I said. "And creating an

impromptu business model that's perfectly suited to your strengths."

Bobby was wearing the universal cockeyed scowl of the angry drunk. I could smell the cinnamon whiskey and piss beer on his breath as he got in my face. I said a silent prayer that I wouldn't pull a Duke Kettle and soil myself.

"Easy there, Bobby," said Lewie.

"At ease, soldier," said T-Bone.

"Anyone got Thorazine to shoot in his jugular?" asked Lewie.

I grimaced and braced for impact.

Bobby wrapped me in a playful bear hug.

"You should have *shh*een your face, brother!" he cried. "What did you think I wa*shh* going to do? Hit you? Come on!"

"Right. Because that would have been so out of character for you," said Lewie.

"An insult-themed bar! I could fucking do that. Obviou*shh*ly being friendly to people ain't working. 'What are the *shh*pecials today, *shh*ir?' 'My foot in your a*shh* and your face on the floor, bitch!'"

"Yeah... we probably need to work on that, Bobby," I opined.

"*Beshht* idea I've heard in ages!"

"Shame he won't remember it tomorrow," quipped Lewie.

"Have a seat then, Bobby," I said, "and I'll tell you something even sweeter."

I turned off the neon Open sign and locked the door.

"Friends," I said, "there's a reason I called you here today..."

"Called us?" said Lewie. "Bobby and I were already here. You ran into T-Bone on the way in. And Kalista brought you. You didn't call anyone."

"Semantics, Lewie," I said. "And regardless of semantics, I have an announcement that you all need to hear."

"She's pregnant," said Lewie. "We've heard."

"No," said Kalista, standing up, "I'm not. And I've already heard this story. Once was enough."

"Wait," I said. "Where are you going?"

She nodded curtly to Lewie and Bobby but smiled at T-Bone. "I'm glad I got to see you again, T-Bone," she said. "Let's do breakfast again. Call me?"

T-Bone winked at Kalista and gave me a coy shrug, as if to say it wasn't his fault he was such a charming old chick magnet.

"Announcement pending, gents," I said. "I'll walk you to your car, Kalista."

"No, thank you," she said. "I'd rather walk alone. I'd rather get mugged."

"I can never tell with women," said Lewie as Kalista stalked past me towards the exit without a word. "Is she angry or just pretending?"

"Ain't been happy since the moment she walked in," said T-Bone. "Take it from the one here with four ex-wives."

"Trouble in paradise, Romeo?" said Lewie.

"Funny story," I said, hurrying after Kalista. "I jumped out of the shower earlier and walked into her home office when she was Skyping with her coworkers..."

"Uh-oh," said Lewie. "Shrinkage?"

"Yes," said Kalista as she struggled with the

unnecessarily complicated door lock. "And then he just kept standing there. Like he was waiting for everyone to take out their graphite pencils and sketch pads."

"I admit it, I may have frozen slightly."

Kalista managed to open the door. "And if you really think that's why I'm upset, V.C., then... I don't know. Have a nice life."

And then she was gone. T-Bone reeled me in before I could chase after her.

"Let it go, son," he said in that deep, soothing voice that couldn't possibly be wrong. "Whatever you did, you aren't going to fix it. Not now, anyway. Let it go."

"Fuck it," I said, convincing no one. "Can I get a drink, Bobby?"

"Pick a bottle, any bottle. Bring it over for the re*shh*t of u*shh* too."

I brought four rocks glasses and a bottle of GrandMa to the table, where I poured Lewie, T-Bone, and me a generous slug and waived the bottle over Bobby's empty glass.

"So, what exactly did you do to piss her off?" said Lewie. "More importantly, does this mean she's single now?"

"Standard domestic squabble," I said. "I suggested she was complicit in Jake's murder. She took offense to it."

"What a bitch," deadpanned Lewie.

"You're the one who put that worm in my ear, Lewie. You're the one who pointed out that her reappearing the same night Jake died was a little too coincidental."

"But I didn't expect you to actually *confront* her with it! Where's your mind, grasshopper? What were you thinking?"

"I was thinking that I was right, Lewie."

I emptied my GrandMa and poured another.

"And I was," I continued. "It wasn't a coincidence. You were right. I was right. Kalista has *everything* to do with Jake dying."

Because the universe has a twisted sense of humor, the background music—"My Girl," by The Temptations—kicked on at that very moment.

"Is automatic," slurred Bobby. "Nine pm on the dot. Can't figure out how to make it quit."

Lewie's eyes were wide as manhole covers, his face unsmiling for the first time since... ever, maybe.

"Are you saying you know what happened?" he cried. "You know who killed Jake? Who?"

I raised my glass, cleared my throat. "A man by the name of... drumroll, please... Sergio Mendoza."

Lewie's jaw dropped open slowly. Bobby hiccupped with his whole body like pre-vomitus drunks tend to do.

"Sergio?!" said Lewie in disbelief. "Kalista's ex?"

"That's the one."

"How do you figure?"

"Simple. I opened my eyes, grasshopper. I looked for the obvious answer. And it came in the form of a girl with an arm full of last week's mail."

"Mail? What? Why would Sergio kill Jake?"

"He wasn't trying to. He came to my apartment to kill me. Jake was in the wrong place at the wrong time."

"Wait, wait, wait. Hold the show, Agent Almond. Jake was killed the night of his quote-unquote funeral, which was a Friday. You and Kalista went on your little date on Saturday. Kalista received that grammatically challenged death threat on Sunday. The timing doesn't add up. He came to your apartment on Friday to try to kill you, then left your lady friend a note threatening to kill you both *afterwards?*"

"Listen, grasshopper," I said. "Kalista only gets her mail once or twice a week. It just piles up in her mailbox. When I took her to *Fromageres*, she had a stack of it that she took off the mailman's hands because her box was too full..."

"That i*shh* ju*shh*t irresponss*sh*ible," said Bobby.

"Earlier today, she walked in with another big stack..."

"Big *rack* i*shh* more like it," offered Bobby.

"How long's he been like this?" I asked Lewie.

"Too long."

"Early today, she walked in with another big *pile* of mail," I continued, "and it made me realize: Sergio didn't leave the note on Saturday or Sunday. He left it on *Friday or even earlier.*"

"Go on," said Lewie.

"Sergio showed up at Kalista's on Friday night, coked out of his skull, demanding she take him back. She refused. He stormed out, but he didn't leave right away. Kalista said she saw him in his car in the parking lot, beating the shit out of his steering wheel. She walked away, looked out the window again, and his car was there, but he wasn't. He must have been bringing the note to her mailbox. She looked again in a few minutes, and the car was gone. He was on his way to the Loop to gut me at the exact time Jake was coming to surprise me."

T-Bone and Lewie sat silent, the latter stroking his

goatee. It wasn't the exuberant response I was hoping for.

"Maybe you're right," said Lewie finally. "Maybe you're wrong. What's your proof?"

"Proof *ishh* in the motherfucking pudding," the ever-helpful Bobby pointed out.

"Beerman's reaction when I wrote Sergio's name down at the police station. Think about it, man. What do you think happened to Sergio after he 'accidentally' killed a mob boss's son? The guy must have left fingerprints, DNA, hair samples, whatever, all over the apartment. Beerman, or Sal, or any number of Big Jamie's friends in authority probably figured out who did it before the sun came up."

"That's not exactly how murder investigations play out, V.C."

"They killed him, Lewie! Sergio is dead. Don't you see it? Beerman and Sal, they cleaned up Jake's body and then killed Sergio. Even if they didn't do it personally, they know that someone did on Jamie's orders. When I wrote Sergio's name, Beerman took it as a threat, like, 'I know who Jake's killer was, and I know what you did to him.'

"It also explains why Sal went ape shit on the phone after I asked him about Sergio. He knows Sergio is a missing person, and he knows why. He probably buried the guy himself. Plus, think about Big Jamie's words at the strip club. 'Some no-name killed Jake,' 'everything went as planned.' Jamie was saying that the plan to fake Jake's death worked, that the person who killed Jake wasn't the people they faked his death to avoid. He was just some no-name.

"It also explains why Sal and Beerman were so uptight about the car that tried to run us down, man. It made them think that maybe the plan hadn't worked after all, that someone suspected Jake was still alive and was menacing his friends to, you know, acquire his whereabouts."

"Meh," said Lewie with a shrug, lighting a new cigarette off the tip of his old one. "It's a theory. And who knows, it might be true. Parts of it, anyway. Sergio *may* have killed Jake. But the evidence is shaky. Even if he did leave that note on Friday, it doesn't prove anything."

"What about Beerman and Sal's reaction to his name, man? Why else would they get spooked by it?"

"Meh," repeated Lewie with another infuriating shrug. "How would I know? They could have sigma-phobia for all I know."

"Sigma...? What?"

"Fear of the letter S."

"Why are you shitting on this, Lewie?"

"Because, V.C.," said Lewie in an unmistakably patronizing tone, "it's not as easy as you seem to think to magically scoop up DNA evidence, run a quick test on it, identify your killer, and then track him down and off him. Even if you are Big Jamie Kennedy. Entire forensics teams spend hours, even days, analyzing a crime scene. Plus... it's kind of anti-climactic, isn't it? Your new girlfriend's—I'm sorry, your new *ex*-girlfriend's—boyfriend did it? Yawn."

"What the fuck, Lewie. I'm sorry it's not Verbal Kint walking off his limp and turning into Keyser Fucking Söze. But it's true."

"Maybe. Maybe not. It's no smoking gun. At best, it's a guy who heard it from a guy who heard it from a guy about a smoking gun."

Bobby took Lewie's words as a cue to break into a hideous rendition of "Take it on the Run." I looked to T-Bone for help.

"Penny for your thoughts, Mr. Bone?"

"I *shh*ay we kick the motherfuckers a*shh*," suggested Bobby, clearly not following along.

"The question you boys need to ask yourself is," said T-Bone, "why the hurry to get rid of the body? Big Jamie was trying to convince the world Jake was dead. Now that he really was dead, why rush to make it disappear?"

An hour ago, I thought I was on the precipice of a quantum leap. Now, after hearing Lewie's doubts and T-Bone's questions, I felt like we'd taken a significant step backwards. I poured myself another GrandMa, hoping to drink my irritation into submission.

"So," said Lewie. "Sergio killed Jake, maybe. That was your little announcement, I assume?"

"No, Lewie, you smug bastard," I snapped. "My announcement is that my nephew Zeke is selling JT's Pizzas for eleven bucks a pop for a school fundraiser. Fuck, yes, that's my announcement."

"JT's Pizza. I should *shh*ell those here," said Bobby, and then, peering into his empty glass, "Wa' happened to my drink?"

"You drank it," I said. "And then you filled it up and drank it again."

"For real? Fuuuuuck me."

"Fuck us all, Bobby," I said, reaching for the bottle. "Fuck u*shh* all."

I couldn't sleep, and not just because Feces Ball, an aptly named three-piece punk band from Edwardsville, was attempting to blast my apartment from Delmar to Skinker. I was irritated as hell. At Lewie for crapping on my Sergio theory. At myself for being such a dolt with Kalista. At Jake for getting himself killed in the most asinine way possible. At Feces Ball's drummer's parents for buying him a drum set when he was nine and encouraging him to follow his dreams.

"Wise man says there's no peace greater than sitting in a quiet room, knowing that you haven't brought harm to your fellow man," I told the Purple Guy as I paced my tiny apartment cagily. "If that's true, there's no anxiety greater than wrestling with a guilty conscious while Feces Ball assails your eardrums."

The one-armed Purple Guy, still sulking about being left to convalesce on the floor with a broken arm courtesy of Sandy Galanos all day, shot me an evil glance.

"Go join the club," I told him.

Feces Ball went on break. I called Kalista. It went straight to voicemail.

"Hey. It's me. V.C.... V.C. Almond," I said dumbly. "Call me back when you can. Just making sure you're OK. And, you know, alive. Bye. Sorry. OK, bye. And mostly, sorry."

I paced some more. A terrifying thought crossed my mind. What if I was right about Sergio killing Jake, but wrong about Big Jamie killing Sergio? What if Sergio was still alive, and he mistook Jake for me that night and believed I was dead? And now it was Kalista's turn to get the ax?

"Death could explain why her phone went straight to voicemail," I said to the little green alien candle with the chipped skull, giving the Purple Guy some space. "On the other hand, even though Sergio hasn't seen me in a couple years, and I only met him a few times ever, Jake and I look nothing alike. Hell, Sergio looks more like Jake than I do. You'd have to be much more than just coked out of your skull to confuse Jake for someone else, especially yours truly."

Near the end of Feces Ball's third and final set, I crashed on the couch and faded into a fitful dreamland where I was drowning in a sea of the letters K, L, and C. I awoke a couple hours later to an eerie silence, parched and sweaty with a rapid heartbeat and a mind's eye fixated on those three letters. My brain was a misfiring calculator. KLC plus KLC divided by the square root of KLC to the KLC degree equals KLC. Maybe my subconscious was trying to tell me something. Or maybe I was having a stroke.

The quietness unnerved me. No silence is thicker than the one that follows an uproar. A chill went down my spine, and I wondered if Jake's spirit really was lingering in my space. I would have welcomed him with open arms. But I didn't feel shit.

"The sad truth is, friends," I said to my inanimate roomies, "we are nothing if not utterly alone."

I stumbled outside onto the balcony. A waning

crescent moon hung high. The empty street glistened with a coat of fresh rain. All the world was calm, a snapshot of perfect serenity. I responded to it by falling to my knees and vomiting three times over the railing.

"Jesus," I groaned. "I didn't know I still had that kind of thing in me."

I was still wiping GrandMa bile from the corners of my lips when a police car rolled to a halt below. A fresh-faced officer stepped out and shined his mag light on me.

"You own the place?" he called out.

I shook my head.

"Then what are you doing up there?"

"Just living."

His radio squawked unintelligibly. I wondered if he was stepping in my vomit.

"*Living*? You live up there? Seriously?"

"Why would I lie?"

"Is anybody up there with you?"

"In the room? Or the whole building?"

"You some sort of smartass?" He sounded more curious than angry.

"In light of recent events," I said, "I'm more of a dumbass."

"In that case... you want a job application, sir?"

We both laughed.

"Seriously, this place is zoned for residential?"

"Sure is," I said. "There's a Form 5211 hanging up in the Korean noodle shop downstairs. Mr. Kun-Woo owns the building."

The officer didn't give any indication that he

suspected there was no such thing as a Form 5211. He wished me goodnight and hopped back in his cruiser, probably to go battle and mingle with other nocturnal disasters while the ninety-nine percent were tucked snug in their beds.

I wasn't happy to see him pull away. The thought of being alone made me want to hurl a fourth time. I called Kalista again.

She answered the phone with a sleepy groan.

"Kalista? Are you there? Are you all right?"

"No," she mumbled. "Some asshole keeps calling me while I'm trying to sleep."

Click.

"Love you too, baby."

I sat on the couch and closed my eyes. A sea of Ks, Ls, and Cs rained down.

And then a shitty little light bulb appeared over my head. I reached for my phone.

"Hey there, V.C.," said Lewie, sounding chipper and awake. "What are you working on?"

"A plan," I said.

"I'm listening," he said over the din of video game machine gun fire. "What kind of plan?"

"A plan to find out who killed Jake."

The gunfire ceased. "Talk to me, partner. How do we do it? What's the plan?"

"We go to Big Jamie's Halloween party tomorrow night and ask him. And while we're at it, we break into the third floor."

Chapter 18

I AWOKE WITH A KINK IN MY NECK AND PUKE STAINS on my shirt. The setting sun was peeking through the window, casting ominous shadows across my room. Live samba music came from the street. The scents of miso soup and marijuana wafted upward through an opening in my balcony door. I felt like death.

I was lying face down on the floor between the couch and the bed with a fresh bump on my noggin. My inner detective deduced that I had attempted to land on something soft, and I had failed.

With a groan, I climbed to my knees. Bad idea. A whiskey volcano rumbled inside me, and I barely made it to the kitchen sink before it erupted like a mash-and-yeast-filled Mount Vesuvius.

"Most important meal of the day," I said out loud.

Two bottles—an empty pint of Old Ezra and a nearly empty half-pint of Old Crow—sat on the coffee table. Evidently, I'd celebrated vomiting over the balcony last night by giving my liver the Hunter Thompson treatment.

The post-it notes that I'd spent so many hours peer-ing at lie in a pile of ashes on the coffee table. Next to them, my cell phone flashed blue and green like it had something important to say. The few remaining drops of poison in my stomach churned. Twenty-four ounces of whiskey and a smart phone is a recipe for irreparable social damage.

Gingerly, like a SWAT officer handling a suspiciously ticking package, I unlocked the screen. A familiar, highly unexpected pair of breasts—my ex-wife's—stared back at me. What the hell. Blurry-eyed, I sat down and scrolled through my text messages. If I didn't have the evidence at my fingertips, I wouldn't have believed that Steffi and I spent the four to five a.m. hours sharing make-up texts and naked selfies. I felt like a barf-splat-tered creep. On the bright side, no proposals were made.

Four voicemails from Tara, my main contact at the resume agency, were waiting for me as well.

"Good news," she said in the first. "We have lots of work available today, just give us a call ASAP. You know the drill."

"Earth to our favorite freelancer," she said anxiously in the second. "Call us. Pretty please, with cherries and dollar bills on top."

"What the hell, V.C.," grumbled Tara in voicemail three. "You agreed to give us twenty-four hours' notice if you're unavailable and to respond to our calls within two hours. It's been six hours, and this isn't the first time this has happened. We've turned down several quality applicants this month because you keep saying you're ready for more work. So, wake the hell up, buddy. If you're sick, dead, or dying, my apologies. Otherwise..."

"Have a nice life," I finished her sentence, deleting the message.

The fourth voicemail was the nail in the coffin. The agency conducted a routine, random review of my file and discovered I wasn't up to date on the myriad certifications inexplicably required to help people find jobs they probably don't really want anyway. "Once you have completed the bi-annual standards training course," said Tara, "and present proof that you have paid the three-hundred-and-forty-dollar Resume Writers membership fee—"

"What a bitch," I said, hanging up before she finished speaking. "I mean, seriously. Who leaves voicemails anymore? No wonder nobody called her back."

I felt like I needed some air, or something high to jump off, so I stepped onto the balcony. Below me, the functioning world soldiered on. A group of giggling teenage girls were taking pictures with the Chuck Berry statue across the street. Gummy Jack—me in fifty years, I half-kidded myself—stood outside Slice Pizza, jabbering madly in his porkpie hat, looking like a ghost. T-Bone manned his usual stoop, chatting with a portly fellow in a checkered tweed overcoat. Probably a fellow musician, I thought.

The samba music was coming from the common area behind Middle City Farmers Market. Its festive *cavaquinhos* and *tamborims* were soon interrupted by a blaring car horn. The driver of a Schlafly beer truck was having words with the driver of a rusty old station wagon. The beer truck wanted to reverse into a loading zone outside Strawberry Mountain. The station wagon wanted him to go fuck himself. After much teeth gnashing and a series of middle finger salutes, the station wagon had the brilliant idea to *go around* the beer truck, and the curtain closed on that drama.

"Some people," I mused aloud, "just aren't very well-adjusted to life on this planet."

I had two hours to spare before Lewie picked me up for Big Jamie's soiree, which I figured was just enough time to get my life together. So, I washed the vomit down the sink and gave the kitchen a Lysol once-over. The Old Crow was next to go. It was mostly a symbolic gesture—there were only a couple swigs of backwash left anyway—but it was a start.

Next, I deleted the naked pictures of Stef from my phone so that Kalista wouldn't find them and get jealous in two years when she started talking to me again. A long hot shower was next. Then, I dragged my bones downstairs to Camilla's for some grub. Weird Hal, the spitting image of a three-hundred-pound Weird Al Yankovic, sat at the door, collecting the five-dollar cover. I reached into my empty pocket, pretending to fish for cash, but Weird Hal was kind enough not to call my bluff and waved me inside. As one of the weirdos who voluntarily lived above the bar, I was something of a celebrity at Camilla's.

A bachelorette party sipping colorful cocktails out of penis-shaped straws occupied the corner section. An orange-vested construction crew sat at the bar, drinking draft beers that probably tasted very well-earned.

Feeling out of place, I opted for the bar downstairs. It was nearly empty. Scotty the bartender was chopping limes and whistling a happy tune. He looked genuinely pleased to see me. Scotty had his shit together—kids, family, Jesus, the whole sha-bang. He was a genuinely good man. I liked him anyway.

He washed the lime juice off his fingers before shaking my hand.

"The usual?" he said. "Guinness and a whiskey?"

"Just a Sprite for now," I said. "Is the kitchen open?"

"We could probably make you something. What do you feel like?"

"Pancakes?"

"Seriously?"

"Or, you know, whatever."

"Let's see what we can do, buddy. Be right back."

Scotty bounced away cheerfully. A bar-back with a handlebar mustache wheeled an ice cart behind the bar and started filling the bins.

"Who's the band tonight?" I asked him.

"Ugh," he groaned. "You ever hear of Cyst Pus?"

"Oh. No. They better than Feces Ball?"

"They've got three years of mediocrity on Feces Ball."

Scotty returned, looking morose. "They can't do pancakes, V.C.," he said. "How about chicken tenders?"

"Sure. Same thing, basically."

The tenders tasted like they spent the afternoon under a heat lamp. Famished, I dug in anyway. I was elbow deep in old grease and honey mustard when a tattooed little hand swooped in and liberated a limp French fry from my plate.

"Hey hot stuff," said the girl with the dragon tattoo. "Come here often?"

She was dressed in leather bondage pants, a spiked collar, and a backless black shirt with skull-shaped cut-outs everywhere. Her face was a pin cushion of rings, beads, and various accessories that wouldn't be allowed on an airplane.

"Hi, Josie," I said. "You're looking... like the poster girl for a fetish website."

"You like, Virginia?" she said, taking a seat. "Have a shot with me, will you?"

"Rain check. I'm on antibiotics," I lied.

"You need to be more careful where you stick that thing, Virginia."

"Noted."

"Pass the ketchup, please. The honey mustard, too."

"Sure," I said, pushing the plate between us as well. "I could use some company, I guess."

"How romantic," said Josie. "How you been? Did you ever figure out who broke into your place? Or why that big bald ogre was there?"

"I did. He was there to steal a dead body."

"Liar, liar, dick on fire."

"If you say so."

"What do you do, V.C.? For a living? Don't lie."

"Not a lot. I'm between jobs, apparently. Resume writing."

Josie scoffed. "Doesn't suit you," she said. "I'm not liking it."

"Sorry to disappoint. What do you do?"

She took off the black medallion hanging around

her neck and swung it slowly in front of my eyes.

"You are getting sleepy. Very, very sleepy..."

"Get the fuck out. You're a hypnotist? For real?"

"For real. I have a Ph.D. in hypnotic therapy with a focus on hypnotic regression."

"You're an academic? The doctor girl with the dragon tattoo? I don't believe it. Doesn't suit you."

"I also do graduations, office events, and BDSM sex parties."

"That sounds more like it. That shit doesn't actually work, does it?"

"BDSM sex parties?"

"Hypnosis."

"It depends," said Josie. "Pass the Sprite, please."

"It depends on what?"

"On whether or not you *want* it to work."

"Ah. So, it doesn't work."

"Come," she said, standing up. "Join my girlfriend and me at our table. She gets jealous when I'm alone with other girls."

"Another time," I said. "I have prior commitme-nts tonight."

"Don't lie, Virginia."

"I'm serious. I'm crashing a crime lord's Halloween party, breaking into a restricted area for quite possibly no reason, and searching for murder clues."

"Fine," said Josie. "Don't tell me. But don't call *me* when you get arrested again."

"I don't even have your number."

"And with that attitude," said my neighbor, walking away, "you aren't going to get it."

I settled my tab, using a nearly maxed out credit card that was looking less and less likely to ever be paid, and made my way upstairs. Lewie was supposed to pick me up in five minutes, which meant I only had two to four hours to get ready. Halfway up the stairway, though, something alarming met my eye: a hulking figure dressed in full Darth Vader regalia pounding violently on my door. He had a light saber on his hip. I had a revolver in my coat. My chances were slim.

"Hey, man," I called, "I think you have the wrong planet or something."

Vader turned slowly and peered at me from under his gleaming black mask. He was carrying a bundle of colorful clothing under one arm. One of us, I thought, is about to die in a rather imbecilic fashion. He raised his free hand and pointed a sinister, gloved finger in my direction. Then he squeezed his hand into a tight fist, as if force-choking the life out of an underperforming subordinate.

"I have been expecting you...V... C ...," said the man, his voice electronically distorted to sound like Vader himself. "You are late. You disappoint me."

He took a dramatic step forward, then another. Only five or six stairs separated us. I fled to the lower landing, taking three steps at a time, ready to burst onto the street, screaming like a lunatic that a Sith lord is on my tail. But then I remembered the equalizer in my coat. I turned and pointed the Colt between Vader's eyes.

Aldous Lewie threw off the mask. With his arms flailing in surrender, he fell awkwardly against the stairway. A wooden baluster under the handrail snapped in two. Laundry flew in all directions.

"Attaboy, partner!" called Lewie from the floor. "Shoot first, ask questions later, just like I taught you!"

"Fuck, Lewie! What are you doing here already, man?"

"Already? It's five minutes to eight. You said to be here at seven, right?"

"I said to be here at eight. You're five minutes early for the first time since birth. What's with the costume, man?"

"Uh, hello," said Lewie, taken aback. "We're going to a Halloween party, aren't we? Help me up, will you?"

"Yeah, we're going to a Halloween party. But not for fifth graders."

With both arms, I hoisted the smiling Sith to his feet.

"Rubbish," said Lewie. "Adults dress up for Halloween parties too, V.C. Snarble it."

"Do *what*?"

"Snarble. A search engine I'm whipping up some day. You know, to give those Google fucks a run for their money."

"Whatever, Lewie." I unlocked the door as Lewie gathered his laundry from the floor. "You're going to be the only person dressed like an idiot."

"Well, not the *only* one."

Lewie starting spreading his clothes—an assortment of used Halloween costumes—across the bed.

"Hell, no. I'm not wearing some ridiculous outfit. I don't think it's that kind of party, man."

"Oh, of course it is."

Lewie put the voice-distorting mask back on his face so that he sounded like Vader again when he asked, "What's your flavor, Jedi? Zombie? Batman? Mullet man? Sexy French maid?"

"Where did you even get this crap?"

"You've met Jimmy Breem, right? He owns that Halloween store I managed for a season. These are from the donation pile. They'll go to charity when we're done with them."

"Charity? What the fuck kind of charity wants a slutty, bloody bride ensemble?"

Even from several feet away, the costume pile smelled like stale perfume and cigarettes.

"Not sure. Pick your poison, though. Let's get this party started."

"Let me make this clear, Darth Lewie. Jacob P. Kennedy and John F. Kennedy have a better chance of walking through this doorway in tandem, singing 'The Monster Fucking Mash', than I do of showing up at Big Jamie Kennedy's mansion in one of these asinine outfits. Understood?"

Thirty minutes later, Darth Vader and a six-foot, polyester-clad middle finger pulled onto northbound I-170. The latter was silently cursing the bastards who torched his car and left him without a retort to his demented cohort's stubborn proclamation that no costume equals no car ride.

"So," said Lewie, still wearing the Vader mask, "what made you finally come to your senses?"

"And pick this stupid outfit? I figured maybe I'd get lucky and someone would take offense to it and shoot me."

"Nonsense. It'll be a hit, you sassy thing."

"As Sartre said, 'Hell is other people,' Lewie."

"Sartre, fartre. What I meant was, what made you

come to your senses about breaking into the third floor?"

"I was drunk. Sober, I'm not convinced this is our brightest move or worth the risk. For all we know, Sal warned me to stay away because there was a fresh coat of wax on the floor. Or, you know, it was overdue for a dusting."

Vader stared me down for several seconds, breathing heavy.

"Sure," I continued, "if one of us happens to get turned around and wanders up there, great. But..."

"Happens to get turned around? You're a barrel of laughs, partner. I *have* a plan, V.C. Take the wheel. I have an ace up my sleeve you'll want to see."

Lewie abandoned the wheel and turned around to search the backseat floor. Moments later, he emerged with the so-called ace: a pair of industrial-strength vacuum cups.

"Voila!" he sang.

"You're going to set up a cupping clinic on the third floor and snoop around between appointments?"

"Close, but not. You know that floor-to-ceiling window on the back side of the house, facing the river?"

"No, not really."

"Clearly, you haven't been studying Google Maps. There's a floor-to-ceiling window on the back side of the house, facing ..."

"The river, got it."

"I'm going to scale it!"

Even from under the mask, the smile in Lewie's voice was palpable.

"Using these suction cups!" he continued excitedly.

"And when I reach the top, I'll just hop over to the third-floor balcony..."

"*Hop over?*"

"... and then I'll open one of the windows, easy peasy Japanesey, and search for clues while the party people sip and snort the night away."

In the Vader mask, Lewie's voice carried a false sense of gravitas, as if the words he spoke were anything but batshit crazy gibberish.

"I see. Quick question, though, Mr. Bond: How many times have you actually been in Big Jamie's house?"

"Including that time for tea, and that other time for Thanksgiving dinner... zero. One less than you. You know Jake and Jamie weren't close, V.C. So, what?"

"So, you've seen the *outside* of the window, but what makes you think the *inside* isn't in a part of the house where people will be, you know, congregating? Don't you think they might notice a grown-ass man in Darth Vader attire scaling the wall with suction cups?"

"Oh, I'm not worried about them," said Lewie dismissively. "Their eyes will be focused on the diversion the guy in the middle finger costume is creating."

"And what diversion is that, Lewie?"

"Beats me. That's up to you, Agent Almond. Be creative. My mind alone can't craft this master plan, you know."

"Hey, Lewie?"

"Yes, V.C."

"I don't think I want you to be my plus-one anymore."

"Nonsense. Tonight's our big night. Tonight, we solve the case of the double-dead Kennedy. I wouldn't miss it."

"You realize you're not going to get five feet off the ground before they drag you off, right?"

"Meh. If they do, I'll just say it's part of the act."

"What act? Since when does Darth Vader climb shit, Lewie?"

"Good point. I guess I should have gone with Spider Man, eh? Ah, well. Jimmy Breem gave me too good a deal on this Vader costume to pass it up. Live and learn, eh?"

"Until you get killed for being an idiot, yes."

Lewie took off the mask and gave me a long, fixed stare. He was wearing his serious smile.

"Can I count on you, V.C.? I need to hear you say that if the need arises, you'll create a diversion. I need to hear that you have my back, V.C."

I knew Lewie too well to waste any more breath trying to appeal to his sense of reason, or lack thereof.

"Fine," I said. "Fuck it. If the situation arises, I'll create a diversion."

"Excellent! That's what I appreciate about you, my good man! You go with the flow. Even when that silly little sensible voice inside you pops up and tells you that the flow is fucked, you go with it anyway."

Evidently, with those words, the planning stage was complete, because Lewie dropped the subject and cranked up some death metal. The 'burbs faded in the rearview as Cannibal Corpse wailed about rearranging faces with a sledgehammer. The Clark Bridge grew closer, the landscape sparser. Strip malls and subdivisions gave way to swampy fields overrun with weeds and muck. Big Jamie's well-lit mansion on the hill rose out of the nothingness, like a rose garden in a wasteland. My stomach turned uneasily.

Lewie killed the music as we began the slow ascent up the winding pathway to the house. The dahlias, I noted, had lost their buds. The mums were going strong.

We came to a stop at the security checkpoint. Two vehicles, a Cadillac sedan and a Toyota Land Cruiser, were ahead of us. The gate was wide open again, but this time, there was no shortage of eyes on it. Two men in black suits stood by the security booth, walkie talkies in hand. Two others were searching the Caddy's interior with flashlights. Beyond the gate, a pair of gentlemen in Security sweatshirts stood guard. The AR-15s clutched to their chests were probably not the costume variety.

"Jesus," I murmured. "I'm starting to doubt we should be here, man."

"No worries," said Lewie, carefree for no good reason. "I'm sure those men with the automatic rifles are just here in case of shenanigans. People like us have nothing to worry about."

"Maybe you should just, you know, throw the car in reverse and get the fuck out of Dodge, man."

"Rambo and Chris Kyle up there might not like that, dude."

"Use the force, Lewie."

We waited in tense silence while the guards picked apart the Caddy. I wondered what they were looking for. I could see the faint outlines of several vehicles parked outside the house and wondered if they were put through the same wringer. Finally, the Caddy was deemed worthy, or harmless, and the guards waved it along. The line rolled forward. A car pulled up behind us. Lewie took off the mask.

"You didn't bring that Colt, did you?" he asked.

"Fortunately, no."

"Well, that's good news."

"Other than the suction cups," I said, "you don't have anything suspicious, right?"

Lewie said nothing.

"Right, Lewie? Nothing suspicious?"

"What? Oh, nothing, really."

"Good."

"Just a .357 Magnum Python in the glove department."

"Shit. Ah, well, you're licensed."

"And a Ruger 10/22 in the trunk."

"Damn it."

"And a couple pump actions..."

"Are you serious?"

"... a Mossberg 930, Kel-Tec PMR-30, a potato gun, some throwing knives, and a couple mouse guns. Oh, yeah, I forgot I still have that Marlin rifle back there, don't I?"

"Christ, man! What are you fixing to do? Occupy Poland?"

"I've been meaning to swing by Connor Ventura's farm in Winfield for some target practice... Oh, crap, I just realized I have that Tiger Moth of Kenny Brodie's back there, too. And also..."

"Tiger what? Kenny who?"

Tiger Moth. It's the bionic sound amplifier the pros use. Kenny Brodie's my FBI guy. I've mentioned him, right? He's a character, you'd like him. He's the one who gave me those files on Big Jamie's people. I'll introduce you some time. You two would get along, he's a whiskey man, too."

"Sounds like a sweetheart." I was starting to panic. "What else is in the car?"

"Hmmm... let's see," said Lewie, tapping his fingers on the steering wheel, thinking or stalling. "We've got some Eye Borg night vision goggles, a couple video cameras, my short stack of fake I.D.s..."

"Fuck, Lewie! We look like CIA, man!"

"Nonsense. We don't look like CIA."

"Oh, really?"

"Of course not. Why would CIA have a collection of FBI files in their trunk?"

"FBI files!" I screamed. "What?"

"Hush," said Lewie. "They could have a Tiger Moth of their own up there."

"The fucking FBI files *on Big Jamie's people* are in our trunk, man? Are you serious?"

I pulled up Big Gay Sal's cell number and fired off a message as quickly as I could: *At gate, need help.*

Moments later, the Land Cruiser was granted admission. A guard waved us forward. Lewie gave him a patently false thumbs-up.

"And a happy Halloween to you, sir!" said Lewie. "Table for two, please."

"What the fuck," murmured the guard, looking stunned as he shined his flashlight between us. He reminded me of a 1970s gangster movie villain: Slick black hair atop a high widow's peak. Bushy eyebrows. Flaming nostrils attached to a pug nose that threatened to take over his entire face.

"We are not the droids you're looking for," said Lewie with a playful wave of the hand.

Pug Nose didn't smile.

"You boys lose a bet or something?" He spoke in a thick New York dialect. Apparently local security wasn't cut out for this event.

"Hi," I said. "We're guests of Big Gay... I mean, uh, Sal..."

"Salvatore Aquino," said Lewie.

"We're friends of his," I added.

"Yeah. Sure. And my granny Faye is the pope's summer mistress," countered Pug Nose.

"That's a... different kind of thing to say about your grandma," I said under my breath.

"And the pope," said Lewie.

"Let's see your invite, boys," said Pug Nose. "Where's is at? You know the rule."

"Rule?" I asked.

"Invite?" Lewie asked.

"Did I stutter? *In-vi-ta-tion*. Come on, let's see it."

"Ours was more of a verbal invite," I said. "Can we call Sal? I'm sure he'd vouch for us."

Pug Nose ignored me.

"Hey, Norm!" he called. "Take a look at these mopes!"

The other gentleman with a flashlight stuck his freckled face through the window. He reminded me of the evil doll Chucky. The two men at the booth also started walking towards us. The boys with the automatic rifles perked up.

"Darth Vader and a giant fuck-you finger, huh?"

said Norm. "Do they have an invite?"

"No invite," said Pug Nose. "They say Mr. Aquino invited them."

"Bullshit," grumbled Norm. "Step out of the car, both of you."

"Just let me call Sal," I said. "I'm telling you, he'll vouch for us, man."

"Out of the fucking car now! Slowly! Hands up!" shouted Norm. The AR-15 boys took it as a queue to rush over, weapons raised.

"This is a mild overreaction, eh?" said Lewie, stepping out.

"Who told you about this here tonight?" demanded Pug Nose, while Norm started poking around in the backseat.

"We already told you," said Lewie. "Sal Aquino invited us. We're friends. Us, Sal, Big Jamie, his son Jake..."

"What the hell is *this*?!" exclaimed Norm.

I detected incredulity in his voice. We were facing away from the car and could only guess which incriminating object he unfurled first. I turned around slowly, half expecting to find him staring at his own federal rap sheet. To my temporary relief, he was merely holding the vacuum cups.

"Suction cups," I said. "You know, to climb buildings and stuff. When we're not Darth Vader and a finger, we're Spider-Man and, uh, you know, uh..."

"King Kong," said Lewie.

"Right. Him. That's the monkey."

"Roar," said Lewie, beating his fists against his chest, Kong-like.

"Shut the fuck up," barked Pug Nose. "Who are you guys? Who told you about tonight?"

"Again, man, Sal..." I began.

"Who told you about tonight?"

"Let me call him on his cell, you'll see, let me just..."

"Who the fuck told you about tonight?"

"*I did.*"

In the chaos, we hadn't noticed that Big Gay Sal had pulled up beside us in a golf cart. He had a beer stein in his hand and a cigar in his mouth. The welcoming committee looked ready to shit themselves.

"Mr. Aquino!" said Pug Nose.

"Mr. Aquino!" said Norm.

"Mr. Aquino!" said the men at the booth and the men with the guns.

Sal jumped out of the cart. There was a crazy glint in his eye. I'd seen it once before—the time he put a gun to my head and pulled the trigger five times.

"What's the trouble, man?" he said angrily. "Why are you wasting my time?"

It took me a moment to realize Sal was speaking to Pug Nose, not me. Pug Nose and Norm shared a nervous glance, shuffled their feet.

"Sorry, Mr. Aquino, but they don't have an invite, and you said that..."

"I don't know what I said? Is that what you're telling me, Brooklyn? That I need you to tell me what I said? Is that it?"

"Of course not, sir. We just thought... well, they don't have an invite, and like you said..."

"What did I say, Brooklyn? Tell me! Tell me what I

said, Brooklyn! Tell me. Tell me. Tell me!"

For the next several minutes, Sal raged at the crew, alternating between English and either Spanish or Italian. I never could tell the difference. From what I gleaned, the gist of the tongue lashing was that yes, Sal said that anyone without an invite should be treated like an enemy, but what did he say, Brooklyn, just tell him what he said, Brooklyn, go ahead and say it, he fucking dares you, Brooklyn, just say it. Brooklyn and the crew said nothing, just stared at their feet. Big Gay Sal was gone. There was only Salvatore Aquino, the man with the flying snake tattoo on his skull.

I took the opportunity to wiggle out of the frying plan.

"I hate to interrupt, *amici*," I said. "Or *amigos*, is it? But this middle finger really needs to use the little phalanges' room, if you catch my drift. How about we parlay in the house, Sal? I mean, Mr. Aquino... sir. We're just going to move along, so... well... bye, all. Happy Halloween."

Sal started to respond to me, but then thought better of it and turned back to Pug Nose to scream more dirty words in a Romance language. Lewie and I crept back into the car and inched forward in slow motion. I feared the gunners would grow weary of Sal's tirade and open fire on us all.

"Well," sighed Lewie, "that was close. Good thing the obviously mentally unbalanced professional hitman came to our rescue and couldn't possibly turn on us later for no reason at all."

My fingers were shaking.

"Sal's not the one I'm worried about, Lewie. *You* are."

"Take a look at his sheet in the trunk and you might

change your mind."

"Would you just fucking lay low in there, man? Let's just talk to Big Jamie and go home. No more surprises."

"Sure, partner. That's going to happen."

We were barely out of the car before Sal rolled up in his golf cart.

"Oh... my... Buddha! Did you see the looks on those gay boys' faces? They damn near wet themselves!"

The glint in his eye and the scowl on his face were gone. He was Big Gay Sal again.

"V.C. once made someone do that," said Lewie cheerfully.

"I am loving the costumes, boys! You are some ballsy mother-brothers. Come in the house, I'll give you the tour."

Lewie gave me a smug, told-you-so look. I gave him a second middle finger in return. Sal led us into the house and through a wide marbled foyer into a coat room the size of my apartment. A man in a tuxedo stood at a podium, scribbling in a notepad.

"Caesar will take your phones and things. No cameras, no phones, no troubles. If you have electronics or weapons under those costumes, cough them up."

Obediently, we emptied our pockets and entrusted our phones to Caesar, who made a notation in his ledger and gave us each a ticket stub. Sal led us into the next room, where another tuxedoed gentleman was monitoring a TSA-style full-body scanner. I passed through it without issue. Surprisingly, so did Lewie. Sal then walked us down another corridor to an ornate, arched door. Voices came from the other side.

"Before we go in," Sal said, "sorry if I was a grouch-azoid on the phone. You caught me in hibernation mode. I overreacted when you mentioned that name. He's not a player on any roster we know about."

"Sergio!" I blurted out, perhaps too fervently. "Is he dead, Sal? We have to know, man."

Sal gave me a coy look that I couldn't quite figure out, shrugged, and opened the door.

"Keep your head on," murmured Lewie.

The room was decorated like a rustic log cabin, complete with deer antlers on the walls and fresh logs crackling in a fireplace. If the dozen middle-aged, sil-ver-haired, power-suited men occupying it were dressed up as anything, it was the League of Conservative Voters. They fell silent when they saw Sal. I was relieved to realize we were only passing through.

"No matter how old we get, we stay in our little cliques, don't we?" Sal said once we were out of ear-shot, maybe. "You boys better stay out of the log room. Fucking politicians," he spat. "They're just here for the payouts. Put them in front of a grand jury, though, and do you think they'd call themselves our friends? Who do you think the no-phone rule is really for?"

Sal stopped and turned to me, expecting a response.

"The politicians," I said dutifully.

"Fragile situation with those fuckers." Sal shook his head pensively. "Can't live with them. Can't kill them off. What can you do?"

"Not much," I said.

"Tough call," added Lewie.

Satisfied, Sal began moving again. We stopped at a

sunken library with plush chairs scattered everywhere. A smattering of somber men in suit coats were staring at the floor, not making eye contact. I recognized one as a state senator whose reelection flyers kept showing up in my mailbox. I used them as napkins. Without pizza sauce on the senator's forehead, he looked especially diplomatic.

In the back corner, a brunette in a business suit sat at a desk in front of a large wooden door. She beamed when she saw Sal.

"That's Jamie office over there. I got you a meeting with him," Sal told me. "Let's go talk to Melody and get you checked in."

Like lost puppies in alien territory, we followed Sal to Melody's desk. He introduced me as Jamie's 11:30. Melody handed me a pager, the kind that vibrates and flashes at a restaurant when your table is ready.

"We'll page you fifteen minutes before your meeting, Mr. Almond," she said.

"Ummm," I said.

"You wanted a meeting with Jamie, right?" said Sal. "I got you one."

"Thirty minutes with Mr. Kennedy is a hot commodity in this town," said Melody, flashing a pearly smile.

"So, a modicum of appreciation for your buddy Sal here wouldn't be out of line," said Sal.

"Or you could just stand there and give him the middle finger," said Melody.

"Oh. Uh, yeah, thanks, Sal."

Lewie was fixated on Melody.

"Has anyone ever told you that you should be a tooth model?" he asked her.

"Who says that?" I said.

"Save it for the girls downstairs, Darth," Sal said.

We followed him past more sitting rooms and bed-rooms than any residence for one should rightfully boast. Finally, we turned a corner and came to a spiral staircase. The upstairs were blocked off by a velvet rope. A man stood guard behind it, presumably to prevent anyone who didn't respect the velvet rope's authority from reaching the mysterious third level.

"Hey, Miguel. Having fun up here away from all the titties?" teased Sal.

"Nah, bro," said the man.

"Miguel here has a pussy problem," said Sal. "He can't get anything done if he's in the same room with it. So, we have to keep him up here by his lonesome. Isn't that right, Miguel?"

"Nah, man. Come on, Sal."

I realized that the man behind the rope was Miguel Zuman, the tattooed Latino who drove Sal and me to Trixie's and later guarded Lewie's hospital room. Until Lewie choked him out with his drip feed tubes, that is.

A plan—albeit an ill-advised, unnecessary one—took form in my head. I snuck a peek at Lewie, as if to send him a telepathic message, but his attentions were else-where. He was staring at the room to our left, a mostly empty space with paintings—including a few Jake Ken-nedy originals—leaning against the walls. But it wasn't the artwork that caught his eye. It was the floor-to-ceil-ing window featuring a view of the Mississippi River and soon, if Lewie had his way, the silhouette of a two-hundred-and-forty-pound, upward-bound Darth Vader.

"That room over there," said Lewie, unable to help himself. "Is that, like part of the party?"

"It's going to be Jamie's private art museum," said Sal. "Second biggest private collection in the Midwest. Are you a collector?"

"Of course he isn't. He's just a nosy Rosy," I said, "who has no business going anywhere near that room. Either side of it. Right, Lewie?"

"Me? Oh, no. Of course not," said Lewie. "What an odd thing to say." I could practically see him winking under his mask.

"Down we go, then," said Sal. "Have fun, Miguel."

We descended the stairs, walked down a long hall-way, and came to a door with a neon stripper clock, like the one at Trixie's, hanging above it. The time was a physiologically impossible ten o'clock. Sal paused before going inside.

"Two ground rules, gentlemen," he said. "One, no tipping. Everything's on the house. Yes, *everything*. And two, everything and everyone that happens here, stays here. It sounds cliché, but we mean it. Agreed?"

We nodded our heads. Sal opened the door. Music and strobe lights spilled out. Lewie went in. Sal stepped in front of me.

"Oh, and one last thing, V.C.?" he said.

"Yeah?" I said.

He leaned in close. The crazy eye glint was back. I smelled Doberman drool.

"That motherfucker Sergio was a dead man before he left your apartment."

Chapter 19

Excerpt from the pilfered journal of Patio Williams, CFO of RW Enterprises, younger brother of Big Jamie's business partner Radio Williams.

I CALLED BIG JAMIE KENNEDY AND TOLD HIS VOICE recorder everything. And then I walked into the FBI and told them everything too. Nobody gave a shit, which makes me more paranoid than ever. What if the FBI people are Radio's people, or Jamie's, or both?

298 pages ago Dr. Chaudhary told me to write down my fears in this notebook and together with enough SSRIs to give me brain zaps when I don't take them for a day my fears will disappear. Maybe Dr. Chaudhary thought with two pages left in my journal I would be living in Buffalo Grove with a kid and a dog and a wife in a neighborhood where white kids ride on Disney bikes on the sidewalk and we have chili in a big pot in the driveway on Halloween and the neighbors give me a beer and crack jokes, "hey patio, why are we doing this in the driveway, not the patio?" and I'd just smile and think to myself how far that I've come, how just 298 pages ago I was a dirty figurehead in my

brother's criminal drug + sex empire and I woke up in the morning with my fingers shaking and fell asleep at night with a brain full of Klonopin and Benadryl even though I don't have allergies. But surprise, Dr. Chaudhary was wrong and all that's changed is nothing, except maybe that I started this journal worried about nothing and for no reason and I'm ending it worried about everything and for excellent reason.

Why aren't I in handcuffs, or witness protection, or dead yet? If only I could talk to the Delgado brothers and convince them it wasn't me, maybe I'd still have a chance to keep on living my life of jitters and dread.

People are starting to notice that Radio is MIA. Someone named Larry from Communications department according to the badge around his neck came in and asked me if it's OK to "renew the same phones as last time." I said "phones? What phones?" and he said "the phones we listen into" and I said "oh, those phones? That's fine." I didn't like the look on his face as he walked away.

I believe I have said too much and I need to follow in my brother's footsteps and disappear.

Chapter 20

Sal walked away before I had a chance to respond. I got the feeling the door wasn't exactly open for feedback on the subject, anyway.

Shocked, I sidled up to the bar to drink sense of things. But then I took a deep breath, and the taste of recycled whiskey scourged my throat. When the muscle head bartender took my drink order, I opted for club soda only.

I needed to talk to Lewie, to share Sal's big reveal and plot our next move, or just go home. My eyes scanned the room. It was respectably full but not overly crowded. Exotic dancers shook their assets on four stages while Nelly rapped timelessly about the elevated temperature in here. On the couch where my face was violated by the Dobermans, a girl was dry humping a man in a cowboy hat. I recognized her as Kimber, the one whose tryout I witnessed at Trixie's. Nice to see she was climbing the corporate ladder.

Beside the bar, there was a large, decorative fountain, the type you'd expect to see chocolate pouring out of at a wedding reception. Instead, a fine white powder trickled down the sides. Two ladies and a former NFL player with a reputation as a party animal approached it. He produced three rolled-up bills, and southward their nostrils sailed. Moments later, they disappeared into a curtained-off section in the corner. Hookers and cocaine. I was beginning to understand the presence of the AR-15s.

A young lady wearing devil horns and nothing else appeared with a tray of hors d'oeuvres. Looked like Italian pinwheels.

"Naked girl salami?" she said in broken English.

What do you say to that? I smiled but didn't partake.

I spotted Lewie. He was center stage, playing the role of gyration station for a resourceful stripper who'd just upgraded from pole to Darth. She was wearing his helmet. He was wearing a goofy grin that made it clear it would take more than a murder confession to drag him away.

Focus, I told myself. I peered into my club soda for answers. Was the case solved? Sergio tried to kill me. Sergio killed Jake instead. Jake's father killed Sergio. Circle of life. Everybody wins. Except for Jake. And Sergio. And, of course, the mystery third body lying in Calvary Cemetery under Jake Kennedy's headstone.

"Fuck the third body. What happened to Jake's body?" I mumbled. Then I remembered the shovel that Sal had the first time I saw him, and it occurred to me that my friend might be buried on this very property. Big Jamie tasked his consigliere to bury Jake's corpse while he was off scouting talent at the titty bar. What a prince. He didn't bother to give his son a proper burial. I remembered how he cried mock tears when we talked about Jake's death, and a shot of 151-proof rage coursed through my veins. Jake deserved better. We needed to leave.

I started walking towards the stage to claim Lewie, but I didn't get far before someone stepped in my path. He had a martini in his hand and a bosomy blond on his arm. The smell of cigarettes and cheap cologne divulged his identity before I saw his face.

"Nice costume, shitbag," the always cordial detective Beerman greeted me.

"Detective," I said. I tried to walk around him, but he blocked me off.

"Lieutenant, actually."

"Oh, yeah? I heard you retired."

"Got a new gig." He raised his eyebrows and nodded at the restaurant pager in my hand. "Full-time."

"Congratulations," I said, hoping to end the conversation. "I hear the 401k is great."

"You're a hard man to find, Mr. Almond."

"Yeah, I'm really not. If you'll excuse me, though..."

"Hold up. This will only take a minute of your time, Mr. Big Stuff."

Beerman laughed at his own cleverness. Mr. Big Stuff.

"OK..."

"You're a hard man to find," he repeated. "I even stopped by your house."

"You could have called me."

"Now there's an idea."

He peered at me with amused eyes and a sideways

grin, like he knew something I didn't, or thought we were covert conspirators whose words were flush with double meaning.

"What can I do for you, lieutenant?" I asked, annoyed.

Beerman turned to his date, or whoever she was. "Go powder your nose, sweetheart." Dutifully, she started towards the fountain. Beerman slapped my back like we were old chums. "I've always wanted to tell a broad that."

"What the fuck do you want from me, man?"

"Whoa, whoa, whoa. Calm down, Almond. You and me, we're on the same team. We're friends now, right?"

"Good to know." I tried to maneuver around him, but he cut me off again.

"Listen to me, shitbag." His eyes hardened. The levity in his voice vanished. "Mr. Kennedy is going to give you something tonight. And I want you know it was my idea. *Mine.*"

His lips curled into a thin smile. I remembered how he went ape shit at the police station when I wrote the name Sergio, perceiving it as a threat. Was he returning the favor? What did Big Jamie plan to give me?

"This is all just a misunderstanding. You see…"

"Zip it, shitbag. Here's how it goes: I picked you up that night because you were acting like a shitbag drunk and causing trouble all over town. You don't know me from the president's dick. You…"

"Huh?"

"… couldn't pick me out of a motherfucking lineup, that's how little you remember. You don't know me, you don't know Mr. Kennedy, you don't know Mr. Aquino. You don't know…"

"This is all a misunderstanding," I said. "Let me explain…"

"Explain? No, no. I've met master manipulators like you before, Almond. I know how you roll, as you hipsters say."

"This again."

"Playing little mind games, spreading rumors, lies. It's all a game to you, isn't it, Almond?"

"Game? I honestly don't know what you're talking about, Beerman. I don't know shit. And I don't care, man. Fuck off, all right?"

My nemesis stared me down, nostrils flaring. Slowly, another thin smile formed on his puffy red face.

"That," he said, "is exactly what I wanted to hear, Almond."

Satisfied, the former SLPD detective and current lieutenant in Big Jamie's criminal empire sauntered away.

Two young ladies took his place before I could take another step. One was short and brunette, the other tall and blonde. The brunette was smiling, the blonde not so much.

"*Looook*, the *fiiiinger* has a *paaaager*. He must be *soooo* important," said the blonde in a thick, eastern European accent, holding onto her vowels like she didn't want to set them free. Her eyes were cold and heavy, her cheekbones high. She reminded me of the singer Nico.

"Oh, be nice, Nadezda," chirped the brunette, bubbly as can be. "Would you like me to sit on your lap?" she asked me. "I promise I'll bounce up and down."

"I'm standing," I said, feeling awkward.

"Ignore her," said Nadezda. "Savannah is so dumb

you could screw her and she wouldn't know it."

"That dumb?" I said.

"American girls are horrible. They are either puritans or whores."

"At least we don't have armpit hair!" objected Savannah.

"You are thinking of the French, darling. See? See?" Nadezda raised her arms to reveal two hairless pits.

"Aren't you just miss *purrrrfect*," said Savannah mockingly.

"I am not," said Nadezda, "but I am not a hairy mongrel, either."

Savannah stuck out her tongue. I sensed a sisterly affection between the two, despite the bickering.

Savannah turned to me. "Are you having fun tonight?" she said. "Do you *want* to have fun tonight?"

Nadezda rolled her eyes.

"Do you girls, like, work here?" I asked, dumbly.

"We are supposed to find the men with the pagers and drool on them like they matter."

"Ignore Nadezda," said Savannah. "She's just bitchy because her lover boy Miguel isn't allowed in here anymore."

"Fuck *yoooo*."

"Miguel?" I said. "The driver... guard... guy who works for Jamie, you mean? Mexican dude with the neck tats?"

"What about him? You know him?"

"Of course I do."

"Nadezda's pissy because she agreed to work tonight just to see him, and now she can't. You know what I think?"

"What do you think?"

"I think," she said in a teasing, singsong voice, "that Nadezda's in love."

"Fuck *yooooo*," repeated Nadezda.

Lewie must have been rubbing off on me, because I felt compelled, in light of this new info, to follow through with the suicidal plan that popped into my head when I first saw Miguel. But then my pager flashed and vibrated, putting my scheme on hold. My table was ready.

Melody, the one who issued me the pager that made me so popular, appeared beside me.

"Mr. Kennedy is running ahead of schedule," she said. "He will see you now."

She offered me her arm. People stared as we passed. Evidently, they'd never seen a business professional escort a giant middle finger out of a seedy suburban strip/sex club. Lewie and his stripper friend, I noted, were no longer on stage. We went up the stairs, past the unhappy Miguel, and through the house. Melody held my arm tight, making me feel as much like a prisoner as a guest. I ran through the litany of things that Big Jamie may give me: A bullet in the ear. A new car. A black eye. A severed horse head. An Imo's Pizza gift card. Could be anything.

The politicos had slithered away, leaving the library unmanned. Herman's Hermits' "Something Tells Me I'm into Something Good" played on the overhead. Peter Noone was more optimistic than me.

"Could you do me a favor?" I asked Melody just before she opened the door to the office. "Help me out of this costume? I'd rather not see Mr. Kennedy looking like a..."

"Jackass?"

Interesting word choice. Not for the first time that minute, I thought about Kalista.

"Exactly."

She unzipped me from the back and helped pull the bulky getup over my head. Then she fixed my collar and even brushed off my wrinkly shirt.

"There's something about you. You're different than the other girls here, aren't you, Miss Melody?"

"Yes, Mr. Almond. I have clothes." She opened the door and stepped aside with a toothy grin. Lewie was right. Tooth model all the way.

The door swung shut behind her with an ominous, echoing boom. The air was thick with the scents of rich mahogany and cigar smoke. Big Jamie stood at a credenza behind a large desk, pouring drinks from a decanter. He was wearing a coat and tie and his few remaining wisps of hair were combed neatly across his vanishing hairline. He looked shockingly unhip, like a tax adjuster or a funeral director—nothing like the slapstick pimp I sat beside at Trixie's.

"V.C. Almond," he said flatly. "Sit, please." He handed me a drink. I guess I was off the wagon. "Your friend tried to visit you the other day, but you weren't home."

I responded with a noncommittal grunt. Joe Beerman wasn't my friend, and I didn't want to talk about him.

Big Jamie took a seat across from me. His tired, baggy eyes came to a rest on a dog-eared Polaroid picture on the desktop. He gazed at it for several seconds while I waited in awkward silence.

"She's a beauty, ain't she?" he said at last, his voice prickly and hoarse.

He slid the photo across the desk. A lanky young man and a short-haired Latina with a bulging, pregnant belly grinned up at me. It took me a moment to recognize the beaming, bushy-haired man as Big Jamie.

"Is she..."

"Your friend's *muthah*." His voice oozed melancholia. "My wife. Suelo."

"She's beautiful."

"Was beautiful. She *was* beautiful."

I squirmed in my seat. "I'm sorry to hear that."

"Thirty-eight years ago today, she stepped into an empty *elevatah* shaft. Can you believe that? That's how witnesses die in *mobstah* films. And it was an honest to God accident."

"I'm sorry," I said again.

"Everyone thought I did it, of course. Up-and-coming *playah* gets tired of the nagging wife, wants to stick his *peckah* in half the city, of course he did it, right? Besides, who the fuck falls down *elevatuh* shafts? Of course I did it, right?"

"Right," I agreed.

Big Jamie shook his head sadly. "I *wondah* how things would be if Suelo lived. Jake would have stuck around, I bet. I just *nevah* knew how to relate to the boy. *Nevah* really even tried too *hahd*, did I?"

"No?"

"People ask me why I'm still in the Midwest. 'Isn't Miami *bettah* for a guy like you?' they say. 'Or L.A.? New *Yahk*? Vegas?' You know what I tell them?"

I shook my head. Why was he telling me this?

"I tell them that my wife's spirit lives in my lonely whorehouse on the hill. And if I move, I'm afraid she won't go with me. True story. And true story."

Blindsided by the subject matter and oddly moved by Jamie's words, I said nothing.

"She loved this house. She was always on the move, always busy, *nevah* at rest unless she was doing something. Suelo used to say that the surroundings here—the highway, the bridge, the *rivah*—made you feel like the house was moving, too. It put her at peace. Does that make sense?"

The image I had of Big Jamie as a cartoonish, ass-grabbing horn dog was crumbling.

"Yes, it does," I said.

"You know how we got to the Midwest? I was an eighteen-year-old kid working as a bellhop at a Holiday Inn in Acton, Mass. Suelo was a maid, ten years my senior. I fell in love with her before she knew my name. I hounded her for months for a date. She got a job *offah* to manage the midnight housekeeping shift a thousand miles away, here in St. Louis. In those days, that was the best a woman could do. I followed her like a lost puppy. Penniless, halfway across the country. My *fathah* didn't approve. Geno Napolitano never liked Mexicans, Japs, kikes, blacks, anyone. He had a fifty-eight-inch chest with the words *Il Duce* tattooed across it. Benito Mussolini, 'the *leadah*.' He said to me, 'James, if you even think about moving to a cow town with a spic maid, you have my blessing. But don't *evah* come back. And change your name, because you are no longer a Napolitano.' It was a no-*brainah*. The next day, I walked to the *govahment* building on Commonwealth Avenue and asked the first bureaucrat I saw how to legally change my name."

Big Jamie took a long sip of his drink. For the first time, his eyes met mine.

"Google me," he said. "That's not the story you'll read."

"No?"

"You'll read this kind of crap." He opened a drawer and pulled out an old copy of the *St. Louis Punk-Disgrace.* "You familiar with this shit rag? You want a laugh? Read this *gahbage*. Actually, read it later. Take it with you. My gift. Bunch of jive-talking mopes who don't know a thing."

I obliged and took it off his hands. Was this the mysterious gift that Beerman told me about? Why?

"That *papah* damn near ruined me. 'Live *lahge* and lay low.' That was my motto. You know who I shared it with? Nobody. That stupid *ahticle* changed everything."

"Sorry to hear that."

"My *fatha* was a *cahd*-carrying Fascist. He didn't hide it. He used to tell me, 'In America, you can get away with anything.' Which is bullshit. Truth is, in *the world*, you can get away with anything. It's just a *mattah* of for how long."

Deep thoughts with Jamie Kennedy. What the fuck was this?

"Do you *remembah* the first time you met me, V.C.?"

"Do *you?*" I said, stunned. Last time we spoke, I wasn't sure the man knew my name.

"Damn near twenty years ago. You and my son came

to the Cicada Club to drink with the big boys. You kids couldn't hold your *liquah* worth a shit."

"You dragged a man out by his ear. You told the bouncer to..."

"Go play piñata with his skull."

"Jesus. You remember that."

"Of course I do. The boy's name was Danny Dyer. He was one of my cooks. I'd just found out he beat his girlfriend's face like a goddamn drum that morning. She used to be one of mine—Stacee, with two e's, danced as Raven. Nice kid. Shitty taste in men, but don't they all?"

"I don't know. With all due respect, sir – why are you telling me all this?"

Big Jamie poured himself a hefty refill. "I've always said that the best drinks are like the best women. Simple and ample." He drank half the glass in one gulp. "Teasing, Suelo, if you're listening, baby."

All around us, I thought, the good people of St. Louis are crawling under their covers, oblivious to the weirdness transpiring at the mansion on the hill. My own loud, lonely bed never felt more welcoming or distant.

"I'm telling you this, V.C., because I'm feeling reflective. And for the first time tonight, I'm not glad-handing or wrist-twisting a money-grubbing *impostah*. And because Jake told me you could be trusted. And mostly, I'm telling you this because I want you to understand that I do have a moral compass, despite anything you may have heard."

"OK..."

"And that's why I've decided that I ain't going to kill you."

"Ummmm... what?"

"By rights, I should. You have a big mouth."

"This is a misunderstanding."

"You didn't think I'd find out about your ex-cop sidekick grilling every friend or acquaintance my son *evah* had? Stirring up *rumahs*, raising doubts about the way he died?"

"Look, sir..."

If Big Jamie was upset, he was doing a masterful job hiding it. "You know too much," he said calmly. "Plain and simple. You have dirt on people whose names you shouldn't know. And you have nothing to *offah* in return. Sure, you had a decent idea once, but it fizzled..."

"I did?"

"You know the *cornahstone* of a good relationship? Reciprocity. I give you something, you give me something in return. What can you give me, V.C.?"

"What do you want?" I said, confused.

"My son did you a *favah*, didn't he?"

"I'm sorry. What?"

"Sergio Sebastian Mendoza."

Hearing the dead man's name gave me chills.

"He wasn't *aftah* Jake, right? Your name and address were in his pocket. He was looking for you. He was in your *apahtment*, right? He wanted you dead, not Jake, right? Not me, right?"

"Right."

"Which makes you indebted to this family, are you not?"

"Sure," I said, not liking where this was going.

"And it would take more than a federal subpoena,

or something along those lines, to make you throw the Kennedy clan *undah* the bus, right? Considering what we've done for you?"

"What? Listen, sir—I don't know what Beerman told you, but I'm not a threat. I don't know a thing about what happened to Jake. I'm in the dark here. I wouldn't say anything to anyone. What would I even say?"

Big Jamie smiled and nodded approvingly. "Good boy. You're not an asshole, are you, V.C.?"

"What? I don't think so."

"And you're not an idiot, are you?"

"Not entirely."

"I can stand idiots. And I can stand assholes. But idiotic assholes? Fuck them. They're everywhere these days. Politics. Business. *Govahment.* The *cornah.* Running the free world. The last time an idiotic asshole crossed my path, I painted my walls red with his blood. Literally."

I was tempted to ask if he then staged a funeral for him and called him Jake. "Smart move," I said instead.

"Jake says you can be trusted." He held up one finger. "You're in our debt already." Two fingers. "You're not an idiotic asshole." Three fingers. "Three valid reasons not to kill you."

"Thank you," I said, unsure how to respond.

"But you know too much." One finger. "You have nothing to *offah* in return." Two fingers. "You have a big mouth." Three fingers. "Three valid reasons to kill you."

"This is a conundrum."

"But I have a moral compass."

"I see."

"And I suspect there's a more, shall we say, *American* solution to all this."

Big Jamie reached under his desk. My heart skipped a beat.

He slid a black leather duffel bag across the desk.

"What..." I began.

"Hush," said Big Jamie.

Slowly, one centimeter at a time, I unzipped it. I gasped at what I saw. The bag was stuffed to the brim with bundles of clean, crisp, one hundred-dollar bills.

"I can't..."

"Hush."

"Look, Mr. Kennedy, I apprec..."

"Hush."

"OK, I get it, but..."

"Hush."

"I wasn't threatening..."

"Hush."

"You don't have to…"

"Hush." With a flick of the hand, he dismissed me. "Hush, little birdie. All you have to do is hush."

Before I closed the door, I took a final look at Big Jamie Kennedy. He was slumped in his chair, tie loosened, gazing at a snapshot of happier days, looking utterly exhausted under the weight of the world and his moral compass. I haven't seen him since.

———————

The library was empty and silent. Melody was gone,

Peter Noone, too. The former had taped a note to the back of the door:

Mr. Almond—call me if you need an escort downstairs ☺

A double entendre? Tempting, but I set off for the basement solo, leaving the middle finger to rot on the floor. Then I got lost in the interminable maze of hallways and was ready to find a phone to call Melody when I turned a corner and came face-to-face with Miguel and the stairway. Miguel was still wearing his grumpy face.

Common sense and instinct both told me to ignore him. I listened to neither.

"You're Miguel?"

He nodded, barely.

"Nadezda's your girl, right?"

He took a step towards me. "What about her, holmes?"

"You want to see her tonight? Right now? I can make it happen."

He stopped scowling, but only for a moment. "Nah, man. I'm working. Step off, *chómpiras.*"

"You have to guard the stairway, right? Make sure nobody goes up there?"

Another minimal nod.

"Does a lot of foot traffic pass through here?"

A minimal shake of the head.

"Who's the last person who came by?"

"You and Mel, holmes. People gonna come and go, they use the door down there. Mr. Kennedy got an elevator in his office goes straight down. This some pointless shit, man, straight *punishment*. For nothing."

"I want to help you. Wait here."

As if he had a choice.

"I'm working, holmes. Shit ain't right, but it's work. Stay away, you hear me?"

Downstairs, Lewie was MIA. His stripper friend was back on stage, sans helmet. I circled the room, feeling more conspicuous with my hush money that I had with the silly finger costume. Security, I noted, was nonexistent. Once inside, you could insufflate and fornicate at will, evidently. This boded well for what I had in mind. But where the hell was Lewie?

I found Nadezda and Savannah sitting at the bar, talking to a portly comedian/actor I recognized from television.

"Hey," I said. "Aren't you..."

"Jon Hamm," he said.

He wasn't.

Savannah was tickled pink. "He's too funny! Isn't he too funny?"

"He is too funny. He has me in the stiches," deadpanned Nadezda, unamused.

"Sorry to interrupt, but I need you." I took Nadezda by the arm. "Now."

The actor whispered in Savannah's ear. I didn't hear him, but evidently Nadezda did.

"Fuck *yoooo*," she said. "You haven't made a funny movie since..."

"Tell him he sucks later, dear," I said, pulling her away. "Miguel is waiting. Quick. Clock's ticking!"

I ushered Nadezda up the stairs, careful to make

sure nobody who looked like they gave a damn was watching. Miguel jumped in surprise when he saw her and ran his fingers through his hair to fix an imaginary cowlick. He'd been transformed into a love-struck schoolboy.

"Look, bro," he said weakly, "I told you, holmes..."

Nadezda shut him up by inserting her tongue deep in his throat.

"Not here!" I said. "Hurry! I'll guard the stairs. Be back in twenty minutes! Go!"

"Come with me, Miggy," Nadezda pleaded.

"Go with her, Miggy," I said.

"Wait, baby," said Miguel. "How do we know this ain't a trap? Or a test, you know?" He looked at me. "Why you doing this, holmes?"

"Because I believe in you crazy kids. And I owe you for what my buddy did to you at the hospital."

Nadezda's eyes grew wide with concern.

"What did his buddy do to you, Miggy? Baby? What happened? Tell me!"

"He sucker-punched him," I said. "Miggy here could have killed him for it, but he didn't. We owe him."

Miguel looked at me with grateful eyes.

"It's a'ight, holmes. We even now."

"Great. Now go! Just don't go..."

They hurried up the stairs, hand in hand.

"... upstairs."

Shit. Hopefully they weren't blood fetishists. If they picked the room where Jake, or whoever it was, got killed, then things could get weird. They slammed a door. I darted upstairs. Giggling came from my right, so I took a left. Bedrooms and sitting rooms lined both sides of the hallway. How many beds did one man need? It didn't occur to me until much later that this really was a brothel and Big Jamie wasn't being facetious when he said he lived in a whorehouse.

I half-sprinted down the hall, poking my head into each room for a split second, hoping to discover a wall painted the color of asshole-idiot blood. No luck. The first ten or twelve rooms revealed nothing more suspicious than the occasional bondage chamber. But then I reached the end of the hallway, veered right, and walked through an arched doorway into a living space that stopped me dead in my tracks.

A rainbow coalition of tropical fish swam in a crystal-clear aquarium under my feet. A school of white and yellow groupers that Google later identified as Neptunes—starting price, six grand—took an immediate interest in the soles of my shoes. An elaborate sectional sofa zigzagged around the room. A giant-screen television occupied an entire wall. In the far corner, the Mississippi River rolled along outside an elegant bow window. Bathed in the brightness of innumerable flood lights, it might have been a Bora Bora lagoon.

The most remarkable feature, though, was the back wall—specifically its fascinating shade of red, somewhere on the color scheme between carmine and crimson. I believe it was referred to as the blood of man.

I stood there frozen for several seconds, debating my next move. Someone had definitely gone to see Elvis in here. The blood splattered on the wall, the ceiling, and the casing of the bow window erased any doubt that a real human was buried in Jake's coffin. But what now?

Slowly, with my heart doing its best Buddy Rich, I moved deeper into the room. I looked under the couch cushions, through a couple closets, even inside the refrigerator. I opened the TV stands, hoping that alongside wires and adapters I'd find a concise note explaining who did what to whom and why. All the while, my inner rationalist urged me to abandon ship. A big part of me felt like a minority at a Ted Nugent concert—facing a mountain of risk, and without much hope for meaningful reward.

I was on the verge of calling it quits and sneaking off to inspect my ill-gotten, newfound fortune when two things happened simultaneously:

Something on the windowsill caught my eye. It looked like a badge of some sort, in a plastic lanyard.

Something on the other side of the window caught my ear. It looked like a man of some sort, in a Darth Vader outfit, suction cups attached to his wrists, legs hanging free. He was knocking his helmeted head against the window to get my attention. There was nothing to break his fall but the cold, hard ground fifty feet below.

"Lewie! Are you fucking suicidal?"

I ran to the window and tried to force it open, but it was stuck.

"Open the window, V!"

"I'm trying!"

I pulled and pulled, but it still refused to budge.

"Come on, man! Neanderthal man could figure this out faster."

"Isn't him be smart!"

Finally, it lurched open. Lewie maneuvered into position and made a desperate lunge for my outstretched arms. He fell through the open window and toppled to the hard glass floor, taking me with him. So much for keeping a quiet profile.

"Hey!" he exclaimed, climbing to his feet, breathing heavy. "There's a bloody wall! Nice timing, partner! Cool fish! Nice TV! Looks like I'm bleeding a little bit myself. I wonder where that's coming from. It's slicker than I thought it would be out there. What's in the bag?"

"What are you doing here?" My heart had gone from Buddy Rich to Lars Ulrich. "Are you crazy?"

"Same thing as you. Investigating the third floor. And mildly, perhaps."

"How exactly aren't you dead? How did nobody see you?"

He held out a hand to help me to my feet. Ever since Jake died, I thought to myself, my friends and I have spent an inordinate amount of time on the ground and bleeding.

"Turns out security's pretty lax once you make it through the gate. Funny considering..."

"What was your plan to get inside if I wasn't here to open the window?!"

"Oh, I figured something would come to me when I got up here. No biggie."

Lewie ran his finger over the bloodstains on the wall.

"What do you think? Art macabre or just macabre?"

"I don't know what that means. Let's get out of here, Lewie. Half the house probably heard us."

"Out? We just got here. What's the rush?"

"What's the rush? Seriously? The rush is that ... what is this?"

I realized that the badge I saw out of the corner of my eye on the windowsill was under my feet. Evidently it was displaced when we crash landed. I picked it up. A middle-aged Afro-Latino with cornrows and beaucoup bling stared back at me. The badge identified him as Radio Williams, CEO, R. W. Enterprises.

"This is definitely the room where Jake version one croaked," said Lewie. "I can feel it. Why wouldn't Jamie clean out the evidence, though? He made sure Seth Rogen disinfected your place in less time than it takes Kun-Woo's soup to give you... damn, what's that stomach illness? I thought I had a good one. What's it called?"

"Dysentery," I mumbled, peering at the badge. For some reason, the name Radio rang a bell.

"No, that's not it. But it'll work. Man, I'm out of breath. That was a rough climb, partner. Maybe he's keeping the blood as, like, a trophy? Maybe he's damn proud of what went down in this room, you think?"

"Dunno."

Something clicked in my brain. A cryptic message I overheard Big Jamie say into the phone at Trixie's: *"The radio is about to get turned off. And be careful or the patio may get torn down, too."*

I looked at the wall, then the badge, then the wall again. Looked like a match to me.

"You ever hear of Radio Williams, Lewie? R. W. Enterprises?"

"What did you say?!" Lewie rushed over and ripped

the badge from my hands. The name had clearly struck a nerve. "Where did you get *this*?!"

"It was on the windowsill. You know him?"

"Know him? Know him? Are you kidding me? Fuck!"

"Calm down. Who is he? Who's Radio Williams?"

"A game changer. Fuck, dude! Fuck fuck double fuck! Infinity fuck!"

Lewie stuffed the suction cups under his cape and made a beeline for the door.

"Fly, you fool!" he called.

"Wrong character, Lewie."

Nevertheless, we flew down the stairs. To avoid raising suspicions, I waited impatiently for the lovebirds to return, then vanished as soon as they appeared at the top of the stairway. Lewie and I collected our personal items from Caesar and walked outside briskly with our heads down.

The retaining wall behind the parking lot was topped with rows of potted mums in full bloom. I checked to make sure no eyeballs were on us. The coast was clear. I climbed on the trunk of Lewie's car and snatched one. Lewie gave me a curious look.

"Klepto?" he said.

"Ask later."

Lewie said nothing as we crept down the driveway, inched past the idiotic guards, and pulled onto the street. Every minute or so, he chortled quietly, shook his head, knit his brow. My own head was spinning. We stopped at a gas station, where Lewie fished a paper and pen from the backseat and scribbled a note: *Turn off your phone. Take out the battery. Put it in the trunk.*

"OK..."

When I returned to the front seat, Lewie was smoking a cigarette and staring into space.

"Peso for your thoughts, man?" I said. "Who's Radio Williams? What the fuck is going on?"

"Partner," he said slowly, "I believe our lives are about to get interesting."

Chapter 21

I WAS BACK AT THE ABANDONED TRAIN STATION, COLD AND naked, waiting for a ride that everybody knew wasn't coming. Kalista sat at the end of the bench, pretending not to see me. She was wearing a hat with the initials KLC on it. A bit vain, but whatever.

"Kalista Lynn Chestnut!" I called.

She turned away.

Gummy Jack nuzzled up to me, unbothered by my nakedness.

"I don't remember where I was when they killed Kennedy," he slobbered in my ear.

Someone else was beside me. A man with a sombrero.

"You're alive?" I cried. "You're alive!"

"Don't be silly," he said.

A robot with a transistor radio for a body rolled up to us. Slowly, it raised a giant war hammer. I dove out of the way as the hammer came down. When I looked up, the robot was gone and the man with the sombrero was lying in a puddle of blood.

I awoke from the dream trembling and screaming.

Someone was knocking frantically on my door.

"V.C.! Are you all right? What's going on?" shouted Hazim.

I opened the door and tried to look at ease.

"Howdy, neighbor," I said.

"Are you OK?! What's going on?"

"Oh, not much. Just, you know, waking up."

"With a blood-curdling scream?"

"Is that, like, unusual where you come from?"

"Ever since the war ended. Were you dreaming?"

"I can't remember," I lied. "Hey, as long as you're here..." I took the pilfered yellow mum from the coffee table and placed it in his arms. "Can I entrust my mum to you for a day or two? Or forever maybe? Lewie and I are taking a trip to Chicago."

"Of course. What's in Chicago?"

"It's more a question of what's *not* in Chicago."

"OK. What's not in Chicago?"

I felt like I was wearing a tinfoil hat, but I couldn't take any chances. Before answering him, I turned off my phone and stuffed it under a cushion.

"Unless I'm very wrong," I said, "a living man named Radio Williams."

———————

Woefully lacking in the luggage department, I stuffed my necessities into the only durable bag I could find— the one Big Jamie gave me. When the band took the stage at Camilla's, 720,000 dollars would be stacked in neat piles eight feet above them, under my bed. An additional twenty grand had already gone to Lewie. Ten stayed in the bag to cover food, gas, and up to one and a half nights at the Peninsula Hotel in Chicago.

Lewie was running late, as usual. For once, I couldn't blame him. After last night, even the gamest pseudo P.I. would have difficulty dragging his ass out of bed before the crack of ten. So instead of calling him and interrupting his slumber, I fired up a pot of coffee and sent Kalista a text:

Big news. Let's meet up!

I waited a few minutes for a response that I knew wasn't coming—did the absent train in my dream represent our relationship?—then lay on the bed and took some deep breaths. It was important, I felt, to start this venture with a good, clean head for once.

On the way home from Big Jamie's party, Lewie told me about the man whose bloody badge we found on the windowsill. First, though, he expressed disbelief that I'd never heard of him.

"What do you mean, who's Radio Williams? How have you never heard of Radio Williams? You call yourself a private detective, yet…"

"But I don't."

"… you don't know the names of the biggest players in the criminal underworld? For shame, partner. For shame."

"Whatever. What kind of name is Radio? Were his parents Top Forty junkies?"

"His mother was a regular junkie. His father was a drug dealer, and a good one. If you bought heroin in the State Street Corridor in the 1960s, there's a seventy-five percent chance you were supporting Mickey Mouse Williams."

"I didn't."

"Radio was his son."

"I get that."

"You're familiar with the Bronzeville turf war between the Trumbull Triggers and the Blood Avenue Babies, right?"

"Who isn't?"

Lewie didn't catch my sarcasm.

"That was Radio," he said. "*All* Radio."

"So, he's a drug dealer in Chicago."

"No, sir. He's *the* drug *kingpin* in Chicago."

"What's his connection to Jamie? Or Jake?"

"Jamie was Radio's mentor. It's all in the files. They own, or owned, some businesses together, shared the same suppliers, ran in the same circles. Jamie turned Radio into a businessman. They were tight, supposedly. Maybe they had a falling out, eh?"

"And why is my cell phone in the trunk?"

"Radio Williams has more roving bugs than the NSA and Kremlin combined. Explains why so many of his enemies have found themselves in unexpected, comprising situations over the..."

"What's a roving bug?"

Lewie guffawed violently.

"What's a roving bug?! We need to get you some proper training, don't we? A roving bug, V.C., is a covert listening device. It allows you to activate a cell phone's microphone and listen to conversations taking place *near* it, even if the person's not actually *on* it. Also allows..."

"Holy fuck." I remembered Big Jamie's cryptic

315

message to me at Trixie's: *"Keep a hundred feet from your phone if you feel the need to talk business. If you know what I mean."*

"And you think Radio has a roving bug on me?" I said.

"You, me, Bobby, Tony, Da'Quan, all of us maybe. Or none of us. Assuming those three nimrods from the alley were Radio's people, we all might be on their radar."

"What do we do now?"

Lewie pulled to the side of the road outside my apartment. The one o'clock bars were shutting down, the street filling up.

"We lay low," he said matter-of-factly. "We get new phones. And mostly, we enjoy the spoils of our hard-earned victory. Hint, hint."

"Ah. Right." I took two bundles from the duffel bag and tossed them in the back seat. "We'll count it later and agree on a more substantial donation to the American Lewie Association. Cool?"

"Cool. In the meantime, I'll get in touch with Kenny Brodie. His former partner, Graham Venables—heard of him? No? I never mentioned him? He works at the FBI field office in Chicago. If Radio's hiding out dead in Jake's grave, he's a missing person in the feds' eyes, and his absence won't go unnoticed. Graham will know something."

"OK. Lay low it is."

Lewie held out his hand.

"You're a good man, Agent Almond. As soon as you want to come work with me..."

I shook his hand.

"Good night, Lewie."

"Get some rest, V.C. Good job tonight."

Up in my apartment, I stacked my earnings into piles and tallied them up on an Internal Reflexions notepad that Kalista left behind. Seventy-three tally marks and seventy-three reminders of the lovely Ms. Chestnut later, I felt wealthier, lousier, and lonelier than ever. Money wasn't shit without a little loving. Someone ought to write a song about that.

I was on the doorstep of dreamland when a loud knock at the door gave me a start.

"Open up, V.C.!" bellowed Lewie. "Why is it locked anyway? It's not like you have a duffel bag full of one hundred-dollar bills in there!"

I opened the door and pulled him inside.

"What the hell. What happened to laying low, man?"

"Fuck laying low! We're going to Chicago!"

"Excuse me?"

He brushed past me, ashing his cigarette on the floor.

"Guess who I just got off the phone with!"

"Queen Amidala."

As he was no longer wearing the Vader outfit, my joke was met with crickets.

"Kenny Brodie!" he said.

"Already? You didn't use your phone, did you?" I realized my own phone was only a few feet away. "Fuck! Wrong number! Scratch that from the record!" I turned it off and stuffed it under the couch cushion. This shit was getting old fast.

"I called him from that pay phone on Delmar and Coolman. You know, the one where the guy in the Lakers hoodie gives you the stink eye like he's going to mug you until you fire a couple warning shots from your Desert Eagle in the air?"

"You're a menace, Lewie. Bullets come down, man."

"Guess what Graham Venables told Kennie Brodie! First, Radio has definitely fallen off the map. And second, just yesterday, his brother Patio..."

"*Patio?*"

"... walked into FBI headquarters in Chicago literally begging to turn himself in. He was in hysterics, rambling about teenage sex slaves, Radio going into hiding, and one... you ready for this?... Jacob. Patrick. Kennedy."

"Jesus. What did they do?"

"Nothing. Treated him like a fart in the Windy City. Radio isn't a terrorist, so as far as the feds are concerned, he's *persona grata.*"

"Jesus."

"Disturbing sign of the times, partner."

"So, we're going to Chicago to...?"

"Follow up with Patio Williams, of course! As field agents in the Chicago FBI, it's our sworn civic duty, yes?"

I sat on the bed and buried my head in my hands. This shit, too, was getting old.

"Sergio murdered Jake," I said. "And he was swiftly executed for it. Isn't it time to stay put and just mourn our friend?"

"Ack! What fun is that?"

"I don't think posing as federal agents to interrogate his business partner's brother is what Big Jamie meant by hush, man."

"Well, then, we'll just have to agree to *fuck Big Jamie.* See you 10:00 a.m. sharp!"

In an even more disturbing sign of the times, Lewie showed up just one hour late, looking well-rested and raring to go.

"Ready for an adventure?" he boomed, even louder than usual. "There's nothing like a road trip down Route 66 on a sunshiny day!"

"I-55 might be quicker. Seeing that it still exists. And it's gray and rainy outside."

"Tomayto, tomahto. Sorry I'm late. You ready to roll?"

"You're *sorry* you're late? As in, you're cognizant of the existence of time and how it works? Damn it, man. The last shred of normalcy in my life is now gone."

Lewie looked hurt.

"What are you talking about? Maybe I've been a few minutes late on rare occasions over the years, but for the most part, I've been..." He paused when he saw my bag. "Seriously, you packed a bag for this?! You do realize we'll be back by mid-evening, right?"

My faith in the order of the universe was restored. Aldous Time was alive and ticking.

"We're looking at a nine-hour round-trip, plus however long it takes to... ah, fuck it," I said. "Let's go."

A drum machine-synthesizer blitzkrieg assaulted our ears when Lewie started the car. I had to think quick before the bowels of Club Car engulfed me. Luckily, the music gods were smiling upon me. The side door of my building swung open and T-Bone stepped outside, plucking an acoustic guitar. I had an idea.

"T-Bone!" I called, waving him over.

"Gentlemen!" he said. "Where you off to?"

"Chicago," I said.

"Chicago? That's my old stomping grounds. River North area. What you boys mixed up with in Chicago?"

"Hop in," I said. "I'll tell you all about it. Bring your guitar."

"We'll be back by dinner," added Lewie.

"Tempting, but Saturday in the Delmar Loop is how T-Bone Jones keeps the cheddar churning, praise the Lord."

"I don't know what that means." I reached into my bag and pulled out five bills. "I'll give you five hundred dollars to come with us."

T-Bone leaned in close and spoke in a whisper. "Does this have anything to do with..."

I gestured to the back seat. "Only one way to find out."

"Thank you for the offer, gentlemen, but..."

"How about a grand? Each way?"

And thus, we were three.

———

"Man, I fucking hate Chicago."

We were actually thirty miles outside of Chicago, sitting in frozen traffic on I-55 near Aurora. Lewie was in rare, agitated form. He was wearing his hangry smile.

"Man, I fucking hate Chicago," he said again.

The first leg of our journey had been pleasant. From St. Louis to Springfield, T-Bone covered every band we called out, from Abba and Slayer (Lewie) to CCR and the Velvet Underground (me). He had the perfect rainy-day voice: a low rumbling bass, like distant thunder. I closed my eyes and drifted into a narcotic-like half-sleep.

About an hour north of Springfield, the drizzle became a downpour. Naturally, Lewie decided the change in weather merited a drastic increase in miles per hour. The faster you drive in the rain, he insisted, the faster the raindrops bounce off your window. Which mattered, apparently. Safety first dictated he drive ninety-eight mph with limited visibility on slippery, unfamiliar terrain.

Later, he put on his psychic hat.

"You're thinking of Kalista," he said out of nowhere.

"What?"

"Kalista. You're thinking of her."

"No. I'm not. I'm thinking about you killing us."

"Bullshit. Sandy Galanos has been teaching me telepathy. He says..."

"You can't teach telepathy. And Sandy Galanos is a fake, man."

"Bullshit. You're thinking about Kalista."

"She still mad at you, V.C.?" inquired T-Bone. "Just because you accused her of killing a man?"

"I didn't accuse her of... We're cool," I said.

"Bullshit," said Lewie. "You're not cool, and you're thinking about her. And just for lying..."

With a villainous grin, he cranked up the techno and bounced happily in his seat while I prayed for a head-on collision.

But then there was gridlock, and Lewie's mood soured.

"I fucking hate Chicago," he said a third time.

"What's wrong with Chicago?" asked T-Bone.

"Seriously? What's not wrong with Chicago?"

"It's got a great music scene. Great food, entertainment, art..."

"History," I chimed in, "night life, sports, wind..."

"Wind?" said Lewie. "Since when does *wind* make a city great?" He blew his horn in frustration. "The only great thing that ever happened in Chicago was when Mrs. O'Leary's cow knocked over a lantern and burned the place down."

"That's a little harsh," I said. "Chicago's got great pizza too, you know."

"Yeah, right. Pizza's pizza, no matter where you are."

"Whoa! I don't even know you anymore. Aldous Lewie, a culinary degenerate?"

"What I mean is, you can get Chicago pizza anywhere these days. You can get it in Chile. I've done it. Just like you can get New York pizza in New Haven, or New Haven pizza in New Delhi, or St. Louis pizza in St. Helens. We live in a globalized pizza market."

"Maybe," I said, "but I maintain that real Chicago pizza *in Chicago* is better than your thin-crusted little brain can imagine."

"I don't know. When it comes to food, my thin-crusted little brain can imagine a lot."

"John Hancock Center's worth seeing," noted T-Bone.

"So's the Field Museum," I added.

"Ever catch a Cards-Cubs game at Wrigley?"

"What are you guys, the city's public fucking relations team?" groused Lewie.

"Hardly," I said. "We're just pointing out that there are some great things in Chicago that should make you think twice about deifying an old lady's pyromaniacal cow."

"Plenty of great things, sure. Like this godawful traffic."

T-Bone started strumming a tranquil tune.

"Let's change the mood, shall we, boys? Tell me about your friend," he said.

"Who?" said Lewie. "Which friend?"

"Jake. I've heard all about his death. Tell me about his life."

"What about it?"

"Anything."

"The day he got his driver's license, he stole a car," I said.

"And then he felt guilty and returned it with a full tank of gas and an oil change," laughed Lewie.

"He literally believed he was Jesse James reincarnated."

"A psychic told him that. And yeah, he believed it."

"He was a modern-day Robin Hood. You ever hear of a state senator called Foster Wardell? He sponsored a bill to make it illegal to vend or even *give away* stuff on the streets after a certain hour. Basically, he tried to make it a crime to give a homeless dude a blanket, or a bottle, or a buck."

"Jake stole his wallet. Then he stole his car. Then his other car."

"He sold them to a chop shop and gave the money to a shelter."

"Then he stole his front door."

"Literally. Wardell came home one day and he no longer had a front door."

"One time, V.C. was having a spat with a friend of ours, Connor Ventura. I can't recall the specifics—something about Connor banging V.C.'s wife like the rest of the bi-state was doing. V.C. and Connor were at the same bar, avoiding each other. Jake picked their pockets and switched their wallets right before they left."

"The idea was, we'd have to meet up to exchange them. Then we'd start talking and kiss and make up."

"Is that right?" said T-Bone, amused. "Did it work?"

"Of course not," I said. "Fuck that guy. But it was a nice thought."

"He was a prankster," said Lewie. "One time when V.C.'s brother Marlin was on vacation, he broke into his house and filled his bathtub with peanut butter."

"It took something like three thousand jars of peanut butter and cost five grand," I added.

We continued sharing Jake memories as we inched into the city. Lewie lucked out and found a parking spot with a full meter near the French Market, a stone's throw from the granite skyscraper that housed R.W. Enterprises. It felt like a positive omen. But then buckets of rain began to fall the moment we opened our doors. The universe was sending us mixed messages.

When we finally pushed through the revolving door into 800 N Clinton in our drenched, wrinkled clothes, we looked more like vagrants than federal agents. Luckily, there was a coffee shop in the lobby where we could dry off, caffeinate our brains, and discuss our plan of attack. Lewie had been coy about it in the car, saying only that he'd brief me when the time came and not to fret. In other words, he didn't have a fucking clue.

"Partners, here's the plan," he said over coffee and scones. "I'll do the talking. Getting people to open up is my chief métier, so to speak..."

"It's that scary smile, ain't it?" T-Bone asked.

"It's that scary smile," I agreed.

"Deep down, you see, nobody wants to tell anybody anything," Lewie said. "You have to..."

"Lewie," I interrupted, "that's the exact opposite of what you told me a few weeks ago."

"Huh?"

"A few weeks ago, you said, and I quote, 'Deep down, everybody wants to tell everybody everything.'"

"Well, that was then, partner. This is now. Times change. Keep up. And let me do the talking. You two, just stand there and look formidable."

"Two?" said T-Bone. "Don't get me wrong, boys, I've got nothing but love and respect for you, but your old pal T-Bone is the music. Not the muscle. I'll wait here."

"Tag along and look mean, and V.C. will throw in an extra grand."

T-Bone hesitated.

"Each way," added Lewie. "And don't worry. We'll call an audible if we don't like what we see. We'll pretend we're selling magazine subscriptions, or Girl Scout cookies."

And thus, we remained three.

"What's a gangsta doing in an office building anyway?" T-Bone asked as we rode the elevator to the forty-third floor. "Did I miss that part?"

"Radio is, or was, a businessman," Lewie explained. "He owns a slew of companies, some legit, others less than. This is corporate headquarters. It's the contact address Patio gave the FBI, which reminds me..."

He pulled an authentic looking FBI badge out of his pocket and pinned it to his coat.

"Exact replica! We need to get you one of these, V.C. Authenticity is key. It's amazing the cases you can solve when the world thinks you're a G-man."

"Why aren't you in jail, Lewie?"

"In the meantime, take this..."

He reached into his pocket and emerged with a plastic toy badge that read Sworn Deputy Sheriff, City of Tombstone.

"Are you out of your mind?" I objected. "Are you trying to get us killed?"

"Oh, don't be a drama queen. Flash it quick, and only if you have to. Nobody pays attention to badges anyway. They're like business cards, or girls named Martha."

It was six o'clock on the dot when we stepped off the elevator. A receptionist behind a desk greeted us with a half-smile and continued packing her things.

"FBI," said Lewie before she could speak. "We're here for Patio Williams."

"Oh, my! Is everything OK? Should I let him know you're here?"

"Not unless you'd like to interfere in a federal investigation, ma'am," I growled, surprising all of us. "Where is he?"

"In his office, sir. Far wall, back corner, on your left. I think he's still here."

We navigated a maze of empty cubicles and came to a double glass door that you needed an access badge to open. Two offices were visible on the other side. The one on the right, belonging to Radio Williams, CEO, according to the placard on the door, was dark.

Loud music spilled out of the other. Craning our necks, we caught a glimpse of a young lady dancing in the doorway.

326

"Ooh, baby! Love me some Pink!" sang T-Bone, swaying his hips and waving his hands in the air.

Lewie knocked loudly. The dancing girl jumped, startled.

"FBI! Open the fucking door, Ginger Rogers!"

"Really?" I said. "What are you, a hundred years old?"

The girl killed the music and hurried towards us. Lewie offered us some final advice: "Stand your ground, gentlemen. Something tells me Patio Williams doesn't crack easily."

———————

Patio Williams cracked easily.

The dancing girl—Jilly, according to her ID badge—led us into his office, where two things stood out about him right away. The first was that he was tall, thin, and handsome, like a guy losing his shirt to a harem in an Axe commercial. The second was that he clearly looked better than he felt, considering he was hyperventilating into a brown paper bag.

"Pat!" cried Jilly. "Oh my God, are you OK?"

"He's having an anxiety attack!" Lewie shouted, rushing towards him and no doubt making it worse. "Stand up straight, you'll get more air! Up, up, up!"

"That's an old wives' tale," I argued. "It's better to sort of slump over when you're trying to catch your breath. Your diaphragm sucks in more air that way."

"If you're out of breath from exercise, maybe. But this man is in the throes of a vicious *mind fuck*! The walls are closing in around him! He's dizzy, lightheaded, thinks he might really die this time, like his brain is going to pop out of his eardrums, like he's..."

"You're not helping!" screamed Jilly.

"Back up, give him some space," T-Bone demanded, stepping between us. "Breathe deep, Mr. Williams. In and out. Just like this. In... and out... in... and out... in... and out... in... and out..."

His voice had an immediate sedative effect. All five of us breathed deep, in through the nostrils, out through the mouth, stomachs expanding and contracting in unison like a synchronized breathing team. It was a bonding moment.

"That's right, Mr. Williams. In... and out... in... and out... You're doing great. Now, listen to me. Stay calm. We aren't here to arrest you... in... and out... And we're not here to harm you ... in... and out... We're your friends, Mr. Williams. In... and out... We just want to ask you some questions. OK?"

"Who are you with?" Patio managed to say between breaths. "The feds? Mr. Kennedy?"

"Yes," said Lewie. "And yes."

Patio nodded slowly and mopped his brow with his shirt. The color in his face was coming back.

"Sorry to keep you late, Jilly," he said. "You can go. I'm sorry you had to see me like this."

She squeezed his hand and tried to hold his gaze. I sensed that she had feelings for him, and he was too wrapped up in his work or his anxieties to notice. For some reason, I really hoped they had a happily ever after.

"You got to believe me, guys. It's just like I told your coworkers at the FBI office. I didn't want my brother to go after the Kennedy kid. Hell, I was hoping Jake got away with it." Patio tapped his fingers on a spiral notebook on his desk. "I even have it in writing if you don't believe me!"

"You were hoping Jake Kennedy would get away with *what*?" asked Lewie, his eyes glued to the notebook. "Pretend we're three idiots off the street. Patronize us."

Patio's fingers shook as he reached for a glass of water.

"It's OK, son," said T-Bone reassuringly. "You can tell us."

"Start from the beginning," I said. "Even if you think we already know something, say it. Tell us what happened to Jake Kennedy."

After a pause, Patio launched into a neurotic ramble, fidgeting incessantly, his words spilling out like whiskey from a drunkard's flask. I didn't know it at the time, but Lewie was recording the audio on his cell phone.

"Jake stole the clean cash Radio lined up to buy those sex slaves from the Delgados. He'd been with Radio for weeks, just learning the ropes he said, and Radio thought he was doing Mr. Kennedy a favor, you know, teaching his son the Chicago side of the business. Radio liked having Jake around, we all did, he was a fun guy, you know, none of us thought he'd sneak in at night and steal three million dollars and then be so bold about it to wink and wave at the camera in Radio's office right after he emptied the safe out. Sure, we knew Mr. Kennedy didn't approve of us buying those girls, he had moral qualms with it, you know, he thought it was bad business, it would upset his connections. But none of us thought he'd send his son to rob us! So, of course Radio was pissed, he saw the safe was cracked and emptied and he watched the camera and lost his shit, jumped in his car to go find Jake and beat the money out of him. He said he'd kill him, just fucking kill him, and he had his gun with him, and I knew he meant it, he was going to start a war. Which is exactly what the bastard did, killing the Kennedy kid and then running off with the money and leaving me here holding the bag and trying to explain this shit. But you guys got to believe me, I really did try to stop him, I sent a couple of the guards here, Eli and a couple others, these guys, they thought they were ballers and they wanted to make their bones, so I didn't give them the details, just told them to go to St. Louis and find Jake, convince him to just give back the money before Radio got to him. I figured everything would be forgiven if he just gave back the money, like it was just a practical joke, you know? I told them to do whatever it takes to find him, track down his friends and family and make them give him up. I even let them drive my car, my brand-new Continental, and I said to don't come back until you've found Jake or I tell you to come back. And then a few days later St. Louis calls and says Jake has killed himself and I know it's a lie, Radio killed him, and Mr. Kennedy has the business sense to play it off as suicide so the competitors and even his own people don't realize Big Jamie, Mr. Kennedy I mean, let someone stroll right into his very own house and kill his son. How bad would that look for the mighty Jamie Kennedy? So, I..."

"Stop. Breathe, man. Go back," said Lewie. "Eli and his friends. What happened to them?"

"They fucked up, got their cell phones stolen and when I tried to call them and tell them to come back because they were too late and Radio already killed the kid, someone else, the guy who robbed them I guess, picked up the phone. When they finally got back they said some street musician tricked them, gave them the wrong address to find Jake and when they got there it was a ghetto and they got robbed, and then they didn't even realize Jake was already dead, they kept hunting him for days, and kept getting their asses kicked, one time by some crazy Marine or something and another time they went to the Kennedy kid's friend's place and they turned the corner to knock down the door and who do they come across, but some murder cop who's one of Mr. Kennedy's top guys and so they run off scared before he sees them. The idiots crashed my car and even burned some other guy's car down on accident, trying to just burn off a tire to threaten him and they ended up setting the whole damn thing on fire. But I tried, guys, you got to believe me, I didn't realize they'd fuck up so bad and I swear I didn't even want Jake to get killed, I *liked* the kid, Jilly liked the kid, and look, here, ask him, speak of the devils, here's one of them now! He'll tell you I wanted Jake alive. Eli!"

A freckled, chubby-cheeked security guard appeared in the doorway. He froze when he saw us.

"You guys! It's them, Mr. Williams!" he shrieked, pointing to T-Bone. "This here's the guy who tricked us into going to..."

It was obvious what he was about to say, but we didn't get to hear it. Last time around, Lewie gave him a draft beer-and-Fireball facial. This time, he planted nine million volts from his trusty Vipertek in his neck.

Lewie snagged the spiral notebook off Patio's desk and the three of us bolted, leaving Eli squirming on the floor and Patio holding the bag again, getting ready to hyperventilate into it.

Chapter 22

WE DROVE UNDER A BLANKET OF RUMBLING GRAY THROUGH an endless gauntlet of corn fields and cow towns. The sky in our rearview was calm. Ahead, there was thunder and fog. Maybe the world was being symbolic. I wasn't in the mood for it.

Lewie drove less ferociously than he did on the way there. Maybe he was concentrating on the words I read aloud from Patio's journal. Or maybe he knew that once we got home, there was nothing left to do but get on with life, sans mystery, sans Jake. And what fun was that?

I read Patio's journal with both fascination and guilt, glazing over the many passages that didn't concern us. Its neurotic content—"Jilly is dancing again and making the un-scratch-able itch buried deep in my brain pulsate in cruel rhythm with the drum beat that makes my heart race dangerously too, I think I hope I'm done for at last"—only amplified my guilt. Invaluable puzzle piece notwithstanding, this journal was clearly not intended for human consumption.

When I finished reading, T-Bone connected the final dots.

"So that's that, huh?" he mused. "The Kennedy boys robbed the Williams boys to foil a human trafficking scheme. Radio confronted the Kennedys and they killed him, then played it off like Radio killed Jake. Then they used Radio's phone to make his brother and his people think he was on the lam..."

"And then," said Lewie, "they tricked the Delgados, probably with Radio's phone again, to make them think their deal was still on. And then they tipped off the feds."

"Damn near inconceivably, the plan worked—only for Jake to find himself in the crosshairs of some murderous psychopath he'd never even met. Lordy, Lordy, Lord. To get away with all that danger, only for a stroke of bad luck to do him in! Mmm-mmm-mmm. What do they call that, V.C.? Irony? Coincidence?"

The rain picked up again. I was sick of it. Maybe it would never end, just wash us all into moldy oblivion. Jake just got a head start.

"Stupid," I said. "They call it fucking stupid."

We stopped for coffee and comfort food at a greasy spoon in Bloomington. The coffee was burnt and unsatisfying, and I savored every empathetic sip. The food was cold comfort. I barely touched it. Instead of feeling exhilarated having solved Jake's double death, I was more let down than ever. Jake risked his life for something. He lost it for nothing.

Lewie didn't have much of an appetite, either. He was wearing a half-smile only. His face looked half-naked. Patio's journal—and the events of the past month, no doubt—had brought him down to earth, at least for tonight.

T-Bone tried his best to boost our spirits.

"Sweet Jesus, I hate to see you boys like this," he said. "Let me tell you about this fellow I knew long ago, one hell of a jazz drummer named John B. Carney. You boys can relate to this. He had a problem like nothing you've ever seen. John B. couldn't control his laughter. For no damn reason, he'd lose his mind laughing, even if he didn't find a damn thing funny. At church, he might crack up. In the middle of sex, he might crack up. It could happen anywhere—funerals, weddings, restaurants, walking down the street. He'd laugh and laugh, and the more he tried to stop, the longer he'd laugh."

"Where you going with this, T-Bone?"

"It practically ruined him. One night, I was playing bass guitar for the great Ali Zane at CC's Blues & Booze. John B. was on drums. Ali was emotional that night. A couple days ago, he put his mama to rest. Between songs, he talked about what a saint she was. Raised four kids on her own, including one that wasn't even hers. Worked three jobs. Chased dope fiends off the front porch so the kids could get a good night's sleep. Marched with Dr. King. An absolute saint. Everyone, myself included, was teary-eyed listening to Ali reminisce about her. He called for a moment of silence in her honor. For a few seconds, it was silent. But then John B. made a noise. I'll never forget looking over and seeing his cheeks puffed out like Dizzy Gillespie, trying like a son of a bitch to hold it in. But he couldn't do it. He cracked the hell up for a good two minutes, cackling like a fool, making an ass out of himself, embarrassing Ali, pissing off the crowd..."

"I do enjoy hearing your voice, T-Bone," I cut in. "But why are you telling us this?"

"Because he got better, man! Eventually, he saw a doctor and got diagnosed with some rare disorder..."

"And you think Lewie has it, too? Because he smiles too much?"

"No. I'm telling you this because *he got better*! The doc gave him some meds, anti-depressants or something, and..."

"So, you're saying we should get anti-depressants?" said Lewie.

"No! I'm saying that *things can get better*, men. No matter how blue you're feeling today, life can always get better tomorrow!"

"Oh. Right. No offense, T-Bone, but next time just say life can always get better tomorrow."

"Fine. Things can get better, Lewie." T-Bone put a comforting hand on my shoulder. "Things *will* get better, V.C. Cheer up, baby!"

A crash of thunder rattled the windows. The lights flashed. A line cook laughed like Dracula.

"I'll get right on that," I said. "Just as soon as the rain stops."

———————

I awoke to a beautiful Indian summer afternoon. Some indie pop band was playing live outside the vinyl shop, gifting a bouquet of jangly guitar riffs and jaunty ooh-woo-woo's to the street. Cheerful banter rose up from the lunch crowd at the tables outside Camilla's. The sky was a cloudless blue.

Ten dreamless hours of sleep under my belt, I felt like a new man. I hummed Nick Cave's "New Morning" while I made coffee. Then, I collected my pilfered mum from Hazim and walked to the MetroLink, only to realize that I'd forgotten cash. I've never been great with money. More than $700,000 under my bed, and it didn't occur to me to bring six bucks for the train. I legged it back home and called for a cab instead.

The driver didn't say much, but he honked his horn gently whenever he passed someone.

"It's the law," he said. "You must honk if you must pass. Most drivers do not know."

I was pretty sure he was dead wrong, but I didn't care enough to burst his bubble. My stomach was in knots. As we pulled into the parking lot of Kalista's apartment complex, I remembered laughing to myself when I saw Miguel blushing like a schoolboy around Nadezda. Karma, I realized, not for the first time, is both instant and a bitch.

There were four ways to get inside Kalista's building. The first, and sanest, was to buzz her directly, and risk being told to go fuck myself. The second was to wait for someone with a key and try to piggyback. The third was to buzz the concierge and try to smooth-talk my way inside. The fourth was the path that I chose. I pushed the buzzer.

"How can I help you?" squawked the concierge through the intercom.

"FBI!" I shouted. "Open up! Now!"

A lock clicked and the automatic door swung open. A woman in a security uniform stood there with her hand on her heart, looking terrified, like she'd committed a crime and knew the gig was up.

"Hey, you!" I said, trying to sound familiar. "Forgot my key again. You should have seen the look on your face!"

She breathed a sigh of relief. "Oh, hardy-har-har. FBI."

"Finally got that mum for my windowsill. You think it's too late in the season for mums?"

"Not if the weather stays like this."

"I know, right?"

"They said it would be in the 70s tomorrow. How lucky are the trick-or-treaters this year?"

"I know, right?"

"You know what they say, if you don't like the weather here, just wait five minutes and it will change."

"It's not the heat, it's the humidity."

"Hardy-har-har." She shook her head. "Mr. FBI."

I took the stairs to the sixth floor, hoping to burn off some nerves. It didn't work. But it did make me not just anxious, but also sweaty—an irresistible combo. I knocked on Kalista's door. There was no answer, but I could hear a hushed male-female conversation coming from inside. Some suave, chiseled bastard would probably open the door in his boxers, biceps bulging, self-assured smile plastered on his face. "Whoever it is, get rid of him quick, sweetie," Kalista would call from the bedroom. "You know how I hate when you leave me alone in here."

I was on the verge of going home to lick my wounds— and then the salt from some tequila shots, perhaps—when

Kalista opened the door. She forced a frown when she saw me, but her eyes, I thought, were smiling.

"You're busy!" I blurted out. "I won't stay, I know you think flowers are lame unless there's a story behind them, and there is. I stole these from a crime boss's garden, and I was wearing a giant middle finger costume, and I had just connived my way onto the third floor and discovered fake Jake's identity, and these guys with automatic rifles who wanted to maim us were nearby, and Lewie was being Lewie, so we... Fuck me, I'm blathering like an idiot."

"Is that a hereditary thing?" said Kalista, looking more amused than annoyed, which I took as a positive sign. "Blathering like an idiot?"

"I'm pretty sure it's a booze and drug psychosis thing."

"Good." Kalista smiled. "You can come in, then."

"Are you... alone?"

"No. The St. Louis Cardinals are hiding in the closet with handcuffs and dildos."

"You're right. Stupid question, I suppose."

Kalista kicked her laundry into a corner while I sunk into the couch. The voices I heard from the hallway were coming from the television. Kalista was watching some schmaltzy Hallmark film. Under different circumstances, I would have ridiculed her fiercely.

"I'd offer you a drink," she said, "but if I can't drink, neither can you."

I didn't follow. "I'm on the wagon. And that's the honest-to-God, one hundred percent half-truth."

She took the flowerpot out of my hands and held it up to her nose.

"Nobody's ever stolen flowers for me before. I guess that makes you special?"

"I've been trying to call you."

"I know."

"I have big news."

"Don't we all."

"About Jake. We know everything. It started with..."

"Save the details. Hit me with the essence."

"OK. Essence it is. We..."

"Who killed your friend? Sergio?"

"Sergio."

"For sure?"

"For sure."

"I'm sorry. Truly."

"It wasn't your fault."

"I'm not looking for pity. But if I wouldn't have told him I was pregnant with your child, he wouldn't have flipped."

"It wasn't your fault," I repeated.

"Where is he now? Dead?"

"Dead."

"How?"

"Big Jamie got to him. Or Big Jamie's people."

Kalista leaned over and reached into my empty jacket pocket. "And your gun?"

"Gave it back to Lewie. Didn't want to shoot my dick off."

"And the person lying in Jake's grave is...?"

"A criminal named Radio Williams. Big Jamie's business partner."

"Ah." I couldn't read the look on Kalista's face. Was

it sadness? Relief? Resignation? Exhaustion? Her next words caught me off guard.

"Where do you see yourself in five years, V.C.?"

"Huh? I... don't know. I didn't realize I had to interview for this position. Why do you ask?"

"I have reasons."

"I don't know. I've got some time to think about it. I came across some money while we were..."

"Enough money for a new crib?"

I shrugged. "My little rat hole isn't always ideal, and sometimes I think it's a little too roomy for just one person, but I don't know, in a fucked-up way, 703 B Delmar is starting to feel like home, you know?"

"Not that kind of crib, V.C."

"I don't follow."

"The soothsayer was right."

My mouth dropped open. "You mean... there's a ghost in my apartment? Jake's ghost?"

Kalista shook her head, exasperated. "No! Do I have to spell it out, jackass? I'm pregnant! For real!"

I stayed at home, thinking and not drinking, for the next few days. It was a volatile combination. I'd been under the impression that Kalista was on the pill, or, at the very least, made regular trips to the hilltop at dusk to perform the barren womb dance to ward off the fertility goddess, Fecunditas. It was time to get my shit together.

Fortunately, one morning, after my usual routine of waking up screaming and then drinking a pot of coffee, pacing nervously, and sharing annoying non-sequiturs with the Purple Guy, an ill-conceived idea popped into my head. I flew out the door to see it through without giving it a second thought.

First, though, I went to the closest car dealership to buy the first vehicle I saw that had everything I needed—four wheels, enough room for a car seat, and zero flames shooting out of it. I'm not a car guy. I didn't take it for a test drive, just counted out three-hundred-and-fifteen Benjamins and asked a polite but flummoxed saleswoman for the keys. Thirty minutes after I showed up, I was driving my brand-new VW Passat off the parking lot to my brand-new job.

Lewie wasn't there, but the surfer dude divorce lawyer with the bleach blonde hair let me in. He was doing tricks with a yo-yo and wearing a beaded peace necklace and tie dye pullover hoodie. He looked less like a lawyer and more like a guy who needed a lawyer.

"I remember you!" he said with a smile. "Did you get married and then divorced already?"

"Still working on it."

"Lewie's not in yet. He keeps strange hours some-times, man."

"I've noticed."

The lawyer stretched, but didn't miss a beat with the yo-yo, sending it sailing in graceful loops in all directions. "I know I should put on my lawyer costume and start the day, but... want to watch me walk the dog? Loop the loop? Split the atom?"

"That's why I'm here."

"Name's Beau, by the way," he said, offering me a fist bump with one hand and walking the dog, looping the loop, or splitting the atom with the other. "Beau Shackelford. My friends call me B.S. My clients call me bullshit."

"Always nice to meet a fellow self-deprecator, Beau."

"You're a friend of Lewie's?"

My next words didn't sound as heinous to me as they probably should have.

"Actually, as of today," I said, "I'm his business partner."

"Cool, bro! You're a private detective?"

I took out a business card and flipped it on B.S.'s desk.

"V.C. Almond. Mastermind sleuth. Jack of some trades. Private investigator ordinaire. At your disservice."

There was a shortage of licensed private investigators in St. Louis. Lewie and I had driver's licenses, which gave us free reign, said Lewie, to market ourselves as "licensed" PIs, as long as we put "licensed" in quotes. I didn't argue. What was the point?

Business was steady. Most of our calls, surprisingly, weren't from suspicious spouses, but instead from conspiracy theorists convinced that their phones, homes, or offices were bugged. Lewie showed me how to conduct bug sweeps to weed them out. We rarely found any. At least once a day, though, we were asked to plant one in someone's boardroom or bedroom. Lewie refused, explaining that such shenanigans are unethical and a federal offense. Then, he'd go wave a fake FBI badge in front of some schmo's eyes and smile at him like a sociopath until he bared his soul.

An elderly woman hobbled into our office one morning and asked us to locate her husband and dog. They went for a walk one afternoon and never came back, she said. The police were no help. She suspected foul play. We uncovered his whereabouts the next day—six feet deep at Bellefontaine Cemetery, where he'd been since 1991. There was no sign of the dog.

Kalista introduced me to her family. Her father, a no-nonsense Army guy who went by "Sarge" to everyone else and "Mr. Chestnut, sir," to me, asked me if I liked the outdoors.

"I'd like to go hunting you some time, V.C.," he said.

"You mean hunting *with* you, right?" said Kalista's pretty, demure mother.

"Yeah. Sure," he grumbled. "That's what I mean."

Patio's journal found a home on my coffee table, darkening my mood every time I saw it. Eventually, I mailed it back to him, along with a note: *Mr. Williams—You are not in danger. You never were. Your secrets are safe. Breathe easy.*

Lewie and I went to Seal the night before Thanksgiving to catch up with Bobby. We hadn't seen him in a couple weeks. He was stocking the beer cooler and didn't hear us walk in.

"Yo, bar wench!" shouted Lewie. "Quit stroking your noodle and get us a couple beers, pronto!"

When Bobby looked up, I knew he was a changed man. His perma-scowl was gone, replaced by a gentle smile. He told us that his new buddy Hazim had introduced him to "Kriya yoga," and it changed his life. His "inner peace warrior," he said, had been awakened. It wasn't just talk. The bar got busy, and Bobby didn't assault or even accost a single drunk. He was the picture of tranquility. Hell had frozen over.

My nightmares faded away. I stopped drinking alone. All was well.

———————

"All is not well," I informed the Purple Guy.

He didn't argue. Deep inside his hollow heart, he knew that I was right.

"At first glance, life is a peach," I elaborated. "It's the most wonderful time of the year. The season's first snowfall is dusting the streets, turning our fair city into a winter wonderland. The future is bright, the coffee strong, the men in white coats at bay.

"And yet," I continued, pacing the room, "something doesn't pass the smell test, and not just the ox blood soup downstairs. The mystery of Jake's murder is solved, yet it feels incomplete. There's a nagging in my noggin that my favorite dead Kennedy does not rest in peace. A crucial piece of the puzzle hasn't fallen into place, and I just don't get it.

"Now, I know what you're going to say: 'Perhaps life isn't meant to be gotten. Don't worry. Be happy.' Which makes for a nice jingle, but I don't want to hear it. Unless you can riddle me this: What in the purple hell are you doing in a dead man's hat?"

For the umpteenth time, I took the hat from his head and turned it over in my hands, studying the faint blood drops splattered on the brim as if they held my answers. It was definitely the hat Jake was wearing when he was murdered. But what was its meaning? Only a few people—Sal, Jamie, and Beerman—could possibly have broken into my apartment and put it there. But why bother with such a bizarre and pointless gesture? Clearly, I was missing something.

It wasn't just the hat that was giving me fits. A grisly scene was playing on repeat mode between my eardrums. In the weeks after Jake's death, when chaos resigned, it was a nugget of noise among many. Now that all was calm, it stood alone: I navigated up the stairs, drunk and woozy. I fumbled with my keys, pushed open the door, expecting... what? T-Bone's shaky voice rang in my head. I took a step forward, turned on the light, saw something... a hat, the same hat the Purple Guy now sported, and blood everywhere... and then I tripped over something... a shoe? an arm?... I descended, in slow motion, and looking down, I saw, for a split second... what? Something. Something important. Something that was now on the tip of my memory, yet hopelessly unattainable.

A strange thing happened that evening. I emptied my mailbox and found, mixed in with the usual stack of junk mail addressed to the guy who used to live there, an unmarked CD. Must be a mistake, I thought. Nevertheless, I popped it into my laptop. I wouldn't have guessed in a million years what I heard:

He rocks in the tree tops all day long
Hoppin' and a-boppin' and singing his song
All the little birdies on Jaybird Street
Love to hear the robin go tweet tweet tweet

"Rockin' Robin?" I said to the Purple Guy. "Rockin' fucking Robin?" I said to ghost Jake. "What in the hell is that supposed to mean?!"

Beau Shackelford, clearly stoned, was rambling about a science fiction novel he wanted to write. He was outlining the plot, which centered around lone shoes on the side of the road serving as portals to an alien dimension, when Lewie barged in. He slapped a faded old newspaper theatrically on Beau's desk.

"Bizarro alert!" he boomed. "In my mailbox! No explanation!"

"Whoa... dude..." I said. "Ummm.... What does it mean, Lewie?"

"Don't know. A threat, maybe?"

"What kind of threat? I don't get it."

"Maybe it's someone's way of saying... fuck, I don't know."

"It was Jake's probably, right?"

"I would think so."

"Did Jamie send it to you?"

"Maybe. But why?"

"Fuck me, dude."

"Fuck us, dude."

"Was it in an envelope?"

"It was loose. Just like you see it."

"Fuck us, dude."

"Jesse James?"

"Jesse James."

"What the fuck?"

347

"I found a CD in my mailbox. Loose, also. One song on it, 'Rockin' Robin.'"

"What? When?"

"Yesterday."

"Which version? Bobby Day? Michael Jackson? The cast of *Full House*?"

"Bobby Day, I think."

"Fuck."

"Why does that matter, Lewie?"

Lewie shook his head slowly. "Jesse James and 'Rockin' Robin.' The Bobby Day version."

"What is going on here? What's this about?"

"Fuck if I know."

"Maybe it's someone's way of saying...Yeah, I got nothing."

"Fuck us, dude."

We stared at the paper in silence for a long time. It was *The Lawton Constitution,* dated May 19, 1948, and it gave me the chills, though I didn't know why.

Jesse James, the headline read, *Alive In Lawton*!

An unexpected storm buried St. Louis under a foot of ice and snow, shutting down schools, businesses, and wills to live. Only the record store in the Loop stayed open. The owner evidently thought that forty-five mph winds and a governor-declared state of emergency weren't enough to keep hipsters from vinyl.

I stood at my balcony door, watching the snow fall and talking to Kalista on the phone. We were discussing options for baby names, which quickly devolved into me making asinine suggestions and Kalista ignoring me.

"What do you think of Doomed? Or how about Maurice Ronald? We can call it Mo Ron."

"Yeah, maybe." Kalista sounded distracted. She was working from home and occasionally muttering profanities under her breath. "Aw, crap. I forgot that goofy hypnotist was coming to the office today to make people cluck like chickens and shit. I bet nobody called and canceled. I hope he realized we're closed."

"Hypnotist, huh?" A light bulb went off in my head. "Call you later. I've got an idea!"

I raced to the other side of the building and knocked on Josie's door. Laughter, electric buzzing, and some riot grrrl band on a stereo came from the other side. I knocked again, then again. Finally, I let myself in. Josie was reclining in a chair, topless. A girl with a ghostly pale Goth face and dark black everything else was giving her a tattoo above her left breast.

"Hypnotize me!" I said.

The tattooist killed the tunes and swung her middle finger, pendulum-like, in front of my eyes.

"You are regretting you came here..." she said slowly. "You are leaving... you are leaving... You are never coming back..."

"Be nice to Virginia, Aliyah," said Josie playfully. "We go way back."

"Hypnotize me," I repeated. "I need to remember something very important."

"Do you like my new tat, Virginia? It's the Chinese

symbol for schlocky whore."

"There's a Chinese translation for that? Isn't schlock a Yiddish word?"

"Aren't you the linguist."

"I need you to hypnotize me."

"She's a certified forensic hypnotist," said the girl called Aliyah, firing up the ink gun.

"I'm already sold. Let's do this!"

"Does this have anything to do with the night the cop dragged your drunk ass down the stairs?" asked Josie, clearly amused.

"I remember my first beer, too," said Aliyah. "I couldn't handle it, either."

"Ignore her," said Josie. "She's only vicious if she likes you."

"Hypnotize me," I repeated. "I need to relive a very important moment."

"Hypnotize me, hypnotize me!" sang Aliyah. "It's his mantra."

"I'll pay you," I said. "One thousand up front. A thousand more if you don't make me cluck like a chicken."

"Cluck like a chicken? I'm a Doctor of Clinical Hypnotherapy, not a third-grade magician."

"She might make you stick your dick to a frozen flagpole, though," said Aliyah.

"I might."

"I'm being serious, *doctor*," I said. "Two thousand, up front."

"Two grand, huh?" Josie shot me a curious look. "I didn't realize a 'between gigs' resume writer made such a killing."

"He doesn't. A drug czar gave me three-quarters of a million dollars to keep my mouth shut about a couple of dead bodies."

Josie rolled her eyes. "You are *suuuuch* a lame liar."

"Three grand. Take it or leave it. And don't act like you're the only hypnotist in this building."

"Fine. Come back at seven. Bring the money. And wear something sexy, Virginia."

We met four times that week. The first night, Josie told me to lay on her couch and tell her everything I remembered about "whatever happened that's got your granny panties in a bunch, Virginia." She didn't interrupt or accuse me of being *suuuuch* a lame liar while I spilled the beans. Maybe she finally believed me. I shared what I remembered, but neglected to mention that the guy whose body I tripped over in my apartment was supposedly the same guy we just put in the ground. For 750,000 hush bucks, I owed Big Jamie at least a modicum of discretion.

"I'm losing my mind, Josie," I said. "Maybe my brain's playing tricks on me, but I can't shake the feeling that I missed something in my apartment that night. Something obvious."

Josie sat in a chair across from me, rubbing Bacitracin on her fresh tat. If my sordid tale shocked her in the least, she was hiding it well.

"Your ego defense could be suppressing some details from your precious little mind," she said lightly. "But don't worry, memories come back from the dead all the time. A man forgets to pay for a coffee when he's eighteen and remembers when he's fifty-five. A mother of four is

351

putting dishes away when she realizes her second-grade music teacher never came back after Christmas break because she must have been fired for teaching the kids to sing 'Maxwell's Silver Hammer' at the school musical. A thirty-eight-year-old is playing Angry Birds on her phone when she suddenly understands the punchline of a joke she heard on *Night Court* when she was eleven."

"That's just Bull," I said with a wink.

"It's true. They're called mind-pops—memories that have been grifting in the limbic system for eons, waiting for the most arbitrary time to pop out. With hypnosis, we don't wait for randomness to happen. We claw into your brain and rip the stubborn little fuckers right out."

"You're very soothing, doctor."

"I am," said Josie matter-of-factly. "It takes a leap of faith to let somebody hypnotize you. People are naturally skeptical. They suspect their hypnotist has dark intentions behind that smiling exterior. With little old me, what you see is what you get. I wear my demons on my sleeve. It comforts people."

"I was being sarcastic. Just picturing you in my head makes me wet myself."

"Hush. Close your eyes. Tell me more about the walk home that night. Imagine yourself walking out of Bobby's bar. Do you see yourself?"

"Oh. We're doing this now?"

"You're walking out of Bobby's bar. Do you see yourself?"

"Sure."

"What are you wearing?"

"Nothing."

"What are you wearing?"

"Fine. A white dress shirt. The one I wore to the funeral. Black dress pants. Stained old tennis shoes."

"Good. Keep your eyes closed. You're leaving Bobby's bar. How do you feel?"

"Drunk." I concentrated hard, trying to remember that fateful night. "Nauseous. Numb. My socks are wet. I'm itchy."

"Feel the wetness in your shoes, the nausea in your stomach. Concentrate on my voice as you push open the door and step into the street..."

I lost track of time. It may have taken an hour, or it may have happened instantly, but at some point, as Josie spoke, my world got fuzzy. I began to straddle the line between consciousness and dreams. Her voice was warm and motherly. She guided me home, past Hare Krishnas beating mridangam drums and pretty girls drinking longnecks at sidewalk tables, past Gummy Jack counting cigarette butts in the palm of his hand, past a fat man in a bowler's hat chomping a cigar in the doorway of the thrift shop. "Look, it's the man with the flying snake tattoo on the back of his skull, rolling the storage trunk down the street!" Was Josie speaking still, or was I? We were one. I felt emboldened and omniscient. I was a man free of time and space, out of body, and Josie was God, and God was inside me and God was around me, "Keep it up, V.C.," she said, "you're doing great," and I smiled, what a girl, what a God, calling me by my real name and walking along-side me, keeping me on my feet, guiding me home... And now T-Bone spots us, his expression is bemused or maybe just scared. A sandy-haired guy who looks like Matt Berninger passes us and says, "I think they call him T-Bone but I call him Blandalf, like a black Gandalf." "You're just racist, Chip," says the girl on his arm. "How am I racist?" he shoots back, hurt. Then Josie's voice fills the cosmos again, telling me to observe myself, this is just a movie scene, and you're in control, you can slow it down, speed it up, you're the director, the actor, the audience... Jake's funeral program flutters in T-Bone's guitar case while the old busker exclaims, "Your friend, V.C., I saw him! I saw the dead man! He was even wearing that same hat as the picture! He went upstairs towards your apartment!"... I float up the stairs, thinking, "Jake's alive? Jake's alive! Jake's alive!" And though something is wrong—the stairs are too round, cartoonish, damn near *alive*, I feel like I'm tripping—I know everything is OK, because there's the door, and Jake is inside, the door is ajar, the angel thief must have picked the lock, and pure joy radiates underneath my moonshine shroud... Eyes wide, heart racing, I step inside, expecting Jake, but my soul is pierced, I wretch and moan, there's blood everywhere, and Jake's hat on the floor, his skin in a heap, and there is a missing clue in this mess, a golden elusive puzzle piece, I can sense its being... Is it the weapon? A person hiding in the corner? I look down and my gaze nearly falls upon it, but then a flying shoulder rocks my kidneys and a knee burrows into my spine. It's Beerman again, that son of a bitch, "I'm not going through this again!" I scream, "I came here to find my friend, not you, goddamn you, you are not my friend you are not my friend you are

not my fucking friend! You are *not* my fucking friend!
You are *not* my fucking friend! You are not my fucking
friend! You are not my fucking friend!"

"I am your friend! I am your friend! It's me, V.C.! It's
OK! It's OK! I'm your friend! It's OK!"

When I came to, I was lying on the floor, flailing
and kicking. Hazim stood above me, trying to pin my
shoulders and talk me off my mental cliff. Josie stood
beside him, eyes wide in alarm.

"Howdy, neighbor," I said. "How's tricks? What
brings you here?"

"You just flipped the fuck out!" exclaimed Josie. "You
were mumbling, then screaming, then *really* screaming.
Hazim heard you from his room. You were going crazy!"

I sat up slowly, feeling like I'd been under for hours.

"That's, like, normal, huh?" I said.

"No!" Josie's hands trembled as she squeezed a bottle
of black Sambuca between my fingers. I felt a demented
sort of pride knowing that I rattled her. "Drink this.
You'll feel better."

"Ack. I feel fine."

"Drink!"

I shrugged and chugged. "You're the doctor."

I was sleeping it off the next morning when there
was a loud knock on the door. Groggy and irritated, I
opened it just wide enough to see my hypnotherapist's
middle finger telling me that I was number one.

"Good, you're still sleeping," she said, pushing past me.
"I wanted to catch you with your defenses down. We're

trying a more conventional approach today. And at the scene of the crime, no less. Ready for this, girlfriend?"

"Ummm..."

Before I could object, I found myself staring at a penlight on the wall while Josie intoned hypnotic instructions in my ear. Listen to her voice and stare at the light, she told me, listen to her voice, blink a couple times, stare at the light, listen to her voice, blink a couple times, stare at the light, stare at the light, and so forth. And then for several minutes she told me to relax, close your eyes, breathe deep, shut your eyes tight, squeeze them tighter, and tighter, and tighter, feel them stuck together like glue, listen to her voice, listen to her voice, now go back in time, now listen to her voice, now put yourself at the scene, now describe the world around you...

I played along, trying to force something, but the hypno-powers that time-warped me yesterday were impotent today. To Josie's credit, my attempts to fake it—"I see, uh, people, a lot of people, and Sal, with the, uh, you know, crate thing with Jake in it, and hey, look, it's T-Bone"—didn't fool her for a second.

"To be continued another time," she said. "I guarantee, we'll figure out what's inside that precious little head of yours, darling. Even if we have to get a little... creative."

The next evening, she showed up with a devilish grin, a bottle of store-bought moonshine, and a glass pipe packed with sticky green and purple buds.

"Let's get a little shitty, Virginia City!" she sang.

"Oh, yeah?"

"Conventional wisdom says heavy drinkers and the mentally unstable make dangerous candidates for hypnotherapy. The lines between memory recall and hallucination are too easily blurred. I say conventional wisdom is stupid. Let's experiment with your little brain, shall we? It'll be fun!"

"Ummm..."

"Now, I don't have salvia divinorum like your friend had in his moonshine, but strong weed can have a similar effect. Let's simulate your state of mind from that night and then put you under and see what crawls out. What do you say?"

"You're the doctor."

The concept was sound, but the weed merely turned me into a rambling, incoherent mess. Fleeting thoughts poured out of both of us like all-important prophecies. Most of it was lost from memory at the moment of creation. I do remember, though, rambling about electing a president of the internet to separate the virtual world from the real one. And Josie telling me about a fantasy-horror screenplay she wanted to write—something about the *Farmer's Almanac* being a dark magic spell book coveted by warring factions of Santeria priests. I confessed that my mind was blown, and it was.

The longer we spoke, and the more we smoked, the more we forgot about hypnotizing me. It didn't matter. The missing piece, or so I thought, came to me that night anyway, unprovoked. Josie was packing another bowl and we were listening, fittingly, to *The Winter of Mixed Drinks* when it hit me.

I laughed out loud, though it wasn't particularly funny.

"I think I understand why things went haywire when I was hypnotized and saw Jake on the floor."

"Go on."

"It's because there's nothing to see. You're right, my ego-defense is suppressing something—the fact that the mystery is solved. *That's* the obvious clue I'm missing. That it's over. Jake is dead. The case is closed. The mystery is history. It's time to move on."

———

In my dream, everything clicked. I went through the same old motions—out the door of Bobby's bar, down the street, past the usual cast of characters, up the stairs, into my room. But this time, something was different. Jake lay in his usual spot, his face largely concealed by his ridiculous sombrero, but he wasn't alone. The missing link was there, too. Bathed in blinding light, like Marcellus Wallace's soul.

I stood in the doorway for an eternity, laughing and shaking my head at my own stupidity. For once, I realized that I was only dreaming, and for once, my dream was beautiful. There was no doubting its meaning. Dreamland was gifting me the truth, and I intended to smuggle it into reality.

It was time to preach the good news. With a devotee's zealous glee, I pinched my leg to wake up. Nothing happened, so I pinched it again. Still, nothing. I must have been in the middle of a deep REM cycle. Maybe a noogie would shake me from my slumber...

"What the hell is wrong with you?" shouted Kalista, rubbing her assailed scalp and trying with her meager frame to push me back to my side of her bed. "Did you seriously drive over here stoned through a foot of snow just to pinch and attack me in my sleep? What is wrong with you?"

I bolted upright to share my revelation, but before I could utter a sound, my thoughts dispersed like air from a balloon at the moment it's popped. The truth, if it even existed, passed into oblivion. Kalista rolled over and pulled a blanket over her head in self-defense.

"Loaded question, I know," she said. "Why don't you sleep on it?"

———————

It—whatever *it* was—was on the tip of my brain. It just needed a gentle nudge to squeeze through the threshold into the realm of explicit memory.

I got a blast of déjà vu walking into Josie's apartment. The same Sleater-Kinney knockoff band blared on the stereo. Josie sat topless in the same chair, getting the same tat touched up by Aliyah. The only difference was that Hazim was there, too, sitting on the couch and flipping through an *Inked* magazine.

"Hey, V.C.!" he shouted over the music. "Welcome to the party! I'm just enjoying the ambience!"

"I need you to hypnotize me one more time!" I said excitedly to Josie. Aliyah gave me the evil eye as she turned down the music.

"Oh, honey." Josie's patient, almost pitying smile was at odds with her go-fuck-yourself facade. "What happened to moving on?"

"One more time. I'm closer than ever. I can feel it."

"Give it a rest, V.C. At least for a few days. Let your thoughts settle. OK?"

"Not OK. Let's do this right here, right now. I'll throw in an extra grand."

"I'm not a hooker, asshole. If I hypnotize you tonight, V.C., I swear to God you're sticking your dick to that flagpole."

"You can at least get some ink while you're here," suggested Aliyah. "I only charge fifteen-hundred dollars a square inch."

"Great idea!" said Hazim. "You should get that beautiful girlfriend's name tattooed across your chest, V.C."

"Or at least her initials tattooed on your arm," added Aliyah.

"May as well," I said, "considering..." I thought about the many KLCs that rained down on me so often in dreamland. "Wait." Something clicked. "What did you say? Say that again."

"Me?"

"You!"

"Her initials," Aliyah said. "I said you should get her initials tattooed on your arm."

"Jesus." My head spun. A bolt of enlightenment struck me. I remembered everything. "That's it. Her initials."

"Are you OK, V.C.?" said Hazim. "Do you need to sit down? You look pale."

Excitement, disbelief, and clarity fought it out upstairs. "That's what I saw, Josie. Her initials!"

Josie shook her head, confused. "OK..."

An indescribable feeling washed over me. When I was a child, I dreamed that my house burned down with my family inside. I was the last to go. Crumpled in a corner, flames licking my skin, I prayed for an expedient demise. When I awoke to find us breathing, I wept in joy and relief. My life had been obliterated, then made whole again. That's how I felt in Josie's apartment that afternoon.

Elated, I took Aliyah's face in both hands and planted a kiss on her lips. Before Josie could object, I gave her one, too. Before Hazim could finish his joke—"The girls get kisses, why don't..."—I gave him one, too. I could have kissed the devil.

I ran to my apartment, grabbed my phone from the charger, and started calling Lewie. Then I thought better of it and hung up. Despite our new, likely untapped phone lines, this was too big to risk. I ran into the street and looked to Seal. The lights were on. I sprinted down the sidewalk in my socks, unfettered by the slush and snow, and barged through the door. Bobby was alone behind the bar.

"V.C.! Come in, brother," he said cordially. Evidently, he was still on his Zen kick.

"Get the gang together, Bobby! Use the bar phone!" I exclaimed. "I have news you'll never believe."

"Really? Try me."

"Jake Kennedy," I said, nearly hyperventilating. "He's alive, and hiding out in Lawton, Oklahoma!"

Chapter 23

WE HIT THE ROAD. UNLESS YOU'RE JACK KEROUAC OR intoxicated, the drive from St. Louis to Lawton, Oklahoma is uninspiring. Endless miles separate landmarks. It's a nine-hour trek through the bosom of America, dotted with corn silos, cow towns, and stretches of highway adopted by the John Birch Society. Billboards advertising Jesus and guns are everywhere.

Somewhere near Mark Twain National Forest, a "scenic view" offered a panoramic view of a picnic bench and a dumpster. Maybe it was someone's idea of a joke. Lewie and I found it hilarious. Our born again-dead again friend was born again. We were an easy crowd.

Near the Missouri-Oklahoma border, we drove past a pudgy white farmer in overalls working in a field near the road.

"Hey, look!" exclaimed Lewie. "It's T-Bone!"

I was embarrassed as hell about how badly I misconstrued the dead-guy-on-the-floor situation, but that didn't mean Lewie was letting me off the hook.

At a gas station outside Lawton, he told the cashier, after making sure I was within earshot, "Ma'am, you are the spitting image of a friend of ours in St. Louis. Your name's not Kalista too, is it?"

The woman was nearly as round as she was tall and pushing sixty years old.

I suppose I deserved all the ribbing Lewie could dish out. I did, after all, miss a terribly obvious fact the night of Jake's funeral: the corpse I tripped over on my kitchen floor wasn't Jake Kennedy.

It was Sergio.

I'm not sure what hit me. Maybe the hypnosis had a delayed effect. Maybe I had one of those "mind-pops." Or maybe it was nothing more enigmatic than the fact that you can only stare down the obvious truth for so long before it flicks your nose and says, "Boo, bitch!"

Embarrassment would come later, but at that moment in Josie's apartment when everything clicked, there was only elation. Something indeed had caught my eye as I careened towards the floor that night. I could suddenly see it clear as day.

An arm. Crudely burned into it were the initials KLC.

Kalista's words at Fromageres came back to me: "Did I ever tell you that Sergio burned my initials into his forearm with a grill lighter?"

Everything suddenly made sense—Beerman's confusion after he was forced to arrest me. His sense of urgency to eliminate the evidence. His fiery reaction when I wrote down Sergio's name. His insistence that I keep my story to myself.

I envisioned that night from Jake's perspective. Sneaking into my apartment to surprise me... getting waylaid by a psychotic stranger, whom he was forced to kill in self-defense... fleeing in a panic, leaving his hat behind... reaching out to his father, who promptly dispatched his finest cavalry... hopping in his car and racing across the Show-Me State to a life of quiet anonymity in a town he once read about in an old newspaper...

Beerman, I realized, wasn't at my apartment to arrest or investigate. The case was already closed. He was there to help Sal dispose of the body. Had everything gone as intended, I would have come home to an empty, bloody apartment. Beerman may have showed up the next morning to feed me the same asinine story he gave Mr. Kun-Woo about animals getting stuck in the ventilation and bleeding out all over the place. I may have even believed him.

Big Jamie wasn't speaking in code at Trixie's when he marveled how I "read the situation and called an audible." He figured I realized that Jake killed Sergio. Now, he thought, I was suggesting that we fake Jake's death a second time. After all, if Jake was under attack mere hours after the funeral, the Jake-for-Radio body swap had clearly not fooled anyone. Try, try again. Only, it didn't matter. Radio's people didn't go after Jake. It was some no-name. The plan worked.

When Big Jamie told me at his party that my "friend" tried to visit me the other day, he didn't mean Beerman. He meant his son—who, incidentally, took the Purple

Guy's sombrero before he left. For some reason, perhaps to alert me he had been there, he left behind the
blood-splattered one that Sal must have salvaged from
the crime scene after hauling Sergio away.

Radio Williams, meanwhile, couldn't possibly have
tipped off the feds about the Delgado deal. He was
already dead. It was the Kennedy boys who thwarted
it all along.

"Remind me again, how exactly did you mistake your
dead archenemy for your second-best friend?"

We were sitting in a hotel room in Lawton, feeling
cagey, listening to "Rockin' Robin" on repeat mode,
wondering what the hell it meant and how we should
go about locating Jake. Flashing his picture at gas
stations and grocery stores for two days had yielded
nothing but suspicious stares.

"Not this again," I groaned. "I told you, Lewie. I
made a mistake. And in my defense, I had a head full
of moonshine laced with salvia something…"

"Divinorum. Salvia divinorum. Sage of the Diviners,
they call it."

"So, yeah, I had the Sage of the fucking Diviners in
my head, man. And T-Bone had just told me that Jake
was alive and heading towards my apartment, so I was
expecting Jake. And then his sombrero, which must have
come loose in the scuffle, was lying there, and it must
have been obscuring Sergio's face, and they have, you
know, a similar build and skin tone…"

"We need to work on your hallucinogen tolerance,

partner. We can't have you mistaking John Doe for Joe Blow every time someone slips a little something in your drink."

"Shut it. And play the song again, will you? There's a clue in there somewhere. Got to be."

"One Bobby Day song coming up, Mr. Magoo."

Lewie opened the curtains to check out our dazzling parking lot-freeway-corn field view.

"I'm not going to lie, Steven H Wonder. Lawton is not what I expected."

"Probably because our knowledge of the place consists of what we read in a newspaper from 1948 about events that took place in 1882. What were you expecting, a one-horse town with two dirt roads, a schoolhouse and bank on one side and a jail and saloon on the other?"

"Yeah, little bit."

"And we'd waltz into the saloon with our six shooters drawn, spit on the ground, and demand some yellow-bellied cur tell us where the Kennedy boy is hiding?"

"Now you're being ridiculous. I didn't bring a six shooter. This is .45 ACP territory."

"Well, sorry to break it to you. But times change, even in Oklahoma."

Lewie shook his head, disappointed. "Christ, man. There's fro-yo across the street."

I opened another beer and perused the *Lawton Constitution* from 1948 for the twenty-third time. If nothing else, it provided some interesting reading material, fictional or otherwise. Officially, the Missouri outlaw James was killed in 1882 by Bob Ford, a member of his own gang who was never fully accepted by the rest of the bandits. In truth, said the article, the man Ford killed was Charley Bigelow, also a member of the James gang. Jesse and his brother Frank, after a great deal of pleading, convinced their mother to identify the body as her son. Legend has it that James, a "two-fisted, gun slinging Robin Hood who never let down a friend in need," sang at his own funeral, sounding off with his deep, mournful baritone voice. Fact, meanwhile, has it that Jake Kennedy played the saxophone at his.

"Jaybird Street!" said Lewie suddenly, jumping to his feet. "'All the little birdies on Jaybird Street/ Love to hear the robin go tweet tweet tweet.' Maybe there's a Jaybird Street in Lawton, and he's there!"

"Didn't you already Google 'Lawton, Oklahoma Jaybird Street' twice and come up blank? If there's a clue in that silly ass song, it's buried deeper than that."

"Silly ass song? Dr. Teeth and The Electric Mayhem once covered it!"

My cell phone rang. It was the landline at Seal. Probably Bobby calling to tell me that if I want to climb a mountain, begin at the top, or some other slice of unsolicited Zen.

"Let me guess," said Lewie. "It's Jake. He's decided to throw us a bone."

"Right. He doesn't have our new numbers and he's obviously concerned that Radio's listening in, or else he would have called us months ago, but yes, it's Jake."

"Tell him to meet us here. And wear a name tag so you know it's really him."

"Namaste, Bobby," I answered the phone. "How you doing?"

Maybe I'm just a damaged human being, but I was pleasantly surprised by his response.

"Li*shhh*en here, you are the forgetfulle*shhh*t, I mean the blinde*shhh*t, I-don't-know-what-I'm-looking-at – i*shhh*t fucker in the world. And I fucking ju*shhh*t love you anyway, you hear me? And tomorrow me and Hazim and thi*shhh* here T-Bone motherfucker, we're coming up there, and we're going to find Je*shhh*e Jame*shhh* for you, you hear?"

"I look forward to any company that's not Lewie's."

I hung up the phone with a smile.

"Good news, Lewie. Jake's not the only one back. So's Bobby."

———————

It's 8:00 p.m., and Lewie, having knocked back a case of beer, is snoring like a tugboat with a megaphone.

I decide to take a walk. Lights flash in the distance. Could be a mile, could be three. I head towards them, jump a fence, walk along the silent freeway, cut across a pasture. I find myself on a winding gravel road. How many roads must a man walk down before he calls himself hopelessly lost? The answer is three.

Not that I mind. Being lost in the countryside at night feels cathartic, spiritually humbling. My fate is in the hands of God or chance. Or, if I really get desperate, GPS.

The moon is lower and brighter than it is back home. Mother Nature feels larger, more real and human here.

I imagine her fluttering her eyelashes and sending me flying to Kansas. Ashing her cigarette and covering the land in dust. Shedding a tear and turning this land-locked kingdom into a seaside resort.

Gravel crunches under my feet. Coyotes howl in the distance. I feel like a speck of near-nothing on the surface of the everything. I whistle a happy tune.

The lights are closer. I trudge through a weedy ditch. Cross another field. Fight my way through a thicket of bushes.

I wind up on a quaint little Main Street like you find all over rural America. The shops are closed, but I hear music nearby—an old cosmic country tune. Gram Parsons, "The New Soft Shoe."

I don't know if I believe in fate, or a Higher Power, and I don't mean the President of the United States, Snoop Dogg, or Willie Nelson. But something from above is lighting a fire under my ass tonight. It propels me towards the music, past thrift shops, jewelers, antique stores, a realtor, café. And it drops me off outside the flashing neon lights of a hole-in-the-wall with the terribly obvious name of Rockin' Robin's Ale House.

I feel like I'm dead or dreaming as I take in the scenery inside—the over-served ladies at the bar singing along to the song on the jukebox... the snaggle-toothed, smiling bartender with the wife-beater tee and tribal tattoo on her triceps... the beautiful Georgia peach walking out of the restroom, freezing in her steps when she sees me... her boyfriend, the benevolent madman, raising his glass in my direction for a split second before his eyes dart back to the bar top, where six or seven shiny quarters are spinning in elaborate figure eights...

I sit beside him and order a Grand Marnier. He flicks the sides of several coins as they begin to lose momentum, granting them new life.

"Don't have Grand Whatever," says the bartender, gawking in amazement at the bar top. "Want a beer?"

"I'll just have whatever this guy's having."

It tastes like scotch and something. Club soda, maybe. The madman in the Purple Guy's hat and I say nothing as the coins spin on, nearly colliding each time they cross paths before pirouetting to safety at the last split second.

Finally, the coins fall in an impossibly straight row. The madman clinks his glass against my own.

"Thanks for stopping by, V.C. Great to see you," he says.

"Hello, Jake."

Acknowledgements

FOR THEIR LOVE, INSPIRATION, ENCOURAGEMENT, EXPERTISE, legal assistance, abstract purple statues, or one-liners, I'm forever indebted to: Missy and Jewelbug, my partners in crime; my parents, Mark and Rita; Terry Lewis; Curt Wiele; Carol Wieduwilt; Bobby Frauenglas; Phil Schiff; and Andy Dandino.

Eric Whelchel disproved the theory that an editor is someone who takes something great and turns it into something good. Instead, he took something almost passable and turned it into something barely palatable. Cheers, bro.

A special thank you to David Ross and Kelly Huddleston at Open Books for being damaged enough to decide to make this monster a reality. If you didn't already live on a remote island, now would be the time.